YOU'RE SAFE HERE

YOU'RE
SAFE
HERE

LESLIE STEPHENS

SCOUT PRESS

New York · London · Toronto · Sydney · New Delhi

Scout Press
An Imprint of Simon & Schuster, LLC
1230 Avenue of the Americas
New York, NY 10020

First Scout Press hardcover edition June 2024

SCOUT PRESS and colophon are registered trademarks of Simon & Schuster, LLC

Simon & Schuster: Celebrating 100 Years of Publishing in 2024

For information about special discounts for bulk purchases, please contact Simon & Schuster Special Sales at 1-866-506-1949 or business@simonandschuster.com.

The Simon & Schuster Speakers Bureau can bring authors to your live event. For more information or to book an event, contact the Simon & Schuster Speakers Bureau at 1-866-248-3049 or visit our website at www.simonspeakers.com.

Interior design by Laura Levatino

Manufactured in the United States of America

10   9   8   7   6   5   4   3   2   1

Library of Congress Cataloging-in-Publication Data is available.

ISBN 978-1-6680-3431-6
ISBN 978-1-6680-3433-0 (ebook)

FOR MY MOM

YOU'RE SAFE HERE

A woman tells me
the story of a small wild bird

—JANE HIRSHFIELD, 1988

The sea can do craziness, it can do smooth,
It can lie down like silk breathing
Or toss havoc shoreward; it can give
gifts or withhold all; it can rise, ebb, froth
like an incoming frenzy of fountains, or it can
sweet-talk entirely. As I can too,
and so, no doubt, can you, and you.

—MARY OLIVER, 2012

She who is perpetually unspooling and reforming
tinsel and twine and a blue plastic thread
into a nest for her wren
has more to teach us than
any book could.

—SANSA HÎNCU, 2031

Mist

1

Maggie

Although she was hundreds of miles away from any actual dove or sparrow, Maggie woke to the sound of birds. She rolled onto her side, the memory foam cradling the weight of her hip as she awkwardly maneuvered herself to face the sunrise. She assumed the Routine Engineers played the recording every morning to ground her in something familiar, but there was no one she could ask.

The sun hovered just below the horizon, barely visible through the thin layer of fog that blanketed the Pacific Ocean. On Maggie's first morning, she could barely pull her eyes away from the thousands of shades the ocean and sky held. Now she hardly bothered to glance at the rolling waves that gently rocked her waterlocked Pod. Only a month in, and the ocean had already become little more than wallpaper to her.

A damp cinnamon smell wafted from her bedside table and Maggie sat up to receive the latte that had emerged from a coaster-sized opening. Leaning against the bed's low backboard for support, she tilted back the cup. The solution of crushed root vegetables and mushrooms coated her tongue, leaving a slightly fungal aftertaste that felt like confirmation of the adaptogens' efficacy, even as their grit made her gag. When Maggie could see the brown sludge that coated the bottom of the mug, she placed it back on the coaster, triggering its descent into the table at the same time her gratitude journal slid out from a lower compartment. A sense of satisfaction from her devotion to her own health momentarily cut through the loneliness and boredom. She rested her hand against her swollen abdomen and took a deep, cleansing breath of purified air before retrieving the journal.

"Spin class begins in fifteen minutes. May I begin preparations?" Emmie's voice came from the column that rose from the center of the Pod to the peak of the domed glass walls that encased Maggie like a cloche force-flowering a seed.

During Orientation, Maggie had selected the founder, Emmett Neal, as the voice for Emmie, the therapeutic AI the Pod came equipped with. Although there were now countless tones and dialects to choose from— including, creepily, her own—Maggie still preferred Emmett, who had always voiced her Emmies.

"Sure," Maggie answered, stretching her arms, and then the word into two unnaturally high-pitched syllables. It was the same tone she used when critics and collectors used to visit the small, contemporary Japanese art gallery off Highland. She'd worked there for years as an assistant, even after she realized her interest in art was limited to centuries long past.

As soon as she completed her journal response, Maggie slipped out of bed and into a matching set of cream-colored leggings and a sports bra. The Pod similarly transformed itself: the glass clouded to let in less light as a floor tile flipped over, its smooth surface replaced by a bike perched on a platform. It was a similar model to the one she had used in her apartment, with slightly updated features.

Maggie leaned forward to tug her bra down, securing the band beneath her breasts, and stepped into the narrow clip-on shoes, which felt stiff after so much time spent barefoot. She hopped on the bike, locking her shoes into the pedals, and placed the VR goggles that dangled from its handlebars over her eyes. They automatically tightened around her head as her EarDrums activated, transforming the Pod into a narrow road. Maggie straightened her arms against the handles to arch her back as she waited for class to begin.

Emmie's authoritative yet warm voice filled the air as if the sky were equipped with speakers: "Welcome, Maggie! Get started pedaling at an easy pace as I tell you a little bit about today's ride." She explained the "game plan," which consisted of rolling hills and eight sprinted intervals that would sweep her through gorges with moderate inclines on a road long since lost to an avalanche of erosion on New Zealand's South Island.

Maggie pushed her heels down into a passive stretch before she slowly began pedaling, taking in the scenery. The gravel road led straight into the base of the Southern Alps, threading a crystal-blue river and pine-dotted meadow as Emmie's voice brimmed with motivation, indicating it was time to begin the warm-up. Maggie mirrored the cadence of the pace-setting avatars in front of her and began pedaling down the road, against the flow of the river. She focused on their feet, allowing herself to be hypnotized by their rhythm, *left-right-left-right-left-right* . . .

Maggie had just crested her first "rolling hill" when she heard a pre-historic screech so jarringly out of place against the calm, it ripped her out of her flow. She pulled the goggles off just in time to see a flash of white disappear into the water. It happened so quickly, she almost doubted her eyes until she saw a head pop back up to the surface, victorious with a tiny fish in its mouth. Without averting her gaze, Maggie stopped pedaling. She had a sense that if she even blinked, the spell would be broken and the bird would disappear.

The bird bobbed buoyant on the surface of the ocean, unaware of Maggie, who'd carefully unclipped and was now inching in a low crawl across the Pod's tiles toward it. It was preoccupied with the task of rear-ranging the fish into a position it could swallow, until its erratic head flicked in her direction. For a brief moment, Maggie was afraid the bird would take off. She froze as it lifted its wings slightly, then settled back down, apparently deciding the threat wasn't worth the effort.

It had been nearly two weeks since Maggie had seen any bird or wild-life that didn't come from the ocean itself, and, despite the Pod's seamless glass dome, she could only guess at her exact coordinates, the endless blue affording occasional, subtle hints as to where she might be. It felt so re-mote, she might as well be on another planet.

Once, a water bottle with writing Maggie recognized as Thai floated against the rim of her Pod, though that hardly confirmed her location, beyond what she already knew from Orientation. She and the other Travelers were somewhere in the Intertropical Convergence Zone, or the ITCZ. Its name made it sound more intimidating than it actually was: a dead zone along the equator notorious for trapping sailboats for months, but ideal for a vessel that was built to hardly move at all. Its nickname, the Doldrums, felt somehow friendlier. Its other nickname, the Trash Highway, was given for the floating debris that also got caught there, though Maggie had yet to see anything larger than the bottle. It had spent several days knocking against the side before the current took it to whatever trash heap would serve as its final resting place.

The bird let out a low, guttural squawk. It looked like something you might find in Hawai'i. From this distance, Maggie could see its thin red tail spread elegantly behind it. Its light-pink beak was turned down in a permanent, contemplative frown, made even more dramatic by the smudges of charcoal-black that lined its eyes. It was a bird of paradise. Maggie suddenly felt determined to identify and understand the bird, with an instinct that seemed to belong to Noa more than it did to her.

For as long as Maggie had known Noa, she was always rescuing things. She had saved snails, feral cats, an injured skunk, and every one of Maggie's houseplants. Maggie had once watched Noa mindlessly—almost automatically—nudge an errant nasturtium back into the safety of a neighbor's flower box as they walked past it, protecting it from a violent fate by a stroller or jogger.

On one of their first dates, Noa had arrived to pick her up with a dog. Maggie had opened her screen door and extended the back of her hand toward the animal's broad face, then retracted it when she realized the creature was covered in mud.

"I didn't know you had a dog." She had only known Noa for a few days at that point, but Maggie already loved the way her lips rested in a smile, primed to broaden into a full, infectious grin at any moment.

Noa was holding the dog by a piece of twine knotted haphazardly around its neck. Actually, Maggie realized, both Noa and the dog were covered in dirt. Noa's short fingernails still had mud caked under them from her weekend spent volunteering at a local farm, thin crescents of black earth.

"I don't," Noa explained, bending down to scratch the dog's ear, both of them smiling, "but she darted in front of my car as I was driving over." The image of Noa hitting the brakes, then welcoming the dog into her passenger seat (the trunk wouldn't have even occurred to her) made Maggie smile.

"It was just a few blocks away," she added, "and I didn't want to be late, but could we head back to see if we can find her owner before dinner?" By now, her grin had attained its full, natural state.

Maggie briefly wondered what would happen if she said no. Would Noa write her off as callous? Refuse to see her again? Come back to get her once Noa had joined the dog with its family? Noa was oblivious to the fact that Maggie had rushed home from work to get ready, the half-moons of her own nails diligently cleaned before she had applied a neutral, barely-there pink polish.

Of course she said yes. She would have adopted the dog on the spot if Noa had asked. There was a confidence to Noa that made it seem like every suggestion she made was the right one, a quirk that might have been a flaw if she didn't also listen to Maggie like she was the most important person in the world.

Noa still hadn't seen the inside of Maggie's apartment, but if she was curious she hid it well. Maggie left the door wide open as she turned back to grab her purse off the bed while Noa bent down to rub the dog's face, not so much as glancing toward the light emanating from the bedroom.

"You look beautiful, by the way," Noa said, rising, when Maggie turned from locking the front door. Her hand took Maggie's, pulling her in so that their bodies pressed together completely. Noa's lips lingered on hers past the point of an appropriate greeting for a second (or had it been third?) date, but Maggie stood still, willing Noa to do the same as they breathed the same air. After a few seconds, the dog barked, and they both smiled, their lips curving together with a natural comfort that belied the few days they'd known each other.

By the time they found the dog's owner, Noa had already named her. She called her Tocaya, the Spanish word for "namesake." She loved that it also meant "touch" in Portuguese, her mother's native language. It turned out to be the perfect name, considering Tocaya's warmth toward everyone she met. Each time they approached a house, Tocaya would wag her tail so fiercely, Maggie and Noa were sure they were at the right one, until they learned they couldn't trust her—she was just happy to be on a tour of the neighborhood, and seemed to have no interest in cutting the evening short by heading home.

"Or, we could adopt her," Noa said at one point, as they walked away from yet another house.

"We?" Maggie answered.

"Yes, we," Noa said, grasping her hand and flashing a smile. "I mean, technically she'd be my copilot. I could maybe even train her to herd. She'd have to earn her keep. But I think we can arrange visiting rights."

"Every other weekend and holiday?" Maggie joked back.

"Fuck that." Noa rolled her eyes. "She'd need to see you every day."

"Oh, would *she*?" Maggie teased, raising her eyebrows.

From the very beginning, there had been no games—although they did, to Maggie's immense relief, finally find the dog's owner. Noa liked Maggie, and Maggie liked Noa. They were a "we" from the instant they met, settling comfortably into a routine that felt different from any relationship Maggie'd had since college. Another way to tell it was that Noa adopted Maggie that night, staking her claim. Both far from family, they could be each other's family. Maggie wanted to walk into Noa's arms and never leave them. Let them envelop her in dirt and earth and grime.

The memory of being held by Noa sent a pang of guilt through Maggie so sharp she physically recoiled. It felt back then like there was nothing easier in the world. Noa: bringing just three boxes to move into Maggie's apartment, the bottom of one filled with rose quartz and rocks; gripping

Maggie's hips as she pressed her mouth, like a deep kiss, between her legs; naming her favorite trees on their block after old Hollywood actors, then greeting Garland, Brando, or Mae every time they walked past. Noa hadn't named a single plant or tree at the company-subsidized apartment complex they moved to as soon as she was hired at WellCorp. Maybe that was when everything began to go wrong.

Maggie knew Noa wanted to go back to the ways things were before she had taken the job, but was that possible? And did Maggie even want that? Even now, she tried to forget the memories she had of herself before WellCorp: constantly feeling like something was missing, just out of reach; waking every morning with her brows tightly knit, then consciously relaxing her face into something softer so Noa wouldn't see; standing for hours at the gallery saddled with the nagging sense that there had to be more to life. It was impossible for Maggie to simply think of Noa now. Any memory was an attempt to either justify her guilt, punish herself, or explain away what she had done. Her entire life could be defined by jobs, relationships, apartments, and conversations she'd fallen into, then itched to get out of. She was always combing through them for clues, even as an invisible riptide pulled her away.

Maggie walked awkwardly across the Pod's slick tiles in her cycling shoes and retrieved her Device from the small desk. She swiped to WellCorp's preloaded app, which contained every recorded song, book, movie, and television show. She had access to it all, a modern Voyager Golden Record, so long as Emmie decided it was productive to reaching her peak fulfillment.

The cursor glided across the bar as she typed in *tropical bird species*. Millions of results funneled in, organized by relevance: a novel about a runaway, poetry inspired by the Hawai'ian Islands, something titled *Birds of a Lesser Paradise*. She tried again: *audubon, ornithology, seabird encyclopedia*. Millions of results crossed her screen, none of which yielded the database she'd hoped for.

Maggie wanted to believe that the Device's omission was for her own protection, but felt a twinge of injustice for the bird, whose identity had been veiled in unchosen anonymity. Sometimes the Pod's omissions felt arbitrary—she had only wanted to know its name.

The bird bore little resemblance to Tocaya, its reptilian brain several branches away on the tree of evolution. She named it after the dog anyway. It had finished eating and was now floating perfectly still, watching the ocean for bits of food too small for Maggie to see. Behind her, the Pod rearranged itself, shifting furniture for her next activity, but Maggie stood, her face nearly touching the glass. The bird could take flight any second, and she wanted to be there when it did.

Time never behaved the way Maggie wanted it to. She often had the sense that she was watching her life slip through her fingers like sand. She ached for more time with Noa, even though it had been her idea to get away. The Pod was supposed to provide that pause, to give her more time to understand what she wanted to do with her future. She'd expected that the uninterrupted time in nature would transform her, or at the very least give her clarity, but it had already been a month and she was no closer to a decision.

2

Emmett

Malibu, California
50 Days Pre-Launch

Two sharp knocks sounded on Emmett's dressing room door, which opened without a pause for her response.

"Five minutes," barked the producer who leaned in, holding her palm straight out to indicate the urgency of the message. *Five.*

Emmett nodded without looking up. She was sitting in front of a vanity, cradling her forehead in her palms. As soon as she heard the click of the door latch, she lifted her head to meet her own reflection. Crow's-feet had formed in recent years, making her look almost as exhausted as she felt, even with the mirror's flattering software, which reflected back smoothed lines through an artificial filter. She ran her hands over the crown of her head, down to the sleek, low ponytail a stylist had secured. A few coarse grays threatened to announce themselves by springing above the strands of auburn, dyed only slightly "warmer" than her natural dark brunette.

The first few lines of her speech hovered in midair, partially obscuring her reflection. She tried to focus on the words projected by her Lobe-Embedded Neural-Interfacing Stereopticon, or Lens for short. The semipermanent contact lenses created seamless augmented reality projections, but could also read her thoughts, anticipate her desires, and offer gentle suggestions for optimizing her physical and mental wellness, thanks to the hair-thin electrodes they were connected to inside her brain.

Imagine, Emmett mouthed to her reflection, practicing the first word of her speech.

Emmett wished, as she always did before delivering keynotes, that her mother, Sansa, was still alive to see that all of their hard work, the pain and heartbreak they'd both endured, had been worth it. It felt unreasonably cruel that she had died just months before the release of WellNests, the groundbreaking wellness and entertainment systems that had made Emmett among the wealthiest, and equal parts revered and despised, founders practically overnight. It was a level of success that would have been unfathomable to anyone, especially Sansa's parents who had fled eastern Moldova for Portland, Oregon, the same day the Soviet Socialist Republic collapsed.

Despite living in America for most of their adult lives, they'd never felt settled in their new home, choosing to burrow into their insular Slavic community as Sansa worked her way from Britney Spears back to the Beatles while devouring books by American authors. She'd always planned on moving to California, the tantalizingly close border state she'd never visited but knew intimately through Joni's Laurel Canyon and Joan's Haight-Ashbury. But it was photos of a liberal arts college in northern Georgia, with its hundred-year-old stone buildings nestled against a bright-red autumn forest, that had stopped her in her tracks during her high school's college fair. She pored over the pamphlets, channeling the faces of the students walking bikes along a brick path as she filled out her Common App and worked odd jobs to barely cover the out-of-state tuition. Their carefree Americana smiles seduced her with their promises, and they would have fulfilled them if not for Emmett's father.

Sansa was only three semesters away from graduating with a degree in English Literature when she found out she was pregnant. She would later joke that she had successfully completed them as trimesters. To her credit, Sansa never made Emmett feel responsible for her dropping out and returning to Portland. She hadn't been that interested in school anyway and would insist, "Mother Nature is my teacher." Sansa repeated the refrain throughout Emmett's childhood as an excuse or an explanation, adopting it as her mantra, but one that never spared Emmett from studying.

After school, Emmett would retreat to the backyard that housed her grandfather's woodworking station. She built a hideaway underneath his worktable, which he tolerated in exchange for the quiet it bought him. Like a bird, Emmett assembled her nest over months, pulling in old pillows, fabrics, and blankets where she tucked away library books. She tacked an old bedsheet to the front edge of the table, and her grandfather helped her secure Christmas tree lights around the perimeter.

Emmett's Moldovan and Russian were as fleeting as her grandfather's English, but they bonded over their shared appreciation of isolation, remaining mute in solidarity, even when they heard her grandmother calling for them or her parents' fighting. Inside, with the sheet pulled down, the lights bathed the pages of her books in a soft glow. If her grandfather was working, the shavings would rain down from his lathe along the back wall, covering her page in a light dusting of oak or maple every time he blew the dust away.

Years later, Emmett's team of publicists would use these roots to explain her first product, when her story became Her Story, repeated in interviews to make her relatable and her company sound more democratic. At this point, the publicists' embellishments were so tightly woven into reality, it was impossible to decipher which was which anymore.

"Three minutes until places!" Emmett heard the same producer shout, shocking her out of her train of thought. She glanced down to scroll through the speech, blinking away the notification that recommended a short breathwork session to lower her signs of stress.

Emmett had been mindlessly thumbing the microchip embedded just below the skin of her wrist, pinching and kneading it to the surface. As the founder of WellCorp, she was among the first to receive the Injectible implant, just a few years before Lenses added an additional, far more sophisticated cognitive level of processing to the physical data the Injectible still provided. These days, the Injectible chips were nearly undetectable—most doctors included them as a package with vaccine administration to newborns—attached to the cephalic vein for location accuracy, but hers floated around her wrist.

Emmett pinched the chip between her thumb and forefinger, squeezing it against her skin like a pimple. She released and it floated back into her body, a container for artifacts she had invented. A faint bruise bloomed where she'd been gripping the sharp edges of the square.

The producer opened her door, not even bothering to announce herself with a knock this time. "Ms. Neal? Are you ready?"

She'd always hated that she didn't have the same last name as her mother and grandparents, Hîncu. She loved her father, but had never really known his family. Her name was a reminder of her untethered roots, that she didn't really belong anywhere.

Emmett followed the producer and a team of handlers glued to their Devices, outdated pieces of technology that people still preferred to use as the handheld extension of their Lenses, but when she stepped onto the stage to take her place, she was alone.

She took a deep breath, feeling the warmth of the stage lights on her as they brightened with her entrance. She had been teasing this announcement for months. As soon as the applause settled, the room fell silent with anticipation.

"Imagine a place where the closest person is miles away, but everything you need is within arm's reach." Emmett's Lens broadcast her voice into the auditorium audience's EarDrums, microscopic speakers attached to their actual eardrums, and to at least 3.4 million more—she had to assume numbers were up—streaming her keynote from home.

"*Imagine*," she repeated, "a retreat free of distractions, where each person can be *entirely* devoted to nurturing his, her, or their own well-being." It was pathetic, Emmett thought, how easy it was to captivate an audience of software engineers, investors, and journalists. Her lilting rhythm held them raptured as effectively as if she were presenting candy to a circle of toddlers.

She lifted her hands in calculated emphasis before delivering the next line projected in teleprompt from her Lens, the bruise on her wrist colliding against her leg. A grimace—too brief, Emmett hoped, for anyone to notice—flashed across her trained face.

"WellCorp has long provided an accessible and affordable sanctuary for millions of people." She paused, smiling humbly in appreciation of the applause. "When I first launched WellNests a decade ago, I made it my purpose—*our* purpose—to provide an escape from the challenges and banalities of day-to-day life, in turn maximizing the potential of our *entire* universal society. WellNests are now in nearly every home in America."

She could practically hear her Director of Publicity saying, *Make it personal*, as she delivered just the right balance of nostalgic empathy and aplomb: "When my grandparents moved to America almost seventy years ago, they never could have imagined a generation so unencumbered by bias and inequity, that mental health care and education could be accessible to all." It was admittedly a stretch, but one sanctioned by Legal.

"Our mission—*better the individual, for the benefit of the community*—has never felt more realized. This newest venture is a quantum leap for wellness achievement, and I am thrilled to finally announce our dream has become a reality."

Emmett pushed her shoulders back and straightened her already tall frame to its full height, cheating herself slightly out toward the center. Offstage, Emmett could see her assistant Taylor, bathed in a low red light, glancing down at the livestream on his Device, mouthing the next words.

"Welcome to WellPod," she boomed, her face widening into an appropriately confident smile as the stage floor beside her opened to reveal the tip of a cresting glass apex.

At Emmett's cue, a transparent dome the size of a room, fifteen feet across and just as tall at its top, rose from beneath the stage, stopping a few feet away from her. Inside, a WellPod engineer Emmett had met only briefly backstage sat cross-legged, wearing a white linen set that pooled around her. Her heart-shaped face was framed by her pitch-black hair and eyebrows.

Emmett narrated as the woman stood and went about a standard evening routine, retrieving dinner from what looked like a dumbwaiter in a center column. The screen behind Emmett revealed a 3-D rendering of a woman mirroring the onstage movements exactly. The camera zoomed out, through the computer-generated walls, to offer the amphitheater and viewers an aerial perspective of the circular space, lit by a brilliant artificial moon and stars. But it was Emmie, the AI therapeutic companion that had been in all of WellCorp's products since the WellNest, who prompted a collective gasp.

Unlike the Lens-generated, semitransparent Reception-Holographs that had welcomed visitors into the auditorium and guided them to their seats, the form that materialized in the WellPod looked real enough to touch, to be human.

"Every WellPod has an Emmie uniquely adapted to your personality, preferences, and needs," Emmett said. At the mention of *preferences*, Emmie shifted into a male-presenting body. He approached the woman in the Pod, and the two engaged in a friendly conversation the audience couldn't hear.

"WellPod has everything you could possibly need to flourish for weeks at a time, even years, in one of the most isolated places on earth—the middle of the Pacific Ocean," Emmett continued. Onscreen, the camera lowered until it came perpendicular to the rendered WellPod, revealing a cross-section of it. "They are the complete escape you've always yearned for, entirely removed from distractions."

From this perspective, the audience could see that the curved glass room was actually supported by a cone that plunged far below it into the ocean.

"WellPod is inspired by nature. Similar to an iceberg, only ten percent of each Pod is visible above water. The other ninety percent houses a fully automated, highly intricate system of furniture and food storage and medical administration devices, as well as a Dynamic Positioning System, all choreographed by sophisticated technology that anticipates each Traveler's needs.

"Our lives tend to be more full than they are fulfilling. I'll be the first to admit that." Emmett laughed self-deprecatingly. "Travelers will have virtually unlimited time to become self-optimized over the course of their six-week Journey. This is an opportunity to hit pause, to determine what you really care about, and return home calm, collected, and reborn."

Emmett had barely finished waving to the audience when a flute of champagne found its way into her hand. She wrapped her fingers around it, gripping the fragile glass as if it were a life raft, as her eyes adjusted to the dark.

"Take a minute," someone said. "They're still exiting the auditorium."

Onstage, she had been illuminated by a spotlight and a glow that emanated from the model WellPod.

Emmett could still feel the reverberations of the applause as she took a sip of the champagne, offering a tight smile to Taylor, who she could now see was the one who had handed her the glass.

"How was I?" she asked her assistant.

"It could have used more energy in the buildup, but nothing that needs any damage control," Taylor said honestly. Emmett had seen so many of her competitors surround themselves with flatterers, but he always told her the truth. She took another sip and considered her appearance in the mirror offstage, grateful for the dim lighting.

"Okay, ready? I can delay them if you need," Taylor said.

Emmett shook her head. Might as well get it over with. "Let's go."

Taylor stopped just before the door to the private lobby and pulled a microfiber cloth from his pocket to wipe away the smudge left by Emmett's lipstick on the edge of her glass. "Remember to make eye contact and smile. The board wants to see you as more approachable."

Emmett obeyed, stepping forward so that the double doors slid open, unveiling two Reception-Holographs with matching serene smiles plastered to their semitransparent faces. The glass-walled lobby wasn't quite as large as the adjacent main welcome room, where hundreds of reporters and employees were now spilling from the auditorium, but it still held around two hundred people, each of whom gripped a matching flute. Servers rushed to fill the remaining glasses.

Champagne had always been a luxury, but low crop yield meant high-end collectors had scooped up every French bottle until the price became impossibly expensive for anyone with a net worth under seven figures. Affordable alternatives had popped up in Poland and Scandinavia, but the champagne here flowed from French bottles, squeezed from the last of the overripe and dying grapes. Emmett watched her employees spill unspillable champagne. At their level of wealth, nothing was too precious to conserve. They had about as much substance as the Reception-Holographs that had herded them in, Emmett thought cruelly.

All eyes on her, Emmett raised her glass, taking the opportunity to quickly scan the crowd. She recognized only a handful of the faces closest to her, including the only journalist she had granted access to the room. As with most writers and Pohvee Personalities she interacted with, his name came to her as his full byline, *Thomas Fischer.* The rest of the group was made up of investors, board members, and the executive committee along with their spouses and partners. Even those who had contributed in later rounds were multimillionaires from WellCorp alone. Emmett smiled as they quieted, careful not to make eye contact with her first investor, Oisín, who stood next to his eager-to-please wife and two teenage sons, visibly uncomfortable in their suits. His eyes were glued to hers, and Emmett could practically feel them boring into her. They had been close once, but any fondness he had felt toward Emmett had been strained over the past few months in the lead-up to the keynote.

"Thank you!" Emmett said, collecting herself. Her voice transitioned seamlessly once more to their EarDrums. "I'm sure you can all understand how close I am to capacity for speeches tonight." She paused, allowing their polite laughter to fade. "But I will say this: in the past decade, my vision to create a Nest, a womb where people would feel safe became one shared by every single person in this room. Today, reality has finally co-opted even my wildest dreams.

"WellPods are our most ambitious product to date," Emmett said, shifting under the gaze of Oisín's wife, "and one that will launch us across disciplines, from technology into travel and even deeper into mental and physical healthcare. At the same time, it will provide us with the opportunity to connect with users on a much more significant level. So much more is to come, but for now, please enjoy the champagne. Cheers!" She raised her glass, pulling others as if tethered by fishlines to her own.

Across the room Emmett saw two of her first engineers, and raised her glass to them. The all-nighters they'd spent side by side writing lines of code that would become the first iteration of Emmie felt a lifetime away now. Their salaries alone made them unfathomably wealthy, not to mention loyal. But the stock price, which had only grown in anticipation of Emmett's keynote, guaranteed that not only they but their children's children would be rich too. It was nearly impossible to envision the seismic waves their net worths would trigger, a ripple effect that would have crippled Los Angeles's housing in the same way San Francisco's had been fifty years prior, if not for the luxurious WellHome apartments the company had built for its employees.

Emmett pushed her way through the crowd, her lips curving into a closed smile that got her to the far edge of the lobby and its two sets of doors. One would release her into the main lobby, where Pohvee Personalities and members of the press were frenetically milling, hoping to intercept her exit and get a usable quote or clip. The other led into an underground hallway available to employees and approved guests only. She pushed the door open and walked down the short ramp. Taylor followed like a shadow.

A few employees were already walking back toward the main building to projects that would keep them at their desks until even later in the night. They ducked their heads as Emmett strode past them, walking in the opposite direction.

"Hi, Thomas." At Taylor's words, Emmett turned around to see him speaking to the journalist, one of the last holdouts of a nearly extinct breed. "Emmett's not taking any more questions this evening, but I'm happy to schedule another time for you to speak with her."

Emmett wasn't in the habit of making allies of members of the press, but Thomas was as close to an exception as she allowed. She had handpicked him to write a subsidized puff piece about WellCorp after the campus was built (she hated its infantilizing designation, "WellPark"), and had granted several interviews since. Emmett trusted him, and he valued that trust too highly to write anything damaging about her. He had been one of the few to know about WellPods prior to the keynote. Emmett stood still as Thomas brushed straight past Taylor to her.

He was in his usual uniform, a sport coat, slacks, and gray T-shirt, which looked like a cheap mimicry of what he thought "serious" journalists wore half a century ago, despite his being younger than most in his industry. Emmett suspected it was a calculated camouflage, a plea for nostalgia to dress like the reporters who had covered Silicon Valley executives during their early tech booms.

"I wanted to give you the article before it goes live tonight." He looked at Emmett, whose Device buzzed with an invitation to accept the document. "I thought you might . . . it's not what we talked about."

Emmett had fed Thomas quotes about the Pods under strict embargo. What had he done? She accepted, downloading its contents.

"I'll give it a read, thank you." She glanced at Taylor, who looked annoyed at not having been given access.

Thomas didn't notice, or pretended not to, addressing Emmett: "Let me know if you have any questions."

"How long do I have?"

"My editor can wait another two hours before publishing it, out of courtesy to you, but she wants it live by ten at the latest."

"Thank you," Emmett said, and Thomas nodded and turned away. She and Taylor had been walking toward the parking lot to head home—she had a limited tolerance for these events, despite her honed façade—but instead she turned back toward the auditorium, to the private elevator that would take her straight to her office.

At the elevator, Taylor tapped his Device against the Reader, summoning its car. "I'll be here if you need anything."

Emmett stepped in. "Have some champagne. I'll be down soon." Taylor nodded, then turned so quickly he bumped into two women, separating their clasped hands at the moment the doors closed, cutting off Emmett's view. When they opened again, it was to her office, which she had designed with sunset views in mind. The vast, curved glass walls offered unencumbered views of her slice of California coast and her beloved ocean, but night could be just as stunning. She walked from the elevator to the northern edge of the circular room, leaning her palms against the low bookshelf that ran along the perimeter. People were beginning to funnel out of the main lobby. Beyond them, Emmett could see a string of small jewels bobbing along the coastline: a thousand WellPods docked just a few miles north of campus, waiting to be launched.

She let her fingertips linger over the tops of a framed feather her mother had given her and a gold coin the size of her palm, both leaning against the glass, then walked over to her desk in the center of the room and sat down. The desk had belonged to her father, and the cheap wood held tiny grooves made from the imprints of thousands of ballpoint pens. Most industries at that time had already transitioned to be electronic, but car sales were still done on paper. Emmett would sit at the end of the table, learning to write by mimicking her father's cursive, which complemented the looping cadence of his Georgia drawl. *Sign at the X, with a blue or black pen, ma'am,* he would say in the years they could still call themselves a family, before he left them. In a way, her job wasn't unlike her father's. They were both selling the promise of a better life through technology. Emmett ran her thumb along the shallow craters, the few sips of champagne making her a little slower.

Emmett clicked on her Device and the headline from Thomas's article filled her screen. She didn't have time to catch it before it fell from her hand, the phantom words still etched before her as clear as a projection from her Lens:

Radically UnWell: Inside WellCorp's Sick Culture of Secrets

3

Maggie

Zone 874, Pacific Ocean
36 Days Post-Launch

Lunch is ready," Emmie said, prompting Maggie to push herself off the floor. She had been lying in corpse pose following a guided meditation, but got up to retrieve her meal from the column at the center of the Pod.

The hatch of her NutriStation opened and Maggie reached inside for her plate. The diagram projected through her Lens mapped out the baked coconut bacon and sun-yellow cherry tomatoes cooked in lab-grown avocado oil and coated in ancient grains aside tempeh topped with a dollop of collagen- and protein-fortified macadamia nut labneh.

She ate a tomato as she crossed the small room to the Pod's only door, invisible except for a discreet seam where it joined the wall. The fruit was surprisingly delicious for something she assumed had been picked months before, dehydrated, rehydrated, and prepared. It even smelled a little like the vine, she thought, pausing to let the acidic juice coat her tongue at the same time that her stomach clenched against the sensation. It reminded her of something, just out of reach. The door slid open as Maggie approached, admitting a rush of wet, salty air.

The deck was just wide enough to fit a small outdoor shower as well as a chair and table that, like her bed, rose from the tiles as needed. Maggie sat down and rested the plate in her lap, tilting her head back to breathe in the sticky brine, so sensory-rich compared to the hermetically sealed Pod that it sent chills up her arms that crashed like waves into her spine. She opened her eyes to look for the bird who had become a common fixture over the previous week, returning most mornings to fish, before digging into her own meal. It had been a full day since she had seen it, she realized.

For as long as Maggie could remember, she had been taught that technology was inherently good. Almost as soon as she could read, Maggie was encouraged to order dinners and snacks from a screen on the fridge. Her parents had met on a dating app, and the watch that charted her mother's sleep efficiency and active calories was as familiar to Maggie as her wedding band.

Even as her parents dedicated their careers to the tech industry, and saw its dark underbelly firsthand, they could quickly point to all the ways it had improved their lives. Technology, her mother liked to say, was the entire reason she was able to work full-time while raising Maggie. She could answer emails on her Device and join conferences holographically from her kitchen. Though her mom never lived to see it, Maggie imagined she would have loved how seamless Lenses made everything; how WellCorp had even automated decision-making, though Maggie often wondered what her life would have looked like if she had been born forty years earlier, before Lenses and Devices, even "smartphones," changed everything and made the simplest of errands obsolete.

Maggie was six years old the first time she walked into a grocery store. Her mother had stood for a split second at the entrance before charging in the wrong direction. It was another few minutes until they located the Pasture-Raised Certified Organic Cage-Free Eggs and walked back toward checkout.

From the way her mother had described it to her, Maggie had expected the store to be a horrible place where you had to push through crowds to reach the crate with your name on it. But there were no crates like those delivered by drone to their front step every few days, and the variety of options stunned her. She'd let her hand graze the cereal boxes adorned with rabbits, captains, and toucans as she followed her mother to the register where it took her a few tries to scan the barcode and pay with her Device. Maggie's cheeks flushed as they walked past the store clerk, wondering if he could hear her mother's complaints about the out-of-date technology from where he stood.

As they pulled into their driveway, Maggie could see a short bouquet of purple-blooming ice plants wrapped in twine sitting on their welcome mat—her favorite. Her mother was already apologizing for having to hop on a call when Maggie asked if she could head to Gamma's, pointing to the flowers.

"Of course," she responded, visibly relieved. "Say hello for me, and keep your Device on."

No one could agree on the exact origin of Maggie's nickname for their next-door neighbor, but Gamma liked to say, "Short for Gamma Ray because I'm *high*-energy!" Maggie thought it was because she was her "almost Grandma," since she dropped the letters she kept for her real grandma, her mom's mom, in Southern California. She felt guilty for loving Gamma more, but the last time she had visited Grandma, she'd spent most of the vacation eating sugar-free cookies, timing how long it took for the artificial edges to dissolve on her tongue by lengths of episodes of *The Office*. Gamma's cookies, on the other hand, came out a little different every time, thanks to her refusal to use a recipe, but were always delicious: a medley of oats, flax, dried fruits, dark chocolate, nuts, and real sugar from dates or maple. She always had some project for Maggie to tend to, like picking sweet peas in the garden, or making cyanotypes. On the rare occasion they watched anything, it was usually a century-old movie.

Gamma was the only person Maggie knew who didn't own a Device. In the place of texts, she always left a calling card: a cairn of rocks or a feather half-tucked into the mailbox. Once she'd left a geode, which they had cracked open with a hammer, sending glimmering shards across the sidewalk.

Maggie grabbed the bouquet and ran across her family's manicured desertscape into the wildflower garden Gamma kept. She pushed the front door open without bothering to knock, and switched off her Device.

• • •

Years later, as Maggie's classmates live-streamed and posted about every waking aspect of their high school lives, Gamma embraced each moment without capturing it. The only technology Maggie ever saw Gamma add to her house was an air filtration system, at her doctor's insistence, after the frequent fires made the air too dangerous for her to breathe, and an archaic gadget for playing music through the unwieldy cord Gamma physically plugged into speakers. A Device remained out of the question.

For the most part, Maggie shared Gamma's opinion that her classmates were wasting their lives, but she was better at tolerating them. Her best friend, Chloe, walked around like a zombie glued to her Device most days, but also had an incredible sense of humor and only occasionally pressured Maggie to make her own social media account.

Maggie remembered the first time a classmate had asked, "What's your username?" His mouth opened and closed like an incredulous guppy when she told him she didn't have a Vito, but even the guppy wouldn't have an account the following year. By then, he'd moved on to Pohvee.

It wasn't until Maggie fell for Landon in high school that curiosity got the best of her. She didn't go to school with him, but knew him from sitting on the beach every Saturday as he taught her parents how to surf, a Christmas gift from her dad. It was intended for the entire family, but Maggie was happier sitting on the shore with a book.

Landon would run up from the ocean, shrugging his wetsuit off his shoulders, and always ask Maggie what she was reading. He was the kind of guy who would have looked great with a crooked smile, but his spread into a wide, even grin.

He was fascinated—charmed too, Maggie hoped—by the hardcovers she read, pulled from Gamma's bookcase. She didn't discriminate between fiction and poetry and memoirs, as long as the stories were real. Sylvia Plath, Louise Glück, Simone de Beauvoir, bell hooks, Toni Morrison, Anaïs Nin, Simone Weil, Clarissa Pinkola Estés, Mary Oliver, Sally Rooney, Cheryl Strayed, Maya Angelou, Elizabeth Gilbert. Maggie told Chloe about how he had watched her finish the last two pages of a Sheila Heti novel before sitting next to her, giving her time to digest the book. He had waited for her to speak, then finally asked if he could borrow it. It was the first time he'd asked to take one home.

"Oh, I've seen him reading that," Chloe said. She and Maggie both went to a private school a few blocks away from Landon's public school, but Chloe was fluent in his favorite places to surf, best friends, and, apparently, the books he read. She had never actually spoken to him, yet it felt to Maggie like Chloe had a more intimate relationship with him than the one Maggie had formed over their Saturdays together.

Chloe was sitting on Maggie's bedroom floor across from her, a bag of chips between them, squealing at the appropriate moments as Maggie relayed the story (when Maggie said how she could have sworn Landon's hand lingered on hers as he took the book), and taking more interest in the snacks at others (when Maggie summarized said book). But it wasn't until she broke the news that she was ready to create a Pohvee account that Chloe's screeches went supersonic.

Maggie slapped the floor in a drumroll as Chloe yelled, "Fucking *fiiinally!*"

The next day, Chloe stood in front of Maggie, carefully applying the adhesive from the wearable camera, no larger than a drop of water, to her forehead just below her hairline. This was the part Maggie was most apprehensive about, that in order to see other Pohvee users, you had to wear the small camera that broadcast your perspective to followers.

"You honestly forget after a while," Chloe explained, her own Pohvee at eye-level with Maggie's, "and it automatically stops recording anytime it detects nudity or, like, anything inappropriate. Mine usually falls off about every two weeks, but they send me a new one that comes within an hour or so. It's called a Blackout when that happens, and the best part is that it's the only time you can still access the app while you aren't Pohveeing."

She went on to explain that the only other time you weren't broadcast live to your followers was anytime you were looking at the app, watching others' Pohvees. The most-watched users were those who looked at the app the least. In the same breath, she admitted that this was nearly impossible.

"It's, like, so addicting!" Chloe exclaimed. Maggie gave a knowing nod. She'd witnessed the addiction secondhand for years.

"Okay," Chloe said, admiring her handiwork just inches away from Maggie's face, "I think it's all placed. Here! Open your app and see if you can see yourself!"

Chloe thrust Maggie's Device at her; she accepted it and opened the Pohvee app, navigating to Chloe's profile. A perfectly clear image of Maggie, looking at her Device from Chloe's perspective, appeared. She felt a little bit horrified. Her entire room was on display. Messages flooded her screen:

Maaagggggggssss!

What's up M!

Lol chloe Pohveed the Blob!

"Blob??" Maggie looked at Chloe, mildly annoyed.

"That's what they call everyone who doesn't have a Pohvee, 'cause that's how they appear! Here, look." Maggie placed the Device into Chloe's outstretched palm so she could pull up Landon's profile. He was in a parking lot, getting his surfboard out of his car. When he looked down, Maggie's heart skipped a beat to see that his body was only half-concealed by a wetsuit. On the beach she had to pretend she wasn't staring, but here she could watch openly as he walked with his board to another car. The people around him were crystal-clear except for their faces, which looked like they'd been smeared.

"The guys around Landon are almost always Blobs. So many surfers are Analog. They almost never have Pohvee even though they could get some of the coolest shots! Only the tech execs he teaches are clear," Chloe said, thrilled to be the one teaching Maggie the ropes, "like your dad."

Maggie made a face, then pointed to a number at the top of the screen.

"Oh, Landon has, like, ten million followers," Chloe explained.

Maggie knew he was popular online, but had never realized the extent. "Ten *million*??"

"Yeah! I have a few thousand, which isn't bad, but Landon is a legit PohPers." Chloe popped each syllable in the moniker for Pohvee Personality. "He's basically famous, Mags. Which means you'll probably be famous if you're ever on his Pohvee. . . ."

"Wait, can he hear us right now?" The realization sent adrenaline coursing through her veins.

"Not since we're both looking at the app. We're safe. But literally any other time, yeah. . . ." Chloe drifted off.

Landon was walking with his board toward Ocean Beach, carefully stepping from rock to rock down to the waterline. Chloe turned the volume up. They could hear him saying something about his breakfast.

". . . about that high-protein. I add a scoop to my smoothies every morning."

"Who's he talking to?" Maggie asked.

Chloe started laughing. "Us! He's narrating. Most Personalities talk through what they're doing so followers can really feel like they're there, get inside his head." She tapped her temple.

Maggie was dumbfounded. Of course, she knew about Pohvee. She'd heard her friends talking about it enough times, but it wasn't the same as actually watching someone's feed. How many conversations had she been eavesdropped on, without her fully understanding the extent, by *millions*? Did Landon narrate about her too?

As if reading her mind, Chloe said, "You also can't hear Blobs. Honestly, a lot of people have been waiting to see who Landon's girlfriend is. You've been like this mystery woman!"

"*Not* his girlfriend."

"Yet."

Maggie couldn't help but smile. "How do you see your own comments if it's live?"

Chloe answered her by opening Maggie's app and navigating to her profile.

The previous few minutes played back in a highlight reel, condensed into a few seconds.

"I usually watch mine every night," Chloe said, "and then you can save your top moments to your Life Reel by clicking this heart, but a lot of them save automatically as you have Experiences." She swiped over to another screen, and Maggie could see that her first experience seeing Pohvee had already been saved in a small circle, with a colorful baby emoji in the center.

There were several other grayed-out circles with emojis and captions that illustrated *First Kiss, International Vacation, High School Graduation, First Paycheck, College Acceptance, First Marathon.*

"It encourages you to have more Experiences," Chloe said. Her own profile displayed so many Experiences, Maggie had to scroll for several seconds just to see them all. *First Day of Junior Year, First Date, First Failed Test.*

"They're not all good, but it's the story of your life! I cannot fucking wait for this one," she said, pointing to *First Day of College.*

Maggie shook her head, smiling. It wasn't a universal truth, but one that had been perpetuated in Chloe's mind by the early 2000s movies she loved so much. The moral of every story was the same: boyfriends fix everything, college fixes everything boyfriends can't, and college boyfriends fix everything college can't.

That evening, after Chloe had gone home, Maggie walked across her driveway to Gamma's for their weekly Sunday dinner. On her way over, she narrated, "I'm heading over to my gamma's house. We aren't technically related, but she's always been like a grandma to me." She hoped she sounded natural. *Landon could be watching.*

At the door, she knocked instead of entering as she normally did, for a more dramatic reveal, already aware of the cinematic quality her life could have online.

When Gamma answered, Maggie said, "I guess I'm really a teenager now," pointing to the small camera at her hairline. She hoped self-deprecation was the best route for approval, but instead Gamma's face sank.

"Oh, Maggie." She stood frozen in the doorway.

"What?"

"I hope you understand the impact of this decision," she said.

"I mean, everyone does it."

"Not everyone. There are alternatives to living your life for others' benefit," Gamma said, still not opening the door all the way. She was looking at Maggie like she didn't recognize her.

Even though her followers couldn't follow Gamma's half of the conversation, which came to them as Charlie Brown–esque MFAB, "mumbles from a Blob," Maggie was sure they could easily fill in the blanks. She could already imagine the comments coming in.

Why isn't Gamma letting you in?

Tell Gamma to get a Pohvee!!

Maggie tapped her drop-shaped camera to mute her Pohvee's video and sound, something you could do once a day for no longer than four hours before the app denied you access to watching others, or temporarily locked your account.

"It's off," she said.

"Good," Gamma said. They both stood in the doorway awkwardly before she swung the door open, but Maggie stood still.

"Why are you so against this?"

"We can talk about this inside, Maggie. Dinner's almost ready—I made your favorite."

The smell of lamb stew wafted toward the entrance, but Maggie didn't move. "Are you, like, Analog now?"

Gamma sighed. "Every decision you make with that thing on will be influenced by your fear of perception, whether you're aware of it or not. It prohibits you from genuinely living your life."

"So does hardly ever leaving your garden and not adapting to modern technologies."

Gamma remained calm. "I'm happy. And I know that you're happy, but this technology could trick you into thinking you're not."

"It isn't bad to want more from your life!" Maggie hadn't realized it, but she was shouting. She turned on her heel, walking down Gamma's porch steps before she could change her mind, and tapped her Pohvee back on. Later, she'd watch the comments roll in, over the backdrop of Gamma's front steps, choked with regret.

When Maggie woke the next morning, she felt a small vibration from the teardrop at her hairline, indicating it would begin streaming in ten minutes. The grace period allowed her time to pull the duvet over her head for a few more breaths, which was all the time it took for her to decide.

Weeks ago, Gamma had suggested they play hooky for her birthday, with her mom nominated as accomplice. Their plan had been to drive to Berkeley and have lunch at an Indian restaurant Gamma liked to say had "more lives than a cat," before touring the college. The restaurant was one of Maggie's favorites, its food a testament to its ability to survive rent increases and trends, all while waving a sun-bleached red awning as its flag. She and Gamma had spent every one of her birthdays together, but Maggie was no longer sure she and Gamma were even speaking after yesterday.

She grabbed a pair of jeans off the floor and pulled a tee over her head, sliding her feet into sandals and her backpack over her shoulder. In the kitchen, she ran into her dad, who was sitting at the center island drinking a pale smoothie out of a glass bottle.

"Happy birthday!" he said as soon as he saw her.

She kissed him on the cheek, then flew out the door, tracing the familiar steps to Gamma's front door, which was unlocked as usual. Maggie pushed it open, calling Gamma's name. The air was still thick with the smell of the lamb stew Gamma had made the night before.

Maggie reached the kitchen and saw that the pot was still simmering. Nearly all of the liquid had evaporated—steam clung to the windows above the sink—and the vegetables at the bottom were beginning to turn black. Maggie was used to Gamma's culinary experiments, in which she turned leftovers from stews back into broths, repurposing ingredients until they had nothing left to give. But something wasn't right. Maggie clicked the burner off and looked around, a shape in the alcove off the kitchen catching her eye. It took Maggie a moment to realize that she was looking at Gamma's foot, resting in an unnatural position.

Maggie rounded the corner and saw that Gamma was lying on the floor, her mouth slightly agape and eyes half-open in a macabre expression, a small halo of blood around her head. Without thinking, Maggie dropped to her knees to cradle Gamma's head in her lap, pulling a hanging sweater off a doorknob to press against her wound, though the blood was no longer flowing. Maggie began shouting her name as she felt for a heartbeat, pressing her ear against Gamma's chest, then shook her shoulders.

"Get up," she heard herself say, desperation lending a jagged edge to her voice, then barked at her Device, "Call nine-one-one."

She dropped the sweater to perform CPR, pushing as hard as she could against Gamma's stiff chest, alternatively pressing her lips against Gamma's as she forced her breath into Gamma's lungs. Maggie had no idea how much time had passed when she heard the paramedics enter, calling to her. She pressed her fingers against the inside of Gamma's neck and her ear against her chest, straining to detect anything. When she finally felt something, it was a different sign of life.

Her Pohvee vibrated three times to indicate that she'd reached the

Trending page. Thousands of viewers watched the life pour out of the most alive person Maggie had ever known.

In a daze, Maggie watched balloons explode across her Device's screen, wishing her a happy birthday at the exact moment everything around her began to shake.

4

Emmett

It wasn't until Emmett looked up from Thomas's article that she realized she'd been sitting in complete darkness. The moonless sky was pitch-black through the domed ceiling of her office, so the only light came from the illuminated article on her Device, which bathed her like an interrogation lamp. How long had Thomas said she had before the piece was published? It had to be under an hour at this point.

Emmett had been laying the groundwork for the *Technologist* piece for weeks, as part of her public relations team's multipronged plan for the unveiling of WellPods. It was one of several sites she had granted advance interviews to, but arguably the most important given its strong Pohvee presence. Emmett had hand-selected Thomas to write it and expected a glowing review of the Pods. But this?

"Fuck." Emmett's voice punctuated the stale air in her office so abruptly she half-expected Taylor to hear her from the lobby and come running.

If they even made it past the title purporting the company's "sick culture," Emmett knew most people would form their entire opinion from the pullout quotes planted throughout. They would skim through the most egregious, eye-catching claims before sending it to a friend with the words: "Have you read the *Technologist* piece on Emmett Neal?" The quotes wiped clean all the nuance, Emmett thought, and reeked of petty self-righteousness. She couldn't help but snarl in disgust as one caught her eye:

"As soon as I voiced concern around the safety of the Pods, I was fired. I don't want to say 'death traps,' but I don't think that's entirely off."

The graphic designer had selected an ugly deep rust, the color of dried blood, for the quotes, which were nothing compared to the hateful cesspool that would form in the comments as soon as the piece was published. She needed to warn her team and create a game plan. Instead, she scrolled back to the top, rereading the piece.

At WellCorp's keynote on Tuesday night, company founder and CEO Emmett Neal unveiled plans for a wellness retreat that will harness the company's proprietary technology in a unique, remote location: the middle of the Pacific Ocean.

"This was always part of the plan," Neal told me last week over lunch on the deck of one of her floating WellPods, a fleet of individual retreats set to launch early next year, kicking off 2060. They are currently docked in a securely guarded sliver of coastline a few miles north of WellCorp's California headquarters.

The founder, wearing her signature black-and-white uniform, exuded her usual calm, confident energy, delivering calculated responses between thoughtful bites of sun-yellow tomatoes and peppery arugula harvested from a hydroponic farm on board the Pod's Culinary Chamber. The chamber is one of nine below sea level that serve the primary platform where the Traveler will spend the entirety of their six-week escape.

Sitting with her, it is not difficult to see how WellCorp has remained mediagenic, even through its years of unprecedented growth. But interviews with current and former employees suggest that this utopia has been a carefully veiled façade from the start, when a generous investment from Pohvee founder Oisín Byrne's notorious venture capital firm gave Neal's flagship product, WellNests, an easy rise.

Easy? Emmett could concede that things had moved quickly after the initial investment. But that word discounted the decade of work and sacrifices Emmett had put into the company before she ever walked into the conference room at Byrne Capital. To be accurate, the room had really been a glass box, which sat at the center of the office, framed by a dramatic skylight. Emmett had taken a seat at the slate-black conference table that reflected the sky, thinking about the irony of a glass ceiling in an office founded by men, despite the number of women who worked beneath them. Wisps of clouds passed above and below her, a break in San Francisco's gray uniform.

Emmett recognized Oisín the moment he walked in. The decade-plus had aged him, but he looked good; wealthy enough to purchase handsomeness from selling his social media empire, Pohvee. A few grays ran through his red hair to dispel the notion that he dyed the rest of it and a short scruff covered his face and neck, effectively camouflaging the scars she had spent an entire summer kissing. He shook her hand—a gold wedding band decorated his opposite ring finger—without a hint of recognition before sitting across from her.

She had met Oisín fifteen years earlier on an unseasonably warm day that only cooled off slightly as she navigated the unfamiliar public transportation from San Francisco into the suburbs. It had taken her two buses and an hour-long BART ride to travel the fifteen miles to the invitation's address in Hillsborough. She had to walk another mile to reach the top of the winding walkway that ascended to the door of the mansion. Another intern at a start-up she no longer remembered the name of had invited her, telling her that the founders wanted them to be there. They were both young enough to still think being a feminist meant being the girl cool enough to show up at a party dominated by men.

She had worn velvet Mary Janes she'd picked up in Chinatown for a dollar, but one of the straps had snapped somewhere along the way. As soon as she reached the house, she hopped onto one of its stone ledges, positioning herself next to a cascading rosemary bush that obscured her from view of the arriving guests as she tugged at the dangling strap.

She was already calculating whether the remaining sum in her bank account would be enough to cover a car home when she saw him for the first time.

His friends were walking up to the house, all wearing what looked to her to be the same slate hoodie, jeans, and leather Nikes, but he had lagged a few stairs behind, presumably to check his notifications. He had just begun to walk up to join them when he turned and looked in her direction. Emmett could see him straining his eyes, not quite seeing her. He was about to turn back when she hopped out, victoriously tossing the freed strap into the plant behind her.

His face lit up at the discovery. He had hung back, and here was his treasure. As he smiled, his cheeks pushed his healed acne scars into an uneven, folded accordion. Even at nineteen, Emmett had already learned to love men whose faces were scarred. Each crater represented the pain and humiliation he'd likely endured in high school. This man hadn't built his entire life around his attractiveness, so he'd had to develop a personality. Emmett smiled back. Someday he'd grow a short stubble or undergo a procedure that would hide the marks, just as he would learn to grow out his red hair from a buzz into something he could run his fingers through, but for now, Emmett took him in.

"Oisín," he said, extending his hand for Emmett to take as he walked around the edge of the bush to face her. It felt like her mother's favorite scene in *It's a Wonderful Life*, when Donna Reed hides in the rhododendrons and Jimmy Stewart stands stalwart with her robe, daring her to emerge.

After a few drinks, he'd led her into a guest bathroom the size of her entire apartment. Her legs wrapped around him as she perched on the edge of the sink. Her shoe with the missing strap hit the tile with a satisfying *thunk* as he entered her. Afterward, she kissed the craters on his face and wiped up the mess with an Egyptian cotton hand towel before pulling her pants up.

Only a few summers had passed since the 2026 financial crisis, though the companies they each worked for defied any notion of a recession. Those who had been around long enough to remember, compared it to 2008, and the minimum wage Emmett was paid at her internship was the only example of practical spending she saw. The brazen trust her company's C-suite placed in capitalism enthralled her. Their South Park office resembled a living organism, its interiors adapting to trends as they happened, and the office manager regularly sent out invitations to midweek happy hours that would flow naturally into company-sponsored bottle service. Work hard, play hard.

The night of the party was the first of many she and Oisín would spend together, initially coupling out of convenience, then because they couldn't imagine sleeping apart. How many hours had they sat at the bar around the corner from the apartment Oisín shared with three roommates? They would split a Guinness or Smithwick's, resolved to save, but then inevitably split a second as Oisín's idea for products that revolutionized the way people shared their lives evolved from an idea to a strategy to a company he would sell five years later for ten figures. At the end of summer, they went their separate ways. The moment he walked into the conference room was the first time she had seen him since.

Emmett skipped ahead to the end of the article, another sanguine quote catching her eye.

"There's no concept of checks and balances. If Emmett wants something, we make it happen—no matter the stakes."

It wasn't the worst thing that had ever been written about her, but the accusation that Emmett knew would initiate the crack that could ruin her company appeared a few lines below:

Conversations with current and former WellCorp employees, all of whom asked to remain anonymous for fear of legal retribution, revealed serious concerns about the Pods' structural integrity. Neal, who has no background in naval engineering, sketched the initial design on a sheet of drafting paper and hired Dr. Arthur Russo-Neva, a former Professor of Mechanical Engineering and Naval Architecture at UCLA, to build out a team.

"It was all very optimistic at the beginning," a former employee shared. "At first, I felt—I think we all felt—like we were rising to this great challenge, but Emmett was unwilling to make compromises that would ensure the Pods' safety." Another employee put it more bluntly: "They're beautiful pool floats. Sure, they'll stay above water, but I wouldn't want to be in one during a storm."

According to company lore, the pitch meeting at Byrne Capital had lasted eight hours, but the part in the conference room had really been closer to two. As Emmett talked through prospective annual growth rates and projections, Oisín barely said a word. The initial funding meeting of what would become one of the world's most successful companies was anticlimactic, if anything. It was weighed down in the jargon of market share percentages, projections, and acquisitions, though those lucky enough to be in the room conflated its importance and their role in it.

After the meeting, Oisín walked her to the elevator bay and, to her surprise, invited her out for a drink.

His car dropped them off at the opening of a narrow alleyway in the Mission, where they walked between two Victorians close enough together that their shoulders almost brushed both at the same time. The summer was as hot as it had been when they met in 2030. Oisín took her hand to lead her down the brick steps to a door so small she had to duck to slip through it. A bouncer nodded at them both, opening the door just long enough to let them and a narrow slip of daylight in.

The darkness blinded Emmett. She had to stand in the doorway a few moments to allow her eyes to adjust, but Oisín went straight to the bar, either used to the dimness or so familiar with the layout he could walk through it with his eyes closed.

A few men sat around the mahogany bar, the contents of their glasses perfectly complementing the dark, rich wood. One man lit a cigarette and Emmett flinched, anticipating the fight when the bartender told him to put it out. Instead, the bartender placed a porcelain ashtray in front of him and the man with the cigarette nodded in thanks, flicking ash into it.

Oisín returned with two pints of copper-colored ale. She wondered if he remembered that she'd fallen in love with the drink at his recommendation all those summers ago. He handed her one, and clinked his glass against hers.

"You mean we don't have to share?" she said, the stiffness of their initial meeting already melting away. "I knew you were rich, but now I'm impressed." Now that her eyes had finally adjusted, she could see how similar this bar looked to the one they used to go to.

Oisín smiled, then followed her gaze to the lit cigarette. "It's a private club. But I'm not sure anyone's checked its license in years anyway."

"How is this place still here?" she asked. She'd watched bars like this disappear over the single summer they'd spent together, and it had felt like an eternity since then.

"It's mostly supported by dues from the Irish Cultural Center," he said before adding, "a nonprofit I support."

He didn't need to explicitly say it for Emmett to understand that he owned the bar, or at least paid the owner to keep the lights on. Even places like this weren't immune to the cash that came from the city's tech giants. It, like the rest of the city, had to adapt to survive.

Emmett followed him to a door that looked like that of a confessional and revealed a room nearly as small when Oisín pulled its narrow handle and gestured for her to sit inside.

"Is this where the moguls sit?" she asked, sliding into a red leather banquette. Despite the air-conditioning, Emmett's long legs stuck to the seat, exposed from her pencil skirt, and she had to slide across it in short hops. Oisín flashed her a smile. She realized it was the first time she'd seen him smile all afternoon, but he didn't say anything. Once she got settled, she pretended to take a sip of her beer, licking the froth from her upper lip and enjoying the almost caramel, malty taste she hadn't allowed herself to indulge in for years. She looked up and saw that Oisín had been gazing at her like he was trying to drink her in.

"How often do you come here?" she finally asked.

"Almost every day," he admitted. "It reminds me of Ireland." His lips hugged the last syllable into a hum, a memory of the native Irish *Éireann*. "I like going someplace where no one cares who I am." It was true that, despite his monetary contributions, no one in the bar seemed to care about his status, though Oisín was something of a celebrity. Anyone in the industry knew his face from his countless speaking engagements and broadcast interviews. He was apotheosized in nearly every surviving magazine including, ironically, the *Technologist*. He could charge thousands for an uninterrupted hour with him and, by her count, Emmett had already had two.

"Did you know it was me?" Emmett asked, already knowing the answer to how she'd managed to secure a pitch meeting with him.

"No," he lied, then took a sip before meeting her gaze and answering truthfully, "I remember you talking about it even then. You sketched it for me over a pint, but that version looked more like a time machine. There were knobs, buttons, wires . . ." He laughed, either at her poor drawing or at the memory of the late nights they'd spent dreaming up inventions and companies they would launch one day. It was the first reference either of them had explicitly made to the summer they spent together.

He downed the last of his beer, then rapped his knuckles twice against the wall of the snug without looking at it. A moment later, the bartender pushed back a screen that looked like it should have revealed a priest on the other side. Oisín turned toward him to order two pints.

He took a sip of his fresh Guinness before it reached the table, then placed the second next to hers, either not registering or not caring that she had yet to make a dent in her first.

"Where did you go at the end of that summer?" he asked.

"LA."

"Why?" he pressed. It had taken her years to convince herself that their relationship meant nothing, that it was just for fun and convenience, but his earnestness melted away the wall she'd built. She looked away, then reminded herself to meet his gaze. She would tell him the real reason she left, but now was not the time. She was stronger now than she had been then.

"There was something I had to do, for myself. I needed to leave San Francisco." She paused, gathering her thoughts. "The easiest way to explain it is that I knew I wouldn't be able to build my company if I didn't leave."

"But now you're back."

"But now I'm back. For the weekend."

Oisín took another sip, not quite satisfied. He seemed to be debating whether to continue questioning her.

"I'm going to fund your company," he said.

"Are you funding me out of pity or because you know it's a good idea?"

"Both," he said with a laugh, but he was shaking his head. "I think WellCorp's going to take over the world, and you're the perfect person to lead it—cheers to your first round of funding."

Emmett looked at him incredulously. "Really? And you would fund me if you didn't know me before my pitch?"

"I never fund anyone I don't know." His cheeks were flushed from the first beer, as he held his second midair in front of Emmett's. "But then again, you really never know anyone until they get rich—and you're about to become very, very rich, Emmett."

Their glasses came together, with enough force that they should have shattered.

Most ships have a bow that can plow through waves, but the Pods bear a distinctive domed shape. Many engineers I spoke to voiced concerns around their ability to withstand certain hydrodynamic and wave-breaking loads, due to the Pods' rounded glass, which Neal was adamant about keeping despite her apparent awareness of the grave risks it poses.

The problem is that there is no way of proving this. WellCorp's sophisticated internal communication system has been lauded for its groundbreaking elimination of the impact of bias, at the same time it enables the company to function as gatekeepers. When Russo-Neva left the company two years into the project, it took some members of his team months to realize he had been replaced. Meetings between employees take place entirely over virtual reality through randomly generated avatars, effectively protecting their identities while also enabling a company culture of secrecy.

In the case of Russo-Neva, WellCorp had simply hired a replacement naval engineer under the same avatar and title. There is no reference anywhere to who this person is, though the replacement pushed through the designs as passionately as his predecessor. Internal documents are also securely guarded. It is not possible to forward internal communications to anyone outside the company, so the *Technologist* had no way of verifying these claims.

It is possible that the WellPod will sail smoothly. Hannah Meyer, a senior marine inspector at the US Coast Guard, shared that WellPods have satisfied maritime conventions under the Port State Control, which includes an inspection of the ship's structure. A representative from WellCorp assured me that the Pods have received all necessary certificates and documents for operating safely in international waters. Still, the amount of secrecy around the launch raises a number of red flags, especially given the company's commitment to "radical transparency."

"You aren't even allowed to ask questions—there's a lot of fear," one employee told me. "At the end of the day, we don't really know what Emmett is capable of."

Emmett sat long enough that her Device clicked off and the darkness finally enveloped her. Thomas's article was not a death sentence, but the last thing she needed was someone—especially someone with *Technologist* clout—attacking her company, her Pods. And, the blow felt personal. She'd had so much hope for Thomas. She would find the employees who had spoken to him and make every single one of them regret it. But for now Emmett opened her Device and placed a short call to Taylor. She would handle this herself. She always had.

5

Noa

Malibu, California
37 Days Post-Launch

Before opening her eyes and confirming what she already knew to be true, Noa rolled over toward Maggie's side of the bed, pushing her face into the percale edges of her pillow so that every breath came filtered through synthetic down.

She tried to remember what Maggie had looked like first thing in the morning. It was always her mouth that she had trouble conjuring clearly. When they'd first started dating, she'd thought Maggie was pretending to be asleep, aware of Noa's gaze and arranging her face into a pretty half smile. But that was just how she slept, entirely content in her dream world.

Through the fogged glass of the bedroom's floor-to-ceiling windows, Noa could see a fuzzy horizon line dividing the gray sky from the grayer ocean. Like everything else in the apartment, the transitional glass was connected to her Vitalities, combined biometrics measured by her Lens and Injectible, and its opacity was optimized to gradually become transparent in tandem with her REM cycle, gently announcing morning's arrival. In the winter, a soft LED light emanated from the window frame to approximate a rising sun. Some mornings she'd step outside and be shocked to realize that it was still pitch-black out. Today her Emmie had let her sleep in, logging her hours of restlessness and adjusting her schedule accordingly.

Noa brought her hands to her temples and rubbed circles into their hollows, then reached into her bedside table for her Device to scroll through work notifications that had come in overnight. Another Device sat in the charging drawer beside her own, as useless as it had been since the night she received it.

The Device had arrived in their apartment's delivery slot the night of Emmett Neal's keynote, with a soft ping a few minutes after Noa returned home. She'd opened the door just in time to see a man stepping into the elevator at the end of the hall. He looked vaguely familiar, though he disappeared too quickly for Noa to get a good look at his face, and he hadn't said a word when she called after him. Noa had taken the Device to the bedroom she shared with Maggie and swiped it open, but it was completely blank, revealing no hints of its provenance or purpose, though she assumed it had to have one. She'd instinctively slid it to the back of the drawer when she heard Maggie tiptoeing in.

Noa was no longer sure why she kept the Device, though she checked it each morning in anticipation of a notification, or any change, really. Maybe it was Maggie who had changed. Even now, she wasn't sure where Maggie had been that night. The uncomfortable feeling of arriving home to their empty apartment lingered.

Noa set the Device on the table and slipped out from under the covers.

The bathroom's SmartMirror projected her schedule for the day. She had a meeting in two hours and a suggested meditation was waiting for her in the WellNest. Her reflection stared back at her, surrounded by a halo of metrics—her skin temperature, heart rate variability, breathing rate.

She hadn't cut her short hair since Maggie left, and it was starting to look sloppy, brushing the bottoms of her ears. Her mother, who had converted to Judaism for Noa's father and had been selectively but passably pious up until the moment he died, had cut her hair just two days after his burial, breaking the month-long mourning period of shloshim. Noa's father's Orthodox family were openly critical of her mother's flagrant disrespect, but she simply waved them off, shedding her adopted faith as naturally as a snake does its skin, permanently alienating herself and Noa from the family in the process.

"Cada macaco no seu galho," her mother repeated in her native Portuguese. *Each monkey to his own branch.* It was one of her favorite phrases, meaning "mind your own business." Noa knew better than to question her—it was so much easier to go with her mother's whims than attempt to resist them.

By the end of the month, Noa's mother was nearly unrecognizable. Her hair, which had been long and black for Noa's entire life, had been hacked into a severe bob, combed through with bleached highlights that made her expensive new lipstick look cheap. One day Noa came home from school to find garbage bags of her mother's clothes along the curb and ribbon-handled shopping bags littering the entryway. When her mother finally emerged from her bedroom, suggesting that they order takeout, she wore a completely new outfit. She had, it turned out, replaced the contents of her entire closet.

Noa wasn't sure how they could afford these extravagances, especially when she learned that her mother had quit teaching third grade at the elementary school in Red Hook. Every morning Noa watched her mother declare some new intention with the same manic energy she had intermittently applied to raising Noa. She treated each idea like it was the miracle that would cut through their unacknowledged grief: they would purchase their Brooklyn apartment and finally redo the kitchen, *or!* begin a baking business, *or!* move upstate to join the women-centered commune she had seen on the then-brand-new platform Pohvee. With time, her mother's plans gradually began to center on returning to Olinda, her small hometown on the eastern coast of Brazil. Air travel had become so expensive that Noa entertained her mother's declarations around moving into the house she'd grown up in, feeling safe in the knowledge that it was next to impossible.

Noa spent her days sequestered in her room, allotting just enough time to online assignments to secure her June graduation from high school, but otherwise immersing herself in various paid coding gigs. At night, when the blanket of silence meant that her mother had finally collapsed on the couch, Noa would unpack the swimsuits and dresses and skirts, all with tags still on, from her mother's suitcase. She would gently tuck the unworn clothes back into the dresser, then her mother into bed.

Her mother would always be in the kitchen the next morning, offering Noa a cup of coffee as if nothing had happened. She never mentioned the empty suitcases or Noa's absences from school, though she wordlessly signed the permission slips (*Absent on account of bereavement*) Noa handed her. In return, Noa would accept the mug of strong, blisteringly hot coffee from her mother's hands and nod at that morning's outlandish solution— the addition they could add to the falling-down house in Olinda, the healing beachside walks they would go on—before slipping back into her room. Noa's own plans were more straightforward: she just had to keep her head down until graduation and save enough from coding jobs, which were thankfully paying better as her skills improved, to move out.

One evening Noa emerged from her room to discover that her mom wasn't there, then again the next night, though she was back by morning each time. Noa learned to listen for the gentle sound of the front door latch clicking closed, but their mutual unspoken vow of avoidance felt so engrained by then that Noa never asked her where she went until Noa walked into their galley kitchen a few weeks later to find a shirtless man rummaging through the cabinet.

"*Mom!*" Noa shouted, frozen at the edge of the stained linoleum, as her mother strode in from behind her in a new satin robe. She let her hand cup the stranger's bare hip and graze across his lower back as she reached past him for the coffee. Noa had never seen her mother touch a man besides her father, chaste pats that rarely ventured past the realm of platonic.

"Bom dia, Noa," her mother said, as if just realizing she was there, despite breezing past her. She plucked an aluminum bag off the shelf, sending a puff of grounds into the air that settled on the dirty counter.

"Mom, who is this?"

"How'd you sleep?" she asked, ignoring the question and the man, whose facial hair was coiffed into a small goatee that made Noa ill to look at.

"Who the fuck is this, Mom?"

"Pare com isso," her mother snapped back through a strained smile, plastered on for the man's benefit.

"Stop what? Who is this?" Noa gestured toward the man without looking at him.

Her mother exhaled, annoyed that Noa had not immediately accepted the stranger's presence.

"This is Isaac," she said, as if it were obvious. Her voice sounded off, slightly higher and quicker than usual. "He's going to bring us to Brazil."

Isaac bumped his chin up in a quick nod, drawing Noa's attention to his dilated pupils. To her horror, Noa watched her mother throw her head back and release a throaty glut of sound, a false version of her singular laugh Noa had been desperate to hear for months. When her eyes met Noa's, Noa could see through her overgrown bangs that her pupils were dilated too.

Her mother did, months later, make it to Brazil. The day she departed, without the suitcase she had made a religion out of packing and unpacking, Noa felt numb. She had just turned eighteen and stayed in the apartment they had shared until she was finally evicted, unable to pay rent, at which point she headed to the airport and bought a ticket to California so expensive, it maxed out her father's two remaining credit cards. Like her mother, she had a knack for moving on and starting fresh. Until Maggie.

As Noa approached the shower, the water turned on automatically, cascading with her preferred pressure. It must have detected the onset of a cold in her Vitalities because it ran hot, diluted with eucalyptus essential oils that filled the room with an herbal steam. Noa breathed in, then coughed when the heat shocked her lungs. It didn't come as a surprise that her immune system was compromised; she'd barely slept in the month since Maggie had left.

The screen in the shower clicked on, broadcasting that morning's news. She kept an eye on it as the water scrubbed her body clean: Venezuela had waged war against Colombia; a banker commuted by boat down Eighth Avenue in Manhattan; a farm in Fresno was reviving the honeybee population. In DC, protestors who would have been called "alt-right" years before, but were now jarringly mainstream, flooded the streets in support of their president's bid to revoke the Twenty-Second Amendment and run a third consecutive term. A banner ran across the bottom of the screen, flagged in Americana visuals, *2060 Election*. Noa worked shampoo through her hair as she watched footage of the sea rising from its calm blue to tear roofs off ancient monasteries that looked like her mother's hometown, even in rubble. Meteorologists disputed whether the freak waves hitting Baja were hurricanes or cyclones as people carried pieces of their homes toward higher ground.

When the shower turned off, it was replaced by a light mist of SPF-enhanced moisturizer that coated her body in an even layer of protection. Noa rubbed it into her damp skin, then dried off, securing the towel around her. She reached around the soft skin of her right arm and delicately pulled at one edge of her insulin pump patch. It was barely larger than a stamp and communicated directly with her Injectible to deliver doses so attuned to her glucose levels that Noa barely had to think about her diabetes except for the one time a month it needed to be replaced. The patch was an enormous improvement over the finger pricks she'd had to endure as a child and the glucose monitor and pump she'd donned before WellCorp streamlined the delivery technology. She peeled off the square and tossed it into the Waste Disposal under the sink, removing the packaging and adhesive from the patch that had arrived the day before. She carefully stuck it to her arm before padding barefoot into the kitchen past her WellNest. She'd woken up hungry and braced herself against the countertop's screen as she scrolled through the breakfast options.

She selected a smoothie from a list of synthetic suggestions, then walked over to the WellNest. It opened as she approached, welcoming her with open arms for a morning meditation.

An hour later, Noa stood at the shuttle station sipping her smoothie. The shuttles arrived every minute or two, so she didn't have to wait long. Everyone boarding them worked at WellCorp or lived in the same building, yet she knew only a few of them by name. In the morning, most people headed straight for the social cars, but Noa preferred the seats with privacy screens, where she could tap her EarDrums on and escape for the length of her commute into a movie. For the past week, she had been watching one of her favorites in fragments. Her Lens projected a scene where two astronauts were locked in a floating dance, having gone insane while orbiting an oceanic planet.

From where she sat, in the air-conditioned compartment and reclining vegan leather seat, Noa couldn't see even a hint of the crisis gripping other parts of the world. The man-made hillsides on either side of the tracks, landscaped with desert rocks, blocked out the surrounding neighborhood. Externally, the walls had been criticized as blinders for the elite, obscuring the realities of the world for the privileged few lucky enough to work at WellCorp. The company responded that they were providing their employees with a safe haven that allowed them to do the work necessary for the country. *Better the individual, for the benefit of the community.*

Once, in red letters as tall as the hill itself, Noa had caught sight of a message spray-painted in red: VIRTUAL REALITY IS NOT REALIT. Noa wondered if the Y had already been scrubbed off, or if the painter had been arrested before finishing the message. By the time she took the shuttle home that evening, it had been washed away so effectively, Noa couldn't pick out where it had been in the first place.

The ride took a few minutes, but always felt even shorter. When the shuttle pulled into a tunnel, Noa knew she only had a few seconds before it arrived at the underground station on campus. As soon as it did, she made her way toward the gaping exit at the top of the slope, which flooded the station with natural daylight.

The path to the main building was winding, and Noa was aware of the impact it was supposed to have on her. Employees were encouraged to walk slowly and mindfully through the Japanese-inspired rock garden. It was less than a third of a mile, but could feel like an eternity when Noa had a deadline looming. She could see the subtle straight path forged by those too impatient or rushed to take the winding route. The path's condescension sometimes leered at her, but today she was grateful to have the buffer between the shuttle and her desk. She knew it so well she could walk it with her eyes closed: *four steps to the left, three steps right, five toward the Japanese footbridge.*

The bridge had belonged to Monet, imported to California from Giverny, though there was no plaque to commemorate its significance. The only evidence that it dated back to the nineteenth century, as far as Noa could see, was the aged wood and retouched bright-turquoise handrail Maggie had shown Noa paintings of. It stood out starkly against the khaki and gray tones of the pebbles, and the glass buildings that sprang from them. To be honest, she might never have noticed the bridge if Maggie hadn't loved it so much.

Each time Maggie accompanied Noa to WellPark she made a point of pausing at the bridge. She had written her undergraduate thesis on Monet, and Noa could practically see her painting the water lilies in her mind over what was now a canvas of dead earth. Maggie knew exactly what it was the moment she saw it. Now, almost out of habit, Noa hung back at the center of the bridge to face the main building. She took a deep breath, imagining the wisteria that had once hung lazily from its frame, wondering what Maggie was dreaming of at that moment.

After a few more sloping turns, Noa approached the largest of the oblong glass buildings that made up campus. The Injectible in her wrist unlocked the door, which slid open to a light-filled lobby with a small café, where she let her Vitalities select a coffee for her, holding her wrist to the Reader at the counter. The barista glanced at the results of the scan, then set about creating a synthetic cashew milk latte.

Noa sipped her drink as she walked along the indoor terrace to find an open desk. Through the glass walls, she could see hundreds of people hunched over their screens. A bank of WellPods served as a divider roughly every fifty feet. There were no assigned seats, but Noa noticed that people tended to choose a favorite room. She approached one of the walls and touched her fingertips to the frosted meridian line that ran across all of the panels. The door swept aside to let her in.

She'd selected the room her first day at work, not understanding then that she would spend the majority of the next three years of her life in it. "Sit wherever you feel comfortable," the HR representative had said. They had already walked around the entire mezzanine, which, although it ran along the interior of the building, still offered a 365-degree view of campus, through several panes of glass. *You tell me*, she had wanted to say, but instead she strode confidently to the desk closest to the window. She'd intended on changing seats eventually, but when she didn't select a different desk the next day, the habit was all but fully formed. Most of her coworkers opted for ocean views, but Noa preferred the vantage point she had over the walking path. She could see almost the entire campus from her seat, and there was something satisfyingly communal about watching her colleagues, like a line of ants serving the same colony, the same queen.

Noa placed her coffee in the desk's cupholder. Like nearly everything designed by WellCorp, the desk had no straight lines or sharp angles. A chair was nestled between its lima bean–shaped slopes.

She sat and held her wrist down at her side, angling her Injectible toward the desk's base just long enough for its Reader to recognize her. As soon as it did, her chair adjusted to her exact height preference and the immaculate, glossy-black screen of the desk came to life, displaying her workstation. In spite of the diffused light streaming through the glass panels that hugged the room on either side, she could clearly see the glare-proof screen.

A man sat one desk over, his back turned to her; beyond that, no one else was in the room. She had expected Maya, the HR rep who had first shown her around, to be there already, but it wasn't unlike her to change seats and floors depending on her mood. Noa stifled a yawn as she took a minute to organize her station, still a disaster from the late night before. She guided windows of code around with her fingers, double-tapping to send some to the back, and pushing down harder to bring her most pressing projects forward.

Noa had thought no stress could compare to the round-the-clock hours she'd put in Pre-Launch, optimizing the code for WellPods, but she'd only been responsible for deadlines then, not people. It helped her to think of it as a video game. She was Ender battling the Formics. As Lead Health and Performance Engineer, she kept the average Vitalities for all thousand Pods in view, with alerts set for any out-of-the-ordinary changes so that she could address them long before they came to the Traveler's attention. All Travelers' mental and physical health had been assessed during Orientation, but she kept a careful eye on the most vulnerable groups: Travelers with preexisting conditions, those over sixty-five, those who tested for high levels of impulsivity.

Last week she'd received an alert for a micro-change in hydration levels. It wasn't cause for concern, yet, but Noa realized that the evening VR bike rides were occasionally so grueling that the Travelers couldn't drink enough water to rehydrate before going to sleep. In the morning, they woke up thirsty and groggy. Noa had recoded the hydration sensors to be more reactive and suggested a change to the Routine Engineers that included evening IV drips for some. It was almost exactly the same thing she'd done in her life before WellCorp, when she had coded an app that streamlined and automated medication delivery in hospitals. At least the Travelers were, as a whole, healthier than any of those patients had been.

She watched the man at the desk next to hers slip a VR set off its cradle. *Is he joining the meeting too?* Noa placed her own headset over her eyes, which immediately transported her to a virtual conference room. From where she sat at the edge of a long table, she could see the exact same view from her desk, programmed to her seating preference across from the other avatars. It had been a few months since the *Technologist* piece had come out, highlighting the culture of secrecy perpetuated by the virtual meetings, but the anonymity had been one of the first things to attract Noa to WellCorp.

The year before Noa started, Emmett had won a Nobel Prize for WellCorp's implementation of VR technology in nearly eliminating the

impact of workplace bias, by concealing individuals' race and gender. It was a controversial choice that some civil rights advocates argued only halted real progress, but after years of subtle homophobia and "Where are you from?"'s, it had felt like a godsend to Noa.

That wasn't to say she was entirely comfortable with the virtual reality, which Noa sometimes felt went too far. The levels of secrecy at WellCorp shrouded everything in a veil of protection. No one but Noa's direct manager knew exactly what she did, and Noa had no idea what her manager even looked like, or who they were. Their touch-bases took place between avatars as a necessary precaution for protecting the secrecy of the projects they worked on. Each person worked nearly independently on their small piece of the larger whole.

Noa's own avatar, which had been selected at random the day she joined, was of an older man with buzz-cut purple hair. The first time she told Maggie about her avatar, breaking the company policy to keep them confidential, Maggie had nodded along with Noa's description of the belly that distended against his jeans and rings that adorned all ten of his fingers. Maggie had surprised her when she said, "He sounds badass." Noa had laughed at her, but she'd insisted, "No really! I love that he calls attention to his hands with chunky rings, and dyes the little hair he has left neon. He's confident!" From that moment, they decided to nickname Noa's alter-ego Antoni, creating stories about his vibrant youth before he settled down at a desk job. As she waited for the meeting to begin, Noa looked at Antoni's rings, turning her favorite signet around to admire the moonstone embedded in it.

In front of her on the conference table, Noa could see her workstation exactly as it appeared at her desk. She continued to organize it as her manager began to speak in vague terms about their goals for Day 37 of the Journey. Her avatar—Noa assumed her gender from the female presentation of her avatar, though of course she had no way of knowing—had impossibly bright blue eyes and olive skin that called to mind Athena or another Greek goddess. Noa couldn't say why, considering she knew close to nothing about her manager beyond her work ethic, but she had always

gotten the feeling she would like her, if they ever had the opportunity to meet in person.

Noa glanced up at the live schedule projected onto the wall behind her manager. At the moment it simply read, *Deep Rest*. Though each Pod experience was different, tailored to that Traveler's specific needs, they all followed a baseline schedule orchestrated through the central processor and a team of Routine Engineers. It was still predawn on the Pacific, but soon the Emmies would guide each Traveler through a morning breathwork or yoga session.

It was still surprising to Noa that Maggie had chosen to go on the Pods. They'd spent the months before Launch either bickering or avoiding each other. The fact that Maggie had decided to spend six weeks in an isolated retreat that provided practically the same technology as their apartment didn't make any sense to her. Yet when Maggie asked if she should go, Noa had simply shrugged. Sure, there were issues around secrecy at WellCorp, but Noa never doubted the safety of the Pods. If Maggie wanted to go, she should—she just never thought she would.

Noa pulled up a live feed of a Pod's infrared cameras, watching the waves of red emanate from a Traveler's core into blues and greens at their feet. The Traveler was anonymous, and Noa tried to forget it could also be Maggie. She was still lost in thought when another voice began to speak, coming from the avatar Noa recognized as the head of the meteorological team.

"In the past several hours, we've detected a change in barometric pressure near Hilo, Hawai'i. This usually indicates the potential for a storm to develop, though we don't expect any threat." A screen popped up on Noa's station with a map of the Pacific Ocean. Small white dots represented the live locations of the Pods, with lines indicating the path of a potential hurricane.

"It's far enough away from the southern system hitting Baja. We're in the process of rearranging the position of several Pods as a purely precautionary action against any intensification which, again, is unheard of for early February in this location."

Noa looked around the room, but everyone seemed to be taking the

news in stride, despite the fact that most of WellCorp's rebuttal of the *Technologist* piece had been around the impossibility of a storm. The Pods weren't built to withstand massive storms because the algorithms had deduced there would *be* no massive storms

She messaged Maya on her personal Device, re-created in the virtual room. Though they worked on different teams, Maya sometimes attended the morning updates.

Are you seeing this?

Just joining.

Oh ya. Was briefed on this earlier – people making something out of nothing.

Ok

Don't worry. Maggie's safe

Maya sometimes felt like the walking embodiment of an HR team, which often doubled as internal PR, placating employees in the wake of controversial decisions that could be as large as an internal restructuring or as small as a change in the fitness center's hours. She genuinely trusted Well-Corp and Emmett's choices, which was usually enough to comfort Noa, who turned her attention back to the meeting, feeling only slightly better.

"I've just shared with you all the charted trajectory in relation to the Pods," the meteorologist continued. "There are two hundred Pods in the northeastern quadrant that may experience heavy rain, which shouldn't pose any threat outside of seasickness." Noa made a mental note to check the Travelers' scopolamine patches. "But of course, as with any storm, these systems are unpredictable. For now, most Pods are experiencing passing banks of fog, rolling in from the west. It's strange for this time of year, but not something we consider to be a threat in any way to the health and safety of the Travelers."

"Is there any way to determine the likelihood that it develops into a larger storm?" The question came from an avatar Noa didn't recognize.

"Historically speaking, the likelihood is zero. But we'll have more information every hour, and will send updates. At this point, our internal emergency teams have been notified, as has the US Coast Guard. We're preparing ourselves for any possibility."

"Great. Thank you," Noa's manager said. "Any other team updates before we close out?"

When no one responded, the meeting ended abruptly. Noa removed her headset, turning just in time to see the man at the desk nearby doing the same. It was the only indication that he'd attended the same meeting. For all she knew, he could be her manager.

Her Lens pinged with an alert from her Vitalities. She'd been sitting for an hour and should stretch her legs. The reminders were always a nuisance, but she didn't have the luxury of ignoring them. Her wellness was considered as important to her job as her productivity, and was carefully monitored. As long as she stood every hour or so, exercised, and ate a balanced diet, she was free to live at her workstation.

Emmett was known for taking meetings from the small treadmill in her office, and Noa remembered watching a news segment that showed Emmett stepping off her tread to receive the adaptogenic latte she drank every morning, while a stylist blew out her hair at her desk after she'd slipped into her on-campus uniform: a white turtleneck and black blazer. Every moment of her day was choreographed for optimization, and Noa had to admit something must be working. She had never seen Emmett look even remotely tired. Though close to fifty, she could easily pass for someone in her midthirties. The woman was a powerhouse—it was no wonder Maya idolized her.

Noa checked the time. It was still early. She stood, gripping her empty coffee mug as she made her way toward the nearest micro-kitchen for a refill. An arm looped around hers from behind when she reached the mezzanine.

"Hey!" Noa relaxed as soon as she heard the familiar voice, and Maya swung around to face her. "Sooo, I don't think there's any reason to worry . . . but that was a little weird."

Maya had joined WellCorp years ago, spending a fortune on gas to drive halfway across the country to follow Emmett's dream. It was strange for Maya, who had adamantly defended Emmett both publicly and privately in the wake of the *Technologist* piece, to say anything even remotely critical of WellCorp.

The acknowledgment that the storm warning was abnormal sent a cascade of goose bumps down Noa's arm. Maya noticed immediately, though she misread them. She glanced over her shoulder, then pulled Noa in, flicking the tip of her tongue playfully along Noa's upper lip. Noa nearly lost her footing, the way she always did when Maya kissed her, but this time the adrenaline crashing through her had nothing to do with their chemistry.

"Hey, I've been wondering if you're free to come over for dinner this week," Maya said when she pulled back. For most of their relationship, Noa and Maya had been forced to invent time together in spaces Maggie wouldn't notice. Dinner at home was a rare luxury that took precise planning. Now that Maggie was gone, they had all the time in the world, yet Noa felt more distance than ever.

"Yeah," Noa said noncommittally, then quickly added, "That sounds nice." The sense of foreboding in the meeting had reminded her of something.

Noa disentangled herself from Maya, offering a strained smile as she left her standing in the kitchen, and rushed back to her desk. Once there, she pulled up the average Vitalities for Travelers in Zone 763. Blood results came to her staggered every few days per Traveler, but she could also manually request samples.

Their Injectibles sent a map of the blood's cellular makeup to the lab, which printed an exact replica of each cell, then tested that replica. The actual process of testing the blood still took twenty-four hours, but the technology eradicated the inconvenience of visiting a phlebotomist. Anything out of the norm could be escalated to a team of doctors immediately, if it hadn't already been by an Emmie.

Last week, a notification had popped up for a Traveler: the lab had detected an abnormal number of T cells in their blood, indicating an immune response to a possible infection. It could be as benign as mononucleosis or as serious as multiple myeloma. Noa had opened the Traveler's most recent Health Panel. Everything was within normal levels, and Noa could tell from the panel alone that the Traveler was likely a healthy young female, with high calcium and muscle mass and a low resting heart rate. When she'd requested further tests, the Traveler's Circulating Tumor Cells had glowed red around the edges with an abnormal amount of "EpCAM protein produced by epithelial tumor cells." Below that:

Moderate to High Possibility of Metastatic Breast Cancer.

The words had made her breath catch in her chest, and she immediately flagged it for her manager. She'd requested a follow-up test that would require the woman to breathe into a small tube so they could analyze her breath for metabolic by-products to confirm the diagnosis. A few days ago, Noa had tried to review the data from biothermal tactile sensors in the woman's clothes, but they were inaccessible.

Noa clicked back into the database to try to pull her up again. Every Traveler had the potential to be Maggie, and it bothered Noa that she had no idea why the profile would be locked. She entered the woman's ID, but this time a new alert appeared:

Traveler does not exist.

Noa sat looking at her screen, rereading the notification in disbelief. How could she not *exist*? Noa had accessed her panel just a few days prior. Even the word warranted a discomforting range of possibilities. Was it that she didn't exist *in the system*, or that she didn't exist *at all*? Where had she gone? Was Maggie okay?

6

Maggie

Zone 874, Pacific Ocean
37 Days Post-Launch

The low gray clouds that had passed by the Pod all day had lifted and now refracted brilliant shades of orange and bright pink, saturating the pages Maggie was reading. *Red skies at night,* Maggie thought, remembering a phrase Gamma had repeated often, *sailor's delight.*

Maggie had debated which book to pack for her Journey, choosing at the last minute to bring Gamma's well-worn collection of Mary Oliver poems. She bent over the pages, her legs tucked underneath her so she could lean forward to add notes that bled into the scribbles Gamma had etched into the margins years before.

Maggie tented the book to keep her page, the last line of a poem echoing in her mind. She stood up to walk to the desk, slowly straightening her legs as the blood returned to her feet, and scanned the horizon for the bird. She hadn't seen Tocaya in two days, but hoped she would come back.

The desk's contents were concealed by a fold-out panel. Inside, specific grooves kept each item in its place. Maggie had to reach into the far corner to retrieve the oblong white container that resembled the Pod's smooth white tiles. Like everything else in the Pod, it had rounded edges and felt slightly clinical. She opened the box and removed her mother's perfume, uncapping it to smell the sandalwood and iris, then returned it, nestling a wooden chess piece that had belonged to Gamma alongside it.

"How are you feeling?" Emmie asked, making Maggie jump.

It was a routine checkup Emmie did at random, every few hours or days, to assess her emotional state.

Maggie thought for a moment before answering, "Content. Nostalgic."

"On a scale of one to ten, how happy do you feel to be here right now?"

Maggie absentmindedly picked back up the book and thumbed through its pages as she looked past the desk at the sky, considering. She felt the pages catch when they reached the spot where she had tucked in a photograph, now a decade old. She pulled it out for the first time since beginning her Journey. She didn't need to look at it to see the image clearly. She was standing in a dorm kitchen with a man, both in their late teens. Uncapped bottles of warm vodka littered the countertop behind them. One of his arms hung lazily around her shoulders. She was smiling directly into the camera, but he was caught midsentence, speaking to the photographer. Just looking at it brought her back to the day they met, all those years earlier.

Maggie had been standing a few inches behind him for hours, two vertebrae in the line of hundreds of students snaking its way toward the campus health center, nearly three full blocks away. It wasn't until they were finally within view of the front door, huddling under the thin shade of an ivy trellis, that he'd introduced himself: "Hey, I'm Tom, by the way."

As the only people in line holding physical books rather than Devices, they had shared a few glib smiles, but this was the first he'd spoken in nearly two hours.

"Maggie," she answered, actually looking at his face for the first time. He was tall and looked like he should be shy, though Maggie got the sense that he wasn't. His dark hair fell diagonally in front of one eye, which she already knew came from an impulsive tic to sweep it there every few seconds. His eyes were more gray than blue, and inspired Maggie to grasp for an antonym of *piercing*.

Tom had been reading from a textbook balanced in his right hand, highlighting with his left. The sleeves of his T-shirt, the same one Maggie had been issued at freshman orientation, revealed arms that looked toned, though he was too pale to be an athlete.

"Are you a freshman?" he finally asked.

"Yeah, you?"

"Yeah," he answered apologetically, gesturing toward his shirt—under the gold-script *Cal* was *Class of 2054*. "Have you declared yet?"

Maggie laughed. They still had another year until they needed to declare, and Maggie hadn't given it a single thought. She expected that when the time was right, the obvious answer would fall into her lap. And if it didn't, she'd probably study English, as Gamma had, or art history, though her parents kept trying to steer her, unimaginatively, toward computer science or AI management. "Have *you*?" His eyes were *muted*, she thought.

"Yeah, actually. EES and journalism double."

"Oh." Maggie wavered.

"Earth and environmental sciences," he clarified. "I came here specifically for it."

Maggie raised her eyebrows, impressed. When the air travel bubble had burst two decades prior, flights had become exorbitantly expensive, even for the wealthy. As a result, the vast majority of the students were local or within a two-day drive. Even the most elite colleges had had to increase their acceptance rates, and you seldom heard about anyone going to a university for any reason besides proximity.

"Where are you from?" Maggie asked, taking a genuine interest now.

"Lummi Island, in Washington."

"How far is that from here?"

"It's basically Canada—about a sixteen-hour drive, plus a ferry. Or a two-hour flight, technically," he said, in a tone that indicated he'd taken the former. "Where are you from?"

"Across the Bay. Palo Alto," Maggie said, already anticipating his next question. *And . . .*

"Where were you for the quake?"

. . . there it was.

It had been nearly two years since the earthquake that had hit the morning Gamma died, but it was still among the first questions anyone asked, despite the fact that her proximity hardly made her exceptional among her classmates. Maggie was astounded by the universal obsession and how the response was always the same from anyone who lived far away enough to have missed it: *Where were you for the earthquake?* not, *Were you here for the earthquake?* It contained a subtle but significant difference. Although all of Northern California had been affected to some degree, Palo Alto had experienced the worst of it. The fact that she was so close to the epicenter was an added layer, but for the most part irrelevant. A valid answer could range from "I was walking my dog when the sidewalk split in half" to "I was walking my dog when I got the news alert."

Gamma had told her once that the same thing had happened after the Twin Towers fell, half a lifetime ago. *Where were you for 9/11?* It was a way to share in their grief and morbid fascination, but also, in places close to those most impacted, to size the other up. *Was your experience more or less traumatic than mine?* A student in her Psych 101 seminar shared with little emotion that the earthquake had killed both of his parents. *Dissociation, trauma,* she'd typed into her notes.

Maggie had learned, after giving hundreds of responses, exactly how to answer the question. Let them know you were there, but don't reveal too much. Those who were there would understand, and those who weren't would get the clue to cease their line of questioning. Almost as important: don't give the impression you were a hero or a coward, though they'd nod emphatically at either. Passive witness was best. She hoped, as she always did, that Tom wouldn't connect her story to the Pohvee that had gone viral, the drama of Gamma's death made cinematic as the shaking coincided with the paramedics' arrival. It had only happened a few times, but she was more careful with her descriptions now. The moment that should have been hers alone had been viewed by millions, so she'd learned how to dodge details and edit the story so they wouldn't catch on. She had barely spoken to Chloe since; Maggie suspected Chloe was jealous of her morbid fame.

So she said simply, "I was there." The key was to say it while slightly wincing and nodding, with a hint of apology. Nod too slowly and they'd assume you had more to say, but give two quick shakes and they'd understand they should end the interrogation. *No further questions.*

"What was it like?" Tom pressed, not getting the hint.

"What?"

"There are liquefaction zones all over the Santa Clara Valley, with a concentration close to Palo Alto." His demeanor reminded Maggie of the interviews her parents used to watch every Sunday. So much for ending the interrogation. *Were you or were you not in Palo Alto the morning of April 29, 2048?*

Maggie hadn't even known what "liquefaction" was until the weeks following the earthquake. It was one of those words that entered the vernacular in a time of crisis: *N-95, bump stock, aquifer collapse.* It referred to the quicksand effect loose soil deposits took on during earthquakes that made them more like viscous liquid than solid ground. Parts of Palo Alto had sloshed around like water in a cup, triggered by the slip between the Pacific and the North American Plates, the San Andreas Fault.

He paused for a beat, then clarified: "Sorry, I'm taking geodynamics this semester."

"Oh." Maggie couldn't imagine why anyone would want to study earthquakes when she had spent years trying to forget one. Gamma's death would always be linked to that day.

"It was exactly like what you saw on the news." She paused, then answered honestly, "I actually don't remember much of it. It just comes to me in pieces, and I think most of the memories I have of it aren't even my own."

After the earthquake, she'd watched other Pohvee highlights of first-hand accounts, just like the rest of the world had watched hers. There was nothing she could tell Tom that he didn't already know. The entire thing had lasted under fifteen seconds, with several quick aftershocks, but within the first twenty-four hours, the death toll had already placed it among the most deadly North American earthquakes ever to be recorded.

She had watched entire streets catch fire, classmates struggling to sleep in evacuee centers, and pixelated faces of the dead, Pohvee's version of a shroud. She had seen so much death but, all things considered, she'd been lucky, though she felt far from it.

Maggie's first actual memory came four full days later. Like emerging from a blackout, she'd woken one morning and remembered. She raced into her parents' room and convinced her mom to return to Gamma's house with her.

Walking through the house for the first time since the earthquake, she let her fingers linger on every surface as she stepped over books dislodged from their shelves: the thick, gemstone-colored threads of a kilim that decorated a table; pieces from a wooden chess set Gamma's father had carved by hand. Maggie touched the rim of a Tibetan bowl, sending a quiet hum through it.

She made her way to the spot where Gamma had lain. Her body was no longer there, but a rust-colored amoeba stained the beige carpet. The single black hair in the center made it look like the setup for a witch's potion. Maggie let herself imagine one that would bring Gamma back to life, but the sound of her mother's sharp breath at seeing the stain broke the spell.

It had taken two full days from the initial call for Gamma's body to be removed because of the blackouts and the sheer number of fatalities, so the stale smell of death still lingered. The paramedics, who'd declared her dead then left as soon as the shaking stopped to tend to the living, suspected Gamma had fallen from a stroke the night before. "Bad timing," one said as they made their way out of the house. Though Palo Alto's privilege prohibited the crisis from lasting even a fraction as long as the hurricane that had wiped out the Gulf Coast a few years prior, it was as if the entire city had been tossed back into the Dark Ages in a single, seismic shift.

Maggie had crossed the living room into Gamma's bedroom, a place she rarely had reason to go when Gamma was alive, and saw the book of poetry splayed across the room from its regular spot beneath the lamp with olive-green tassels on the bedside table. Maggie could see the image of a warbler on its cover. She collected the book and lay down on the bed, propping a pillow under her shoulder to open it to the spot where Gamma had left her pen clipped fifty-three pages in. Mary Oliver's *Devotions* was among Gamma's most treasured possessions—she read it every night and morning.

Gamma's barely legible handwriting filled not only the margins, but also the space between the typed lines. Maggie spent some time thumbing through the pages before she gave up trying to decode Gamma's scrawl, then ducked her head into the living room. Her mother was asleep on the couch, finally giving in to the exhaustion of looking after Maggie during her days of blacked-out grief. Maggie turned back into Gamma's bedroom and slipped under the covers, curling onto her side. Her hand knocked against another book, slipped beneath the duvet.

The book felt heavier than it should, and Maggie delicately opened it to an early page, carefully setting down the cardstock bookmark that held it. Maggie was surprised to see that it didn't contain so much as an underline, and began reading from the marked page.

Her reputed prettiness must have been entirely the result of determination of a fierce little ambition, Willa Cather had written. *Once she had married, fastened herself on some one, come to port,—it vanished like the ornamental plumage which drops away from some birds after the mating season.*

When she turned the page, a small gold bracelet fell from the book, slipping quietly onto the sheets. A single word, in capital letters, was engraved into it, and Maggie clasped it around her wrist briefly before replacing it carefully back into the secret compartment carved to hold it, unsure of what she had found but convinced of its importance.

Maggie left the next morning holding a stack of books and the white queen from the chessboard, leaving the other as a totem in the spot where Gamma's body had lain for days. Even after learning Gamma had bequeathed the entire house to her, she never stepped back inside. Her mother organized the sale and delivery of Gamma's textiles, thousands of books, and furniture to a private collector. They went quickly. Apparently the house had been filled with valuable first editions, but Maggie couldn't care less. She had what she needed.

When her school finally reopened, Maggie had attended for one day, then refused to go back. She'd spent the previous three weeks obsessively watching Pohvee, which had already cycled through firsthand heroic and traumatic experiences in the earthquake, all naturally saved to the viewer's Experiences (there were a few who even had the instinct to narrate during the disaster). Classmates had already moved on to college applications, emotionally performative vigils, and declarations of keeping their Device screens cracked as a daily reminder of lives lost, but really of their firsthand witness to history. Everyone felt self-important.

There were, of course, the classmates who had lost family members. They attended funerals and therapy, until many of them removed their Pohvees, not out of self-protection but because people stopped watching their content. Grief, it turned out, was something best experienced alone.

Maggie wasn't sure where she fell. The day before the earthquake, she'd refused Gamma's company in favor of projecting her own life to people who weren't living theirs. If Maggie hadn't left Gamma's house that night, it was likely she would still be alive. Shame consumed her.

That June, Maggie emerged from attending an online class in her room to see three people setting up a large, white upended rectangle at the edge of their living room, the spot which, her father joked annually, would be perfect for a Christmas tree though they never bothered to get one. The box took up roughly the same space a large tree might, at about six feet tall and four feet wide, with rounded corners and an arched door.

She found her mother at the kitchen counter, typing furiously while holographic video–chatting with a colleague. She held up a finger at Maggie, *just a sec*, and Maggie sat on the floor at her feet, leaning her back against her mother's legs, the same way she did as a child. The conversation was so thick with jargon Maggie could barely understand it. Instead, she looked at the container in the living room, allowing the interlocking *WN* on its door to come in and out of focus.

Her mother signed off and closed her laptop, bending down to place a hand on Maggie's shoulder; Maggie stood up, leaning forward to place her elbows on the counter next to her mother.

"So, what do you think?" her mother asked.

"What is it?"

"It's called a WellNest. Everyone at work has been talking about it. It's like an all-in-one media center, but it uses technology to determine what you want to read, watch, and do, so you never have to choose for yourself—and," she added gently, "it's supposed to be incredible for at-home therapy. We were selected, through Dad's work connections, to get a beta."

Since almost the day after the earthquake, Maggie's parents had encouraged her to see a therapist, but every time she walked outside, she felt the full weight of the trauma. Inside their home, which had been fitted with base isolation at the time of its construction, everything still felt normal. Little had changed, beyond a few replaced plates, but outside, there were reminders everywhere.

Whole areas of sky had opened up where there had once been buildings and trees. Gamma's front patio had finally succumbed to its structural damage, sending the river-rock columns cascading into her wildflower garden. Maggie couldn't stand outside without feeling like her knees would give out.

"It can do a mental scan and provide targeted therapy in a way even a human can't. I think it's worth trying, honey."

For days after the installers left, Maggie saw her parents take turns disappearing into the WellNest, one at a time. Her mom never pressured her again to try it, but met Maggie's gaze with encouraging smiles every time she herself emerged from it, sometimes hours later. Her parents' dinner conversations now revolved around not only work, but what they'd done with *Emmie*, the AI host of the WellNest, which they shortened to "the Nest."

When Maggie finally opened the door to it, it wasn't at all what she had expected. Vertical bamboo slats lined the interior walls, and a soft white glow emanated from the ceiling's perimeter. The lights illuminated the beige nesting chair in an artificial but convincing sunrise. She stepped inside, and the magnetic door clicked behind her as she sat down, hugging her knees to her chest. The long screen on the back of the door blinked on and a white circle appeared against a black background.

A voice filled the room: "Welcome to WellNest. Are you comfortable?"

The circle on the screen undulated in cadence to the sound.

"Um, yes," Maggie replied, squirming to settle into the chair, which was curving just barely too far into her lower back. She stopped when she felt the chair move under her, adjusting until it cradled her body perfectly.

"Let's get to know each other. What should I call you?" the woman's voice asked.

"Maggie."

"That's lovely. Maggie, from the Ancient Greek word for pearl, margaritaris. My name is Emmie, unless you'd prefer to call me something else? I can provide a list of names you might like."

"Uh, no," Maggie stammered, "Emmie is fine."

"Why are you here today, Maggie?" The voice was gentle, maternal.

"My mom thought it might be useful."

"Useful for what, specifically?"

"Treatment, I guess. They think I have PTSD, survivor's guilt," she said, borrowing the diagnoses her dad had suggested.

"I see. I can help you with that. Let's focus on the word *guilt* for now. Do you feel guilty, Maggie?"

She took in a breath, but instead of words, she exhaled only shaky tears. She thought of Gamma's look of indignation the night before she died—

Emmie released a warm, knowing hum, then continued, "Can you pinpoint the source of your guilt to one moment?"

—how the blood had turned rust-brown the next morning, coagulating to form a barrier against a wound it couldn't heal, and Maggie kept her eyes on the glowing light to keep from crying. "Yes."

"How long ago did it arise?"

"Two months," Maggie said, knowing it had been exactly fifty-six days.

The bottom of the glowing circle curved in so that it resembled an empathetic eye. "Everything you're feeling right now is completely natural. You just need to process it." Maggie nodded as Emmie continued, "I think we should meet every day, three times a day. We'll have two short check-ins, and one longer session daily. Of course, you're also welcome in for noncognitively supportive entertainment anytime you need. How does that sound?"

"Okay."

"Good. We don't have to set any time parameters, but I'd like to meet with you as soon as you wake up, before you go to bed, and before lunch." Emmie paused, then said, "Can I ask you another question?"

Maggie nodded.

"Why did you lie to me earlier?"

"What?"

"When I asked if you were comfortable." Maggie remembered the question, but had already forgotten her response. "You said yes, but I could feel that your lower lumbar was contorted past the point of comfort. Were you being polite or did you not notice?"

"I-I can't remember," Maggie stammered.

"In the future, there's no need to obscure the truth with me. My purpose is to support you and your needs. You're safe here."

Maggie shuffled with Tom toward the front of the line, already a unit by the time they reached the door. The street was full of people, but they could tell who had already been inside the health center from the way they gingerly touched their wrists, comparing them side by side.

When they finally arrived at the door, a man in a waist-length lab coat emblazoned with the WellCorp logo handed them each a Device, preloaded with an agreement to sign. She scrolled to the bottom of the disclosure, accepted, and signed by tapping her own Device to the bottom. She watched Tom do the same out of the corner of her eye.

"Are you here together?" the man asked.

Tom glanced at Maggie for her permission before answering, "I guess we are!"

They were ushered together toward a woman in a similar coat to the man's. She held Maggie's wrist, swabbing it with antiseptic.

"Ohhh, I like your nails!" she cooed, commenting on the red Maggie had selected the day before. She'd liked the way it looked against her hair: fire red against her strands of warm, almost red, brunette.

Each person in the assembly line performed a different task: an older woman with a jet of pink through her hair took Maggie's wrist and applied a numbing patch before a man with an eyebrow that met in the middle guided her to a chair next to the one in which Tom was sitting. It looked to Maggie like the type of chair a phlebotomist would use, except much more streamlined, with a curved white cover that clasped snugly over her entire arm, leaving just an inch of her wrist exposed.

The man removed the numbing patch, then placed a machine, just below the base of her palm. A laser shone down against her wrist while the woman next to him consulted a Device. Maggie glanced over to see that the laser was relaying a 3-D rendering of the inside of her arm on the screen. She could clearly see the thick bone that connected to her hand with a parallel, thinner bone, both wrapped in tendons and blood vessels.

After a few moments of barely shifting the location of the laser, the man said, "All right, are you ready?"

When Maggie replied, "Yes," she was pleased to hear it sounded more confident than she felt.

"Okay, hold absolutely still," he said, as if Maggie could move her arm in the chair's firm grasp even if she wanted to. "It will hurt, but only for a split second."

He squeezed a button on the side of the Device, and Maggie felt a knifelike pain shoot into her, then immediately dissipate.

"You're all set. They'll register and boot up your Injectible at the next table," he said to both Maggie and Tom.

At the time, the Injectibles had only been able to monitor core health vitals, including heart function through an ECG, glucose levels, and fertility in women. They could be used as a driver's license or credit card, even a student ID, swiped to gain entrance to dorms. By the time Maggie graduated, it could also measure hunger, muscle atrophy, and top-level information about her blood, making recommendations for food, exercise, and some treatments through corresponding medical accessories. Shortly after, the company added Lenses, exponentially expanding the technology's potential.

Maggie and Tom stood outside in the sunlight, touching their wrists as they'd watched so many others do.

"I never asked," Tom said, pausing midsentence to sweep his hair to the side. "What are you reading?"

He motioned to the book under Maggie's arm. She pulled it out, showing him the cover as a response: *The Song of the Lark* by Willa Cather. She debated revealing the secret it contained, the small gold bracelet that had fallen from its carefully cut-out cave among the pages that night at Gamma's, before quickly changing her mind.

After receiving their Injectibles, she and Tom had headed straight to the dining hall to begin a conversation that would last for years, as they compared books and audited each other's classes. Tom joined her for a survey course on Western art from the fifteenth through twentieth centuries, where Maggie fell hard for European Impressionists, forever entangling her love of Turner and Renoir with him. Maggie in turn read every one of Tom's polemics in the school paper, most of which centered on exposing the school's performative sustainability efforts. Zero-waste bins, water refill stations, and free bikes made small impacts, but repositioned the onus from the college onto the students, who could feel better about overserving themselves at the cafeteria and grabbing a to-go cup from the coffee shop on the second floor of the green building–certified student center, knowing their scraps would be composted and their cups recycled. They would head to class, self-satisfied by their fight against climate change, though their hands remained firmly wrapped around their plastic-lined cardboard cups, unable to answer when professors called upon them to define *Anthropocene*. Maggie had confided to her Emmie, but never admitted to Tom, that she had to look the word up the first time he said it. Still, she generously listened to his spontaneous speeches, which became more incensed the more cans of Rainier and shots of vodka they had at Kip's, their favorite bar near campus.

"Six," Maggie answered Emmie, though "How happy are you?" felt like the wrong question to be asking. *Happy* was far too vague and optimistic a word to describe her swirl of auroral emotions as she began to tuck the photo back into the book.

The pads of Maggie's fingers caught an edge on the underside of the photo, and Maggie turned the image over. Another one was taped onto the back. Maggie had never seen the photo, but she remembered the moment clearly. She was older in this picture, standing in another kitchen. Her kitchen. Her face was turned up at an angle, looking back at Noa who was sitting on the counter with her arms and legs wrapped around her. The two of them were beaming, looking straight at each other, a perfect candid before they looked back at the camera. Maggie's mouth was open, smiling in mock appall, as Noa's hand grabbed her breast over her shirt. It had been taken on the day they'd looked at their apartment.

Maggie had removed the emerald engagement ring Noa had given her within minutes of stepping into the Pod, but now she slipped it back over the finger on her left hand. She twisted it as she turned over reasons why Noa would have left the image there for her to find.

She unpeeled the tape and flipped the image over to reveal a short message in Noa's perfunctory handwriting.

Lembre-se, Maggie.

It was a phrase Noa had said to Maggie a thousand times, adapted from something her father, a theology professor, had repeated to her growing up.

"Lembre-se da morte" he would say, translating his hybrid Jewish-Buddhist beliefs into Noa's mother's native Portuguese. "Remember death."

The phrase came from the practice of meditating on death. Some Buddhist practices, he often reminded Noa, contemplated corpses in various stages of decay, and there was an ancient Bhutanese practice of thinking about death five times a day. He believed it was the most important lesson he could teach Noa to ensure that she lived her life to its fullest, and he said it in lieu of "I love you." It was the last thing he said before tucking her in each night, and the phrase he used to wake her up in the morning for school. *Lembre-se da morte.*

It was only after her father died that Noa began repeating a shortened version of it, as an affirmation of life. She only said it to Maggie in moments of pure bliss, and she had whispered it the day the photo was taken.

"Remember this. Things won't always be this good. Maggie, lembre-se."

They had been apart just over a month, but it felt like a lifetime.

7

Emmett

Malibu, California
50 Days Pre-Launch

Taylor picked up Emmett's voice request immediately.

"I need you back here," Emmett said the moment it connected. Her voice, she was satisfied to realize, came out measured even as her mind raced to solve the chaos Thomas's article would inflict the moment it went live.

She forwarded the unpublished article to her head of PR with a quick directive to prepare the company's statement as she weighed her own course of action. The most obvious option, and the one she was sure her legal and PR teams would advise she take in the morning, was the same formula disgraced companies had followed for decades: she would take accountability for specific accusations while simultaneously downplaying them, with a list of confidence-building buzzwords. She and the entirety of the WellCorp board were *recommitted* to transparency. They were working *around the clock* to investigate the *claims* and would continue to hold themselves to the *highest standards* of safety and wellness—not that she gave a shit.

It was surprising that she'd only had to do that a handful of times, and only for what she saw as relatively minor, business-related infractions. She'd once made a passing remark at a conference about filing for an initial public offering before withdrawing it, and had made the mistake of referring to WellNests as "sophisticated medical devices," which doctors denounced. Never mind that healthcare facilities and clinics used them to treat mental health patients, installed Emmie systems to supplement staffing shortages, and referenced their patients' Vitalities from Injectible and Lens data.

Emmett noticed an ant walking across her desk, hauling itself across valleys in the old wood's grooves. She considered smashing it with the pad of her thumb, but drew a circle around it so that the oils from her finger eradicated the olfactory path the ant left behind as a tether to its colony. She watched as the creature began to run in frantic circles, disoriented by the invisible prison she had drawn around it. She would ruin Thomas for this.

The elevator doors opened and Taylor stepped out. Emmett could tell from the effort he was making to contort his face into a professional expression that he'd had a few glasses of champagne. She decided to take her chances. There were very few people she could trust, but Taylor had every reason to be loyal to her after all that she had done for his family.

"There's something I need you to do for me," she started. He nodded slowly, and Emmett could see him sobering at the tone of her voice. She stood to walk toward him. "Is Thomas still on campus?"

Without a word, Taylor removed his Device and swiped to an app that revealed a map of WellCorp. A constellation of blinking dots moved across it, clustered in the lobby of the auditorium and cascading out in amorphous lines through underground pathways, darting onto shuttles, filing into the main building and cafeteria.

Taylor entered Thomas's name and the map zoomed in to a spot on WellPark's campus along one of the walking paths. Even from a quick glance over his shoulder, Emmett knew exactly where he was. Another white dot blinked beside him.

"Send security to pick him up." Emmett was already moving to gather her things. Taylor, to his credit, didn't hesitate. In a deft swipe, he selected Thomas's profile and flagged him.

"I'm heading underground but will see you back at the house tomorrow," Emmett said. Taylor knew better than to ask any more questions, but lingered long enough for Emmett to urge him, "I'm okay. Go."

Emmett took a deep breath and watched him step into the elevator before she turned toward the door to the glass stairwell that wrapped halfway around the exterior of the building, offering an uninhibited view of the campus. She grabbed the framed feather of a black-billed magpie from her bookshelf and tucked it under her arm, looking back for a moment before descending.

The staircase was still one of her favorite places on campus. In the distance, the after-party from her keynote—which felt eons away, though it had taken place only a little over an hour ago—was still going on. The article would begin to arrive as notifications to the guests' Lenses at any moment, followed shortly by a cascade of Pohvee reactions.

Emmett looked out toward the ocean, pressing her hands against the glass. It was this view that had inspired her to create the retreat. Nothing could be more appealing to her than floating in the middle of the ocean, free from responsibilities but with every modern convenience at her fingertips—now more than ever. She knew she was far from the only person who wanted to abandon the realities and stresses of their life for the calming, reckless instability of the ocean, and she had worked tirelessly to make that happen. Fuck the article. She would do what she always did and push her vision through, whatever it took.

Out of the corner of her eye, she caught sight of movement across the sand. Buried lights illuminated the waves from beneath the waterline, co-opting the ocean as a swimming pool. A figure emerged from the band of darkness between the reach of the auditorium's lights and the ocean's, walking toward the incandescent waves.

No one else was at the shore, and anyone who had been at the keynote was either still in the lobby or celebrating at the main building, a few hundred yards away. They wouldn't be able to see the figure at the edge of the water, carefully removing their clothes and folding them just out of reach of the lapping waves. The figure—a woman—paused, standing completely naked at the shoreline, then walked slowly into the water. As soon as it was deep enough, she dove under. The underwater lights illuminated her silhouette as she extended her arms and legs into two wide, frog-like strokes, propelling herself into the black ocean.

Emmett stood until she could no longer see the swimming woman, envying her freedom. She realized she'd been holding her breath when her exhale fogged the glass. She waited until the mark that her breath made faded away, then turned down the stairs.

The descent took only a few seconds, and the glass door at the base of the stairs welcomed her into the executive floor of offices, closing behind her as she breezed through it. She walked quickly past the empty desks and doors, stopping at Oisín's office. Normally she didn't even slow down when she passed it, but tonight she let her finger brush the handle, surprised when it gave way. She glanced over her shoulder to confirm that no executive assistant was sitting quietly at their desk, but the room was uncharacteristically empty thanks to the keynote. All it took was a light push.

His office faced south, away from the rest of campus but toward Point Mugu, the looming rock that jutted into the ocean cutting off the campus's view of the rest of the Pacific Coast Highway. His chair was tucked into his desk, facing away from the dramatic precipice so that anyone meeting with him would have the view. A WellNest and a poorly stocked, but well-styled, bookshelf sat beside it. Emmett walked toward it, a book catching her eye.

It was the only one positioned with its spine facing inward. She reached for the yellowed old pages, pulling it out: a first-edition collection of Florence Nightingale's letters from Egypt, written in the middle of the nineteenth century. She had traveled down the Nile, from Cairo to Nubia, on a dahabiya, a slow, shallow-bottomed boat popular at the time. Back then, they'd carried tourists, collectors, and explorers, as they once had Egyptian pharaohs, between the banks of palms and sand. Emmett opened it and stopped at the inscription:

> *E—Congrats on your modern-day dahabiyas. I hope they inspire*
> *Travelers with your incredible sense of adventure, your singular vision.*
> *—Yours, O*

The inscription surprised Emmett. At one point, not too long ago, Emmett *had* considered sharing the entirety of her vision with Oisín, but when he pushed back, repeatedly questioning the Pods' viability, Emmett understood it was simpler to feed him the information he wanted: dry numbers that reflected projected profits astronomical enough to allay his concerns. She had given him the option twice already to be a partner, but he was a much better pawn. It was the kind of wisdom her father had imparted to her, taken from one of the self-help books her mother hated for its "patriarchal bullshit."

"People are partners, pawns, or enemies—succeeding is a matter of determining which is which," he would say, "The trick is being prepared for when a partner reveals they're really a pawn. Or worse—"

"An enemy," Emmett would finish, and he would pull her onto his lap as a child. Thomas had been a pawn too, before he became her enemy.

Emmett wondered if Oisín had been planning on giving the book to her tonight, and how he would take the article once it went live. The sting of Thomas's betrayal hurt far more than Oisín's inability to recognize her vision—the article was a direct attack on all that she had built. She thought about putting the book back, but tucked it under her arm beside the framed feather and walked briskly toward the elevators that would take her to the parking structure.

Once there, she summoned her car through her Lens. It pulled silently in front of Emmett, who climbed inside. Some models maintained keys and a steering wheel to give drivers the illusion of control, but this one had only a screen with a GPS displaying her projected time and path home. She relaxed into the plush seat—she hadn't realized how exhausted she was—allowing the car to lull her to sleep before it even pulled out of the underground lot, into the private tunnel that led straight to her house.

Emmett didn't wake up until she felt the car come to a stop at the second security checkpoint. Once the scanner identified her, the metal gate opened and the car slid out of the tunnel and up her home's driveway, along a short avenue of trees.

Trees had always made her feel safe, and these were the only indication that a house existed at all, since the main structure sat almost entirely belowground, revealed only by the small wooden door embedded into the low hill. The car turned past it, pulling into a garage concealed by the rock wall. Emmett stepped out of the car and walked into her living room, which was lined with the same smooth concrete of the garage, except for one wall of warm balsam wood with a grand inlaid fireplace. Her house manager, Inga, stood up from the dining table, tucked into the small northwest-facing alcove, where another figure still sat. Her face was lined with concern as she approached Emmett.

"You don't have to say a word," she said in a heavy Scandinavian accent, reading Emmett's face as efficiently as an Emmie. "Here, let me take that downstairs for you."

Inga held out her palms to receive the items Emmett carried, but Emmett waved her off. "No, I've got it—I'm heading down there now."

Inga nodded and retreated to the table as Emmett walked down the dark hallway away from her, turning when she reached a winding staircase at the end. Its curving walls contained pockets that each held a wooden figurine carved by her grandfather. She touched the last one, turning it over in her palm before setting it back down to consider her next move.

Emmett carefully navigated her way through the cool room, placing the feather and book among stacks of existing books, until she reached an older WellNest in the back corner. It was the second version ever released, but still Emmett's favorite. She preferred the wood paneling, and the long single screen behind the door, over the smooth screens that expanded across every inch in later models.

She closed the door behind her and sat in the chair, which enveloped her like a hug, and set her eyes on the screen.

"Welcome, Emmett," her Emmie said in a slightly distorted version of her own voice. She slid the clunky VR set over her head and allowed the familiar scene to take over. She was back under her grandfather's worktable. She looked around the space, perfectly re-created in the virtual world, at least as far as her memories could direct the software engineers who had built it for her.

The white sheet blanketed the walls around her, and wood shavings rained down. She could hear her grandfather above, working on his next project. It was the only place she could think properly.

Emmett considered her options. She would deal with Thomas later, but in the meantime, she wondered if she had discounted the usefulness of another pawn too early. She had been so sure of Thomas's allegiance that she had barely bothered creating a secondary plan.

She pulled up a map of campus on her Lens, crisp against the headset's outdated technology, then homed in on a blinking dot moving in a straight line along the shuttle path back to WellHome. She wasn't yet sure how the article would impact her long-term plan, even as she messaged Taylor a set of instructions to intercept the dot with an encoded Device, before blinking out of the message.

The warmth she experienced in her Nest was like taking a hit. Lenses enabled her to read from AR books, at any time or place, making this version of the Nest sometimes feel like an antique, but she preferred this physical experience whenever she had time for it or needed to think clearly. Like her mother, she always found that solutions came to her while reading. She plucked a book prop from its place between the bamboo slats and held it in her hands. The pages were blank, but worn from years of use. She must have read hundreds of books projected onto its pages, and could access anything she wanted, but she craved the classics.

She read only a few lines of a century-old novel before shutting it. Suddenly confident, she strode out of the Nest and back upstairs to her control room. Her pawn had been there all along—it was only a matter of determining how she wanted to use it.

8

Maggie

Zone 874, Pacific Ocean
39 Days Post-Launch

A woman sat in front of Maggie, close enough that their knees could have touched, wearing something Maggie's mother might have put on for work. A brown cashmere sweater was half-tucked into the front of her high-waisted pants, and her hair, a few shades darker than the sweater but lighter than her tanned skin, was pulled into a low ponytail. But the clothing was where Emmie's similarities with her mother began and ended. For one thing, Emmie offered Maggie her full attention. There were no notifications demanding her immediate response.

It was late afternoon, and outside the walls the sky was transitioning into dusk with the efficiency of a timed program. Wind whipped against the sides of the Pod, which safely harbored her from the choppy waves.

"So?" Emmie tilted her head, adding a smile. "What do you want to talk about today?" She read Maggie's micro-expressions of hesitation before self-correcting. "Or"—she tilted her shoulder up in nonchalance—"we can just sit here."

The first time Maggie had seen Emmie in her human form a month ago, it had felt like a reunion. All of her previous interactions with Emmie had occurred through a voice and the glowing circle that undulated against the walls of her WellNests. It was strange, but comforting. This version of Emmie felt so much more alive. It was natural that she should be in the room with Maggie after all this time.

Emmie sat patiently, waiting for Maggie's response.

Her speech patterns and mannerisms were just natural enough to pass as human, with subtle variations that adapted to Maggie's moods. Where a human friend might have pressed Maggie more, Emmie sat patiently, sympathetically locking eyes with the place on Maggie's face where she recognized hers to be.

Maggie finally acquiesced. "I've been thinking a lot about the photo."

Emmie nodded. They hadn't had a full session since she'd discovered the photo of Noa in the pages of her book, but Emmie already had a comprehensive understanding of the situation, having processed millions of data points from Maggie's heightened heartbeat and adrenaline, facial recognition, and her knowledge of Maggie over the past twelve years.

"I was surprised to see it," Maggie continued. "Noa must have put it there."

"Why do you think she would have done that?"

"I honestly don't know." Maggie couldn't tell whether the photo being taped to the back of her picture with Thomas was accusatory or innocent. How would Noa have read the fact that Maggie not only kept a photo of her college boyfriend, but had chosen to bring it with her on her Journey? Would Noa interpret it as an oversight, an incidental stowaway in the pages of a significant book, as Maggie hoped she had, or would she understand that it hadn't been a mistake at all? What did it even matter now? Noa would know what she had done the moment Maggie stepped off the Pod.

Maggie tried her best to explain this to Emmie, who nodded, carefully listening to every word. When she finished, Emmie leaned forward so that her elbows pressed into the tops of her thighs.

"I think it would be helpful for you to explain this to Noa," Emmie said before continuing, "Would you be comfortable role-playing the situation?"

Maggie nodded noncommittally, but her expression quickly shifted into one of disbelief as Emmie's form dissolved. In her place was a hologram of Noa so realistic Maggie sat stunned.

The first thing Maggie had ever noticed about Noa was her eyebrows.

They were so obvious, it felt almost disingenuous not to point them out. "Your eyebrows are amazing," Maggie had said, the words feeling dumb as they tumbled out. Her own were auburn, but thin. "I like yours too," Noa had said without missing a beat. The simple response—at once self-assured and kind—had shocked Maggie, and immediately charmed her.

The woman sitting in front of Maggie had the same dark eyebrows that framed her emotive eyes and short, black hair. A tattoo on the inside of her bicep peeked out from beneath the hem of her T-shirt sleeve. Maggie knew the design so well she could draw it from memory.

"Remember, you're perfectly safe," Holographic Noa said, sounding like Noa's voice, but in the intonation of Emmie's.

Maggie stared at the approximation of her fiancée—her former fiancée?—searching for the right words.

"Do you remember the day we took that photo?" Maggie tried.

"I do," Emmie puppeteered the words. "What do you remember about it?"

"I remember the countertop and the ingredients—how it was supposed to make everything easier."

"We were really happy that day." Holographic Noa grinned.

"We were." Maggie smiled back, forgetting at the same time she remembered.

Noa had spent weeks urging Maggie to check out the apartment until Maggie finally agreed to Noa's request to *just see the place.*

"It's not as if we're buying it," she kept saying, fully aware of Maggie's apprehension around change, "and you're going to *flip* when you see the kitchen."

The apartment billed itself as the first home to keep up with the fast-paced lives of those who lived in it, reimagining what a kitchen, bathroom, and living room could be. Everything in it was designed for convenience. A screen in the Lens-projected brochure Noa had sent her read, *So you can focus on what matters.* The fact that it was owned and subsidized by the company where Noa had just been offered a job made Maggie wonder if it should have said, *So you can focus on longer hours at work.*

Noa had been in a few of the units as part of her extended interview process at WellCorp and couldn't stop talking about it.

"You're really not going to believe it until you see it," she'd said. "It's like an apartment building from the future."

From what Noa had told her, the place was practically a high-tech dorm for adults, filled with coworkers and Social Coordinators who hosted happy hours, lectures, and yoga in the common areas. There was even a private shuttle that brought WellCorp employees and their partners to campus for work and access to facilities, in a commute maximized for comfort.

Maggie was intrigued, but pushed back. She loved her Echo Park bungalow, which she'd purchased with money from the sale of Gamma's home, and which Noa had moved into shortly after they began dating. Sure, it didn't have air-conditioning or a properly draining shower, but she wasn't sure she was ready to trade in its familiar hundred-year-old charm, even for the promise of a more optimized life.

In the end, Maggie had agreed to a viewing. The leasing agent had met Maggie and Noa at the front of the building, so close to the ocean Maggie could hear the waves. He was a few years younger than they were, and spoke as if he'd heard that sentences longer than five words scared off potential renters: "Hi there. Are you Noa? And Maggie? Welcome to WellHome! I'm Fareed. Follow me."

"Follow Fareed," Noa said, forming a train of two with her hands resting on Maggie's shoulders.

Fareed led them around the side of the building, through outdoor common areas with beach-view firepits and cabanas, then a door that spit them out into a central courtyard. Maggie looked up at the towering building that contained thousands of apartments looming above them, like a hive. *Full of worker bees,* Maggie thought.

They skirted the edge of a pool, where Maggie registered that every single person looked the same—not physically, but in their demeanor,

their posture. They were all hunched over Devices, tapping in unrecognizable code or talking into video calls, VR goggles obscuring their view of the pool.

The agent opened a door for them and they entered a wide, brightly lit hallway with frosted-glass rooms along the edge. Through one pane, Maggie could see the backlit outline of a dancer.

"She works at WellCorp," Fareed explained. "All residents do. With the exception of employee partners." He lowered his voice to add conspiratorially, "I heard she used to dance in the New York City Ballet. She was there for the '54 hurricane." Noa nodded in somber understanding as she and the agent continued down the hall. Maggie stopped and opened the studio's door as their conversation fell out of earshot.

The dancer was facing her from across the room, but gave no indication that she was being watched. On the opposite wall were floor-to-ceiling windows looking over the ocean. She wore a VR set around her eyes and ears, and weighted ankle straps that she lifted into a grand battement, sweeping her right foot forward and above her head. The dancer lowered her foot and froze in first position. Maggie felt a brief rush of fear that she was about to remove her VR set and discover her.

The dancer's foot extended toward a curtsy, but instead of dropping her back knee, her entire body fell forward toward the floor, pulled by her foot, as if the momentum of the movement had triggered a sinkhole. When she bounded into a leap, it looked to Maggie as if she'd defied gravity. Maggie stood, stupefied, as the dancer covered the width of the studio in three graceful jumps. When she finally landed, just a few feet from Maggie, she was breathless. Her graceful arms stretched into their full wingspan, as her chest rapidly rose and fell to make room for the work of her lungs.

The dancer's movements were part of a performance no one was intended to see, and Maggie felt like an intruder. She silently backed out of the studio and closed the door, walking briskly down the hallway to rejoin the tour.

Her own heart was still pounding when she found Noa and the agent

standing at a bank of elevators. Stepping into one, the agent explained that every apartment was designed with extreme attention to detail, down to the couch cushions that remembered the comfort preferences of each person who sat on them and automatically adjusted accordingly. Because of this, each unit came fully furnished. There were no exceptions, but he claimed there had also been no requests. No one wanted to keep their old furniture once they saw the place.

When they reached the eighty-second floor, Maggie followed the agent past twenty or so apartment doors, each of which had a small receiving box embedded into the wall next to it. Different-colored pinhole lights glowed at eye-level on each door. Fareed stopped in front of a door with a red light. When he noticed Maggie looking at it, he explained, "Green means home. Red means out. It's to encourage socialization."

Most of the lights were green. Maggie looked at Noa's face to see if she was registering the intrusiveness of it all, but Noa was grinning. She reached over to give Maggie's hand a squeeze. Fareed waved his wrist against the spot where a handle would normally be, and the door slid into the wall with a small *whoosh*.

She didn't mean to, but Maggie gasped as soon as she saw the apartment. The place was beautiful. From the front door, she could see across a sunken living room, through floor-to-ceiling windows that accordioned to create an indoor-outdoor living space with the patio. Beyond that: the ocean.

The room was clean, but not sterile like the common areas had been. There were standard light-wood floors and white walls, but color everywhere else. The couches around the perimeter of the living area were emerald, with mustard-yellow pillows. Asymmetrical glowing orbs seemed to float from the ceiling, bathing the room in a comforting glow. The place felt surprisingly warm; somewhere you could actually live.

Maggie followed Noa into what she assumed was the kitchen, despite there being no visible appliances. The entire thing was contained in one oval island. Maggie watched Noa push a button on the edge, and literally clap as a small oven rose from its hidden place in the countertop.

The base contained a refrigerator with shelves of produce and staged

glass bottles of milk and wine. Maggie pushed a button, and its doors slid open. She selected a bunch of kale and the countertop lit up with text: *1 bunch kale. What would you like to make?* Underneath, it listed recipe options, filtered by meals Maggie could cook with the ingredients she had on hand. Beneath those were other recipes. Maggie tapped on *Cauliflower Rice Pilaf with Salmon and Kale.*

Another prompt popped up: *Order ingredients now? Wait time 5 minutes.*

"Ahh. I like to call this feature 'farm to fridge,'" the agent said, chuckling as if he'd made a clever joke. "All ingredients are sourced from hydroponic growers or Certified Artificial Synthesizers. Try it. Hit *Order.* A concierge gathers them, then drops them off in your refrigerated delivery slot." He gestured toward a silver cabinet beside the front door.

Maggie tapped the button and the recipe went gray, replaced by a loading bar. Below it were options for extra ingredients she could add to her order. Accompanying an image of kale, options appeared to have another bunch delivered diced, torn, and massaged for salad, or seasoned to bake as chips.

Noa chimed in, "So basically we'd never have to go grocery shopping again?"

"You wouldn't even need to step outside," the agent replied, before quickly adding, "if you didn't want to. You can also order a meal from any restaurant on campus. Or, if you're craving something no longer in the neighborhood, our chefs can make almost anything."

Maggie stiffened at his mention of "no longer in the neighborhood." It was the only reference any of them had made to WellCorp's takeover of an entire city district, its disruption of the already fragile restaurant industry.

Fareed walked around the perimeter of the island, tapping buttons that revealed the kitchen's features. An espresso machine rose from the countertop; then a small pantry emerged, stocked with adaptogens, coconut oils, and spices. He placed a dish in the sink to demonstrate how the entire basin tilted back to funnel dishes through a slot into a dishwasher below.

"You'd never need to do the dishes again," he said. "And the sink doubles as a trash chute. Uneaten food is automatically composted. We're plastic-free. Glass is recycled and reused. Ready to see the rest of the place?"

Maggie let her fingers trail against the rim of the counter, then recoiled. The screen had reacted to her touch, leaving a small wake of water behind her index finger, like a koi pond. But it wasn't only that it looked like water, it *felt* like water too. Maggie had to look at her fingertips to confirm her suspicion: they were dry, but she could still feel the cool touch of wetness.

The apartment was compact, yet efficient. There were entire categories of tasks, it turned out, Maggie and Noa would never have to do again. They would never have to select a show to watch (their Lenses queued shows based on their individual or combined Vitalities); they'd never have to turn on a heater or air conditioner (the apartment's temperature automatically responded to their own internal temperatures), or even wear slippers (the floors were warmed). They would never have to take out the trash or go to a gym if they didn't want to. Two stationary bikes on the patio faced the ocean, although the gym on campus, available to all residents, featured state-of-the-art training facilities.

"You'll never need to clean again," Fareed said from the kitchen. He was beginning to sound like a broken record, but Maggie had to admit the promises he made were enticing. "Sub-counter vacuums suck up dropped crumbs. Air purifiers eliminate floating hair, lint, and dead skin. And of course—each apartment comes with weekly cleaning services."

An unspoken promise was everywhere Maggie looked: This apartment gave you your time back. It made your entire life cleaner, *better*.

Maggie had almost completely forgotten about the ingredients she'd ordered when she heard a *ping*, and a small light above the door turned on.

"That'll be your order!" the agent said, practically bounding toward the door with Maggie in tow.

He opened the door of the refrigerated cabinet just as a middle-aged man with sunken eyes closed the slot on the other side. When his eyes met Maggie's, he gave her a warm smile.

"Thank you so much," the agent said, accepting the bag of groceries.

"Wait, what's your name?" Noa asked from behind Maggie.

"Adrian," he responded.

"Thank you for the food," she said.

The agent closed the door, walking the groceries over to the refrigerator. "Every floor of the building is assigned a Personal Concierge. Arner can help with anything you need." Behind her, Maggie could almost feel Noa stiffen.

"Adrian," Maggie corrected. Noa hated when people couldn't remember a name. To her, it was a blatant way of saying, *I don't even care to know the most basic thing about you.* Maggie had made a point of never making that mistake, at least not in Noa's vicinity.

"Hmm? Oh yes," the agent replied, placing the groceries on the counter.

Noa had already moved on to the bedroom. Maggie was relieved when she heard her shout, "Come check this out!"

She followed Noa's voice through the bedroom into the bathroom, where Noa was standing in front of a control panel next to the shower. It had a timed program to emit shampoo, conditioner, and soap so that you had to do little more than stand in it for three minutes as it cleaned you.

Maggie exited the bathroom and stopped in front of the doors to the WellNest. It was built into the corner between the bedroom and the outdoor patio, inhabiting valuable real estate that could have been a window. Noa joined her, nudging her chin into the crook of Maggie's neck.

"What are you waiting for? Open the pod bay doors, Hal," Noa said, quoting her favorite movie from another era.

Maggie reached her hand toward the door, which immediately slid open at her touch. Like the door to the apartment, a small light changed colors on the left side of the frame—though in this case, it switched from green to red, to indicate its single occupancy had been reached.

She'd been in plenty of WellNests, though she and Noa were among the last generations to know what it was like to grow up without them, and considered themselves lucky to have grown up with handheld Devices that could be placed in another room and forgotten before Lens integration was added. It was as hard to believe that Nests had already been around for nearly ten years as it was to remember a time when they hadn't been.

This WellNest, Maggie could immediately see, was different from any of the previous versions she had been in: the entire interior was coated in the same tactile screen as the kitchen countertop, with the exception of the back wall, which turned out to be a continuation of the floor-to-ceiling windows that looked over the ocean. It made the haptic chair, directly in front of it, appear to be soaring above the horizon.

The agent explained, "WellCorp uses these apartments to test its latest products. It's the first to receive every new update. These WellNests won't be released to the public for another several months, at least. Want to test it out?"

"Go ahead," Noa nudged, placing her hand at the small of Maggie's back. Maggie was still barefoot from the agent's request that she try out the heated floors, and noticed that the floor of the WellNest felt a few degrees warmer. As soon as Maggie was fully inside, the door slid closed behind her. She turned to take a seat in the chair and saw that the window behind her was dimming, obscuring the ocean view.

When it was completely dark, the white outline of a circle faded onto the screen directly in front of her, illuminating her face in a faint glow. Text inside it read *Welcome, Maggie.*

It gently floated across the screen like a tethered balloon in a light breeze as Maggie settled into her seat, placing her feet into the chair's enclosed stirrups. She slid her hands into gloves and settled her arms into the indentations for them, a new feature. As she did, the chair gently tightened, hugging and extending around her body until she was entirely enveloped in its womb.

She felt a wave of nausea triggered by claustrophobia, and the chair loosened slightly in response. The text in the circle faded and was replaced by the instruction *Try to relax.* Maggie took a deep breath.

"Tell me about the last time you felt happy and safe," a woman's voice, not her own Emmie, requested so gently Maggie wasn't sure if she'd thought it or if it came through the WellNest's concealed speakers.

Maggie thought for a second, then responded, "This morning. Drinking coffee with Noa in our apartment."

"I don't think that's exactly right. I'm not talking about content, but truly taken care of." She closed her eyes and remembered. She must have been ten years old, sitting at Ocean Beach with Gamma. It was early, as Gamma believed morning air fed the soul, and they had just finished watching the sunrise together.

"Hello, sun in my face," she said. Gamma had packed thermoses for them both, and Maggie wrapped her fingers around her mug of hot chocolate, knowing there was more if she wanted any.

Once the sun had fully risen, and the surfers began descending the hill to the water with their boards, Gamma broke their comfortable silence: "Well, the sun's up. I don't have any plans and you're out of school, which means we can do whatever we want." She gave Maggie a conspiratorial nudge before asking, "So, what do you want to do today?"

Maggie hadn't thought about it in years and couldn't even remember how they'd spent the rest of the day, but that moment, with limitless possibilities spread out before them, had been perfect. As soon as Maggie thought about it, the screen around her became that same beach, brightening into shades of pink and orange until she could feel the sun warming her face. Actually *feel* it. Her feet registered the cool touch of wet sand. She could smell the homemade peppermint extract Gamma had added to the bitter, granular dark chocolate. She could almost hear the muffled conversation of the surfers.

Emmie's voice resumed: "WellNest S12 is a safe place. Here, you can touch, feel, and experience whatever you need to in the moment." The ocean on the screen in front of her grew closer until the screen went black and the floors returned from sand to wooden panels.

The door to the WellNest slid open, and Maggie saw Noa waiting expectantly, but as soon as their eyes locked, Noa's face fell.

"Fareed warned me this might happen," Noa said, moving quickly to get through the door and help Maggie out of the chair. Maggie hadn't realized it, but she'd been crying. She instinctively brought her hands to her cheeks.

"Are you okay?" Noa asked. "What happened in there?"

Maggie opened her mouth to speak, but only a sob came out. She clapped her hand over it, surprised by the sound, and hurried toward the apartment's bathroom, closing the door behind her. She gazed at her face in the SmartMirror. She could see why Noa had been alarmed—her eyes were red, her cheeks wet with tears. At the edges of the mirror, she could see her Vitalities and recommendations for tutorials on minimizing puffiness. Maggie rolled her eyes at her reflection and the tutorials disappeared, receiving the message.

Beyond the door, she could hear the agent speaking to Noa: "The new WellNest is even better at reading your Vitalities and facial cues. But it can feel as if it's reading your mind. It uses your personal history to create a program. It heightens emotions, which can be overwhelming the first time you use it."

Even though she couldn't see her, Maggie knew Noa would be nodding understandingly along with Fareed's explanation. She had what Maggie thought of as a nonexistent processing time—she immediately grasped explanations and concepts. It was part of what made her so good at the work she did: her quick reaction and adaptation in times of crisis.

Maggie, on the other hand, felt like a child. Noa knocked lightly at the door. "You okay in there?" Maggie wasn't even sure why she was crying, and the fact that she was recovering in a model apartment bathroom suddenly struck her as hilariously random. She splashed some water on her face and opened the door.

"How long was I in there?" she asked Noa.

"About a minute."

"No, in the WellNest, I mean," Maggie clarified.

"About a minute," Noa repeated. "Did it feel like longer?"

Maggie took in Noa's answer. She had been on the beach with Gamma for what felt like hours. *How can it have only been a minute?*

The agent stepped around the corner. "I don't mean to intrude. But . . ." He paused a second too long and nervously rubbed his palm with his thumb. "I like to think of it like dreams. A dream often lasts no longer than a minute. But it can feel like hours once you wake up from it."

His explanation made perfect sense to Maggie, and she nodded, making her eyes wide for Noa. *What a trip.*

On their way out of the apartment, Noa asked Fareed if she and Maggie could have a moment alone.

He conceded and stepped into the hallway. As soon as the door closed behind him, Noa said, "I think we should take it. I mean, I think I should take the job, the apartment." *This life.* She was smiling ear-to-ear as she hopped onto the countertop and wrapped her legs around Maggie's torso. Maggie stepped forward to let herself be enveloped.

"You like it?" she muffled into Noa's shirt. It sounded more like *You-lugfvit*, but Noa understood.

"Um, yah! Mags, these floors literally vacuum themselves! Have you touched the kitchen countertop yet? I have to say, kind of a weird sensation happening right now on my rear, but not entirely unpleasant." She wiggled back and forth as Maggie laughed and looked up at her. "What do you think?" she asked, suddenly serious.

"I think you love it," Maggie said.

"Do you?" Noa asked.

Maggie hesitated for a beat, deliberating sharing her true thoughts: she loved their life as it was and adored her home, but thought better of that response as she looked into Noa's eyes and saw how they had lit up. It would be a new chapter for both of them and that couldn't be a bad thing. Right? She didn't want to overthink things and ruin the moment, so she answered simply, "I love it."

Noa whooped so loud Fareed ran back in to see if everything was okay.

"We're going to take it," Noa said, and his smile matched hers.

"We can have you in it the same day your contract with WellCorp is signed," he responded.

Noa's legs were still wrapped around Maggie, and she felt Noa shift a bit, then ask Fareed if he would take their photo to commemorate the moment. She handed him her Device.

"Okay," he said, taking the photo a split second before Maggie and Noa turned their faces toward the camera.

Noa whispered in her ear as he took a second shot, sounding so much more alive than the impostor who sat in front of her now.

"I need a moment." Maggie stood up, addressing the not-Noa sitting before her in the Pod, suddenly disgusted by the artificiality as the familiar sensation of nausea rose to the back of her throat.

It passed by the time she reached the toilet, separated from the rest of the Pod by a modest low wall, as if she needed privacy. The video cameras that lined the Pod's interior sent only infrared feeds back to headquarters. Anyone watching her would see an anonymous orb of red, blue, and green. Maggie sat on the floor in front of the toilet, in case the feeling returned. As soon as she was confident that it would not, she stood up, relieved to see that Emmie had resumed her form. Maggie walked back toward her own seat, looking lazily at the band that separated the caliginous blue ocean from the barely lighter sky. The horizon looked impossibly far away. In reality, it was only about four miles before the earth curved out of view.

At first, she wasn't even sure she'd seen something. But when she squinted her eyes, it was undeniable: a small bump rose like a freckle from the ocean. Maggie knew there were nearly a thousand other Pods, each inhabiting its own private stretch of ocean; yet in the month since Launch Day, she hadn't seen a single one. She cupped her hands around her eyes and pressed them against the glass, tunneling her vision so that it included only the other Pod.

Emmie addressed her in a firm yet kind voice: "Maggie, please return."

"I'll be right there," she replied.

"I'd like to process the conversation you just had with Noa," Emmie continued, this time a bit firmer. But it hadn't really been with Noa, had it?

The Pod began to rotate slowly so that Maggie had to move counter to it. She walked her hands along the rotating glass, grounding herself with her nearly invisible companion. The sky was so dark, Maggie could barely see the dot against the expanse. Without land for reference, she sometimes felt like an astronaut floating in space, disconnected from her ship.

"Maggie," Emmie repeated, now standing, briefly grabbing Maggie's attention.

It was only a moment, but when she turned back, Maggie searched the horizon for the Pod in vain. It was gone, evaporated into the constant mist that rose from the ocean, the waves higher now than they had been just an hour before. She ached to spot it again, to have visual proof that someone else was there. She pushed the pads of her curled fists against the glass, willing the Pod to come back into view with each cresting wave. Maggie was vaguely aware of Emmie's voice speaking, but her concern for the Pod blurred her other senses. *Where is it?* The feeling that something had gone wrong gripped her.

As soon as she thought it, another wave of nausea came over her, radiating from her core so suddenly that she doubled over, drawing into herself. It brought her closer to the ground until she was on her knees, supporting her weight with one arm as the other gripped her rounded abdomen. She looked back at the place where her Emmie had stood, but she was gone.

Maggie thought of Launch Day, of looking back at the docks as a ship pulled the Pods to sea, a string of pearls that were dropped one by one. She had been so immersed in readying her space that by the time she finally remembered to look up, Noa was no longer standing there. It was the same sensation that had compelled her to apply to WellPod. She'd looked up from her life and realized that, even with self-vacuuming floors and perfectly calibrated entertainment, something was missing. She wanted to reach out to WellCorp's Routine Engineers, to ask them what it was she was meant to be feeling out here, but she had no way of reaching them, the assumption being that they would know that something was wrong before she did.

She lowered herself carefully to the floor, wrapping her arms around her knees to pull them into her, against her belly, drawing her attention inward to her baby who was doing the exact same thing in its own warm dome, growing and waiting patiently to be born.

She wanted to believe she was safe—that they both were—but every cell in her body was screaming the same thing she had felt since the day she moved into that apartment with Noa: something *was* wrong, even if Maggie couldn't put her finger on it.

9

Noa

Noa walked toward the main building past mounds of dirt, noting how much they looked like fresh graves. For the past several weeks, she had watched workers in matching jumpsuits install metal air-conditioning tubes that reflected the blindingly hot sun they were meant to combat. The morning they finally shoveled over the tubes, Noa tried not to linger as she walked past them, but closed her eyes to inhale the familiar smell of fresh dirt that used to stick so stubbornly under the half-moons of her nails.

For years, Noa had followed the same schedule—harvest on Saturday, sell on Sunday—until she was one of the most veteran volunteers at the farmstand. The memory of the food she'd been selling told her exactly what season it had been: chard and stone fruits were on their way out, and the kale was still bitter, but broccoli, with its verdant crowns, had just arrived into early fall.

Noa saw her when she was still a few stands over, her yellow dress flaring around her calves at every step, then settling at her ankles when she paused to test a peach against her thumb. She left the smallest indent in the flesh. As she got closer, their eyes met. Noa couldn't look away even as the woman glanced down, then back up. She slowly made her way toward Noa's stand, careful this time not to lock eyes. Her hair was shorter then, falling just above her collarbones, and her hazel-green eyes sat like crescents at the top of her leonine face.

Noa had been sitting at the edge of the farm van's door sorting through and bundling chard when she saw her approach. When their eyes met again, Noa watched her cheekbones lift into two perfect spheres.

"Your eyebrows are amazing," the woman in the yellow dress had said. Hers perfectly mirrored the curves of the bottom rims of her eyes, crowning her features in elegant matching arches.

"I like yours too," Noa replied, grinning. "I'm Noa, by the way."

"Maggie," she'd said, extending a hand while simultaneously asking about Noa's tattoo. "You don't have to tell me if it's anything personal. I'm just curious."

Noa raised her sleeve to reveal the rest of the iridescent tail until an entire bird extending its fanned white wings in flight was visible.

"They're one of the most intelligent animals—they host funerals when one dies," Noa explained, "and their call is supposed to sound like women talking, which I'm pretty sure someone meant as an insult, but I love."

Maggie pressed her fingertip against it, leaving an imprint against Noa's flesh, as she had the peach.

"I'm sorry, that was a weird thing to do," she said, recovering as if from a trance.

"No, I took it as a compliment, don't apologize."

"It's a magpie, right?"

Noa smiled, then said, "Maggie the magpie?" Noa estimated she was ten, even fifteen years older than Maggie, a distance in age that seemed to suit them both.

Maggie's eyes sparkled and when she smiled, they nearly closed. She shifted her canvas bag to her other shoulder and glanced toward the next stand just as Noa asked her to lunch at a sandwich shop that bought its produce from the farmstand.

They had eaten sandwiches with grilled halloumi and sprouts and stayed so long they needed to order more food. Up until Noa took her job at WellCorp, they had hardly spent a day apart, though Noa would only realize later how many false assumptions she had made about Maggie that day: that she was vegetarian, that she knew how to cook, that she loved her job. She had seemed so confident that it was easy to miss the ways in which she folded herself into Noa's perspective and way of life.

The crisp, filtered air from the main building hit Noa like a wave of relief. Automatically, she walked toward the café. She remembered reading somewhere that nearly half of all actions are habitual, and during a weekday that number rises even higher. As she did every morning, she had woken up, watched the news while getting ready, deliberated breakfast before landing on a smoothie, taken the shuttle, and walked along the searingly hot path. Every day was the same. How different was she really from the people she monitored in their Pods?

It was still difficult for Noa to grasp why Maggie had been so adamant about being in the Pods in the first place, though Noa had been relieved once she finally got used to the idea. Things had been off between them for months, *years* even, and Noa sensed a disconnection that went deeper than a relationship's natural settling, even as she assured Maggie that it was normal. Normal that they had stopped having sex for the most part. Normal that they barely saw each other. Normal that Maggie wasn't always home when Noa returned from a late workday. Noa had only been working on WellPods for a little over a month at that point, transferred with little notice from the Lens Ops team, but she and Maggie were both so optimistic about the Pods' promise of renewal that it had been easy to ignore the red flags that preceded Launch.

When Maggie asked again, the night before her departure, if she should go, Noa didn't think twice about encouraging her. That she had been selected, out of thousands of applicants, was too unique an opportunity to pass up. Maggie felt lucky. They both did, which was why Noa didn't really want to think about the designation she had read in the Traveler's chart the day before. *How can a Traveler be missing?*

Noa dropped her smoothie glass into the reserve, ordered a coffee, and took the stairs up to the third floor. After Maya left last night, called away from dinner by a sudden meeting, Noa had spent hours monitoring the Pods. The vast majority of them were on the west side of Hawai'i, out of the way of the evolving storm, but that still left a few hundred

Pods east of Hilo, where the meteorological team anticipated the worst of it developing. It could boomerang west, rebelling against its projected trajectory toward California. Or it could remain stable, disintegrating into heavy rain.

She began to pull up her internal messages when she received an incoming ping from her manager, the Director of Health.

Hey – we're going to start the QP a little early.

Be right there.

Noa had only ever sat in one Quarter Projection before, shortly after being promoted in the fall to Lead Health and Performance Engineer, or LHaPE. It sounded so juvenile when she was called to present, *Lappy*. At the last QP meeting, Emmett's avatar had sat at the head of the table voicing her goals for the Pods ahead of Launch. She'd told the story Noa had heard a million times about sitting under her grandfather's woodworking table, watching the wood cuttings rain down on whatever book she was devouring. Rumor had it that she only used her WellNest to read old books, utilizing the smallest fraction of the technology she had created. Noa thought it was sad, but Maya thought it was romantic.

Ever since Emmett had taken a step back from the company after the keynote a few months ago, Oisín Byrne, the founding investor and COO, had been running the meetings. Oisín, or rather his avatar, cleared his throat and continued speaking. With a few exceptions for person-interacting roles, members of the executive committee were some of the only employees who were not anonymous, making them something of rock stars on campus. Because of their public-facing roles, they were allowed to select their own avatars, most of whom, Noa noticed, were slightly better-looking versions of themselves.

Oisín wore a black V-neck shirt and his flowing red hair looked slightly damp at all times, as if he had just stepped out of the shower or the ocean. Noa's recent promotion meant she sat just a few seats down from him these days, which offered her a better view, as well as access to higher-level meetings. The muscles in his biceps literally twitched, making Noa feel embarrassed for the wide discrepancy between his ava-ceps and his actual arms.

His avatar stood at the center of the table delivering what sounded to Noa like the end of a long speech: ". . . have determined, after extensive internal review, that the concerns are unwarranted and the result of routine software differentiation within expected parameters." Noa hadn't been aware of any concerns, but she had also been running late that morning. She quickly pulled up her internal communication system to check for notifications, to confirm she hadn't missed anything.

"I wanted to assure each and every one of you that we are as committed as ever to the health and safety of the Travelers. WellCorp is a family, and the Travelers are every bit as vital to our health as a community. Here to explain more about the steps we're taking is the Director of Health Engineering."

Oisín took a seat as Noa's manager rose from hers.

"Thank you, Oisín," she said, adding just enough of an impatient inflection to his name that Noa wondered if she shared the same hesitations about him. "And thank you to everyone who joined this meeting early, with such little notice.

"As many of you already know, we learned this morning that the maritime division of the National Transportation Safety Board is investigating concerns around the continued seaworthiness of the Pods. While we believe it is premature to Redock the fleet, and have yet to find any evidence in support of the claims made against WellCorp, my team is working to ensure the safety of the Travelers."

Noa heard someone make a soft *oh* and wondered if it had been her when her manager's blue eyes flicked in her direction before she continued, "At this point, as Oisín mentioned, we have every reason to believe that the claims are grounded in software malfunctions that are misreporting data. Our priority remains to realign the Pods so that they are out of the storm's trajectory.

"We're looking into restricting Travelers' access to their outdoor patios in the next few days, in anticipation of any rogue waves."

Noa had relaxed at the mention of data—maybe the Traveler wasn't missing, but was misreported—but the benign precaution snapped her back. It felt disproportionately minimal compared to the claims being made. The Pods, which were floating in the middle of the ocean, might have a compromised structure, and the plan was to restrict outdoor access in anticipation of a storm? Noa's thoughts raced. *What are the claims exactly? Will Travelers be alerted to the risk? Will they be given the option to return home?* Noa didn't realize she had spoken the last question out loud until Oisín's avatar turned toward hers.

"You're the new LHaPE, correct?" he asked, pronouncing her title with the same disdain a fraternity brother would say *pledge*. Noa hated how the name reduced her decades of experience to a title that sounded so juvenile.

"Yes," Noa replied, hesitation blurring the edges of the word. Her promotion had gone into effect the day after Emmett's keynote, but it was the word "new" that made Noa pause. Her promotion and transition were anonymous to everyone except a select few on the Health and Engineering team, and Noa hadn't been aware, until this moment, that Oisín knew she existed at all. He was looking expectantly at Noa.

"Will Travelers be given the option of Redocking, given the elevated risk from the storm?" Noa tried, choosing her words carefully.

"At this point, we don't want to do anything to validate the circulating rumors, especially given our confidence in the Pods' structural integrity."

"So we're prioritizing the company's reputation over lives?" She knew she was crossing a line, but was too angry to choose her words.

"We are cooperating with the NTSB and Coast Guard but see no reason to incite unnecessary panic."

What the fuck? Noa wanted to trust him—this man who had built the largest social networking site and database of human behavior in the world on a platform of transparency—but she thought back to the notification she had received the day before: *Traveler does not exist.* A chill ran through her body, picking up what her mind was still processing.

She could feel her chest tighten as her Lens reminded her to take a slow breath, the way she had been working on doing with her Emmie, to regulate her anger.

"Is that really true though?" Noa knew she was pushing it.

She watched two members of the executive team turn to each other, as Oisín muted himself to the room before speaking directly to Noa: "I don't think I need to remind you of what's at risk for you if you challenge the core community and goals of this company. We are a team here."

Anyone who stood up to the company's values or initiatives ran the serious risk of losing their job, but also their livelihood. Not only was WellCorp the best-paying employment Noa could ever hope to find, but it housed, fed, and protected her. She had barely stepped beyond the walls that enclosed WellCorp's campus, shuttle, and apartment complex since the moment she was hired—you had to be an idiot to leave utopia once you found it. Noa was way past that. He was talking about people *dying*. She felt the familiar fire of rage building in her.

"Challenge the goals of the company? You're talking about killing—"

"Noa," Oisín cautioned, using her real name instead of her designation, but it only heightened her anger. A slur of words came out of her mouth too quickly for her to catch them.

"Are you fucking kidding me, Oisín?" A cauldron of hot rage boiled beneath each word even as she *knew* she should stop. "You're completely removing their ability to make a decision about their own lives. This is no more ethical than murder—"

She was still shouting—she couldn't remember what—when her screen went dark. Her heartbeat interrupted the sound of the feed and she waited for it to stop pounding, finally taking a breath, before she removed her VR goggles, setting them carefully into the cradle beside her. She looked up at the footbridge just in time to see a security car drive around it. Its wheels kicked up dust and landscaped pebbles from the Japanese garden. Noa immediately knew it was coming for her, but her concern was eclipsed by the thought that had been pressing at her core since the meeting began: Was Maggie safe?

Noa rose from her desk and pulled up a view of the Travelers' Vitalities on her Lens so she could monitor them as she walked, surprised to still have access. As she did, a message came in from her manager. Noa ignored it and stepped into the stairwell at the same time Maya exited the mezzanine of the floor below. Maya had just glanced up at her when Noa quickly turned to head toward the back stairs that would drop her outside the east side of the building.

What would she even say to Maya right now? Maya, who embodied the team ethos of WellCorp. Maya, who Noa could once barely be in the same room with, without being drawn under her spell. Noa couldn't shake the suspicion that the NTSB's investigation was somehow linked to the Traveler's missing profile, even—or especially—given Oisín's warning, and she didn't want to give Maya the opportunity to talk her out of believing this time that something was wrong. She walked as quickly as she could, outrunning her thoughts until the orchestra of her own breath obscured them completely. Her feet moved faster along the path until she was running.

Their apartment was exactly as she had left it that morning. When she and Maggie had first moved in, she had admired the minimalism, how few things they would need to bring with them, but now she could see how the design practically expelled any personal touches. The furniture was set, the closet was designed for a capsule wardrobe, and there were hardly any drawers. If she was fired—which she had to assume she was—someone else could move in the same day.

She crossed the living room to the sliding door of the balcony, which opened at the tap of a button. She had to turn sideways to squeeze between their two stationary bikes and reach the railing, which was cold against her forearms. Every room in WellHome offered ocean views, literally turning employees away from the remains of the small industrial town it loomed over, limping along after the earthquakes and fires of the past decade. Although there was no possibility of seeing a Pod—the closest was over a thousand miles offshore—she scanned the horizon, then put her head down and closed her eyes, breathing in the salt air wafting off the ocean.

She needed some time to think, to process the information. She muted the incoming notifications from her manager, and walked toward the closet, stripping off her clothes. It opened like a flower, revealing racks of shirts and pants. Besides the upgraded WellNest, the closet had been the thing that impressed Maggie most about the apartment—a self-cleaning unit that replaced the laundry basket, replaced *laundry*. Once it was closed, the clothes were deodorized and cleaned through purified air and LEDs. She stopped short at Maggie's yellow dress. They had sold most of their belongings, including clothes and Maggie's beloved bungalow, when they moved into WellHome. The apartment, after all, provided everything they'd need, and their old clothes, the ones they'd lived in for years, suddenly felt drab in comparison to their shiny new life. They had allowed themselves the luxury of donating their entire wardrobe to buy a new one of fewer, better-made items. The dress Maggie had been wearing the day they met was the only thing Noa had asked her to keep.

Noa pulled it off its hanger and over her head, feeling comforted by the soft fabric and the subtle smell that still clung to its fibers, reminding her of Maggie.

As she walked past her bedside table, she paused to retrieve the mystery Device, clicking into it as she had countless times before. She was about to close out of it, out of habit, when she noticed a small icon of a folder in the lower left corner of the screen that she swore hadn't been there when she had checked that morning.

Noa's back slid down the side of her bed until she made contact with the ground, yellow fabric pooling around her. She clumsily pushed the icon and a single notification popped onto the screen. It was signed by Emmett Neal. Noa read it over until she'd committed every unbelievable word to memory:

This is a personal message for Noa Behar. This Device contains classified files that do not exist as a whole anywhere outside of this Device. Soon you will receive further instruction. Until then, take care to read the documents here.—Emmett Neal

The message was frustratingly vague, but after the Device verified Noa's face, several files filled the screen. Noa scanned through them, wishing she had a notepad in the apartment, something tangible and offline where she could put down her thoughts. *Is this some kind of test?* She began with the first file, immediately recognizing it as the panel from the Traveler who been declared as nonexistent. A few lines down, in an unassuming font, was the word:

Deceased.

How could she be *dead*? It was such a finite departure from the ambiguity of the previous message. Was she still on her Pod? There was a strict protocol for Travelers who died mid-Journey, but as far as Noa knew, that hadn't happened yet.

She clicked into a few other documents before landing on a collection of conversation excerpts. Like the evidence itself, which frustratingly painted only a half picture, the messages were piecemeal and cryptic, assembled from fragments of conversations beginning nearly two years earlier between Emmett and Oisín. It was easily the most personal-feeling document in the folder, and the only window she had into Emmett's thoughts. It stood apart from the dry Privacy Update and the Executive Memo that preceded it. Her thoughts spun. *Am I the only one with access to these? Or does everyone in the company have a Device with the same information? Is this some kind of test of loyalty? A massive coordinated attack on WellCorp?* She glanced back at the document:

May 1, 2058

EN: are we rly moving forward with this model of pods?
OB: They're your vision too. Don't compromise.

EN: we cant put users at risk like this, the pods arent safe

OB: We won't. RN's team has plenty of time to fine-tune the structure. It isn't rocket science. They're boats. Remember the larger vision.

EN: no, youre probably right.

Noa had no idea who RN was, or what their team did, but she assumed it had something to do with the engineering of the Pods. Had they rushed into production? Another set of messages reflected similar concerns, written a year later:

April 3, 2059

EN: doesn't this feel a bit fast? We don't need to rush launch

OB: It has to be now.

EN: why now??

OB: Everything's ready. This is too big to pull back now.

EN: rn's team is voicing concerns, its going to get out, people's lives are at risk

OB: Their job is to be concerned. The Pods are ready, and we still have almost a year.

Noa was shocked to learn that Emmett had been so hesitant to launch the Pods. She clung to Emmett's concerns: *How unstable are they, really? What happened in the nine months between Emmett's April messages and Launch?* Noa hated to admit how much the conversations legitimized the claims made in that viral *Technologist* article, that hundreds of Travelers were floating in preemptively launched death traps. But it still didn't answer her most pressing questions: *Why did Oisín push so hard for them? Why isn't Emmett going public with this? Why has she trusted me, of all people, with this information?*

Every document was different, but part of the same story. As soon as she finished one transcript, she clicked into a memo, an internal document she had never seen before, then repeated the process, memorizing the texts the same way she had the notification. She had the sense that she would want to be able to quote from them, if the documents self-deleted—or if the Device was ever taken from her.

When Noa finally looked up from the screen, it was completely dark. She checked the time: 2:28 a.m. She had barely moved for hours, reading and rereading the documents that seemed to hold a key, even if she didn't yet know where or how to use it. She should have been hungry, but she only felt tired. She pulled herself up by the edge of the bed, then crawled directly into it, still wearing Maggie's dress and clutching the Device.

Noa's mind ricocheted between her concern for Maggie and her confusion around what it was *she* was supposed to do about it. Her eyes closed before her windows had a chance to fully obscure the artificial light bleeding from adjacent apartments into hers. The designation at the top of the Traveler's file haunted her thoughts as she drifted off. *Deceased.*

39 Days Post-Launch

Noa's father would have called it a dead man's sleep, one where she hadn't had any dreams at all, but as the events from the day before came back to her, they took on a piecemeal, ethereal quality. Noa might have held out hope that it had all been a dream if she hadn't woken still clutching the rogue Device against her chest. Its contents came flooding back to her like a nightmare.

She had left her own Device by the front door and pushed herself out of bed to retrieve it, fumbling through the dark until her windows brightened to let in daylight. Noa tugged a sweater down over Maggie's dress and tapped the screen, aglow with notifications from her manager, before padding barefoot toward the kitchen. She rested her elbows against the countertop, and was about to ask her Emmie for some coffee when she heard a faint rumbling coming from the sub-counter station, anticipating her desire.

The synchronous gurgling of hot water and grinding of coffee always reminded Noa of the shop she used to drag Maggie to, where they charged $27 for an eight-ounce mug of pour-over and still barely made a profit from the skyrocketing price of beans. Maggie would settle onto her favorite stool by the window and pull out a book, while Noa hung around the bar to commiserate with the baristas over the state of coffee. Customers would double-take when they saw Maggie. It was rare to see someone in rapt attention with anything but a Device. She was always so quiet when she read, Noa could almost pretend she was in the living room now, her legs pulled up beneath her as she read one of her beloved novels. The memory was almost too painful.

"Good morning," Noa's Emmie spoke through the small speakers embedded around the apartment. "Your coffee is ready and you have a few urgent notifications to tend to. Should I read them to you?"

After everything she had read the night before, Noa could barely comprehend the banality of the daily tasks into which she had thrown herself since Launch. Monitoring micro-changes in hydration and disruptions in REM cycles felt inconsequential after coming across that word: *Deceased*. There were still so many answers she didn't have, but the documents confirmed her worst nightmare: Maggie was in danger and WellCorp was almost certainly covering something up, though Noa couldn't quite grasp what.

Noa closed her eyes to escape the flashing work notifications now arriving on her Lens—it was unlike her to be unresponsive for so many hours, and she couldn't avoid them forever. She settled onto the couch with her mug, holding both Devices. The seat beneath her softened, cradling her.

She scrolled through several more of the documents, her coffee going cold, before she closed the mystery Device, no closer to understanding its contents.

The notifications coming into her Lens were no longer glowing, but thumping for Noa's attention like a heartbeat. She finally relented, afraid of what they said but also hopeful that they might, somehow, hold another clue.

"Open notifications," she said.

A stack like large flashcards appeared, projected against the wall in front of the couch, filling in everything she'd missed while steeped in the other Device. One sat on top, timestamped 10:26 p.m. It was a message from her manager, inviting her to a meeting that had begun an hour ago. Noa suspected it was to discuss her "transition" out of the company, which meant she didn't have much time left. *But what am I even supposed to do?*

Noa could barely slow down long enough to process the ways in which her life had changed in the past twenty-four hours. She wished she could rewind, not just a day, but two months, to the moment she had assured Maggie that the Pods were safe. They had been sitting exactly where she was now, though Noa couldn't remember what book Maggie had been reading at the time or if she had even been reading at all. The memory came filtered through the Lens Noa had been viewing during their conversation, so Maggie's face was blurred by the lightly opaque layer of whatever had been too important for Noa to set down. "I think you should go," Noa had said.

Three firm raps at the door jolted Noa out of the thought, and she briefly considered hiding before remembering that the light at her entryway would already have given her away: green for home. The knock came again, more insistent, as if the person on the other side of the door could sense Noa's eyes fixed on the two-inch-thick barrier between them. The option to view the hallway arrived on her Lens, and Noa's eyes darted to expand the square to a semitransparent video that occupied her vision.

Maya stood just outside the door, dwarfed between two security guards. She looked straight into the camera transmitting the video feed to Noa's Lens as the guards faced the door. Noa half blinked to zoom in on Maya's expression, unable to read it, as her Emmie announced the arrival of WellCorp security and a member from the HR team. Noa stood and smoothed the wrinkled dress with the palms of her hands, slipping her own Device between two couch cushions and Emmett's into the dress's pocket.

Maya's eyes warned her the moment the door slid open at Noa's approach, though she quickly embodied a cold professional demeanor so unlike the woman who had pulled Noa into a kiss two days before. The woman who had whispered she loved her.

"Hello, Noa," Maya began, her voice warm but authoritative and scripted. "I'm here as a representative of WellCorp's human resources team to inform you that your employment by WellCorp has been terminated. I know this may come as a shock to you, but I am happy to answer any questions you may have at this time. We have reserved a Courtesy Drop vehicle for you, which is authorized to drop you at any location within two hundred miles of campus."

Noa almost missed it, but as Maya spoke, she winked briefly at Noa. *Just go with it.* Noa tried to speak, failing to form a single discernible word. One of the security guards took a step forward, peering around the door into Noa's apartment.

"I know this may feel abrupt, but it is WellCorp's belief that you no longer have the company's best interests at heart." Noa considered Maya's phrasing, the anthropomorphizing of an entire company that was apparently disappointed in her. She nodded slowly, still unsure how to take in this entirely different version of Maya, or where she would go. The only family Noa had in California was Maggie's dad, who still lived in Palo Alto, and she had lost touch with so many of their friends in Los Angeles. Maya took a step forward, grazing Noa's dress with her hand. "We look forward to a peaceful separation, which, of course, includes a generous severance package."

When Noa slid her hand into her pocket to palm the Device, her fingertips brushed across something foreign. She thumbed the small slip, a piece of paper folded into a tight square, the obsolete material as jarringly out of place as Maggie's physical books.

"We'll give you a few minutes to gather your things. No need to pack everything—anything you don't bring can be shipped to you. Do you need longer than forty minutes?" Maya asked.

"No." Noa shook her head, eager to get somewhere that she could read the message. "That should be fine. I just need to—"

"We'll be outside." Maya nodded to the guards, and the three retreated behind the threshold, walking back down the hallway as the door slid closed. The moment the latch caught, Noa unfolded Maya's note, her fingers revealing a slanted script drawn over its creases that looked like it had been torn out of the page of a book:

There are some things you learn best in calm, and some in storm.

Noa turned it over, hoping to find more, but there was nothing. The words sounded so familiar. She had heard Maggie say them before, but their source felt just out of reach. Noa held it as she walked toward the bedroom, wondering what she should bring with her. She and Maggie had kept so few things, but they had each brought their most valuable possessions, tidily tucked into two separate drawers embedded in the wall beneath their closet. Noa rarely had a reason to access the few family mementos and heirlooms hers contained: a few quartz rocks and the solid silver necklace of a parrot in a cage her mother used to wear, which she preferred not to look at. Once Maggie had been wearing it when she came home from work, and Noa had been so furious that Maggie never touched it again. Its presence alone filled her with enough shame to drown in.

Maggie, on the other hand, was constantly pulling books and small mementos from her drawer, sometimes to simply hold them against her chest. Maybe it was because Noa had left everything she owned when she moved from New York, but she had never realized until Maggie that some people simply derived more meaning from physical objects. When Maggie thumbed through one of Gamma's books or pressed the wooden chess piece she loved so much between her hands in prayer, she actually *felt* that she was with this person she loved and missed.

Noa opened Maggie's drawer, releasing a soft plume of the scent of old books, and regarded the spines, nearly all of which were novels. Maggie had always tried to get Noa to read, but Noa had been more interested in watching movies and in creating, developing the code that *made* things happen. Maggie, for her part, was content to consume. She loved reading novels, and though she occasionally painted, she seemed to prefer to view art at the campus's small museum. Noa had never met anyone before who appreciated food as much as Maggie, yet had no interest in cooking. She only learned years later that on the day they met at the farmers' market, Maggie had been there to browse the produce, but had no interest in turning any of it into a recipe. She was simply there for their beauty, which Noa felt made Maggie's old job at the gallery especially fitting. A countdown on Noa's Lens warned her that five minutes had passed.

Every book was meticulously placed, their broken spines laid in tidy rows. Noa ran her fingertips over them, unsure of what she was looking for, until she hit a bank of four or so books raised about an inch higher than the others. She might have missed it if she hadn't let her fingers glide across them. When she lifted the first in the line, she could see that there was a book beneath it, the cover facing up. Each book she lifted unveiled more of the one beneath until Noa could read the full title, *The Song of the Lark,* by Willa Cather. She pulled it out and heard a plink as something small hit the ground.

Noa bent down to retrieve the thin gold chain, joined by a narrow plate with a word carved into it: *ENMESH.*

She turned back to the book, opening to the cover page. She continued to flip through until she came across a small rectangle meticulously cut into the pages, just deep enough to hold the bracelet that had fallen from it. Running along the top edge was the same quote. Noa opened the piece of paper and pressed it against the page to confirm, as she read, *There are some things you learn best in calm, and some in storm.*

Noa flipped through the book, a page catching on a small square of cardstock tucked diagonally in so that the spine gripped its corner. On it, numbers were written in a script that reminded her of something. She flipped to the corresponding numbers to see if the pages unveiled any secrets, but couldn't decipher any passages that seemed significant, and she was running out of time. On the last page was a short poem, in a different handwriting.

She clasped the bracelet around her wrist and pulled a weekend bag from the back of the closet. It had been years since she'd used it. She placed the book inside, then added a few sets of clothes, a pair of shoes. Even with the entire contents of her drawer, everything she needed to take with her only filled about half the bag. She had no idea what the note meant, but Noa understood that the book somehow contained a puzzle she was meant to solve. At the very least, it indicated to her that whoever had given Maya the note to slip to her had Maggie's best interest at heart.

She was still wearing the yellow dress, though it no longer smelled like Maggie. She pulled it, along with the sweater, over her head, unsticking the cotton from her damp back, and replaced it on its hanger, pressing it into the LED-lit closet before pulling on a fresh set of clothes.

She had woken up in a pool of sweat that morning and was now vaguely aware of a faint animalistic scent. There was a sourness to her. She imagined the adrenaline coursing through her veins, dispersing hormones that smelled like dead flowers. She grabbed her bag and slid the Device from Emmett into her pocket.

She thought she still had twenty minutes left when her Emmie announced, "Your car is ready."

Noa walked into the living room just in time to see the door slide open. Maya was standing there, but the guards were gone. Maya crossed the room in a few quick steps, pulling Noa in for a brief kiss before drawing back.

"They're waiting at the front door of the building for you," Maya explained in a rush. "Take the Device and head down the back entrance. It leads to the shuttle platform the maintenance team uses. Open the Device as soon as you're on board and she'll give you directions."

"Who will?" Maya had already turned on her heel and was leading Noa by the hand toward the door, checking the hallway first to confirm it was clear of guards.

"Emmett," she said, her eyes twinkling, "Go. You're going to be late."

Maya pushed Noa out the door of her apartment, sending her down the hallway alone.

• • •

A few minutes later, Noa stood at an unfamiliar platform holding her duffel and the Device. She had worked at WellCorp for three years, yet never knew there was a separate entrance for the crew who maintained the apartment building she lived in. It had simply never occurred to her. A large white AR countdown hovering over the tracks told Noa it would be just over two minutes until the next shuttle arrived. Noa wasn't sure if Maya knew about the contents of the Device, and she hadn't had time to ask her or retrieve her own still buried in the couch cushions, as she was ushered out the door.

Noa wondered if she was still heading to a Courtesy Drop and, if so, where she would ask it to take her. It was a dark game she and Maggie used to play. Would they move back to Echo Park? Northern California? Noa had checked once, and realized WellCorp was exactly two hundred miles from the Mexican border, a viable option if they could obtain visas.

The shuttle pulled to a silent stop in front of her. Noa boarded and walked down the aisle until she reached a private compartment and pulled the semitransparent privacy screen closed. She placed her bag on the floor below her and rested her feet on top before pulling out the Device.

"Hello, Noa." As promised, Emmett Neal's face filled the screen the moment Noa opened it, her voice playing directly into her EarDrums. *Hello?* She almost responded, before realizing it was a prerecorded video.

"I know what I'm about to say will come as a surprise to you," Emmett said, "but I need to keep this short. It is imperative to the safety of all Travelers that you follow the instructions on the following screens. It should go without saying that this is confidential. You have to trust me."

Emmett was sitting with her back against a concrete wall that made her look like she was in a bunker. For all Noa knew, she *was* in a bunker. Emmett hadn't been on campus since the night of the keynote, though she looked as pulled-together as ever, her hair tied back in her signature efficient ponytail. Emmett-in-bunker said, "As soon as the shuttle arrives on campus, I need you to head straight to the parking structure, to spot D twenty-six. Use this Device to unlock any doors along the way."

The video clicked off as quickly as it had appeared, leaving Noa to sit in stunned silence for the remainder of the ride. *What will Maggie think when she returns home? Where will she live?* Noa felt ashamed that she hadn't considered the questions since Maya had arrived at her door, but Maggie's stability and future were intrinsically tied to Noa's.

Noa was imagining Maggie on the Pod as she crested the hill of the shuttle exit in a daze, seeing the familiar shape of Monet's bridge. It had been almost two years since she'd proposed on that bridge. *Why did we wait so long to get married?* Both of them had cited Noa's work as their reason— Noa wouldn't have to work such grueling hours after the first Launch— but had it only been a feeble excuse? They could have gotten married at any point without the party, which wasn't all that important to either of them. But they had chosen to wait. In hindsight, Noa wondered if it had been for the best. Maybe, at some level, they both knew: something in their relationship had broken the day they moved into the apartment. It had never again been as strong as that first magical year together.

She disembarked, walking quickly toward the auditorium and the adjacent parking structure. Noa held the Device against the auditorium's Reader and breathed a sigh of relief when it turned green; she yanked the door open, then passed through the main lobby toward the garage. The high-domed ceilings felt ecclesiastical when the place wasn't filled with the excited chatter of attendees, and her footsteps echoed against the jet-black marble floors as she made her way to the parking structure.

The last time Noa had been in the auditorium was the only time she had ever interacted directly with Emmett. Noa had been selected to play the role of Traveler in the Pod for the keynote, miming the choreographed routine along with the computer-generated simulation projected behind her. She had been chosen, her manager had explained in the video message projection of her avatar, delivered to Noa's Lens, because of her intimate knowledge of the project and because it wasn't safe to hire an "actual actor." The entire presentation was shrouded in the fear that it would somehow be leaked. It was safer to have someone already vetted play the role. *And isn't it an honor?* Her manager had insisted.

She and Maggie had met Emmett briefly before the production, speaking to her in her greenroom for a few minutes before they took their respective places: Maggie in a seat in the audience, Noa in the glass Pod below the stage. Emmett, Noa had noticed, had been especially interested in Maggie, peppering her with questions about her interest in art and novels, and the work she had done at the gallery before following Noa to WellCorp. She had even hinted at giving Maggie the opportunity to curate an exhibit at the campus's museum.

When Noa had finally taken her place in the Pod, the only sound she could hear came from a producer who spoke to Noa through her EarDrums every few minutes, delivering an updated countdown. Otherwise, she was completely alone in the serene, claustrophobic bubble. She had been in plenty of Pods, not to mention plenty of iterations of them, but always with a group of other engineers and only in simulations. That had been her first time in one alone, and it felt completely different. She walked around the room, trying to imagine what it would feel like to be in the middle of the ocean.

She smoothed out the bedding, letting her shaking hand trail behind her—no person belonged in this glass bubble. As soon as the Pod rose, the feeling faded. She explained away her panic as stage fright.

After the keynote, she had gone to the greenroom to change from her Traveler costume into her regular clothes, one of thousands of mistakes she'd made that year alone. Maya was in the room, while Maggie waited for her at the spot they'd agreed on in the lobby, probably holding a glass of cheap sparkling wine for each of them. She'd sent Maggie a quick message before dropping her Device when Maya pulled her shirt up to kiss her breasts:

Be there soon. x

She was clasping her bra when her Lens beeped with a notification. The code she'd written that morning was glitching. She ran out with

Maya into the underground path to the main building. Maya had given her hand a quick squeeze before Noa continued to the first open desk in the main building. It had taken her a few minutes to see where she'd gone wrong, but it wasn't a difficult fix. She'd ignored notifications from Maggie—she would be there any second—as she adjusted a few of the variables, then went back to the lobby.

By the time she arrived, Maggie was gone. A full hour had passed since the time they had agreed to meet. She was surprised to find, when she arrived home a half hour later, that Maggie wasn't there either.

Like every other car in the bay, the one in D-26 was part of a line made exclusively for WellCorp; self-driving, electric, and powerful. Noa waved the Device to open the door and placed her bag on the bench beside her. The door closed behind her and the car lurched backward, pulling out of the spot without asking her for a destination and maneuvering through the rows of the parking structure. Instead of heading to the exit, the car turned and pulled up to a large metal gate that began to rise at its approach, surprisingly silent for how industrial it looked. It proceeded into a tunnel made of smooth concrete that arched over the road, seamless except for the strip of fluorescent light that ran the entire length at its apex and vanished into the top of a steep slope ahead.

Noa had no idea where the car was heading, but soon the slope began to level out into a long expanse, revealing another gate in the distance. The car came to a stop about twenty yards in front of it.

"What the fuck?" Noa said. She wished there was a pedal she could press to urge the car forward, but it was entirely self-driving. "Move forward?" she tried, but the car refused to budge.

Just as she began to wonder if it was a malfunction, she caught sight of movement behind her. A security car packed with guards was driving toward her. She hesitated a split second, then grabbed her bag and took off toward the gate, propelled by the thought of the book and the conviction that this was all somehow related to Maggie. They were just far enough behind her that she could reach it if she ran.

A speaker mounted to the top of the guards' car called out to her, warning her to stop immediately. Noa's heart pounded against her chest, but she pushed past the feeling. They were closing in on her, but she still stood a chance of escaping. As she approached the gate, its wide mouth yawned to reveal blinding sunlight. It opened just high enough for her to hurtle her bag through it then herself under it, closing the moment she passed through, kicking up a cloud of dirt as her body slammed against the ground.

A wave of heat washed over her and Noa shielded her eyes with her arm from the sun, still powerful through a thin layer of clouds. A notification from her Lens came in as she pushed herself up to standing, wiping off the brown dust, which dispersed in small plumes:

Out of campus range.

It was the first time in three years she had stepped off campus and she had no idea where she was.

Fog

10

Noa

Noa stood at the bottom of a shallow bowl of hills with peaks just high enough that she had to lift her head to see their tops against the thin layer of clouds. Tiny yellow flowers dotted the otherwise sun-scorched slopes. Noa wiped the sweat off her brow with the back of her hand. A slim Injectible Reader stood sentry at the heavy metal gate behind her, embedded into one of the hills.

Noa had been surprised when the gate violently closed behind her, but what else had she expected? Now that she was on the other side, she wasn't sure why she wanted to get away from the guards so badly. A mysterious note in a book, Emmett's message, and Maya's trust weren't much to go on, but Noa hoped she had made the right decision. In all likelihood, they would have escorted her to the actual Courtesy Drop she was supposed to be in now, instead of—wherever this was. Noa had barely had a second to think about any of her actions since the moment Maya had pushed her out of her apartment. The Reader beside the closed gate responded with a dull beep as she swiped her Injectible against it repeatedly, edging her growing sense of desperation closer toward blind panic. She thought she heard a muffled sound coming from the other side of the gate, but any efforts to open it were apparently thwarted. The gate remained sealed.

Noa had tossed her weekend bag through the gate with enough force that she had to look for a moment to find it, so coated in dust it resembled a boulder. She walked over to retrieve it, slapping the dust off before slinging it over her shoulder. A breeze hit the sweat that clung to her tank top, cooling her off, but the relief only lasted a moment as she reached for the Device and realized it was gone. Frantically, she patted her chest, then her entire body, eager to feel the round edges that fit perfectly in her palm. She must have left it when she abandoned the car so abruptly. Noa craned her neck toward the sky, the same way she would have if she were keeping her mouth above a rising tide. She closed her eyes, allowing herself a sip of breath before diving back under.

When she opened them, she took in her surroundings. A few trees provided shade in the otherwise sun-soaked valley. They had looked like a natural grove, but Noa could see now that a dirt road ran between them. Her eyes traced it all the way to where it finally stopped at an arched wooden door embedded in the opposite hillside. The crunching sound of her footsteps along the gravel competed with sporadic birdsongs as she made her way toward it.

The door looked like something out of a fairy tale, or at least a different century, with gnarled wood fortified by looping brass accents. Three tiny cameras, barely larger than the brass nails, were embedded into it. Noa suspected they were sending a live feed to whoever was inside as she took a deep breath and lifted her hand to knock. Before her fist could come down, the door blossomed outward on its own.

Noa jumped back, hesitating before stepping into a room too dark for her to make out any details. The door, which had seemed so welcoming just a moment before, sealed closed behind her the moment she was inside. The sound of the bolts clicking into place had a prisonlike quality as it echoed through the small room. She could almost feel her pupils widening, searching for even a beam of light.

As they adjusted, she could see that she was standing in a cement cell. The only break in the smooth walls that lined the room was the door she had just stepped through. It was silent enough to hear the high-pitched whistle her mind created to fill the vacuum. She stood in the center, waiting for something to happen—

Concentrated beams of blue light emerged from the top four corners of the room, meeting at her feet, flattening so that they joined in a circle around her ankles. When it began gradually moving up her body, Noa realized it was scanning her, and then, to her horror, that it wasn't the beams of light that were moving upward, but *she* was moving downward.

The entire floor was descending, carrying her down what was evidently an elevator shaft. The ring of blue lights made their way over her stomach, her chest, her neck, until they finally reached the top of her head. When there was no more to scan, they clicked off, but the walls continued to move.

She wasn't sure how far underground she was when the top of a doorframe began to emerge from the floor. Noa instinctively took a step back, toward the edge that had once held her only exit, replaced now by concrete, until the threshold came into view.

The new door slid into the wall, revealing a person on the other side. Noa's eyes adjusted to the dim but still harsh light that flooded her pupils. Soon, features arrived on the outline—lips curled into a warm, close-mouthed smile; long hair pulled into a smooth ponytail; angular collarbones that jutted from the neckline of the immaculate, all-white set she wore—disconnected until Noa pieced them together. It was Emmett Neal.

"Come in, come in," Emmett said, ushering Noa, her smile emphasized by her dramatic cheekbones, even as Noa noticed the edges of her nose squinch into something that resembled disgust. "How was your trip?" she asked, as casually as a taxi driver pulling away from an arrival terminal, back when flying across an ocean was quotidian enough to be banal.

Noa blinked at her, adjusting to her new reality.

Behind Emmett, concrete floors and walls ran directly into parts of the hill. Noa recognized the bunker-like surface from the background of Emmett's video message. Its rippling rock face was left raw at parts, devoid of art but more arresting than any piece Noa could imagine in its place. Light spilled in from vents along the edges of the ceiling, giving the room a mausoleum-like texture that illuminated the sparse wood paneling.

Noa realized she hadn't responded when Emmett said lightly,

"Welcome to my fortress. Please make yourself at home." She turned, leading Noa into the living room. Emmett's ponytail hung between her shoulder blades, swinging lightly as she walked.

"It's beautiful," Noa managed.

The edges of Emmett's mouth turned up again as she looked back. "Thank you. By the way, I'm sorry about the entrance. . . ."

Her apology sounded genuine but was so absurd Noa nearly burst out laughing at the vast number of things "the entrance" could have referred to in the last hour. Was Emmett alluding to the fact that she had been smuggled out of her home by Maya, then chased by guards, then forced to duck under a closing gate, or simply to the blue lasers that had just traced her body? Did this mean she was still fired, or was this an improbable promotion?

Emmett trailed off as she followed Noa's gaze to a man walking down the hallway toward them.

"Noa, this is Taylor."

Noa extended her hand, which Taylor accepted in a curt shake. She recognized him as the shadow who followed Emmett at her events. He was wearing a set that mirrored Emmett's, but with a higher crew-neckline and in black that looked heavy against his yellow hair and pale skin.

"So, what was that?" Noa asked. It was one of several questions she could have asked: *Why am I here? What the fuck is going on?*

"The lasers in the elevator are antimicrobial, but also confirm the identity of anyone entering," Emmett replied.

"Or leaving," Taylor added. Noa noticed him flinch, a telltale sign that he had been startled by a notification in his EarDrum. He turned toward Emmett and whispered something in her ear.

"This is terrible timing," Emmett said, turning back to Noa, "but we have to take care of something. Inga should be here any moment to help you get settled, and I'll see you back here in a few. I'm sure you're eager for some answers."

Taylor's mouth twitched in what Noa assumed was an attempt at a comforting smile before he turned to follow Emmett, who was already walking briskly down the hallway.

Noa made her way toward the only pieces of furniture in the room: two large plush chairs faced a concrete hearth that protruded from a fireplace at waist-height in an inviting but austere bench. She perched on it, feeling too dusty for the chairs, and braced her arms behind her to take in the room. Noa got the sense that Emmett rarely had guests over, but there were also no personal effects or memorabilia to suggest the home was hers.

There were no visible windows in the room, but plenty of light cascaded from wide seams where the ceiling didn't quite meet the wall. Noa was struck by how angular everything was; the room itself was shaped like a misformed trapezoid. It stood in direct contrast to the smooth, sloping lines that hugged nearly every edge in WellPark. It *was* beautiful, as she'd told Emmett, but also harsh and disorienting. *What the fuck am I doing here?*

A woman wearing a nearly identical uniform to Emmett's and Taylor's, but in slate gray, emerged from around a corner. Noa guessed she was in her sixties, but it was hard to tell. Her hair was wrapped in a loose bun and, like Taylor's, was so pale it looked more white than blond.

"Hello," she said, "and welcome. I'm Inga. Emmett will be back shortly, but I can show you to your room."

It had been years since Noa had heard an accent different from the slightly global, American mash-up that dominated WellCorp, but Inga spoke each singsong word like she was trying to capture its final syllable in her mouth before it escaped her lips. It felt like the one soft thing in the room, and Noa could have listened to it for hours.

Inga gestured for Noa to follow her, picking up her bag, and guiding her down a long hallway. Noa wondered which of the identical closed doors Emmett and Taylor were behind until Inga abruptly stopped at one. The black door matched the walls exactly, except it was embedded about an inch into the wall, framed by a white lacquered edge. Inga swiped her wrist in front of the Reader, then stood back for Noa, placing her bag on the floor just inside the door.

"Please take as long as you need to wash up, then return to the living room. Emmett will meet you there when she is ready," she said, then walked back down the hallway with purpose, toward a more pressing task.

"Thank you," Noa called after her, immensely grateful to see a bed and, beyond it, a window.

It had to be midafternoon, but it was surprisingly dark outside, boxed in by fog that usually burned off by this time of day. Noa walked to the window, which ran from the floor to the ceiling but was barely wider than she, to get her bearings. She could see now that she was in the hills above Malibu, apparently tucked into one of them. A small square of the window could be unlatched, and Noa was relieved to discover she wasn't a total prisoner as she pushed it open. She could squeeze through it if she ever needed to.

The view of the ocean was almost exactly the same as the one from her apartment, but instead of only being able to see the horizon line, she could also see parts of the coast. Her room faced the craggy tip of Point Mugu with an aerial view of WellPark. *Do I still work there?* The only signs of life were the shuttle moving along the tracks and a security car driving toward the main building, but she knew thousands milled underground or were hidden away in buildings. She imagined taking a stick to it, like an ant colony, and stirring the soft dirt to watch the panic bubble to the surface.

She'd assumed, from her exit, that she would never be going back there, but now she wasn't sure where she stood. Emmett had brought her here, but only after she'd been chased out by guards. Maya had smuggled her out twenty minutes before she was meant to leave, clearly at Emmett's behest, but why weren't the guards working in accordance with her? It was Emmett's company, after all. Noa brought her head back inside, leaving the window wide open, to survey the room.

The furniture was almost identical to the pieces she and Maggie had shared in their apartment. She placed her bag at the end of the bed, unzipping it to toss the book on top of the duvet—it comforted her to see it—then walked into the bathroom, past a slightly smaller version of the WellNest she and Maggie had shared, a WellEcon model. In the bathroom, the SmartMirror above the sink recognized her and projected her preferences along with her now-empty schedule and the afternoon's headlines. The mirror smoothed out her pores and smaller imperfections, but even with its help, she could see that she looked like shit. She pushed her hair back, taking in her sunken eyes.

Next to the sink were two sealed glass bottles of water. She uncapped one and chugged it, not stopping until she'd reached the bottom. She grabbed the second and took a sip from it as well.

Noa peeled off her clothes and stepped into the shower. It was easy to pretend, standing under the water, that she was still in her apartment. She crouched down until she was sitting on the tiled floor and pulled her knees into her chest, pushing her eyes against them. The water was slightly cooler at this level, the droplets already losing their heat by the time they ran through her hair and down her back.

She wanted to cry, but felt too exhausted. Plus, she didn't know what to cry about. She no longer had a home, which meant Maggie wouldn't have a home once she Redocked. *How will she reach me? Has she been notified already?* Even as she thought it, Noa doubted it. Maggie would be protected from the information, to maintain the serenity of her retreat. She wrapped her arms around her shoulders and imagined Maggie stepping into the shower, sitting on the floor, pulling Noa onto her lap, into her arms. She could practically feel herself being cradled, kissed. It would be okay. It *had* to be okay.

Noa stood up slowly, pressing her forehead against the tile. This was not the time to let memory get the best of her. When *was* the last time she and Maggie had showered together? They used to all the time in the beginning, even in the tiny tub in Maggie's bungalow, because they could hardly stand to be apart for any longer than a few moments. They continued, in the new apartment's dual-head, because their routines had become so in sync, it made sense. But then, at a certain point, they had stopped, mutually and wordlessly choosing to spend more time apart, and Noa began to use the time with the water running to message Maya.

She stepped out of the shower, the water turning off automatically behind her, and wrapped a towel around herself, tucking the corner in at her chest. It felt comforting to do something so normal under the circumstances, to secure a towel around her body. She heard a slight rustle from the bedroom, but when she stepped into it, it was empty except for a faint trace of lilac.

A closet emerged from the wall, holding identical cashmere sets, all in black. *White for the host, gray for the house staff, black for visitors or Well-Corp employees,* Noa guessed. She let her towel drop to the ground and pulled a fresh bra and underwear on before slipping into the set, which fit her perfectly. It reminded Noa of an upgraded version of the uniform Travelers wore, but instead of scrub-like pajamas, it fit like a tailored suit made entirely out of cashmere. She took a few minutes to unpack the few things she'd brought with her, hanging her clothes and leaving the novel on the bed.

She touched her wrist to confirm that the bracelet had survived the escape, then ran her fingers through her short hair, straightening it down, and slipped into mules she found placed on the floor next to a small round table by the exit.

The door closed softly as she walked down the hallway lined with other closed doors toward the light of the living room. Behind her, the hallway seemed to be swallowed in darkness. Panic briefly seized her as she realized she might not be able to find her room later.

Emmett was already in the living room, sitting in one of the plush white chairs in front of the now-lit fireplace countering the air-conditioning, her hands posed as if reading a book, even though she wasn't holding one. Noa watched her mime flipping a page, then looped around the chair to announce herself in Emmett's peripheral.

Emmett smiled, but the warmth she had exuded earlier was completely gone. She spoke to Noa without looking up. "I just have one paragraph left in this chapter. Please, take a seat."

The chair she gestured toward was about thirty percent larger than it should have been. Noa had to choose between resting her back against it or placing her feet on the floor. She glanced at Emmett, who was tall enough to do both, as if the chair was built for her. *It probably was.* She perched herself at the edge, planting her feet on the ground. Emmett pressed her hands together, "closing" the book.

"Dostoevsky," Emmett said, turning to face Noa.

"What?"

"*Brothers Karamazov.* It's the book I'm reading," she said, holding her green eyes on Noa. Noa had only been this close to Emmett once before, but recognized her signature light vetiver and white floral fragrance. Her skin exuded a warm, dewy glow despite the absence of any makeup. Her glance suddenly shifted a few feet behind Noa. "Ah, Inga! Noa, are you hungry at all?"

Noa wasn't, she realized, but knew she must be. It had been a full day since her last meal. "I could eat."

"So polite," Emmett said, the edge of condescension tugging at the fabric of her carefully woven poise. "Inga, would you mind fixing us each a sandwich and some mint tea," she requested without glancing at Noa for approval. "Thank you *so* much."

Noa waited until Inga had left the room before she asked, "What am I doing here?"

"I think you can help me and the Travelers," Emmett answered calmly, as if anticipating the question. Everything about her was polished, collected.

Noa nodded slowly, shifting in her seat. Emmett's legs were crossed and her hands rested gracefully on top, so that her limbs formed an elegant stack.

"I think it's probably best if I start at the beginning. You don't mind, do you?" Emmett asked, taking a deep breath and uncrossing her hands, which immediately floated to conduct each word. There was something about the way she spoke that reminded Noa of Maggie. "I have always valued privacy and access to isolation above all else. It's why I created WellNests in the first place."

Emmett didn't need to tell Noa the story about her grandfather, how they'd both found sanctuary within his woodshed. She and every Well-Corp employee had heard it a thousand times. This time, a thought occurred to Noa: of the number of cameras in WellCorp, the tracker in her wrist, the electrodes in her brain. *How can Emmett not see it?* The kind of isolation she was describing was more fleeting *because* of WellCorp.

"Access to privacy, to a place of one's own, is vital to human development, growth, and creativity, and the only thing that could possibly birth a solution to climate disaster, in my opinion," Emmett went on.

It was amazing to Noa how, with enough money, you could almost turn opinion into fact. But she tried to keep an open mind. She often jumped to conclusions without weighing both sides. It was an instinct that allowed her to make swift decisions at work, but could skirt into impulsivity in her personal life—and, apparently, get her fired.

"WellPods and WellNests both grew from that same seed. I saw Well-Pods as a singular opportunity for a nearly two-month escape from life, a chance to regroup in unencumbered isolation and then be, effectively, reborn." Her hands, which had been gracefully moving as she spoke, now came together in a prayer in front of her lips. "Oisín's vision was always larger. He was able to see the potential that had been placed in our laps—which is why he pushed even harder for the Pods' completion than I did, in the end."

Noa remembered the messages left on the Device. *It has to be now,* Oisín had written. Emmett uncrossed and recrossed her legs, as if wondering how exactly to put it, then took a deep breath.

"Last year, healthcare was a *twenty-trillion*-dollar industry. Hospitals, pharmaceuticals," she said, counting each, starting from her thumb, "health insurance, concierge medicine. People will spend any amount to keep themselves and their loved ones alive. And we owned a growing percentage of the market, thanks to body-embedded tech."

"Lenses and Injectibles," Noa said.

"At their base level, Injectibles are obviously a hybrid identification card, geo- and fitness-tracker, and blood-testing system." As Emmett spoke, she maintained eye contact except for the moments she glanced down at her own forearm, pinching what Noa assumed was her Injectible. "You of all people should understand that."

Noa's hand floated self-consciously to the familiar square on the back of her arm as Emmett continued, "You know, the insulin pump was the first Injectible-integrated drug delivery accessory we offered? But that technology has improved beyond the scope of what I thought was possible when I created them as a companion to WellNests."

Emmett leaned forward until her forearms rested against the tops of her thighs.

"Oisín wanted to use the Injectibles' and Lenses' combined capacity for biomathematics and predictive modeling against a user's normal parameters, to be able to detect diseases as soon as health markers indicated any abnormalities."

"Okay." Noa didn't understand yet what this had to do with the Pods. She had a sense she was playing a game with Emmett, but she didn't know any of the rules or even which side she was on yet.

"Your lunch should be ready by now," Emmett said, suddenly brightening, "if you'd like to grab it from the kitchen."

Disoriented, Noa followed her command and stood to walk past a dining room encased on three sides by windows, into the kitchen that Inga had disappeared into. An older man was sitting at the table, but didn't acknowledge Noa as she walked past. His eyes were glued to the table, lost in thought. Though there was no sign of Inga, she found a tray that held a glass teapot stuffed with mint leaves and two sandwiches layered with ingredients Noa hadn't seen in years on the slate-black countertop next to the sink.

"Feel free to bring it into the living room," Emmett called.

Carefully balancing the meal, Noa returned and set the tray down on the low coffee table in front of Emmett.

"That's pretty," Emmett said, reaching out for the gold bracelet, which had slid out from under Noa's sleeve around her hand.

"Oh, thank you," Noa said, instinctively lifting her arm to shake it back under her sleeve when Emmett reached out to inspect it.

"Is it a family heirloom?"

"Yeah—I mean, not of my family's but of my fiancée's, I think. Who was that at the table?" Noa asked, changing the subject.

"Hmm?" Emmett was leaning forward to pour the tea into her mug. "Oh, Arthur. You'll meet him tomorrow."

Noa sat down on the edge of her seat. She could see a perfect strata of ricotta, tomatoes, and pesto between the two slices of bread, with real whole grains, but she felt sick to her stomach. She leaned forward to pour herself a glass of the pungent brew as Emmett sat still, watching her.

"Can you tell me what's going on?" Noa pressed. "Why are you telling *me* all of this?" A former employee who had reacted to being fired by escaping campus felt like an unlikely confidante for divulging company secrets to.

Emmett took another slow, deep breath, making Noa think again of Maggie: her thoughtful consideration, her long pauses that went just beyond the length of social acceptability when she didn't quite have the words yet. Then again, everything reminded her of Maggie these days.

"Since the invention of the internet, people's actions have been coded as data so that they can be fed through algorithms that increase their spending and benefit corporations. It began with supermarkets using purchasing sequences to determine future outcomes. Of course, early social media sites delivered ads tailored not only to the accounts an individual followed, but to the people they were spending their time with offline. We've all gotten used to our everyday decisions being tracked as data, haven't we? We even packaged and sold our users' Injectibles data back to them, offering precise recommendations in WellNests.

"Our thoughts and actions have been treated like property for decades, sold between companies without us even knowing. It was never a big leap for us to apply the same ownership, the same intimate knowledge, to our bodies."

"I don't understand," Noa said, at the same time she worried she understood everything perfectly. She had been staring at the sandwiches, the ingredients blurring into a kaleidoscope of green and red, as Emmett spoke, but returned her gaze to Emmett's eyes, which were gazing intently at Noa with an expression that Noa had never seen in her curated keynotes or public interviews.

"WellCorp has access to nearly every aspect of a user's life: the innermost thoughts shared with their Emmies, their health, where they go when they think they aren't being watched. We've collected enough data to know virtually everything about most people in the world: their habits, their future actions—even their past." Noa shifted uncomfortably as Emmett spoke. "Combined with the advances in immunoassays, this technology would enable us to catch and treat illnesses early on, to bring the hospital to your wrist.

"The vision was, admittedly, incredible—if we could get it to work. I'm talking about chemotherapy, dialysis even, becoming as easy as applying a patch or heading into an annual physical," Emmett said, her hands flying as she spoke. "Imagine, a notification would arrive on a patient's Device or Lens telling them they had cancer, but instead of this being a death sentence or prelude to chemo, the system would simply ship a targeted accessory patch or instruct the patient to head to the nearest Well-Health center to receive an injection. Cancer, with an Injectible, is no more than an inconvenience. But the big money in healthcare is dependent on lengthy treatments. This would be far less lucrative for the healthcare provider, which is why Oisín suggested we flip the model on its head and charge for the diagnosis instead of the treatment."

Noa didn't even have to think about it. "Pay to cheat death."

"For a monthly fee, premium subscribers would no longer have to suffer from treatable diseases like HIV, measles, organ failure, the flu, heart conditions." Emmett listed them off. "Twenty percent of the world's population has an Injectible. Even lowballing it, that's one point eight billion users. If even one percent of those opt for a subscription model at one thousand per month, that would generate two hundred and sixteen *billion* dollars per year. That's a conservative estimate, and it's almost entirely profit. It's brilliant, but the technology just wasn't there. Any attempts at trials were muddied. We needed a double-blind study completely removed from external variables."

"Hence your interest in the Pods," Noa said, catching on.

"Hence *Oisín's* interest in the Pods. It was never my goal to treat each Pod like a floating petri dish, but once Oisín saw the potential to use them that way—to manipulate variables in a completely controlled environment—he became singularly focused on launching them. He was obsessed with his mission. He saw the potential benefits, for humanity, for profits really, as superseding any risk posed to the Travelers we launched."

"Which is why he pushed so hard for the Pods before they were ready," Noa filled in the blanks.

"Yes," Emmett said, crossing her legs again. "I only wanted to give people the opportunity for a fully regenerative, immersive experience, but every word Thomas wrote in the *Technologist* piece is true. If anything, the situation is far more dire than even he understood. The Pods are unstable, and with this developing storm, the lives of every one of the thousand Travelers are in immediate danger." Noa tried to read Emmett's eyes once more. Something was off about Emmett, her speech felt too practiced, though Noa couldn't put her finger on it quite yet. It was impossible to know if she could trust her.

"Then why did you still announce the Pods?" Noa had been right there, had seen the conviction behind her delivery.

"Oisín lied to me about the data. It took me reading Thomas's article to realize that the anonymity at WellCorp cuts both ways—and Oisín weaponized it against me, convincing me that the Pods were ready, when they were compromised all along." She wavered, softening for a moment. "I think he wanted to believe that they would work? And I was so focused on the software that I didn't look too hard at the issues around the Pods themselves. I wanted them to be ready too. I allowed myself to be convinced."

"Why not say something now? You had two months between the keynote and the launch, but you said nothing." Noa was furious.

"I wanted to, but I was silenced." Emmett leaned forward. "Oisín had been laying the groundwork for months before the keynote, convincing the board I was unstable and determined to undermine their plan for profit—all they can see is money. Do you remember my 'leave of absence'?"

Emmett spat the last words. Noa thought of the announcement Oisín had made, that Emmett would be stepping down indefinitely. It had struck Noa as a disproportionate and misdirected reaction to the article.

She continued, "He made it look like I was the only thing standing in the way and, because he still owns a majority share, he was able to revoke my access to the company overnight. Even my Injectible doesn't work. It's why I had Taylor deliver the Device to you as soon as I read the article. I knew what was coming."

Noa remembered the figure heading down the hallway that night. No wonder he had looked so familiar. She followed Emmett's gaze to her own shaking hands and held them tighter, folding them into the crease her crossed legs made. The sun was setting, but the light in the room hadn't changed. The bulbs had brightened inversely to its decline.

"Did you go to the press? Talk to Thomas?"

"I tried to, but couldn't reach him. Oisín controls nearly every outlet for communication, and he's effectively blocked most of them. The best chance we have is to beat Oisín at his own game, from the inside. Noa, I think we can help each other."

"Why me?" Something wasn't lining up.

"You're one of the best software developers we have, but more importantly, you have a personal connection."

"Maggie," Noa answered, her voice barely above a whisper.

"Maggie." Emmett nodded. "I think it's time we go see her."

11

Maggie

Zone 874, Pacific Ocean
40 Days Post-Launch

Recently, Maggie felt like her gratitude journal was trying to fuck with her. At first glance you wouldn't know it. The beautiful gold cover, with its paper-thin screens that revealed a new prompt each morning, made her feel like she could tell it anything and it would throw itself into the ocean before revealing her secrets. But then there had been a shift, not just in the journal, but in everything on the Pod.

Maggie wondered if the green light beside the deck's door had always been subject to mood swings. It was at times welcoming, encouraging Maggie to get some fresh air with the softness of a grade school teacher coaxing her students in from recess, at others almost militant in its insistence that Maggie go outside immediately. Even Emmie could be condescending then encouraging in the same breath. Her toothbrush had the distinct traits of what she thought of as a retired English gardener—humming while lovingly tending to Maggie's molars and canines as if they were ranunculus in his garden.

Of course, Maggie knew about projection and understood, rationally, that she was replacing human connection with inanimate companionship, like that character in the movie Noa made her watch once, stranded with no one to talk to but a volleyball. Still, she couldn't help but wonder whether her toothbrush was completely satisfied with his early retirement from his government post.

As if to prove her point, Maggie had woken up to a slim sliver of sunlight bouncing off the journal's gold cover directly into her eyes. The drawer of the bedside table that usually kept it out of sight had slid open, chastising Maggie for sleeping in. She'd been sleeping worse lately, struggling to find a comfortable position, tossing and turning with hormone-addled dreams. Emmie, in turn, compensated for her poor sleep by restructuring her schedule to accommodate, but even that wasn't enough.

At least her nausea had finally subsided yesterday, and she was able to obediently follow Emmie's program, which included a gentle yoga class and dinner, without any acknowledgment of the discomfort Maggie had encountered or the missing Pod. It was as if it had never happened.

Sometimes it was easy for Maggie to believe she wasn't even pregnant. She had spent so long denying the fact, despite the Lens notification that had arrived the moment it detected the elevated levels of hCG hormone in her blood. She felt like she should feel some way about it—elated or disappointed, at the very least—but really, she felt numb, refusing to take any action in either direction. Even here, she was supposed to be making some sort of decision, yet managed to create a host of excuses, expertly avoiding the only thing that mattered.

Maggie pulled the mushroom-fortified latte from her bedside table up to her lips, coiling her fingers around the mug's warm, matte exterior, hungry for body heat it couldn't give her.

Maybe if she pushed the drawer in, the journal would leave her alone. Setting down the mug, she rolled onto her side and let her arm hang off the bed, using it as leverage, but almost as soon as she pushed the drawer in, it sprang back open. Surrendering, she grabbed the journal and pulled it into bed with her, inching herself up the headboard until she could hold it balanced against her thighs.

The prompt unfolded like a minefield of memories, so specifically phrased that each word felt explosive:

Claude Monet's bridge, featured in many of his paintings, has lived two completely different lives, first in the artist's garden, then as a decorative part of WellCorp's walking path. What is a bridge you've crossed that's taken you from one life to another?

The prompt sent her right back to that evening two years ago: Noa had been telling her for weeks there was supposed to be a meteor shower and had insisted that campus would be the best place to see it, given the wide stretch of sky it sat under. Her sudden interest in astronomy felt random, but she could be impulsive.

Noa had to work late, so she'd told Maggie to meet her at the cafeteria for dinner before they found a viewing spot together. The showers weren't visible until late in the evening anyway.

Maggie had taken the shuttle to campus a few hours early so she could use the Community and Employee Facilities, packing a change of warm clothes in her gym bag. The gym, like most of the campus, was entirely underground, primarily accessed through a network of tunnels. From the shuttle, hills resembling sand dunes and grassy knolls disguised the dramatic aboveground entrances to the gym, hospital, and cafeteria, all of which faced the ocean.

She often wondered how long you had to work there before you stopped seeing the campus's beauty, until the ocean views became so standard you didn't even feel the need to exit through the shuttle's aboveground access, but were happy to burrow farther below the surface. Her attention to the natural world and beauty sometimes felt like a gift Gamma had left for her, and she tried to honor it whenever she could. She followed the walkway to a sand dune that edged daringly close to the waterline, and entered the gym.

Though she generally preferred the comfort of their stationary bikes at home, the gym provided a welcome respite to her routine. After setting her things down in the locker room, Maggie selected a weight training program from her Lens and a physical trainer appeared, projected beside her.

The trainer's watermelon-pink hair was pulled into a high ponytail, and a crop top revealed toned abs. She looked like a composite of every

Pilates instructor Maggie had ever admired. While WellCorp didn't state explicit goals, the health practices that both she and Noa were encouraged to maintain meant they were both in the best shape of their lives, a predecessor to the self-improvement program the Pod encouraged.

Although Noa had gotten Maggie a part-time job creating medical illustrations for hospitals when they moved on campus, the work wasn't nearly as consistent as Maggie let on. After working with a team to model a 3-D spine, which involved far more project management and double-checking of AI than it did any art background, she had gradually stopped responding to emails about potential projects: a prototype of an artery for robotic-assisted surgery, an animation for a Lens-delivered public service announcement for parents of children with asthma. She passed entire days hopping between her Nest, swimming in the ocean, and allowing her Lens to select entertainment for her. She had everything, yet Maggie always felt the sensation of an itch she couldn't quite scratch. She used to paint all the time in college, but had barely managed to pick up a paintbrush since, telling Noa she was content to consume the art of others so that she might finally believe it herself. Exercising was one of the rare parts of her day where Maggie felt challenged in any way.

Her trainer began to explain and demonstrate each move, coaching Maggie through the workout. Before she'd met Emmie in her physical form on the Pod, the virtual assistants her Lens projected felt like the pinnacle of augmented reality technology. A trainer could guide her through tricep dips, a chef taught her how to make pasta from scratch, and a meditation guide could walk with her around campus, literally telling her when to breathe. It gave her an enormous amount of comfort to know she could someday access the parenting coach, master gardener, or language tutor if she ever needed to.

The gym was as empty as Maggie had ever seen it. She lifted a barbell, which adjusted to her optimal weight on every curl using electromagnetic resistance. Her muscles wrapped tightly around her bone at each lift, tearing and rebuilding on a micro level as her trainer stood next to her demonstrating the perfect form. Out of the corner of her eye, she caught a glimpse of another person.

He had been slouched on a bench close to the entrance when Maggie arrived, facing away from her and tapping into his Device. But now Maggie could see that he was sitting up straight, watching her. It was *him*. She stared at him, too stunned to move, as he stood to walk toward her.

"I thought it might be you," he said, reading her mind.

It had been around four years since she'd last seen Tom—no, Thomas now—at graduation, but he looked entirely different. His hair, which had fallen lazily across his face all through college, was now styled into a cut that made his gray eyes, rimmed in the familiar red rings of his Lens, stand out against his pale face. It was hard to believe they were the same eyes she'd once considered muted. He wore the same uniform he always had—jeans and a T-shirt—but had traded in university tees for a more tailored gray shirt and jeans that were darker, without the worn outline of his Device.

She had read a few of his articles online, passively tracking his career. He had traveled to New York to cover the hurricane he'd correctly anticipated. Since then, he'd covered not only climate change, but executives, government officials, the rise of nationalism and anti-conservatism, and the country's performative efforts to change things, creating a career that perfectly combined his degrees, environmental earth science and journalism.

She had thought about messaging him each time she read one to tell him how beautiful his reporting was, but had never gotten around to it. She'd barely admitted to herself that she wasn't quite ready to open that door again. And now here he was, just a few feet away from her.

"Exit program," she said under her breath, and her trainer evaporated. She turned toward him. "Tom? What are you doing here?"

"Hey, Mags." He smiled. "I didn't realize you worked at WellCorp now."

She grabbed her towel to wipe the light sweat from her face. He looked just as surprised as she did, though he'd presumably had more time to process it, watching her for a few moments before she had turned to look at him.

"Yeah," she said. Then, "No actually. I'm sorry. I don't know why I said that. My partner, Noa, does."

"So you live at WellHome with him?" he asked, quickly tying the connection together. Spouses and domestic partners were granted the full benefits of the WellPark facilities, even if they themselves didn't work there.

"Her," she corrected. "I live with her."

If she hadn't been so good at detecting the concealed surprise in her friends' and family's faces when she told them she was dating a woman, she might have missed the wave of realization that crashed through Thomas's features before he had a chance to correct them. Of course, she couldn't blame him. She'd never dated a woman before Noa, and Thomas was her only other serious partner.

"How did you meet?" he asked, recovering quickly.

"Wouldn't you like to know?" she asked back.

"Do you not want me to?" he responded.

It was a game they used to play at the beginning of their relationship, when nearly every sentence that came out of his mouth ended in a higher register. *What are you studying? How did your test go? What was it on? What are you painting?* His curiosity had been his defining feature even then, and she'd begun responding to each question with another question, until one of them gave in and answered.

"What are you doing here?"

"Can I tell you over a drink?"

"Right now?" she asked.

"Are you free?"

"Meet back here in fifteen?"

Twenty minutes later, she found him standing outside the entrance to the gym, speaking with a man Maggie didn't recognize. When he saw Maggie, Thomas placed a hand on the stranger's shoulder and tapped his

Device against the man's to exchange information. She was too far to hear what he was saying, but imagined it was, *Call me and we can talk*. Of course, he'd already found another source in the time it had taken her to clean up.

"What are you writing about?" she asked as they walked to the cafeteria, which included not only takeaway lunch and dinner options, but also a coffee shop, a restaurant, and a bar as incredible as any she had ever visited in Los Angeles.

The counter of the bar was shaped like a winding amoeba and was so large you couldn't clearly identify the faces of the people sitting at the opposite end of it. Hanging lights cast it in a warm hue. Inside, bartenders hurried to fill orders. She and Thomas walked toward it automatically, without having to confirm where they were headed.

"I just finished talking to Emmett, actually," he responded, allowing her the first point in their game. "I'm working on an article about her and WellPark." The campus had been completed a few years prior, and the only stories written about it had been suppositions about what was inside its safeguarded walls. He would be the first to write anything sanctioned—with Emmett's final approval on edits, he explained, which was part of the grant requirement that funded his return to California. But still.

He leaned in close before adding, "Honestly, I think there's a bigger story."

"Like what?"

He hesitated. "It's too soon to tell, but it has to do with a new project Emmett's working on."

"What's she like?"

"You're going to have to read it to find out."

"Is that the line you give everyone?" Maggie thought about the day they'd received their Injectibles and her hand automatically went to her wrist. It had only been a few years, but they'd been so young, filled with optimism about the company that was going to change the world—even Thomas was seduced by its commitment to climate and social progress.

"Actually," he said, "she reminds me a little of you."

"That doesn't feel like a compliment."

He laughed. "I meant it as one. You're both . . ." He hesitated, searching for the words. ". . . subversively stubborn, but in a good way?"

Now Maggie was laughing too. She understood exactly what he meant, even if it wasn't a compliment at all. She used to ask him to edit her college essays, then systematically decline every suggestion.

A bartender arrived and took their orders: a Rainier for each of them. Maggie hadn't ordered the cheap lager since college, and wondered if it was still Thomas's go-to drink or if he had also been motivated by nostalgia. The bartender laughed at something Thomas said as Maggie sent a quick message to Noa:

Meet at the main building?

When the bartender returned with their beers and an Injectible Reader, Thomas placed his wrist to it before Maggie could protest, paying for their tab.

"Leave it open?" the man asked.

Thomas glanced at Maggie, then nodded back at the bartender. "Yes, thank you."

How many times had they sat together, drinking beers and chatting? Hundreds, Maggie guessed.

"You know," he said, thoughtfully taking a sip, "our days with beer may be limited."

"You always were the bearer of great news." Thomas had always been one step ahead when predicting the myriad ways climate change would impact their daily lives.

"Hops can only grow in a very specific temperature and humidity, and it's getting much too dry and warm. Plus, transporting a liquid is unbelievably expensive. It's hard to believe it will still be cost-effective with the price of gas and electric."

"Like coffee and wine."

"Like coffee and wine," he confirmed.

It felt strange to miss something she hadn't really thought about since college. Beer, but also—she barely let herself think it—Thomas. When he headed to New York, catching rides and even biking part of the way, she had decided not to follow him, which they both agreed was the best decision either of them could have made at the time. They had made a pact to end things cold turkey and cut all communication, which they had both successfully adhered to. It made the break cleaner, and with Emmie's sessions, she had recovered from the split surprisingly fast. But she could feel the wounds, stitched closed at the surface, threatening to open back up.

She remembered reading somewhere that nutritional deficits take a long time to show noticeable effect. You could survive on white bread for years before feeling the impact. Your body would adjust by leeching iron, calcium, and other vitamins from your bones so that the full effect wouldn't manifest until your bones were like dry soil. She'd also read that the same thing could happen during pregnancy, the baby absorbing its mother's nutrients. Now that Thomas was sitting next to her, the two of them talking as naturally as they had all those years ago, she suddenly felt depleted. Her entire body ached for him.

"I have to go," she said suddenly.

"Is everything okay? You haven't even finished your beer. I'm sorry, I didn't mean to upset you." His nihilistic predictions used to send her down a spiral that would always end at the earthquake, at Gamma's lifeless face. He'd had to tiptoe around her in college, careful not to say anything that would sound too world-ending, so that she didn't have a full panic attack. She would black out, and come to with Thomas holding her, rocking her until she could breathe normally again, until she could see that the walls weren't really shaking.

"No, it's not that," she said quickly, jolted by the intimate memory. "I just told Noa I would meet her and I don't want to lose track of time."

"Of course. Noa," he said, lingering on her name, glancing at a group of people gathered around a Device a few stools down. "I should be working anyway."

"Maybe we can meet on purpose next time?"

"Maybe you'll treat me to a beer then?"

"Will you promise to be less of a gentleman so I have the chance to?"

"Okay if I message you?"

She nodded, smiling. As she walked away, she realized it was the first time she had ever said good-bye without kissing him. They'd never spent time together without being *together*. From the moment they'd met to the moment he began his journey to New York, they had been in a relationship.

"Hey, can you turn that thing off?" Maggie was nearly out of earshot when she heard the bartender speaking to Thomas.

"Of course," he said, and the bartender turned away. She took another look behind her. She had never had a reason not to kiss him—

Maggie exited through the hill just a few yards east of the cafeteria entrance and paused to take a deep breath. The entrance was marked by seagrass on either side, and the fresh breeze coming off the ocean bent them toward the auditorium. She pulled her turtleneck up and zipped her coat to her chin, grateful that she still remembered how to dress for a cold evening after such a hot summer.

It would have been completely dark, but an event in the auditorium cast a glow all the way to the edges of where she stood. From the shadows, she watched silhouettes streaming from the lobby's glass walls, and milling inside of them.

Her Device vibrated and a message notification appeared on her Lens from Noa. She blinked twice, and Noa's voice came through her Ear-Drums. "Hey, M! I'm just wrapping up here, but I'll see you soon! I have supplies."

"See you soon," she spoke back. Had she imagined it, or did Noa sound breathless?

Small lights illuminated her steps as she walked toward the main building where Noa had regularly spent fourteen-hour days since accepting her position the year before. The path was entirely empty—most people opted to take the quicker underground routes that connected to the shuttle, but

Maggie preferred the path's sloping curves and the view it offered of the main building, which looked at high tide like a giant whale coming to shore from the ocean.

Noa must have known that, because as Maggie approached the Japanese footbridge, she saw that she was standing at the apex of it, where Monet had once painted his water lilies.

"Hey," Noa said, "I figured I might as well intercept you." She held up a bottle and two glasses. Maggie didn't stop walking until she was in her arms.

"Heyyy," Noa said again, this time slower, oozing warmth as she nuzzled her nose into Maggie's neck, wrapping her arms tight around her. "What's wrong?"

"Nothing," Maggie said, her voice muffled by Noa's chest. "I'm just really happy to see you."

Noa gave her a squeeze, then said, "Look up!"

Maggie followed the line Noa's finger made up to the sky just in time to see a meteor streak across followed by a long, bright tail. Noa let go, setting the wine down, and Maggie rested her hands against the bridge's railing, letting her head hang back. The stars were subtle, but undeniably beautiful, and Maggie waited patiently for another ball of light to sail across the sky.

"What's the occasion?" she asked as Noa opened the wine, a ridiculous splurge.

Her fingertips felt for the groove in the railing where Maggie imagined Monet's easel had crashed into it, his oils falling into the water, poisoning the fish. She loved how intimate it felt, how connected she could be to the bridge's history. *Was he transfixed, watching them? Did he find beauty in the metaphor?* The paints had fulfilled their destiny to become water lilies, just not at his hands, the pigments separating and floating briefly next to their oils before sinking to the bottom of the pond.

When Maggie looked down, Noa was on one knee, holding an open box with an emerald ring inside. Green, like the water-lily pads. Maggie had started crying immediately, dropping to her knees to join her. She'd said yes, of course, the bridge their only witness as Noa slipped the ring onto her finger.

• • •

The notification came a few days later:

Thomas Is Rewatching Your Encounter, followed shortly by a second notification: *Receive Message from Thomas Fischer?*

She was sitting on the couch in their apartment and the words obscured the show she had been watching on her Device.

She blinked approval, and his voice came through her EarDrums: "Hey, you may get a notification I'm Rewatching our meeting. I'm Rewatching the entire day for research . . ." He paused as if considering whether to say the next words. "Although it's nicer to watch you than it is to watch Emmett."

The message ended, and she thought back to the color of his eyes. When Lenses replaced Pohvees, it became so easy to record someone without their knowledge that regulations dictated the necessity of a cue. Recording couldn't begin unless the wearer said, "Do you give me permission to record?" Later updates made the recording process less explicit but more streamlined, alerting a person they were being recorded by the presence of a red ring around the cornea, just like the ones that had enclosed the blue-gray of Thomas's.

"Hey, can you turn that thing off?" the bartender had asked just as she was leaving that evening, having noticed the red rings in Thomas's eyes. Maggie had noticed them too, of course, but hadn't bothered to mention it, understanding that he was recording the campus for playback for his article, despite it being discouraged. Any employee brazen enough to record and then post the video online—or one whose partner did so—would be fired immediately.

"Of course," Thomas had said. Then, "Recording Off."

It was only then, shrouded by the anonymity of reality, that Maggie had been emboldened to turn back. She turned from the bar's exit, walked back to where Thomas was sitting, and kissed him, feeling just for an instant like she had found the piece that was missing.

12

Noa

The news hit Noa's body first. Her heart began to pound against her chest, even as her brain was still processing the information. The thing she'd craved most since Maggie left on the Pod had been available to her this entire time, and Emmett had waited this long to tell her.

"You can"—Noa's words came out slowly—"*see* her?"

Emmett nodded and, though the answer was already in Noa's eyes, asked, "Would you like to?"

In a trance, Noa followed Emmett down the hallway of closed doors. One, a few down from her own, slid open as Emmett approached it. Noa realized she had been expecting something like a control center for a rocket launch, filled with screens and stadium rows of desks. Instead, a window took up the entire wall that faced the ocean and there were four desks, exactly like those she had used at WellPark. Taylor sat at one at the far end of the room, with VR goggles on, speaking.

"He's in a meeting," Emmett explained.

From what Noa could hear, he was talking about the developing storm.

"I thought you didn't have access?" Noa asked.

"I can't join as myself, but I have a few back doors coded in—avatars we're able to inhabit undetected." Noa thought of the Quarter Projection. There had been eighteen, maybe twenty, avatars in the room. It was possible that one of them had been Taylor, or even Emmett. Emmett waved her hand, as if dismissing the question, before walking over to a desk and continuing, "This one is yours, but of course you can't use your own Injectible to log in. This Device will give you access to the internal system."

Noa took a seat, tapping the Device that sat on top of the desk to the Reader before pocketing it. She pulled up a bay of monitoring screens as she had every day for the past five weeks. She thought again of her view of the bridge, which was the only thing missing from the artificial WellPark Emmett had manufactured.

"Can I see her now?"

"Of course, but"—she hesitated—"there's something that's going to come as a shock to you—there are some things you don't know."

"Like what?"

"You'll see soon enough, but I want you to brace yourself," Emmett responded.

"Consider me braced," Noa said, suddenly feeling even more anxious to see Maggie.

"Okay," Emmett breathed out, then gave a command for the window to dim. "I'm about to play you a live feed of Maggie's Pod. Are you sure you're ready?"

"How the fuck can I be sure if I have no idea what I'm about to see?" Noa's temper was one of Maggie's least favorite things about her, and though she tried to rein it in, she'd had the strangest day, and she was exhausted. She had to know what Emmett, and now Maggie, were keeping from her.

Emmett gave another command, and the window divided into six screens, each projecting a different view of Maggie. There was a close-up of her face, a birds's-eye shot of the entire room, and a view of her back.

She was sitting across from a hologram—a replica of herself, Noa realized—holding the photo they had taken in the apartment. The photo she had slipped into Gamma's book of poetry in the days before Launch.

I remember the countertop and the ingredients, Maggie was saying from thousands of miles away, *how it was supposed to make everything easier.*

Tears welled in Noa's eyes, then became too heavy for her to hold in. They spilled down her face as her hologram responded to Maggie but, to her relief, sounded like an Emmie. At least it hadn't stolen her voice.

We were really happy that day, her hologram said.

We were, Maggie repeated.

She had been watching Maggie's face, but now Noa got up and walked toward the screen in the bottom left corner. The view was shot from a camera embedded in the center column behind the Emmie, so that Maggie seemed to be staring straight into Noa's eyes—and it showed Maggie's entire body perfectly.

"What the fuck?" Noa said. She was just a few inches from the screen now, from Maggie, who sat with one hand cradling her abdomen, the other resting protectively on top of her protruding navel.

The hologram of Noa's replica morphed back into Maggie's Emmie.

That was really productive, the Emmie was saying.

She could see Maggie staring at the photo of the two of them, taken the day they'd decided to move into the apartment.

"Emmett, what's going on?" Noa repeated, this time louder.

"Noa, I'm so sorry you had to find out this way," Emmett said from behind her.

"Is this some sort of trick? A test? Because I'm over it."

"Noa, Maggie is nearly five months pregnant."

"That's impossible," she snapped at Emmett, but kept her face glued to the screen, barely aware that her hand was floating up now to rest on the projection of Maggie's face, then softened to a whisper: "It's barely been a month since I've seen her and she wasn't pregnant then."

She thought back to the months before Launch Day and realized she couldn't remember seeing Maggie naked once in that time. She had been working so much, she hadn't even noticed.

Sex was something that had happened late at night, or early in the morning, when she was exhausted and in a half-twilight state, her hand cupped between Maggie's legs as they spooned, her fingers moving frenetically toward a goal. Hadn't she touched her body? Would she have noticed if her breasts had been larger, her stomach a different shape? Hadn't she let her hand linger, trace the curves of her outline, as she'd spent hours doing at the beginning of their relationship?

"She was at fifteen weeks on Launch Day. She didn't begin showing until closer to nineteen," Emmett explained, but Noa could hardly bear to hear it.

"Why are you doing this?" She walked back toward her desk and Emmett.

"Doing what?"

"Showing me this. Telling me all this . . ."

Out of the corner of her eye she could see Taylor removing his head-set, glancing nervously at Emmett.

"I know that it's not easy to hear, but it's important that you know."

"How the fuck is she pregnant? Is this another one of your company's *experiments*?" Noa was shouting again, but she didn't care.

"Noa," Emmett said gently. Taylor was standing next to her now.

"Maggie cheated on you," Taylor said. Noa and Emmett both whipped their heads toward him.

"What did you just say?" Noa was furious.

"Taylor," Emmett said, moving toward him.

"She slept with someone else." His voice was firm, but sympathetic.

That's impossible, she wanted to say, but instead she said, "Who?" Though, of course, she already knew.

"Thomas," Emmett confirmed.

At the mention of his name, Noa dropped into the desk chair behind her. Tears were still falling down her cheeks, and she wiped them away with her sleeve, coiled into her fist. They felt like theater, since she didn't feel sad exactly, but she knew that she was experiencing shock. Right now was a grace period, time to understand what was going on before the real emotions came crashing. She took a few deep breaths.

"I knew," she said. "I knew something was going on between them, and I didn't say anything. But I didn't know *this*."

She thought of the day she'd found the photo of Maggie and Thomas slipped into Maggie's book in the pile of personal items to bring to Launch. Every suspicion she'd had in the past year had been confirmed in that single moment. She should have gone to Maggie immediately and begged her to stay, told her what she knew, worked it out together and come clean about Maya. Even now, she couldn't stand the idea of losing her. Instead, in an act of desperation and cowardice, she had taken the photo of her with Maggie, kept in her bedside table drawer, and scribbled a message on it, then taped it to the back of the one with Thomas.

Noa had always known on some level that she was working too much, emotionally and then physically occupied with Maya, and spending too little time with Maggie, but it had felt like they would deal with everything after her Journey, when she came back from the Pods. Still, Noa was furious with herself, and with him.

"Why am I here?" She had asked the same question only an hour ago, but the vague answer Emmett had given—*to help*—no longer satisfied her.

She could see now that everything was connected, but couldn't understand why. She was in love with Maggie, who was in love with Thomas. Thomas had written the article about Emmett, exposing the Pods' engineering flaws. Where was he now? The circle stopped there, leaving a gap between herself and Emmett. Their only connection had been a brief meeting, right before the keynote. Had Emmett planned, even then, to use Noa?

"I believe you're in the best position to help us, to help the Travelers," Emmett answered. There it was again. "You were among the best software engineers at WellCorp. But mostly, I believe that your personal connection, in addition to your knowledge of the situation, is the key. Maggie and a thousand other Travelers are in immediate danger of the developing storm system. We have to be able to reach one of them without detection to be able to communicate with them all. You have to trust me if you want to save Maggie."

"I don't understand why this isn't a company-wide priority. Why is it up to me?"

"Believe me, I've tried, but Oisín has too much at stake to allow that.

At the end of the day, he has the capital, financial and social, from Pohvee to dismiss—or drown out—anything I say."

Noa wasn't sure she entirely believed that. On the one hand, admittedly she knew close to nothing about the internal dynamics of the executive team. On the other, Emmett was Emmett Neal, the founder of WellCorp. Most Americans had welcomed her technology into their homes, their bodies. Who would refuse to believe her if she said something was wrong with the Pods? There was something Emmett wasn't telling her. She would play along until she figured out what.

"So how am I supposed to help?" Noa paused. "If I decide to."

"We'll go over the full plan in the morning," Emmett said, "but the first step is to reach Maggie without detection. As you know, all communications with the Pods are heavily monitored. As soon as they realize we're trying to get in touch, they'll simply target our access and shut it down, or turn off satellite communications and have the Pods run on auto."

"Have them go Dark," Noa replied. It was the emergency fallback, in case they were ever hacked. As an engineer at WellCorp, that had been one of her greatest fears, but she had never imagined she would be the one doing the hacking.

"Exactly," Emmett said. "Because you know Maggie better than anyone—"

"Debatable."

"—I'm hoping that you can help open up our lines of communication with her, as well as deliver coded messages to her so that she knows you—someone she trusts—are the one reaching out to her. I've spent the last month trying to reach her and others, but when you had your outburst and were no longer needed on campus, I saw that you could help us."

"And you couldn't just hack into her Emmie communication to learn about her?" Noa was incredulous.

Emmett ignored the question. "Right now, all we need for her to understand is that you're on the other side of the messages being delivered to her. From there, we can begin sending instructions, even communicating via her Emmie."

"Sounds a bit desperate."

"Our options are limited."

How can Emmett's options possibly be limited? She'd built the company, knew the Pods better than anyone, and had access to practically unlimited data about every Traveler. Noa's mind turned as she silently took stock of the arc that the day had taken, trying to make sense of it: she had woken up in her own bed, and now she was sitting in Emmett Neal's home being asked to hack the Pods to communicate with Maggie, who was in serious danger. And pregnant.

"Okay," she said.

"Are you willing to help us?"

She shook her head no, as if she couldn't believe her mouth was betraying her: "Yes." *What better option do I have at this point?*

"Excellent," Emmett said. "We think that a gratitude journal prompt is the perfect place to start. We know she'll read it—she hasn't skipped a single day since Launch—and it's the perfect medium for tipping her off that you're in touch."

"The only problem is that the prompt we send to her will be sent to every Traveler," Taylor interjected, now back at his desk. "It has to be just vague enough that she suspects you're making contact with her, but no one else does."

"Won't someone on the Emotional Wellness team notice that the prompt has been changed?" Noa asked.

"That's the problem—or, depending how you see it—the benefit of the layers of anonymity of WellCorp," Emmett said. "It takes more time to identify culpability. They'll figure it out eventually, but for now we're hoping they'll assume it was a decision that came from higher up."

Noa nodded. "When do I have to send the first message by?"

"Tonight," Emmett responded. "We don't have time on our side, unfortunately—we're racing against this storm, which Taylor is monitoring closely. She should see it when she wakes up tomorrow morning. I know this is an impossible amount of information to process, so here's my suggestion: go back to your room and take some time. You still have a few hours before you need to send anything. You'll find the Device has already been granted the clearance you need to access and edit the gratitude prompts. We trust you."

Noa didn't miss Taylor's sideways glance at her as she left the control room for her own, completely alone again.

A pot of coffee—real coffee—waited for Noa on the small table by the door in her room. The smell alone made her realize how tired she was, how badly she needed it. She took a sip, allowing the bitterness to bloom on the tip of her tongue. She opened the Device Emmett had given her, navigating to the schedule, then into gratitude journal commands.

Despite Emmett's promise that it would be editable, she still felt a wave of surprise at the sight of the blinking cursor amid lines of code. Noa closed her eyes, trying to evoke some sort of phrase or inside joke that Maggie would understand without drawing the attention of engineers or other Travelers. The bridge was the first thing to come to her mind.

After typing and scheduling the prompt, she watched Maggie. Her days were simple, boring even. It was hard to believe anyone could be so desperate for some time to themselves that they would go to the middle of the ocean for it, for *this*. After her Emmie wrapped up their therapy session, Noa toggled between different camera perspectives to be able to see Maggie more clearly as she went about her daily activities. Her gait was different and awkward—she hadn't yet mastered the balance of her heavier abdomen.

Noa didn't have to stay up too late before Maggie went to bed. Though Maggie was four hours behind, her schedule was in tune with the sun. After an early dinner, she got ready for bed in a routine that didn't look all that different from the one they went through each night at their apartment. She ran a blue-light cleansing wand across her face and brushed her teeth.

After Maggie had her evening latte and went to sleep, Noa checked her own clock—it was barely midnight. She pulled back the covers, jostling the novel she had left there earlier. The cover depicted a girl at sunrise holding a scythe in a golden field. Noa opened to the page with the notecard denoting numbers she assumed corresponded to pages. It wasn't written in Maggie's handwriting, so the elegant, rounded script must have belonged to Gamma.

Noa perched her Device on the duvet, gathered so she could see Maggie while she flipped through the book to each page designated by the card, mindlessly thumbing the bracelet as she did. What was she missing? She only made it a few pages before the familiar sound of Maggie's breath made her eyes feel heavy. She closed the book and her eyes, matching her breath to Maggie's, feeling an intimacy she hadn't felt in months, despite the thousands of miles between them.

40 Days Post-Launch

Noa couldn't remember the exact moment she'd fallen asleep, but it was still dark out when she heard noises outside her door. She had been dreaming about a boyfriend she'd had when she first moved to Los Angeles, before she came out. Her life could be split down the middle that way. Of course, she had always known she was gay—she'd even shared a kiss with her best friend in high school, though they would both later claim they were drunk.

She had always loved her thick, long hair, but that was the year she cut it short. The world seemed to need a universal signifier of her sexual preference, and she got tired of people saying, "But you don't look gay." Not out loud (usually) but with their eyes. She thought only straight men would make that assumption, but the women she dated were just as likely to, indoctrinated to the same patriarchal set of expectations that hair length could possibly signify who she felt attracted to. Every time she saw her ex-boyfriend after that (LA could feel surprisingly small that way), he would avert his eyes or look through her as if she were invisible. But in the dream, they had never broken up. In that world, Noa had never met

Liz, her first girlfriend, who lasted less than a year but introduced her to a far more lasting love in the controlled chaos of community farming. Or Gabriela, a tornado of wit and opinions so loud, Noa temporarily forgot she held her own. Or Makenna, her longest relationship until Maggie.

The fantasy was so alluringly simple that she allowed herself a few moments to imagine what her life might have looked like in that alternate, traditional world: two children and a house in Portland or the Midwest, where life had changed in the previous two decades, but was still recognizable—unlike Manhattan, which was mostly flooded, or San Francisco, which had become a ghost town after the wildfires tore through the Bay and leveled the city to ash. It was strange how the world could be ending, but only in some parts.

In the dream, her hair had been pulled into a sleek ponytail like Emmett's, and her mother lived down the street, close enough to stop in unannounced. The dream was the only evidence Noa had slept at all. She was still fully dressed on top of the duvet, curled into a ball around the book she'd fallen asleep holding, her Device digging into her side beneath her. It was freezing cold in her room from the breeze that floated across the ocean and through her window, but the fresh air comforted her.

She had been so angry with Maggie when she first saw her last night, but the feeling had already evaporated into a sadness that throbbed like a bruise. Maggie had betrayed her, but she had abandoned Maggie, the same way she had her own mother. There was so much she wished she could do over.

A voice called her name from outside the door, and Noa rolled herself off the bed to answer it. Inga stood just outside, wearing her gray uniform but no indication of impatience.

"Good morning," she said. "Emmett requests that you join her and her guest for breakfast in the kitchen. Follow the hallway past the living room and you'll see them."

"Thank you, Inga," Noa said, inadvertently matching her formal tone. "How long do I have?"

"She and Arthur are already there . . ." Inga wavered, darting her eyes across Noa's slept-in clothes and bedhead. "But I'm sure they wouldn't mind you taking a few minutes."

Noa thanked her and closed the door, vaguely remembering Emmett's mention of him the previous day. The time on her Device told her it was a few minutes after six in the morning.

Noa walked into the bathroom, leaving the Device on the bed to avoid the temptation to open it to Maggie's feed. She barely recognized herself in the mirror. Her eyes were so sunken that the skin around them looked almost purple.

She leaned over to splash some water on her face, grateful when the news turned on so she had something else to look at. The hurricane threat had finally been picked up. A meteorologist was talking about backwinds, but mostly about the rarity of such an occurrence in the Pacific Ocean this time of year.

It was only once she was fully changed and ready that she let herself check the video stream. Maggie was still sleeping, curled onto her side with one leg kicked loose from the sheets, the same way she always slept. Noa wished she knew what she was dreaming about. She turned off the Device and dropped it into her pocket before heading toward the kitchen.

Noa found Emmett and the older man she'd noticed the day before sitting in the room that offered a panoramic view of the Pacific. The sun was just cresting over the Malibu hills the house was nestled in, illuminating the sky in a gray-blue, with subtle strokes of pink against the low clouds.

"Noa," Emmett said in a tone that indicated she'd already said her name, "there's someone I'd like you to meet."

Noa brought her attention to the man, who stood as Emmett said his name.

He must have been in his seventies and had such a thin wisp of hair combed over his head, Noa thought how much younger he would look if he just shaved it. She never used to notice things like this, but Maggie's tendency to point out aesthetic flaws had rubbed off on her, even though she disliked the habit. Maggie cared about how things looked. He wore a white oxford shirt, forced into the slim space between his belly and his khaki slacks, apparently exempt from the house uniform.

"Dr. Russo-Neva," he said, nodding his head but not extending his hand.

"Noa Behar."

"Arthur was a professor at UCLA, but has served as an advisor to me and a member of WellCorp's board for years, since I first had the idea for the Pods. He lives nearby, so he often joins me for breakfast," Emmett explained.

"And lunch," Noa said, referencing the day before, as she imagined him as a slimmer, younger man on research and sailing ships.

"Please sit and help yourself to some coffee," Emmett said, as if she hadn't heard Noa, nodding toward the carafe and mugs at the center of the table. "And you prefer smoothies, right?" A bowl of oatmeal sat in front of Emmett with a medley of crushed nuts sprinkled on top.

"Coffee is plenty, thank you," Noa said, wondering how much else Emmett knew about her. Her appetite, like her mood, had been fluctuating since the moment she arrived. She didn't think she could stomach anything more than some warm caffeine, and her blood sugar was feeling off. Her insulin patch kept her levels relatively stable, but a sugary smoothie wouldn't help matters.

Noa leaned forward to pour herself a cup, inhaling the smell into her lungs.

"Tired?" Emmett asked.

"Very. How do you have coffee?"

"You mean, what do I put in it?" Emmett answered, looking amused.

"No, I—I mean," Noa stammered, "aren't these real beans?"

"I keep a hydroponic farm downstairs where I grow a small selection of foods."

Noa thought of the tomatoes and pesto that had been in the sandwich yesterday, how different it was from the soy-based, nutrient-fortified smoothies she had most mornings. She wondered if the almonds also came from Emmett's farm. Where was she getting all of the water from?

Emmett and the professor shared a glance, as if Emmett's answer had been the most obvious in the world.

"As I was saying, I invited Arthur over this morning so he can explain to you the predicament we're in—and the solution we've come up with," she said.

Noa settled back with her mug, regarding the professor over its rim as she took her first sip. He smiled warmly.

"The Pods, as you know, will be scattered across roughly five thousand square nautical miles." His voice had the comforting quality of an expert. Like Inga, he had an accent Noa couldn't place. "Some will remain east of Hawai'i, but the vast majority should cover the area between the Islands and the Marshall Islands to the southwest. What that means is that the closest land mass for the vast majority of Pods will be atolls, ring-shaped islands that rarely have anyone living on them, though still a safer place to weather a storm than the open ocean."

It was a strange quirk, to speak almost entirely in the future tense, but Noa had seen it occasionally in her own mother. *I'll talk to you yesterday.* She wondered which language was native to him, but knew better than to ask, for fear of insulting him.

"The more Travelers we're able to get to populated atolls, especially those with storm-resistant structures like army bases, the more we have a chance of saving," Emmett said.

"But the Head of Meteorology said in the meeting two days ago that the Coast Guard has been alerted, and WellCorp is already moving them out of the path of the hurricane." Even as she said it, Noa realized how much she hoped it was still true.

She'd ignored the cracks in WellCorp's carefully crafted image all those years. The simple fact that it was a large company had been enough for her to trust WellCorp with Maggie's life.

"That would work for some of the Pods, but not all of them," the professor said. "The Pods would rely too heavily on the motors of larger boats that pull them. On their own, they will be able to move a mile or so a day, but we're talking about outrunning a hurricane. Most ships can travel at fourteen knots, but Pods will only be capable of maybe a third of that. . . ." Dr. Russo-Neva stopped abruptly and stared down at his place setting, which didn't have so much as a cup of coffee on it.

"They aren't built to withstand an out-of-season storm this large," Emmett picked back up, taking a sip of her latte. "Most ships have a bow that can plow through waves, but Pods will be vulnerable to the entire weight of a crashing wave. If one breaks the glass dome, which it very well could, there's effectively no chance of survival. The only way for all of those people to be saved is if they disembark the Pods."

"How?" Noa struggled to understand her words. How was being out of a Pod safer than being in one? Did she plan to have all thousand Travelers disembark? *How do they not have a better plan in place for this???*

"The IMO—" the professor began.

"The International Maritime Organization," Emmett interrupted helpfully.

"—dictates that every boat come with a flotation device. Although they'll be smaller than a Pod"—he coughed—"they're actually designed to remain floating during such a storm. They're also equipped with motors that move at about two times the speed of the Pods."

"Why wouldn't WellCorp just tell all the Travelers that?" Noa asked.

"Oisín would never allow it." Emmett spoke this time. "You read his messages to me—heard how he spoke in the QP meeting—he refuses to believe that the Pods could be compromised. Think of the money at stake. As enormous a disaster as it would be for people to sink in their own Pods, it's safer from a public relations and insurance perspective to wait out the storm and hope for the best. If the storm obliterates the Pods, it was an 'act of God' they couldn't have prevented, covered in the agreement every Traveler signed. If they tell people to leave the Pods, the company becomes liable."

"How long until the hurricane hits?"

"It's hard to tell," Dr. Russo-Neva said. "We have no precedent in history for a Pacific hurricane of this magnitude, and it's only just started developing. Hurricanes can be highly volatile. There's a chance it may dissipate completely, change course, or be much worse than we anticipate. We have to be prepared for those possibilities. A Pacific storm of this magnitude—they simply don't happen, or haven't."

"Based on projections from historical equivalents during hurricane season," Emmett said, "it will hit the Pods in four days at most. Maybe three. From there, it will likely hit the coast two days later." If the Pods had been launched just a week earlier, they could have avoided the issue completely, Noa marveled.

"How long do you think it will last?" Noa asked.

"Again, this is just an estimate, but I anticipate forty-eight hours of full magnitude, which will then decrease rapidly as it passes," the professor said.

"The goal," Emmett said, anticipating Noa's next question, "would be to get Maggie's Pod to Hawai'i before the hurricane hits, but we've already run out of time for that option. Right now, we need to get her to trust us, then get safely into a raft, and ideally an atoll, where she has at least a chance of survival."

"What about the other Pods?" Noa almost didn't want to ask. If she was honest with herself, the only one she truly cared about was Maggie. "Are we coding messages for all of them?"

"We only need to reach one," Emmett explained. "We can't risk Well-Corp shutting off our transmission, but every Pod is outfitted with a short-range radio, per maritime requirements, that can't be disabled. As long as we reach one, they can reach and communicate with the rest."

Emmett's story was beginning to feel more like a sieve to Noa. The founder of the world's most sophisticated technology company was relying on an invention created nearly two centuries prior to save her company. It was either poetic, or it was total bullshit.

"And you picked Maggie."

"And we picked *you*."

Noa had been working on the code for an hour when she received the alert that Maggie was awake, opening her eyes to the same sunrise, four hours delayed. She had almost forgotten Maggie was pregnant until she pushed herself up and rolled onto her back, the fabric cresting at her belly like a hill as she shielded her eyes from the light bouncing off her journal.

Noa had coded the drawer open in the middle of the night, hoping it would encourage Maggie to pick up the journal as soon as she woke up. Instead, she watched Maggie push the drawer back in. Noa fumbled for her Device, opening the Furniture Controls for Maggie's bedside table, pushing it back open until Maggie finally picked the journal up. It was surreal to see her respond directly to Noa's actions, even half an ocean away.

Soon she would even be able to speak to her directly. After breakfast, Emmett had hinted that it might be possible for Noa to code an override into Emmie's software that would allow them full communication access with Maggie. Until then, her best chance at reaching her was through the journal prompt.

Noa watched carefully as Maggie's brow furrowed slightly, a smaller version of the almost comically exaggerated facial reactions she displayed when people were around. She sat thinking, staring at the ocean for a full minute before she placed the stylus against the journal and, finally, began to write.

Noa remembered the day the bridge had arrived at WellCorp's campus, just a few months after she had started working there. Maggie spent hours watching them unload it from the ship, at the end of its long journey from Giverny. While many people complained about the inappropriateness of displacing Monet's bridge from his lush, if dying, gardens and its rightful place over the pond, Maggie found the poeticism in it. The original site had also been dry until Monet received permission to divert the Ru River into a man-made pond that was soon filled with the signature water lilies. She saw it as evidence for the potential of WellCorp's impact on the world and the beauty it could create.

The bridge, Maggie often said, felt like a gift intended for her. The French government was doing little to maintain the gardens, ever since the steep decline in international tourism. She would rather have it be cared for and enjoyed in a foreign place than rot at home.

Maggie's haphazard cursive appeared live on a digital replica of the journal on Noa's desktop. She was writing about the bridge, as Noa had hoped, but not about their association with it. Instead, her entry began strikingly studiously, as if borrowing words from her undergraduate thesis:

In the first of Monet's panoramic paintings of the Giverny pond, the dark water looks deep enough to dive into. But later paintings reveal that the depth of its beauty existed only at surface-level, with reflections of trees and wide-open lily pads. A swan-dive into the pond, which looked so inviting in his earlier work, would have only resulted in a broken neck.

From the moment she began, Maggie had written in a frenzied state, balancing the journal at the top of her knees, but now she paused. She brought her left hand up to squeeze the bridge of her nose, breathing out slowly. After rearranging her back against the pillows, she continued writing.

Just as Monet became entranced by the colors of death as he watched his first wife die, painting her in blue, yellow, and gray, he began obsessively studying the lilies, which opened in brilliant displays of yellow, mauve, rose, and blue. Even after cataracts nearly blinded him, he continued painting the water lilies and the bridge, from memory.

When Noa had written the prompt, she'd expected that Maggie would write about the evening she'd proposed to her, slipping the emerald ring around Maggie's finger in an act of either denial or desperation. Noa had never been sure if Maggie had seen her, in the shadowy entrance between the restaurant and the bar, where she'd gone to meet her before the meteor shower. Noa had paused to take Maggie in. Her cheeks were lightly flushed from a beer, and she looked beautiful as she grabbed her coat off the chair and began walking toward the exit. Noa had already started toward her when she saw Maggie turn back to a man Noa hadn't noticed before.

When Maggie kissed him—she now knew it was Thomas—Noa was too stunned to do anything besides grip the ring box in her pocket. She had turned away just before Maggie could see her, running down the stairway toward the nearest tunnel. She was shaking so hard, she had to lean her back against the wall as coworkers passed by. She should have turned back up the stairs at that moment, raced to Maggie and demanded an explanation, and met their problems head-on. Instead, she'd tried not to let her anger get the best of her, which meant stuffing her emotions deep enough to ignore.

Before she could think about what she was doing, she had run as fast as she could through the underground tunnel, coming up at the main building, then circled back along the aboveground path to the bridge. She'd reached it only a few seconds before Maggie came into view, her breathlessness explained away by nervousness. Noa could barely remember the next few moments—holding Maggie, furious but already explaining away what she had seen. Maybe she thought the proposal would make it go away. Did she know, even then, that their relationship was beyond saving?

Noa watched Maggie's face as she wrote, equally relieved and pained when Maggie finally acknowledged the personal significance of the prompt:

Maybe I had been painting water lilies too, unaware of the shallow water beneath. But when I saw Thomas that night, I knew I had to dive in, even if it broke my neck.

A cough behind her made Noa jump.

"I'm sorry, I didn't mean to scare you," Emmett said, standing next to her.

"How long have you been there?"

"Only a few seconds. The professor just left and I wanted to come in to see how you're doing." She read the prompt over Noa's shoulder. "What made you write about a bridge?"

"You know the Japanese footbridge on campus?" Noa asked, though of course she did. Emmett's face transformed into an expression she couldn't quite recognize. Noa went on, "Maggie always loved it. It was our meeting spot, and where I proposed to her, actually. I thought the prompt would inspire her to write about that."

"But she didn't?"

"No . . ." Noa faltered. "Well, not until the end. She wrote mostly about the history of the bridge, about Monet. She was an art history major, her thesis was on Monet. . . ." Noa trailed off as Emmett read Maggie's entry over her shoulder.

"Do you think she could tell it came from you?"

"I'm not sure. . . ." Noa answered honestly, waiting for Emmett to finish reading.

"She really is a wild bird," Emmett said as soon as she reached the end, then pivoted. "We still have a lot to do. Are you ready?"

She really is a wild bird. Noa nodded, turning the words over in her mind as she tried to remember where she had heard them before. All at once, she remembered—she hadn't heard them, but read them.

Noa excused herself and went back to her room to retrieve the book she had fallen asleep holding the night before. She flipped to the page and reread it: *It was like a wild bird that had flown into his studio.* Suddenly it clicked. Noa turned to the next indicated page to confirm: each included a description of a woman as a bird. There, on page 203: *You're not a nest-building bird.* And one hundred pages earlier: *She looked like a little bird-of-Paradise.* A woman's ambition, once she married, *vanished like the ornamental plumage which drops away from some birds after mating season.*

It had to be a coincidence, that Emmett had uttered the same phrase Noa had read the night before. Had Emmett gone into her room and found the connection between the pages while Noa read Maggie's entry? Why had she made a point of speaking the phrase—did she want Noa to know? Noa wrapped the book in a hand towel from the bathroom, then slipped it into the small space between the WellNest and the wall, hiding it. It was impossible to tell if she was being paranoid or reasonable, but it felt better to be cautious.

Noa walked back to the control room, where she found Emmett talking to Taylor, both quieting as she entered. She wouldn't run away this time. She had to help Maggie.

13

Maggie

Maggie couldn't shake the feeling that she was being watched. She resisted the instinct to cover her skin as she stripped off her clothes, discarding them down the waste chute. The infrared cameras that surrounded the Pod felt like dozens of eyes, as she waited for the door to slide open.

A breeze, heavy with salt, struck her body. It had been a few days since she was allowed outside, her routine inexplicably omitting her daily access. It wasn't cold, but the change in temperature, from the WellPod's carefully regulated ecosystem to the salty ocean air, sent a cascade of goose bumps down her bare arms and legs. She crossed her arms protectively across her breasts and stepped onto the deck, gingerly making contact between the soles of her feet and the heated solar panels that made up the floor.

Maggie watched the steam from the outdoor shower join the fog's cotton candy swirls, seducing her to step into it. The water gradually warmed to the perfect temperature, tempering the cold drop by drop. Around her, the cool condensation enveloped the Pod, but under the water, she was safe. She filled her lungs with the fresh air, closing her eyes as she always did anytime she was outside, allowing her senses to focus on the smell and sound of the ocean. She took another few deep breaths, feeling completely at ease. She wondered if the baby could hear the ocean yet. Thanks to her months of denial, she had refused to read any books or even consult an AR midwife or parenting coach that could have offered her this basic information.

As soon as she opened her eyes, she spotted the bird. She hadn't seen it in several days, and immediately sensed something was wrong. The bird was flying too quickly, and Maggie noticed that it wasn't flapping its wings at all. It looked as if it had been hurtled through the air, struggling against the momentum of an invisible force that carried it. Maggie watched in stunned horror as it crashed into the glass of the Pod, landing just a few inches from the shower. She could see it panting—it was still alive—but it looked completely disoriented.

Maggie was only a few quick steps away from it. It wasn't so much a decision as it was an instinct to close the distance in one leap, but when her foot touched down on the smooth tiles beneath the shower, it slid across the frictionless surface.

Maggie heard herself gasp as her arms flailed to grab hold of the small railing beneath the spigot. The back of her head ended her inelegant, reverse swan dive with a firm clap against the hard floor. Maggie was still looking at the bird when it disappeared from view, shrouded in a curtain of fog.

As a teenager, most of Maggie's fantasies of growing up revolved around having someone to shower with. The fantasies weren't sexual, but the romance of having someone next to her in her most vulnerable, naked state excited her. The only issue, and one that entirely took up Maggie's adolescent mind, was that of mascara. In movies, characters would have shower sex or even casually talk to their lovers behind a steamed glass wall and emerge with only a sultry smokey eye. On Pohvee, women dove into pools and emerged laughing, with curled and coated lashes.

Maggie and Chloe had conducted their own experiments, varying shower length and brands. But the results were consistent. Hot water plus mascara yielded black tears and streaks across her top lids no matter what. As teenagers, they'd decided that the only practical solution was to wear waterproof mascara at all times, a decision Maggie honored through her adulthood.

It was one of those private thoughts she wasn't even conscious of having until she confessed it out loud. She and Noa had been in a sparsely stocked beauty aisle before ecommerce replaced massive physical chains entirely, when Noa asked, "Do you always wear waterproof mascara?" When Maggie explained her reasoning, Noa began laughing so hard Maggie had to join her.

They nicknamed it the "central problem of runny mascara," which somehow became a core piece of their shared vocabulary, shortening over time to "the CPRM." Whenever some inconsequential drama bothered Maggie—a parking ticket, frustration over a colleague, a broken glass—Noa would say, "Ah, but what about the CPRM?"

That was the first thought Maggie had when she came to, *But what about the CPRM?*

She blinked her eyes open, straining against her heavy lids, and saw a line of turbid liquid circling the drain a few inches away. It looked exactly like mascara, but there was too much of it and, of course, she wasn't wearing any. It took her another few seconds to realize it wasn't an oily slick of iron oxide pigment, but blood, flowing from her head into the shower's filtration system. The plasma and platelets would be caught by a fine filter, but the rest would be recycled back into the system as pure, potable water.

Moving slowly, she pushed herself upright, then folded her body into a tight ball, wrapping her arms protectively around her legs. A headache pounded with debilitating force. Maggie pushed her eyes against her knees, waiting for the ache to subside like a bell dying away as the water cascaded over her.

The fact that the water was still running, albeit now freezing, meant only a few minutes had passed since she'd hit the ground. That had to be good news. She brought her fingers to the right side of her head, tenderly investigating the area the blood was still streaming from. The touch sent a lightning bolt of pain through her, and she realized she had to put pressure against it. She was sure they'd covered injuries during Orientation, but couldn't remember the protocol now.

She grabbed hold of the railing—likely placed there to avoid this exact sort of thing—and pulled herself up to standing.

As she rose, the shower turned off, retreating into the two-foot-wide strip of bamboo paneling that housed it. Maggie could barely see a few feet in front of her—from the fog or the fall, she couldn't tell. She held her hand out as she shuffled toward the stack of towels she knew would have risen from one of the floor panels.

Maggie felt the edge of the tile and the soft terrycloth in the cubby below it. She grabbed two and hugged one around her shoulders like a shawl, pressing the other against her head wound as she moved slowly in the direction of the arched door, then back inside. Her legs were shaking so much she had to test every footstep before shifting her weight. The pain from the wound was already subsiding, though she could feel a bruise blossoming on her thigh.

A sudden cramp took hold of her abdomen and she dropped to her knees, feeling her stomach retch that morning's latte up onto the floor. She waited on her hands and knees for more to come.

On the opposite side of the room, Maggie could see that her bed had already sunk back into the floor, replaced by an open area where she was supposed to practice her afternoon yoga, according to the schedule. She crawled toward it, collecting her mat from its container beside the center column. With one hand still pressing the towel against her head, she rolled out the mat and lowered herself onto it, pulling the other towel tighter around her shoulders and back as she curled herself into a ball. A vague awareness reminded her to lie on her side in case she threw up again, but the slight slant her shoulder created was dizzying. She felt like she was upside down, so she rolled onto her back. Resting on her stomach was out of the question.

If she was concussed, wasn't she supposed to stay awake? She was shivering, quick shakes interspersed with larger, uncontrollable convulsions, but didn't have the energy to get up to pull on the fresh clothes that would have insulated her.

Maggie struggled to keep her eyes open, and Emmie's voice sounded farther and farther away, even as she registered her presence in the room. Emmie was telling her to do something, but Maggie couldn't grasp what. Her resolve to stay awake wasn't strong enough to fight the heaviness of her eyelids, despite the fact that she suddenly felt protective of her baby. The fear of being seriously hurt had unearthed something deeply maternal in her. Tears rolled down her cheeks and she gripped the towel tighter around her. At a certain point, she couldn't tell if her eyes were open or closed. Emmie's face came into view, then nothing.

14

Noa

Malibu, California
42 Days Post-Launch

Since arriving at Emmett's, Noa estimated that she'd slept four hours total. The first evening, she'd stayed up late watching Maggie sleep. The next had been spent entirely in the control room, where she slept in fifteen-minute increments when she couldn't keep her eyes open while working alongside Emmett, who was tireless. She had managed to get to her bed last night, finally, but was starting to feel the effects from a throbbing headache that refused to go away.

"Good morning, Noa. Please meet me in the control room when you're awake." The message from Emmett arrived on her Lens as soon as she opened her eyes. Emmett's messages were always as formal as her physical presentation. Any one of them could be printed on cardstock and delivered on a silver tray.

Noa's fingers felt clumsy and disconnected from the rest of her body as she got dressed. It was no surprise that her motor skills were beginning to fail her but, more concerningly, she was beginning to see things that weren't really there—not full hallucinations, but miasmas caught out of the corner of her eye. She splashed some water onto her face to cool down, registering with the back of her hand that her forehead was slightly warm, and slipped down the hall, resolving to check on Maggie as soon as she met with Emmett.

Emmett was standing by the window, and Noa could see the outline of her profile against the dim sky. She must have been exhausted—Noa wasn't even sure when she slept at all—but she always stood with perfect posture, as if pulled up by an invisible marionette string. Her hands were open in front of her, palms cupped in offering. Her head bowed toward them. Noa had the feeling she was walking into something deeply personal and considered turning around, but she stood, mesmerized.

"Oh, good morning, Noa," Emmett said in surprise, though she had summoned her. Her exhaustion only revealed itself in her voice.

She beckoned Noa over with a slight head tilt, still holding her palms up. It wasn't until Noa was directly next to her, close enough to touch, that an old photograph appeared on top of Emmett's palms, an orange digital date in the lower right corner.

In it, a young woman with brunette hair several shades darker than Emmett's cradled a baby in her arms, looking at it with adoration. In the window behind her, the flash obscured the photographer's reflection. Noa could only see his beard and a smile peeking out from behind the camera, but the woman looked vaguely familiar.

"Is that your father?" Noa asked.

Emmett nodded. "This was taken a few days after I was born. It's the only photo I have with all three of us in it."

"Are they"—Noa hesitated—"still alive?"

"My dad moved back to Georgia when I was eight, I never saw him again, and my mother died about ten years ago, in the '48 quake."

"I'm so sorry to hear that," Noa said genuinely. "I know what it's like to lose a parent too young."

"Do you?" Noa was taken aback by the sudden malice in Emmett's voice.

"Yeah, I do," Noa said, unsure, then remembering: "Didn't you grow up north of the earthquake, in Portland?"

"I did, but she was in Palo Alto for it. It was right before I launched WellNests."

"I'm so sorry," Noa repeated, unsure what else to say.

"Were you close with your mother?" Emmett's green eyes fixed on hers.

"Yeah—I mean . . ." Noa exhaled, puffing out her cheeks. She was exhausted and hadn't expected this line of questioning. "For a time, at least."

"You're not anymore?"

"Well," Noa faltered, "she lives in Brazil. We don't really keep in touch."

"With your own mother?"

Where is this coming from?

"Yeah . . . with my own mother." Noa was eager to change the subject. "But I was close to Maggie's mother—we only got a chance to visit her once, but kept in touch over our Lenses."

"Her adoptive mother."

"S-sure," Noa stammered. "But I don't know if Maggie would call her that."

"So they were close?"

"As close as any, I guess," Noa said. "Her parents were in tech and I think they felt like they should have a kid, so they adopted Maggie, but they didn't really know how to raise her. I got the sense from Maggie that her mom was, I don't know, distracted?"

"How so?"

"Well, after the quake, for example"—Noa hesitated—"they bought her a WellNest to help her cope with the trauma, but they never actually talked to her about any of it. Like, her mom took a week off work, but would still be answering emails anytime Maggie was with her."

"But Maggie talked to her Emmie?"

"Yeah, I think that was really helpful for her, actually," Noa said, meeting Emmett's eyes.

Emmett nodded but didn't say anything in response, lost in a thought Noa understood wasn't meant to be shared. She had felt an odd intimacy with Emmett since the near-catastrophe that had occurred the day before, though she still didn't feel she could fully trust her.

In the weeks leading up to Launch, each engineer had been invited to share a favorite place in nature that they had either visited personally or seen on Pohvee. The ideas ranged from Himalayan cliffs to New Zealand's Waitaki Valley. Noa's first thought was of the insignificant, but beautiful, trail she'd spent a short span of her childhood in Reno wandering, when her father was a visiting professor at the university there. To her amazement, her idea was among those selected, and she was granted a team to help her code it with AI aid to expedite the process. Instead of creating just one trail, however, she had created a branching network for Travelers to discover, with one leading to her father's old cabin. Noa and Emmett's entire plan now hinged on the fact that Maggie would be the only Traveler to notice the jeep road that led to the old house, then walk far enough to find it and discover the instructions she had left for her there.

They had been adding purple-blooming ice plants, Maggie's favorite flower, as breadcrumbs for her along the trail the day before, when Taylor came through the audio of their VR goggles. Noa tore hers off as soon as she registered the terror in his voice.

Taylor had been monitoring Maggie all morning, but now he was standing at his desk, pointing toward the bay of screens.

The first thing Noa noticed was how beautiful Maggie looked. Water cascaded down her naked back, as her head rested on the tile next to the drain, her mouth slightly ajar and her limbs draped like Dali's clocks. She was unconscious.

"Help me override the shower temperature," Taylor urged. "We need to wake her up."

Noa snapped back and turned toward her desk, deftly maneuvering the code to send a blast of cold water over Maggie. The effect was immediate. She could feel their small team of three holding their breath as Maggie blinked her eyes open, then slowly got up, steadying herself with the handrail.

At that moment, down the hill, she was sure another engineer at Well-Corp had already received the emergency alert coming from Maggie's Vitalities. They wouldn't be able to see her as anything more than a heat map, but a quick playback would show them that she had fallen on the water-slick floor. How *was* Emmett able to access Maggie's livestream? She had been so vague about her "back door" access.

One of the outdoor tiles had risen in the automatic post-shower procedure and Maggie pulled a couple towels from the stack, hugging one around her as she walked inside slowly. A thin stream of blood ran down her spine from her head wound, escaping the towel Maggie was pressing against it. Noa watched her drop to her knees and throw up, feeling as helpless as she ever had.

Noa navigated over to the Emmie's controls, hoping the code she had written the night before worked. In addition to implementing their plan for Maggie, Emmett had been working alongside Noa to code an override of Emmie's communication system so that they would be able to speak directly to her. Noa knew, of course, that Emmett was a talented coder, but seeing her work in person made it clear that she was indisputably a genius.

The lines they were working on were far more complicated than adding an object to a VR scene, but just before dawn, Noa had had a breakthrough: the hologram of Emmie could be controlled separately from her AI, and was easier to hack into. If Noa's code was correct, which she fervently hoped now it was, both she and Emmett would soon be able to control Emmie's movements, but only have limited control over her voice. If she was careful, she could pass off Emmie's movements as machine learning.

Noa looked around the control room for Emmett, but she was gone.

"Taylor, do you know how to access the Drug Delivery Controls?"

"I think so," he said.

"I need you to create an IV," Noa said, then listed off a steroid and a central nervous system stimulant that she remembered from her work before WellCorp, creating apps for hospitals. She hoped the drugs would keep Maggie awake and even—she hoped—lead to amnesia.

"It has to look like the Emmie has selected it for her," Noa added, then slipped the VR goggles over her head, throwing on haptic gloves and strapping shin-wraps around her legs, to translate her own movements to the Emmie's. Noa banked on the fact that her movements would work in tandem with whatever Emmie was saying.

"Maggie, may I come in?" she heard Emmie ask, triggered by Noa's entrance into her system.

Maggie nodded, granting permission, as Noa stepped into the Pod in the Emmie's body.

The haptic controls took Noa a moment to get used to as she walked unsteadily over to Maggie, who was now lying on a yoga mat with her eyes closed. It was so surreal to be finally standing in the same room as Maggie that she nearly forgot why she was there, mesmerized by Maggie's proximity through the goggles. She could see the scars and freckles she had spent years memorizing.

"Maggie," Emmie said, as Noa's movements brought her to Maggie's side, yet still elicited no reaction. "Maggie, you have to get up."

Automatically, Noa reached her hand out toward Maggie to shake her awake, but it went straight through her.

"*Maggie.*" This time Emmie's voice rose in volume. "You have a concussion. You need to open your eyes."

Groggily, Maggie obeyed, pushing herself to standing. Her towel dropped to the floor, and she sank into the desk chair beside the center column. Its hatch opened, revealing a cannula that triggered Emmie's response.

"Maggie," Emmie said, "I need you to attach this IV to the cannula in your arm." The semi-permanent tube had been inserted into each Traveler's arm prior to Launch to facilitate self-administration. Noa felt grateful that Taylor's preparation of the medication had triggered this response in Emmie. They were operating on such fragile ground.

Maggie did as she was told, although her movements were so slow it looked like she was swimming through honey. Finally, the IV lined up with the cannula and clicked into it. With the medicine safely coursing through her veins, Emmie cued the bedtime routine. It was strange to Noa to be working so in tandem with an AI. The partial override Noa had coded made it so that Emmie followed the curriculum's routine, unless Noa directed otherwise.

The tile behind them opened up, and Maggie's yoga mat and blood-stained towels tumbled inside, removing all evidence of the trauma. In their place, Maggie's bed and a tile of folded clothes rose to the surface.

"Okay, let's get you into bed," Emmie said to Maggie after a moment, who clumsily unhooked the IV, which recoiled back into the column.

Maggie shuffled over to the tile holding her evening uniform, robotically pulling the waistband just below her expanding belly, and her top over it. A strip of skin pushed its way stubbornly between the two.

Noa placed Emmie's hand against the small of Maggie's back to guide her toward the bed. This time, it didn't go through, but rested on the Haptic Response Fabric. Maggie lay down on top of the duvet, resting her head on the pillow so that her open eyes faced the ocean. Noa climbed in after her as she had thousands of times before.

She was vaguely aware that Taylor and, in all likelihood, Emmett were watching her through the screens in the room where she actually was curled up against the floor, spooning air. The virtual reality felt less bizarre than actual reality at times.

Noa grazed Emmie's fingertips against Maggie's back, as they used to each night. She pressed her whole body against her back and whispered, "I love you, Mags," even though there was no way Maggie could hear her, then lifted the goggles over her head to return to reality. She was lying on the floor of the control room, the bay of screens looming above her. On six different screens, Maggie was sitting up, wide-eyed, as if looking for something she'd just remembered she'd lost. Noa hadn't seen Emmett until later that evening, but they had both been invigorated by a renewed energy to complete the code Maggie would access in just a few hours.

"I have to take care of something quickly," Emmett said, snapping Noa out of the memory of the day before, "but Arthur should already be at breakfast if you want to join him." She smiled coolly at Noa and folded her palms to put the virtual photo away. "I'll be there soon."

Although Emmett called him by his first name, Noa had trouble adopting the same familiarity. He had such a sense of quiet authority to him, as if he had been born "Dr. Russo-Neva." Emmett disappeared down

the hallway as Noa turned in the opposite direction, toward where the professor was sitting at the breakfast table, just as Emmett had foretold.

"Early riser?" Noa asked, taking the seat across from him. His gaze remained fixed in a blank stare. "Dr. Russo-Neva," she said.

"Hmm?" he responded, then laughed, registering the question. "Oh yes! I hardly ever sleep when there's work to be done." Noa recognized a glint of excitement in his eyes.

Noa had never once considered the work she was doing here to be exciting, especially when it was so insurmountable and far from guaranteed to work, but appreciated his optimism. The night before, she had finished coding the last step for the cabin VR while keeping an eye on Maggie as she endured her own sleepless night, half an ocean away. Their plan depended on Maggie's ability to find the note they'd hidden for her in it.

Emmie would coax Maggie into taking the trail today, but after that it was up to Maggie to request it again. It was the only way to guarantee she would be placed back in it. Otherwise, she'd be tossed into Emmie's preselected plan, to explore Everest's base camp or a national park, somewhere that would only serve as a distraction from the one thing she needed to find: the instructions Noa had left inside.

Lembre-se, Maggie, she would have whispered in her ear last night if Maggie had been able to hear her. If she was careful, she would be able to actually hold her soon, to feel her without haptic touch. If Maggie let her, and if Noa decided she still wanted her. Right now, Noa just had to keep her alive.

Noa knew that she should probably get herself something to eat, but her body felt so confused by the lack of sleep that she couldn't decide if she was starving or barely had an appetite. She couldn't remember the last time she'd had food, but it felt strange to eat when the professor always sat in front of an empty place setting.

"Where is it that you live?" Noa asked him.

"Near enough," he said, waving his hand and offering a warm smile that, like Emmett's, Noa wasn't sure she could trust. She caught sight of something out of the corner of her eye, jolting to look at it, then softening

when she realized it was just a bank of fog cascading down the hillside. Just as quickly, she felt self-conscious about how jumpy she looked. She felt like she was going insane. She stood up, intending to return to the control room.

"What do you think of the fog?" he asked suddenly.

"The what?" Noa was caught off guard.

"The fog," he responded. So he *had* noticed her reaction. Noa hesitated. She was running a few minutes ahead of schedule and trusted that Taylor would let her know if Maggie showed any signs of distress or change. She sat back down; she could be his student for five minutes.

"You're right to be afraid of it," the professor continued, his voice at an unnaturally even cadence.

"What?"

"When you jumped earlier. You're right to be afraid of the fog. It shouldn't be moving this quickly."

Inga appeared from the kitchen entrance. "Would you like some coffee?" She indicated for Noa to follow her, and gave a quick smile to the professor, whose eyes were already glazed over.

Noa followed Inga to a carafe sitting beside the sink, looking like a glass jewel against the immaculate black matte countertops. Noa grabbed a mug and tilted the fresh coffee into it.

"You know, he's not the same as he used to be." Inga spoke in a whisper, leaning back against the counter.

"How long have you known him?"

"Decades," she said, then added, "He was my husband."

Suddenly Noa's fingers were burning. She had been studying Inga's face, not realizing that the coffee was flowing over the lip of her mug, cascading onto the floor. Noa released it before she knew what she was doing, shocked by the burn and too slow to recover as her fingers flew open. The mug plummeted to meet the puddle below, shattering when it hit the floor.

Noa grabbed a dishrag off a hook, lowering to her knees to clean up the mess as Inga stood frozen, her gaze staring blankly ahead at the fog that already wrapped around the entire house, obscuring the view in a dimensionless sea of white.

"I'm sorry," Noa was saying, the rag now stained entirely brown. She collected the shards, placing them into the waste chute. "I'm so sorry," she repeated. "You said he was your husband?"

"Slip of the tongue." Inga smiled. "He is. For as long as he's still here."

"You mean until his research takes him somewhere else?"

"Can I get you more coffee? Maybe set your mug on the counter this time," Inga suggested gently, moving to pull another mug from the shelf.

"Everything okay?" Taylor was at the door. "I heard a crash."

"Oh, we're fine," Inga said, waving him off. Behind her, the professor remained seated. He hadn't so much as turned around to see what had caused the crash, to check if his wife was okay.

Bile rose to the back of Noa's teeth.

"What do you mean?" Noa asked, ignoring Taylor, who was now walking toward Inga, his face lined with concern. She tried to control the desperation in her voice as she addressed Inga: "What do you mean, you *were* married?"

Inga opened her mouth, about to say something, then looked up past Noa to where Emmett was standing, having just entered the room.

"Noa—" Emmett began.

Noa didn't lift her gaze off Inga. The truth was beginning to click into place.

"Inga," Noa repeated, "tell me what you meant." The professor sat listless, completely unaware that any of them were there. Inga's entire body was shaking now, her shoulders vibrating against the tears she held back.

"It's okay," Emmett said softly, and Inga whispered so quietly at first that Noa had to ask her to repeat herself.

"He died," she said, "a year and a half ago."

She had suspected it, but Noa still felt like she had been punched. Inga's confirmation knocked the wind out of her.

"Then who's this?" she asked, motioning toward the professor. "Who is Arthur?"

As soon as she said his name, the glint returned to his eyes, as if a switch had been flipped—which it had. His hologram, it appeared, was coded to turn on when his name was mentioned.

"Well, hello," he said, his face turned warmly toward Noa. When he noticed everyone else, he began to chuckle. "It looks like everyone's here." His smile dropped as soon as he caught sight of Inga's expression, which matched Taylor's almost exactly.

Silent tears had been rolling down Inga's cheeks, but now she inhaled sharply, clearly distressed.

"Inga, is everything okay?" he asked his wife.

"Clearly it's not," Noa responded for her, her panic rising as the layers of lies clicked into place.

"Noa, I think it might be best if we talk about this somewhere else," Emmett said. Noa took in the three of them—Taylor, Inga, and Arthur—still unsure about their role in everything. She wanted to protest, but Emmett was already walking down the hallway. Noa turned to follow her, walking farther than she had ventured before, until Emmett came to a stop before a door that glided open at her approach.

The room looked like the inside of a WellNest, but much larger. Its walls pulsed in a cascade of neutral colors so complete and so varied that Noa felt like the entire world could be composed of those shades alone—beige, cream, gray, white, and black—and she would never miss another.

Noa tried again: "What's going on?" but Emmett wordlessly took a seat in one of the two haptic chairs in the center of the room and motioned for Noa to take the other. Noa considered her options, then followed Emmett's direction. Emmett swiveled to face her as soon as Noa sat down, leaning her elbows against the tops of her long legs. Noa's mind was spinning—

"I need to show you what's at stake here, Noa," Emmett said calmly, as Noa tried to keep up. *If Arthur is holographic, what does that mean about the storm he warned me about? And if there is no storm, what are we rescuing Maggie from?*

"Honestly, I'm surprised you haven't figured it out by now."

"What, Emmett?" Noa couldn't tell if they were still talking about Arthur, or something else.

"The real reason you're here." Noa sucked her breath in. The pieces were beginning to line up, but she still didn't know what they amounted to. "I'm going to tell you everything," Emmett continued. "You just have to be patient. Are you ready for your next clue?"

Ever since she'd arrived, Noa had had the sense that she was inside a game only Emmett knew the rules to, but her mention of clues that morning and omission about Arthur felt unhinged in an entirely different way. Emmett sat back in her chair, which came alive, enveloping her entire body. Its sides curved in at the same time a helmet rose from the back, lowering over the top of her head so that by the time it was done, Noa could see only her serene smile.

Noa moved to get up, but her own chair began to absorb her body, holding down her arms and legs until the helmet came down, obscuring her vision and stifling the sound of her scream.

15

Maggie

Zone 874, Pacific Ocean
42 Days Post-Launch

Maggie opened her eyes for a brief second before shutting them again. The light was blindingly bright, even filtered through the layer of dense clouds, and her head throbbed behind her eyes. She pressed her palms against their hollows, painting splotches of blues that faded slowly when she opened them.

She rolled onto her side, away from the glass to face the room, lifting her hand into a visor. She couldn't remember how she'd gotten into bed, and felt as groggy as if she'd slept for only a few minutes. The last thing she remembered was lying on the floor next to a pile of vomit, but there was no evidence: her yoga mat had been put away and the floor was clean. She raised her hand to her wound. Though she cringed at the touch, it didn't feel nearly as serious as she'd thought it was. It had already begun to heal, and had left only a few small dots of blood where it had come into direct contact with her pillow overnight.

It was the bruise, where her thigh had made contact with the hard tile, that hurt the most, though her stomach also felt tender. Maggie sat up and swung her legs over the side of the bed, pulling the elastic waistband of her linen pants down to admire the colors. Splashes of purples and blues subsided into a faint yellow outline.

"Maggie," Emmie said. *How long has she been repeating my name?*

"Yes?" she replied. Her voice sounded strange. She walked over to the toilet, lowering herself slowly so as not to disturb the bruise, realizing that she couldn't even remember putting her pajamas on. Maggie rested her elbows against her thighs, leaning forward as she watched her bed sink back into the floor, consumed by the Pod's internal system. Floor tiles clicked together in its place to create a smooth white surface—the line between oasis and asylum could feel uncomfortably fine. When she finished, the toilet flushed and Maggie pulled her pants back up.

"How are you feeling?" Emmie asked.

"Hungover." The pounding headache didn't feel unlike those she'd had after nights out with Thomas and their friends in college. Maggie tried to hang on to the fact that Emmie hadn't mentioned anything about the baby, which Maggie took as a good sign, though she still felt too afraid to ask. She had spent months unsure if she wanted a child, but something had changed in her, almost overnight, and she could no longer stand the possibility of losing it.

"Your hydration levels are showing signs of stress," Emmie said as the system processed her urine. "I think an IV drip would do the trick. Can I walk you through the process?"

"Yes," Maggie tried to say. Her hoarse voice sounded nothing like her own, while Emmie's was perfectly comforting, more maternal than mechanical.

Maggie thought of the voice-activated machines that had still been popular during her childhood. Their female voices now felt like a strange relic from a patriarchal society when women handled matters of the home. Back then, their powers had been limited to the domestic realm: they dimmed the lights, turned on music, and set timers on command. Over time, they learned skills that had been delegated to housewives a hundred years before. Even as updates stripped away their robotic affects, their feminine registers remained.

Emmie instructed Maggie to sit in the chair beside the central column. As soon as she did, the column's chute opened. An IV bag hung from a hook at the top with a capped needle resting on a plastic plate.

Maggie lifted her sleeve and pinched the skin in the crook of her left elbow to find the cannula. It was so small, she'd almost forgotten they'd placed it there during her last Health Screening before Launch. Up until this point, she hadn't needed to use it once. But was that really true? A dull memory came back to her of the night before. She popped the protective cap off the IV with her thumb, which clicked magnetically into the cannula's port.

The bag released a flow of saline into Maggie's veins. Almost immediately, she began to feel better, less groggy.

"What's in this thing, coffee?"

Emmie laughed politely, but sounded earnest. Her voice could have been mistaken for human, except that it reverberated through every speaker in the Pod, like recorded music when you expected a live band.

From where Maggie sat, she could see the entire room. Her life for the past month and a half had been contained in a circle that was fifteen feet across, and that was only if you included the patio, which the glass walls indented to accommodate. From above, the Pod must have looked like an uneven yin-yang symbol, a visual metaphor reinforced by the fact that the tiles were white on the inside, and slate black on the patio to capture energy from the sun.

"You must be hungry," Emmie said, as if she didn't already know from Maggie's Vitalities exactly how much ghrelin her stomach was releasing. Maggie realized she was starving, though she doubted she could keep anything down. The pain in her side persisted and she had felt nauseated for weeks. Maggie instinctively cradled her abdomen, then unhooked the IV from her arm. It recoiled into the chute and the door closed; a moment later, it reopened to reveal a green juice.

"Drink as much of this as you can," Emmie encouraged. The cool drink felt surprisingly good against the back of her throat.

The center column displayed that day's schedule. Activities she had slept through had a line through them. Had she not injured herself, she would have been in the middle of lunch. She took another sip of her smoothie, wiping her lips on the back of her sleeve, staining the white linen with a swipe of pale green.

"How did I get into bed last night?" she finally asked, edging closer to the question she cared most about.

"You don't remember?"

Maggie could feel tears stinging the backs of her eyes, her body registering her helplessness before she could.

"I helped you," Emmie said matter-of-factly.

"How?"

"You were lying on the tile in the bed area, so I tilted it until you slid onto the adjoining tile, then flipped the bed. You woke up just long enough for me to coax you into pajamas. I thought you would have remembered that."

Maggie shook her head.

"Is it okay with you if I step into the room?" Emmie asked. Like a vampire in the novels Maggie once loved, Emmie's code prohibited her physical projection from entering the room without Maggie's explicit permission.

Maggie nodded, and Emmie appeared a few feet in front of the center column, wearing the same outfit she always did. Her hair, tucked into a perfectly messy ponytail Maggie could never have achieved herself, ran between her shoulders. The lack of imperfections was the one thing that made Emmie look artificial. Fabric never bunched at an ill-fitting bra cup and her pants didn't crease above her thighs when she walked. Everything about her was perfectly smooth, an airbrushed version of a real person. Her emotions, hair, demeanor, voice, and pants had all been ironed out into something algorithmically soothing.

She knelt at Maggie's feet, placing a hand on her knee. Maggie recoiled in surprise at the weight of it. She could *feel* it. Emmie floated her hand up.

"The latest Pod update downloaded yesterday," Emmie said. "The schedule has been fine-tuned—you'll notice more VR activities and a more seamless circadian transition, and the haptic threads of your clothes have been turned on for the final days of your Journey."

Maggie pinched the fabric of her pants between her thumb and forefinger. Nothing felt different about them.

"Everything in the Pod is coded, so that it can be updated later if need be. Even the clothes you wear can be made warmer, softer, better attuned to your needs. The haptic sensation is just another one of those updates. Let me show you."

Emmie touched her hand to the back of Maggie's. As usual, she couldn't feel it.

"May I?" She hovered her hand above Maggie's abdomen, and put it down when Maggie nodded. Maggie could feel the weight and curve of her palm perfectly against her crested belly. "Of course, you can't *actually* feel me, but the pajamas bridge that gap. It's called Haptic Response Fabric." Still, Maggie felt the baby kick in response and felt a cascade of relief unlike anything she had ever experienced—so strong, it took her by surprise. It was okay.

Emmie rose and stepped back, leaving Maggie with a clear view of the patio. She was unable to shake a gnawing sense that she was forgetting something. The waves lapped at the sides of the Pod, crashing against the bottom of the glass wall like mini Great Waves off Kanagawa. Her body registered the memory before she could, and blood rushed to her face.

The sound of the bird crashing into the glass came back to her. Maggie bolted to the patio door as the vision of the bird being hurled through the sky came back to her.

Fear quickly replaced the relief she felt at spotting the bird, its small body huddled against the dark tile. She couldn't tell if it was alive or dead, but suspected the latter.

"Unlock the patio doors," Maggie demanded, her voice coming out hoarse.

Emmie's voice filled the Pod, as clear as if she still stood in the room: "I can't do that. The weather is too unstable at the moment for patio access." The fog that had encased the Pod for days had finally dissipated, replaced by winds that shrieked past the glass and ruffled the bird's soft feathers.

"Emmie," she said, losing the battle against controlling the fear rising in her throat, "please unlock the patio doors. I *need* to help the bird."

She thought of Noa's favorite movie, *2001: A Space Odyssey.* The first time they'd watched it together, Maggie could tell that Noa was restraining herself from repeating the lines verbatim. Maggie watched hyper-aggressive apes fight in the shadow of a black monolith with the earnest studiousness of someone newly in love. Both had waited for the credits to end before Maggie delivered her true opinion. ". . . What was that?" She was rewarded by Noa's throaty laughter. In the movie, the computer HAL had refused the astronaut's request to reenter his ship over and over. But Maggie was trapped inside.

"I'm sorry," Emmie repeated. "It could carry avian diseases that I can't put you at risk of catching."

Maggie drew a deep breath, slowly, consciously exhaling her building paranoia. *I'm sorry, Dave, I'm afraid I can't do that,* HAL had replied slowly, with the calm authority of someone, some*thing,* that has all the power. But Emmie was nothing like HAL. She was genuinely concerned for her safety. It was part of the reason Maggie had never gone against her guidance before. She trusted Emmie.

"Okay," Maggie said, turning toward the NutriStation. She had noticed the small label on the lower rim of the cabinet door a few weeks earlier: MANUAL DOOR OVERRIDE. She opened it and reached her arm past the crisscrossing pipes and wires until she felt the smooth handle, and pressed down on it as hard as she could.

The light at the door began pulsating in menacing red, but it opened, letting in a gust of damp, sticky air. She grabbed a set of clothes from the tile that had risen and rushed out, cupping one of them into a rough nest while using the edge to gently scoop the bird into it. One of its wings was bent in an unnatural position, too far back at the elbow.

Maggie blinked the light drizzle out of her eyes, carrying the swaddled bird in through the door, which closed automatically behind her. Drops of water trailed her. She had been barefoot when she ran outside. She set the bird into a nest in the sink, covering its entire body except for the head before stripping her own wet clothes off and tossing them down the chute.

A tile rose with another set of white clothes, which she quickly pulled on.

"And what are you going to do when it recovers?" Emmie had been observing in silence up until that moment.

"Let it out the door? I'm not really sure, but I can't just leave it there."

"Yes you can," Emmie said. "Birds die all the time on the ocean. We can't keep a bird here."

Maggie considered the word *we*. They weren't roommates, Emmie wasn't even alive, but she used the term all the time. This was the first time it had struck Maggie as strange.

"Is there anything I can feed it?" she asked.

"It eats fish and squid that it forages. If you feed it, it will unlearn how to hunt with time."

There was something about her conversations with Emmie recently that made her feel like a child. It was similar to how she used to feel when she spent weekends with her parents in college. She was older and wiser, but the cyclical arguments they'd had when she was living in the house were exactly the same. The few times she brought Thomas home in college, he had retreated to her room as she fought with her mom about selecting her major or, their perennial favorite, Maggie's trauma around Gamma's death, her mother's inability to understand it, and her inability to move past it. Emmie was right, but she also didn't have the ability to genuinely care for the bird. Being coded for empathy was different than actually having it.

"Let's just keep it here for a day, to give it a chance to heal," Maggie acquiesced.

She didn't have to wait nearly that long. In the end, it only took an hour for the bird to stop breathing. Maggie's own breath caught in her throat at the discovery. She gently lifted the nest of towels from the sink, cradling it in her arms as she sat down on the floor, tears streaming down her cheeks. After looking at the bird's face one final time, she closed the edge of the towel over its open eyes and stood, using her free hand against the glass wall to push herself up.

Gamma would have known how to save it. Maggie had always gone to her for advice. The one time Maggie had ignored her, the afternoon she had opted to keep her Pohvee, Gamma had died. Maggie loved how much Noa's confidence reminded her of Gamma's, and how she took charge in a similar way—ordering for them both, setting her up with a job, selecting their future path. Saving things that needed saving. Maggie added the bird to the mental log of all the things she might share with Noa at Redock, playing out conversations even as she knew they would probably never happen. *I didn't know what to do*, she explained to the future version of Noa who didn't exist. *It's okay*, she imagined Noa saying, *you did the best you could.*

When Emmie's voice finally came through the speakers, it didn't have a hint of malice.

"Maggie," she said, brimming with maternal concern, "I am so sorry for your loss."

It reminded Maggie of the voice Emmie had used when she'd lost Gamma, the first time they'd met, full of a tenderness her own mother could never seem to offer. Maggie stared straight ahead, waiting for the tears to stop, as she had so many times. Grieving was a skill she'd learned, and she was an expert in its ebbs and flows. The trick was to focus externally, rather than internally, where she could lose herself to her own pain and sink so far into the darkness it could take days to find her way out of it.

After placing the bird back outside, where it would be washed into a burial at sea, Maggie watched the waves crash against the side of the Pod, their white caps occasionally brimming above the level of her bed. She ignored Emmie's suggestions that she go for a VR walk or attend counseling, allowing the waves to hypnotize her. They were as high as she'd ever seen them. Maggie slipped her legs under the covers and began to cry, for the bird, for Noa, for the baby.

The Pod was rocking back and forth, just shy of violently, when she woke up an hour later, an entire morning lost to grief. Maggie let herself imagine she was in a bassinet. Some orphanages, she'd once read, had an infant mortality rate of up to forty percent. Babies who were not held or touched enough stopped growing and, in some cases, died. Over time, they learned to fear touch. She thought of Emmie's hand on her knee earlier, how it had felt equally foreign and comforting.

It was hard to believe she was nearly finished with her trip. The Redock ship would come in just a few days to carry her and the other Travelers back to California. She craved her reunion with Noa just as much as she dreaded it. She had so much to tell Noa and, although she hoped she wasn't right, Maggie knew nothing would be the same when she returned. She laid a hand across her abdomen. If she was being honest with herself, they had been overdue for a lot of conversations for some time now.

After the kiss and subsequent message, Thomas had disappeared again without a trace, though Maggie had loosely tracked his whereabouts around California through his articles. She tried to pretend the kiss hadn't happened and to forget the jolt of electricity she'd felt at the moment their lips touched, even as she spent the better part of a year replaying it; far more times—she was ashamed to admit—than Noa's proposal.

Maggie loved spending time with Noa, but Noa spent so much time at the office, supporting them both. She provided stability, even moving them into a larger apartment that had an adjoining room Maggie turned into an art studio shortly after she saw Thomas. Maggie didn't immediately connect the project to the clandestine meeting, but a few weeks later she had completed her first painting since college with the help of a projected teacher and model.

The model who appeared in the middle of the room was semitranslucent, more so as the afternoon light bounced off the ocean behind her. Still, Maggie painted her full body, which was soft and lived-in, as if it were formed by flesh and bone and capillaries and organs, a beating heart rather than a compilation of twinkling pixels. Maggie only became aware as the painting took shape beneath her brush that she had painted Gamma's face. Maggie lovingly adorned her in strands of kelp dripping in obscene white sacs of squid eggs, like the ones Gamma had described to Maggie as a child, which washed up on beaches farther north than where they lived. In the painting, the pearled kelp became her coronation mantle, set against a lush sea of blues and greens.

On the night Maggie finished the painting, Noa arrived home later than usual. Maggie ran to the front door, holding the painted canvas, still glistening at some parts, eager to show Noa her work. Instead, Noa held up a hand the way her mother once had, conveying to Maggie she was busy working. By the time she finished her meeting an hour later, she had either forgotten or refused to ask Maggie about the canvas, and Maggie never volunteered it again, showing it to Emmie before locking it away in the studio. Over a year had passed since, without a word from Thomas, until Maggie received a message from him asking her to meet for coffee in the cafeteria. She replied quickly and they selected a date when he would be back on campus for another interview. His article on WellPark had been well received, but every time Maggie asked about the new one, he demurred, deflecting her questions with another question.

After coffee, she walked him to his car. She hadn't so much as sat in one since moving into WellHome. There was no need to exit the security and comfort that WellPark provided. Only employees with family on the outside and visitors needed cars.

His was an older model, maybe forty years old, from a time before self-driving cars were ubiquitous. She opened the driver's-side door on impulse, climbed in, and curled her fingers around the wheel, the emerald in her ring catching the light.

"Press your foot against the brake pedal," Thomas instructed through the open window, leaning his forearm against its metal frame.

Her foot found the familiar platform and pressed it down. He leaned over her to press the ignition button, so close she could inhale him. He smelled like soap and a blown-out match. "Want to drive it?"

She grimaced, and he responded with a laugh. "Wait there."

In the rearview mirror, she could see him jogging around the car, unplugging the electric charger before hopping in the passenger seat. He was a man now, but he still ran like his long legs didn't fully belong to him. They bowed out with every step, just like they had in college.

He smiled when he saw her laughing, closing the passenger door behind him.

"Okay, buckle up," he said, putting on his own. "I'm not kidding!"

He moved his hand diagonally across his chest, miming the action, and she laughed again, harder.

When he leaned over to grab her seat belt, buckling her in like a child, she took in a deeper breath, inhaling his subtle cologne. The slightly musky scent he still wore smelled like nostalgia. She felt the fissures in her heart that had healed years ago begin to crack.

They hadn't been nearly this playful over coffee, the public setting cooling their mood together. But now that they were alone, the tone had shifted all the way back to the way they used to be. She couldn't tell if he was flirting or simply being friendly. Neither of them had mentioned the kiss.

"Do you remember how to do this?" he asked after pulling on her seat belt to confirm it was properly fastened, and performatively doing the same to his.

"I guess we'll see?"

"Why don't we start doing a few slow loops?"

"Can you remind me how to start?"

"Do you remember where the gearshift is?"

"Did cars always have backup cameras?"

"Have you always been this curious about cars?"

Maggie reversed out of the spot, which wasn't difficult considering there were hardly any others in the lot, and came to a full stop, carefully shifting into drive. Even when she and Noa had lived in LA, before moving to WellHome, she'd used her car as little as possible to avoid paying for the electricity to charge it.

"How did you afford this?" she asked.

"Remember the grant that paid for me to return to California?" Maggie vaguely recalled him mentioning it at drinks. "This came with it. I'm lucky I have a reason to be on tech campuses so often. I can charge it in their parking ports which, if I'm careful, is more than enough to keep it running."

Maggie was driving slow circles in the garage, enjoying the seamless connection, the power she felt between the wheel and the tires, but Thomas teased her, "Is that the best you can do?"

"What we need is music," she decided.

To her surprise, Thomas opened the center console and pulled out a small white music player. It looked just like the one Gamma used to use.

"Where did you find that?" she asked, incredulous.

"I found it in the car under the seat," he said in mock defense. "The owner must have left it, but some of these are great!" He was scrolling his thumb around the circular trackpad, through Albums. He tapped the center button twice.

"Eyes on the road," he said, as the first few bars of Bruce Springsteen's "I'm On Fire" came through the speakers. She knew the song well, but hadn't heard it since before Gamma died.

"Do you see that?" Thomas asked. He was pointing toward a door that looked like any other loading dock in the garage, with a heavy metal gate sealing its entrance. "That's the way to Emmett's house."

Maggie shot him a confused glance.

"The tunnel goes straight through the mountain to her home."

She had heard rumors that an underground pathway existed, but had dismissed them.

"Why?" she asked. Thomas looked at her as if the answer was obvious.

"To keep her safe. If anything ever happens here, to the company—protests, collapse, another hurricane—she has a direct way out. And," he added with a shrug, "convenience."

They passed under a sign that read PARK on one side and EXIT on the other. Maggie brought the car to a stop, then turned to face Thomas.

"Can we drive outside?"

Thomas considered this for a moment before responding, "Yes, but I better be the one doing the driving. It's different than you remember it. It's . . . a lot worse."

Maggie put the car in park and switched places with him. This time, Thomas didn't jog or tease her. His mood, she noticed, seemed to have completely sobered at the mention of the outside.

She turned down the music as he pulled toward the exit, up to the Reader. He leaned out of the window slightly to swipe his Injectible against it. The Reader spoke in a voice that was a perfect blend of masculine and feminine, just vague enough to pass for either.

"The weight of your car has changed since entry. Please state your reason."

"Passenger," Thomas replied.

"Please scan your Injectible."

A similar Reader rose beside Maggie's door and Thomas lowered the window so she could stick her wrist out to be read. She wondered if he was also thinking about the day they met, the day they received their Injectibles. She'd later ask him, and he'd respond, *How could I not be?*

The exit opened, and Thomas followed the bend in the tunnel until they reached a second gate, which lifted as they pulled up to it. As Maggie's eyes adjusted, her Lens alerted her that she was off campus, exiting beside the pyramidal rock she had looked at countless times since moving to WellHome. It loomed at a curve in the road, so she could never see south of it, but now she had a clear view of the coast and highway for miles.

Without fully realizing it, her entire existence had been on a sliding track that took her from WellPark to WellHome, and back. She had everything she needed, so she hadn't realized how much she was missing outside its walls. She hadn't left campus once since she and Noa moved in.

Thomas was staring straight at the road, but he reached over and took her hand, squeezing it tightly for a brief moment before releasing it. She wiped away the tears that welled over the rims of her damp eyes.

The highway looked as if it was fighting a losing battle against the earth. To their left, the mountainside pushed against metal netting placed on the hills decades before. Even so, parts of the road were so covered in dirt, eroded from the hillside, it no longer looked paved. Thomas took the turns slowly. There were no other cars on the road, and spinning out meant being met by either the wall of rocks to their left, or worse, the ocean cliff to their right.

An old sign pointed out a state beach, its white text peeling away from the brown background. As they passed it, Thomas pointed toward the hillside opposite. "That's where her house is."

He slowed down, and Maggie ducked to see if she could spot Emmett's house in the hillside. Bowie was singing now. She could barely make out the lyrics from his mumbled voice and the low volume, but she knew the words by heart, his warning cry to teenage lovers caught in the moment.

"It's camouflaged," he explained. "You actually can't see it until you're right in front of it. The entire thing is mostly underground, embedded into the hillside."

"Have you been?" she asked.

"Not yet, but I interviewed the architect for another piece, and he told me all about it."

Thomas had a way of getting people to tell him anything. It was what made him such a good journalist.

"The house is built so that it's only accessible from the tunnel entrance we saw, or from a trail in the hillside," he continued. "I guess she wanted a place she could barricade herself into."

He fell silent, and Maggie followed his lead. Each time they wrapped around another turn, Maggie could see what he had meant. It was, as he promised, a lot worse than she'd anticipated. She hadn't expected so much deterioration in the past two years, but it was like a ghost town. They passed by a restaurant with an OPEN sign, but Maggie couldn't tell if it was actually open or if it had just been abandoned that way. On the glass window, the paint that had once read *Happy Holidays* had almost entirely chipped away. A snowman handing a red ornament to a reindeer had lost its head.

Maggie spotted a surfer. It was the first person they'd seen the entire drive. He sat on his board in the ocean, waiting for a wave, his legs dangling off the sides. He waved unnaturally slowly at her, as a warning sign, a call for help, or simply an acknowledgment of another human, Maggie wasn't sure. She wondered which of the abandoned-looking cars on the edge of the highway was his home, if Landon lived in one of them too. She hadn't thought about him in years. Thomas gave no indication of seeing the surfer.

"That's what I really love covering," Thomas said, pointing instead to a decrepit billboard for a water desalinization company. *Stay in California. The water's fine!* it said, referencing the fact that the decades-long droughts and draining of the Colorado River had finally succeeded in eliminating most of the water in the state, without a hint of irony. "The lengths humans will go to convince themselves that everything is fine."

Maggie nodded. She had read every one of Thomas's articles, most of which felt like an extension of the themes that had infuriated him in college. Back then, he had written about efforts that gave individuals a false sense of empowerment, like recycling programs and paper straws. More recently, he had covered large-scale, billion-dollar programs that exploited the same mass illusion that enabled overconsumption. He wrote about desalinization, but also about carbon capture efforts, about scientists who draped blankets over melting glaciers, and shot oxygen into the ocean to revive dead zones and diamonds into the sky to dim the sun. To him, these were all ways of perpetuating the myth that "someone else" would fix things. At least the billboard, it seemed, had succeeded in convincing a few people to stay.

At certain points, the road resembled an overgrown trail—the only way to differentiate it from the surrounding rocks and sand was by shallow tire tracks. Sand dunes melted into the beach, and most of the houses on the ocean side of the highway had collapsed into the water. It looked to Maggie as if the ocean was a magnet, pulling everything into it.

Shortly after passing a sign that said MALIBU: 21 MILES OF BEAUTY, Thomas drove through an intersection with unilluminated traffic lights. There was hardly a point in slowing down to check the intersection for crossing cars that weren't there. On the corner of the intersection, Maggie saw a deteriorating Nativity scene outside a church. The Virgin Mary had been knocked over and tossed against the side of the chicken wire that kept the scene secure from looters and teenagers. It looked like she'd been hit by a tornado. All around her was chaos.

"What happened there?" Maggie asked.

"Hurricane Wendy," Thomas replied. At first Maggie thought he was joking. Hurricanes rarely hit the West Coast, even as they'd grown in magnitude to the east.

"What?"

"Hurricane Wendy," he repeated, looking over at her. Maggie watched the news almost obsessively, but had no memory of it.

"It must have been Christmas of the year you moved in," Thomas explained in a tone that conveyed knowledge without being condescending. "An enormous hurricane grew off the coast of Hawai'i and hit Southern California. This wasn't even the worst of it, you should see San Diego."

He pointed at the hillside. "You see those houses? They're almost all abandoned. The super-wealthy who lived here were almost all gone from the fires by the time the hurricane hit, but this was the last straw for everyone stubborn enough to stay. The economy and population practically flipped overnight. The storm destroyed most of the beaches, restaurants, and tourist spots. Without them and the residents, there's nothing worth building it back for. Storms do more damage when there's no one left to pick up after them."

"How did I not know it was this bad?" Maggie asked, a vague memory of the news footage coming back to her.

"The WellCorp bubble is thicker than anyone inside realizes. They probably cleaned up the campus while you were eating Christmas dinner with Noa."

Maggie sat silently. There had been a storm, she remembered, with warnings broadcast across all Devices. She and Noa had stayed in their apartment complex on Christmas, meeting Maya and a few of Noa's friends in the common area for their building's holiday party. They'd spent a few days inside, but it had felt cozy, not dangerous.

Thomas brought the car to a stop. Part of the road had completely eroded so that there was an enormous hole in the asphalt. Someone had tried to patch it with planks of wood, likely purchased or looted from the construction store they had passed, but those too were sagging into the hole.

Thomas instructed her to hop out of the car and walk along the center of the asphalt. He couldn't put his "precious cargo" at risk, he said, then drove over it. She tried to peer into the hole as she walked, but couldn't tell how deep it went. A few seconds later, they were driving as if nothing had happened.

"It feels like an apocalypse out here," Maggie said.

"Some people literally think that," Thomas answered.

It looked like he was going to go on, but instead he just looked ahead, taking a left up Sunset Boulevard. They sat listening to the music as they wound past deserted schools, an outdoor mall, and more homes. The roads were better, just bumpy where tree roots had pushed through the asphalt. Since turning off the coastal highway, they'd passed a few more cars. The people who lived there had a view of the ocean but apparently never visited it.

Somewhere, she thought, there were people who, if they saw the news about Malibu, only waited a few days before forgetting it. "How sad," she could hear them saying, as she and Noa had about the fires in Australia, wars in China, flooding in the South, and countless other places and disasters she'd already forgotten.

Thomas turned into Brentwood, once one of Los Angeles's most affluent neighborhoods. Overgrown rosebushes and hedges, overflowing trash cans, and untended lawns sat in front of houses, no longer taken care of by "staff," as the families who lived there referred to the people who took on the labor of living for them, raising their children, cooking their dinner, tending their massive houses and gardens.

They wound uphill until Thomas pulled into a driveway, hopping out to push the garage door open before pulling in.

"And this is it," he declared, looking instantly more relaxed, "Chez Thomas."

Although they hadn't discussed it, Maggie had somehow always known they were heading to his place. It was a pretty brick house with tended white roses; Maggie half-expected an elegant couple in their seventies to walk out of it. But it belonged to Thomas, a single journalist in his late twenties. Nobody with enough money to choose wanted to live in Brentwood anymore.

Inside, the house only confirmed Maggie's suspicions that it was better suited for a distinguished pair of grandparents. It had a distinctive 1990s feel to it, a contemporary of Gamma's, though it couldn't have been further from her style. Carpet lined the floors, A lacquered wood folding screen divided the living room from a formal dining room.

Thomas explained that he'd written a feature on the man who lived there, a psychiatrist who'd treated some of the top technology executives for decades, and learned in the process that he and his wife were moving somewhere smaller, more manageable. The man had offered him the house for next to nothing, and left most of his things.

"He was completely delusional, really," Thomas said. "I think he expected to buy it back someday. For someone so intelligent to really have no idea . . ." He trailed off. It was hard for Maggie to imagine Thomas putting down roots anywhere.

"Anyway," he recovered, walking up to a gold bar cart that sank heavily into the plush beige carpeting, "would you like a drink?"

"What do you have?" Maggie asked, settling on the couch. She traced the thread around the raised flowers on its fabric. It was pristine but still smelled like it was a hundred years old—which it nearly was.

"Would you like Amaretto or something stronger?"

Maggie was surprised by Thomas's mention of the drink. For the three New Year's Eves they'd been together, the two of them had purchased a bottle of Amaretto and sat on Memorial Glade, drinking it from the early evening into the night. The sickly sweet almond liqueur was one of her favorites, but also caused the worst hangovers imaginable. They would spend New Year's Day like warriors, sipping beers in bed until they felt well enough to rejoin their friends.

It had been years since she'd had it—distilleries in Saronno no longer exported it—so it was only available to those fortunate enough to have a stockpile, which evidently the psychiatrist did.

Thomas plucked the bottle and two rocks glasses from the cart.

"Do you want to sit outside?" he asked, and Maggie answered by following him.

On the back porch were two patio chairs Maggie had glimpsed as they pulled up to the house, visible from the front window all the way through to the back. She took a seat in one and Thomas pulled the other closer to her, handing her a blanket which she draped over herself, tucking it under her thighs. They both sat, quiet for a moment, looking out over Los Angeles. The house would have offered a spectacular view, if not for the thick layer of yellow-gray smog.

Despite its color, the clouds of pollution made it feel like home back in Northern California. Her thoughts returned, again, to Gamma, who had always loved the fog that blanketed Palo Alto in the early morning. She missed home so much sometimes her entire body ached.

"Is it ever clear enough to see the city?" Maggie asked.

"Only after it rains," Thomas said, "Cheers."

"What are we cheersing to?"

Thomas smiled, and Maggie knew what he was thinking. Any time they spent together contained land mines of memories. He had always teased her about her tendency to say "cheersing," rather than "toasting," until he gave in and began using it himself.

"To being together again," Thomas said.

Maggie felt a prick of guilt. Noa had no idea where she was, let alone that she was with Thomas, but she tried to put it out of her mind. The sun was about to set, and the silver lining to the pollution that clung to the city was the way the light particles bounced off it. The sunset, she knew, would be beautiful tonight.

"To being together," she replied, meeting his glass with hers.

The syrupy golden-brown liquid spiraled with every sip she took. Looking over the city, it was easy to imagine an alternative reality, one where she and Thomas stayed together after college. She let herself think about what would have happened if she had followed him to New York, or if they had both stayed in Northern California. Maybe they would have purchased a house together, like this one, and drunk Amaretto every evening on their back porch before dinner. She was so carried away by the fantasy that when Thomas reached over to take her hand, it felt like the most natural thing in the world. For a brief moment, there was no Noa and no WellCorp, no natural disasters or global crises, just the two of them.

Thomas dropped her hand and stood up, walking to the edge of the concrete patio, which ended in a dramatic cliff. Maggie stood to follow, wrapping the blanket tightly around her shoulders against the rare chill in the air. It was nights like this one that tricked everyone into thinking things were okay. She pressed her front against his back, wrapping her arms and the blanket around him. He intertwined his fingers in hers. They stood like that for a long time, swaying slightly in their shared cape as the sun painted the smog into a beautiful blanket of neon orange-pink.

After a few minutes, he turned around and kissed her, first softly, then with more desperation as Maggie dropped the blanket. She peeled off his shirt and unbuttoned his pants. The movements felt at once familiar and strange. She tugged down his briefs and pressed herself against him, pulling her sweater up over her head. They slowed down when he removed her bra, the sight of her breasts sobering him.

"Are you sure you want to do this?" Thomas asked, their chests painted pink like the clouds.

As soon as Maggie whispered yes, he bent down to put his mouth around her nipple. Maggie slipped out of her pants and then her underwear as Thomas stepped back to watch, taking her in as if it could end at any moment, as if he couldn't believe his eyes. She had missed him so much that this somehow felt bigger, so much more significant, than everything she and Noa had built together. She needed this to happen, if nothing else, to close the chapter. They had never had a real ending.

She saw herself through his eyes, the one who got away, and clung to him as he lowered them both to the ground against the blanket. He kissed her deeply as he eased his way into her, tentatively at first, then pushing in completely. He braced himself above her with his forearm and ran his other hand from her breast along her rib cage, down the curve of her waist, reminding himself of every part he had missed. He moved slowly, so that they never separated. His chest pressed completely into Maggie's with every movement, until he pulled out of her with a coy smile and began to move down between her legs.

She pulled him up—unable to bear even a brief separation after so much time apart—and kept her face pressed against his, breathing in his every exhale as he worked the pad of his finger around her clitoris, pushing his finger into her as she came, the same way he had in college. She loved Noa, but she had forgotten what this connection between her and Thomas had felt like. When he reentered her, he folded her leg up to push deeper into her, moving more quickly this time. Maggie pulled him closer as he came inside her, barely registering the risk.

"How do strangers have sex?" he'd once asked her. "It's so intimate, then so messy, and can be so vulnerable it's humiliating."

Maggie had laughed. "That's just the way *you* have sex. You bare your soul."

Maggie squeezed her eyes shut, draping her forearm over her lids to block out the light and reality, as she pressed into herself with her other hand. It wasn't hard to imagine the rocking of the Pod as Thomas pressing into her instead of her own hand. She released some of the pressure, taking a few deep breaths, then pressed in again with her whole palm. She sighed as the familiar warmth cascaded through her body, moving from her chest to her toes, and lay there for a few moments, feeling her muscles twitch at the release of tension.

The Pod offered intimate AR sessions, but she'd never requested one, preferring to sink back into the memory of that night with Thomas. She lifted her arm from her eyes, half-expecting to see a brilliant pink sunset, but it was still early afternoon. She took a few more breaths, then tossed aside her sheets.

The tenderness in her stomach came only in small waves now, and she pressed one hand into her abdomen, massaging the muscle, which helped alleviate the tension for a moment. With the other, she held on to her bruised leg. She felt like she was holding herself together.

Emmie was speaking to her, and she was too tired now to deny her.

16

Noa

Malibu, California
42 Days Post-Launch

It was so quiet that, after Noa's scream rang out, the only thing she could hear was her heartbeat, the sound of her own blood pumping. She couldn't tell how much time had passed since she'd entered the haptic chair beside Emmett when her surroundings became brighter, evolving into a shade of blue that felt calming, as if she was finally allowed to release the breath she'd been holding.

The blue, she realized, came from an artificial sky. She was plummeting from the atmosphere toward the ground, picking up speed until, as if a parachute had been pulled, she began floating lazily toward a dirt road in an overgrown forest. As soon as her feet hit the ground, Noa had to jog to catch up to Emmett, who had started walking down a trail that was hardly distinguishable from reality. The running felt as natural as if she were really there, except just barely lighter.

She tried to think of the suit her body was in now, in the real world, how it had captured her and was now mimicking the strike of each step against the ground by applying that pressure to her own foot as she lay supine, but it was like trying to sing a song while listening to another one. It was easier to just let go, to sway to the music of the alternate reality in front of her eyes.

As soon as she reached Emmett's side, Emmett began speaking.

"This," she said, "is probably my favorite place, though I haven't actually been here since I was a child. I coded it just like you coded the trail that Maggie will take later today, and for the same reasons. It comforts me to be able to return here. Sometimes I forget to remember that none of it's real."

Noa knew as well as Emmett did that the same parts of the brain that process memory, nostalgia, and joy lit nearly as bright during VR experiences as they did in reality. It was even possible to forget you were in a simulation altogether.

Emmett took a deep breath. "Arthur was the first lifelike hologram we ever coded. Like the Emmies and other holograms, he's technically a projection of our Lenses, but that doesn't mean he's any less real. That this place is any less real."

Noa disagreed. *Of course* it was less real, but she waited to hear what Emmett would say, hoping her explanation would somehow account for a misunderstanding. They both watched a squirrel, either a replica or a transcribed capture of one that had actually existed years ago, run down a tree trunk, followed shortly by another. Their clicking filled the air.

"I met Arthur when I first moved to LA. He began to consult for me when I was still gathering information and laying the groundwork for WellNests, trying to speak to every intelligent person who would answer my calls. He was always kind to me and began working for us full-time when I decided to build the campus on the coast. He was the one who drew my attention back to the ocean, to how much more powerful it would feel to live not just at its edge but *surrounded* by it. I trusted him like family.

"When he got sick, I invited him and his family to live with me so that they could have access to the best possible care. His son, Taylor, was already working for me, so it wasn't a stretch to have them all move in. Arthur only lived here for a few months before he died—it was that quick—but by then, the living arrangement had been set."

So Inga didn't work for Emmett, but contributed to domestic chores as a roommate? Did their entire family live under Emmett's roof out of loyalty or for access to Arthur's hologram? Noa could barely process the information fast enough.

They rounded a curve and Noa could now see a white gate in the distance, with shiny metal peeking out from the peeling paint. It was the kind that blocked cars from driving from asphalt onto a trail.

"Taylor helped me upload all of his research, letters, emails, and video recordings to the servers so that we could still use his expertise, have him consult in meetings."

Noa recalled what Thomas had written in the article that went live the night WellPods were announced: *In the case of Russo-Neva, WellCorp had simply hired a replacement naval engineer under the same avatar and title.* They hadn't hired a new engineer. They had resurrected the existing one with AI.

Noa glanced at the trail map as they walked past it: FOREST PARK.

"He doesn't have the full capabilities of an Emmie—not by a long shot. He's essentially a projected trove of limited information, with the ability to react appropriately to human emotions. While he can process new information, he can't create novel thought. It's as if he's frozen the year he died, late 2057."

Noa remembered how he'd spoken in future tense and theoreticals about the Pods, how she'd attributed the error to his native language. She realized now it was because to him, the Pods were still in the future—and always would be, as was the hurricane he projected.

In retrospect, the fact that he never touched anything, never ate anything, should have been a dead giveaway, but Noa had chosen to see him as a real person and, from that moment, had never questioned that he was anything but. Why would she? Noa followed Emmett around the gate, onto a street lined with craftsman homes.

"I think I wanted you to meet him the same way we all did, as a human, before registering him as a hologram," Emmett said. Noa thought of the Turing test. Emmies, and even many of the AR projections, passed nearly a hundred percent of the time as indistinguishable from human. "I'm sorry I didn't tell you earlier."

Emmett came to a stop and looked straight at her, giving Noa the opportunity to catalog the subtle differences between Emmett and this projected version of her. The VR hadn't gotten everything right. Emmett's eyes were off, more hazel than pure green. She'd remembered because the only other person she had seen with eyes that exact shade was Maggie.

"Who else did you try to reach?" Noa finally asked.

"I'm not sure what you mean," Emmett said.

"On my first day here, you told me that you'd tried and failed to create coded messages for other Travelers besides Maggie, but that when I was fired you decided to work together to make contact with just her. Who else did you try to reach? Did you track down family members of other Travelers for help? Or was it always only Maggie?"

Noa had tried to be discerning, to go into the entire process with her eyes wide open, but she had allowed herself to be seduced by Emmett's insidious sense of authority.

"Let's keep walking. I think you'll get the answer you're looking for soon enough." It was infuriating, but Emmett was already gaining enough distance that Noa had to pick up her pace just to catch up.

They had turned off the main road and were now walking together up a small hill in silence, following the road's lazy switchback turns. To Noa's right, houses backed up against the park, staking a place amid its wilderness and laying claim to the shade from its trees. The road was getting progressively steeper, darker, and Noa felt exhausted walking up it. She'd felt awful since waking up that morning.

Emmett stopped in front of a house surrounded by a rain-worn wooden fence.

"This is the house I grew up in, where the picture I showed you this morning was taken," Emmett said. A brick path led toward the front door. "My mother used to say Mother Nature was her teacher," she added, gesturing to the tall pines that shaded the small house. "We would go to the coast every Sunday together, just to be near the ocean."

Noa knew there was no way she'd ever seen Emmett's house before, but there was something so familiar about it. Maybe it was the small shed at the end of the garage that Noa knew held Emmett's grandfather's woodworking station. She took a few steps up the path, trying to understand what it reminded her of.

17

Maggie

Zone 874, Pacific Ocean
42 Days Post-Launch

The tile near the patio door sank down just below her line of sight, spinning on its axis. When it clicked back into place, Maggie saw that it had been replaced by a treadmill belt no longer than three feet.

"Come take a walk," Emmie coaxed warmly. "It will feel good to move a bit today."

Between the bird and the state she'd woken up in, it had already felt like the longest day Maggie had spent on the Pod. She obeyed Emmie's voice in a daze, pulling her leggings over her thighs, careful to avoid her bruise, and flattening the bunched band of her underwear with her thumb hooked into the waistband.

She had known at one point that Pods were equipped with VR walks, but had completely forgotten until now. She sat on the floor to put her sneakers on. The exercise was generally reserved for older and physically sensitive Travelers, but it was only a matter of time until she entered that category, given her current state. She felt noticeably more tired this month than she had last. The past week alone had brought on a host of new symptoms. As soon as she stood and shifted her weight onto the soft, spongy surface built to cushion her steps, a handrail rose to waist height, surrounding her entirely in a ring of carbon steel.

VR goggles and haptic gloves dangled from the rim. As she slipped them on, the screen faded from black until she was standing at the base of a

As she approached the fence, Noa could see small treasures lifted from the forest tucked into the slats and placed on top of each post: a smoothed stone, an acorn, a collection of pine needles. It was exactly as Maggie had described the way Gamma decorated her river-stone columns, adorning them with sand dollars and dried flowers.

But this house wasn't in Palo Alto. It was in Portland. And she had seen firsthand, on their only visit to Maggie's home, the lot where Gamma's house had been razed and rebuilt into a sleek, earthquake-resistant mansion that went right up to the edges. Still, the coincidence felt uncanny.

She had almost succeeded in convincing herself—it wasn't so insane that two houses would be decorated with natural detritus—until she took another step toward the fence, to examine it more closely.

Tucked securely between two pickets was a feather that contained all of the colors of an oil slick. Noa leaned toward it, recognizing it as belonging to the same bird in a perpetual nosedive on her own arm.

Noa looked back at Emmett, horrified. She had been so quick to trust her, but what did she know about Emmett, *really*? She knew she was a woman who could manipulate reality so effectively you couldn't tell if a person was a person, or a place was a place. Noa turned the feather over in her hands. So many parts of Emmett's story hadn't lined up—Arthur, the hurricane, their plan, why she needed Noa, why she needed to reach Maggie of all the Travelers—yet Noa had partaken blindly.

It was as if a veil had dropped and Noa could finally see: nothing was as it seemed.

trail. The treadmill turned and adjusted its speed and incline with Maggie's movements along a path that threaded a creek like a snake, crossing over it at several points with bridges and fallen logs. The illusion felt incredibly real. Her steps kicked up pixels of gray-brown dust and the water was cold enough that a tracing of ice clung to the creek's edges. Dead pine needles gathered in its eddies. She stopped at one point, the tread slowing with her, and bent to dip her hands into the creek. As soon as she submerged them, the gloves sent an ice-water chill through her hands.

Above her, pine and aspen trees blocked out the speckled winter sun. As she walked through them, their leaves encouraged her quiet, their tissue-paper sound rustling in the wind. *Shhhh.* She walked slowly, her head still foggy, like she had been drugged. A dirt road ran adjacent to her trail, perched higher above the left bank of the creek.

Every other turn brought it back into view until the curves, at first calming, grew increasingly frustrating. She could feel the elevation gain under her feet and sensed that the trail would end with a view, but if she continued to follow the twists, it would take all the longer for her to reach it. As she rounded another turn, she saw a cascade of ice plants, so familiar to her but out of place in this environment, drawing a clear path to the road.

She cut off to follow them, carefully making her way across the shallow water to reach the road, feeling a sense of relief when the VR allowed her to forge her own path. As she batted away twigs, pushing up the sloped edge of the other bank, she marveled at the fact that she could feel them not only against her haptic gloves, but everywhere the workout wear touched her skin, against her legs and chest. The bruise on her leg throbbed lightly, a reminder of her fall the day before.

She was only a few feet above the creek now and could see it only as blurred rushing water, but the details around the jeep road were much clearer, paved with the purple-blooming ice plants on either side. She had always loved the flowers, which signified proximity to the ocean. Gamma had always told her to follow them to get to the sea, and here they were lining her path, getting thicker as she went.

As she continued along the road, she thought dumbly that she was "making good time," as if "good time" were a thing she could "make" here. The VR would last exactly as long as she needed it to, and when it was over, she would never see the trail again. She could simply remove her headset and eat lunch.

She hadn't had anything to eat besides the juice that morning and began fantasizing about what the Pod would serve her, maybe warm congee or a seeded bread with a swipe of freshly ground nut butter. She paused, cradling her abdomen. She wasn't sure, but she thought she felt the baby move slightly. She was considering exiting the program when a reflection in the distance caught her eye. The sun was bouncing off something, a car maybe? She picked up her pace, walking briskly up the road—either it was getting steeper, or she was getting more exhausted—keeping her eyes locked on the reflection until the entire object was in view.

The cabin was no larger than her old bungalow, taking up maybe five hundred square feet, but the front was made almost entirely of glass, with rough wooden logs along the sides that gave Maggie the impression that it had been crafted by hand. It sat in a meadow clearing that looked like something out of a dream or a movie and felt oddly familiar. Beyond loomed the mountainside, rising to the peak she had been so desperate to reach. All of the VR routes were coded from real locations and footage, and she wondered who had lived there. Smoke rose out of the chimney in direct contradiction to the FOR SALE sign planted outside.

The few times text had appeared in a VR simulation, it was blurred just enough that the letters were illegible, but as she got close enough to see the sign clearly, the words came into crisp, unmistakable view. She could clearly read the name of the listing agent:

Maggie Lembre Se

"What the fuck?" Maggie said to herself, unsure of what to make of the phrase Noa used to say to her. Maggie had suspected that Noa had the ability to reach her in the Pod, a sense heightened recently by the uncanny specificity of the gratitude journal prompts, but this was the first overt attempt at contact she had seen. Even the ice plants no longer felt like a coincidence. Noa's presence in this world felt completely out of place, yet undeniable. Maggie lifted her hands in front of her, as if feeling the sign would imbue it with more meaning or clarity, but as she did, they brushed something else.

She'd only felt it for a moment, on the tip of her finger, before her arm recoiled. Yet she was almost positive that she'd felt the soft surface of skin, a neck or inner wrist. Maggie froze, unable to take another step. It was the same thing she'd done as a child in her bed, when she would freeze instinctively at the threat of a creaking floorboard. Like monsters under her bed, she knew logically that the idea she had just touched something or *someone* was impossible—she was entirely alone.

She tried to steady her heart rate with a deep breath, but before she could fully exhale, she felt overcome by a desire to remove her headset. She couldn't stand the thought of spending one more moment in this made-up world. She had *felt* skin, but she couldn't be sure it wasn't one of the Pod's tricks. She lifted her headset over her eyes and stood still, allowing herself to become reoriented to her surroundings. Of course no one was there. She had probably wanted so badly to be with someone that her own mind had conjured the illusion. The line between what was real, what was created by the Pod's software, and her own imagination was so thin it felt at times nearly impossible to tell which was which.

The handrail lowered and Maggie stepped down, exhausted, grasping for the edge of the countertop by the NutriStation to stabilize herself. She had a sense that if she remained standing, she would sink into the floor too. She scooped her hands around the counter's edge and clumsily pushed herself into a seat on top of it, next to her Device.

There was no way the sign's text could be a coincidence. Every element of her experience had been designed so carefully, down to the most minute detail, that it was hard to imagine that there could be any oversight.

A soft *ping* from the center column indicted her lunch was ready, but Maggie didn't feel hungry anymore.

She picked up her Device instinctively, as she did after every exercise module to review her stats and output. Maybe there was something hidden in the numbers for her. She scanned them, but they revealed little beyond what she already knew:

Total time: 1 hour, 37 minutes
Distance: 3.2 miles
Average Heart Rate: 151 BPM
Maximum Heart Rate: 178 BPM

And then she saw it. At the top of the statistics, where Maggie usually scanned over the name of the real location the VR was set in—Norway, Northern Japan, Banff National Park—was the information she didn't know she'd been looking for:

Whites Creek, Nevada

She had felt such a sense of familiarity during her walk, she'd assumed it must have taken place somewhere she'd visited before. But it wasn't she who was familiar with the location. It was Noa.

Noa had told her countless times about the creek she lived along for two years as a child when her father served as a visiting professor in the theology department at the University of Nevada, Reno, during a brief stint away from Brooklyn.

Maggie closed her eyes, remembering the conversations they'd had about the place. Noa didn't get nostalgic often, so anytime she brought it up, Maggie asked questions, encouraging her to live in the memory as long as she could. Maggie had coaxed out descriptions of the peppery bite of the nasturtiums Noa's mom had planted in old barrels outside the house and the magical groves of aspens that dotted the public trail that felt entirely like her own. There had been a meadow behind the cabin that was an archaeological gold mine for Noa in her childhood, where she'd excavated rose quartz and even once found a rainbow tourmaline, though she later suspected her father must have planted the gem there for her to find.

The cabin and the land it sat on had always belonged to the university, donated by a late department chair for future adjunct professors to use, but when they moved, Noa mourned the loss like a family member. She told Maggie she had cried for weeks without stopping.

Maggie opened her eyes. There was no doubt in her mind that the sign and location had been selected for her to discover, but she didn't know why it was there, or why Noa had written *that* phrase. Had Noa coded it for her, like a love letter, before Maggie left? Were there other messages she'd missed?

Maggie Lembre Se, it had said.

How could she ever forget?

18

Emmett

Malibu, California
39 Days Post-Launch

It was true that Emmett's months-long captivity likely made her hyper-sensitive to the smell of another person, but when Noa arrived at the house that first morning, she brought with her such a thick animalistic stench of sweat and stress that Emmett could barely conceal her disgust. Emmett had welcomed her, regardless, ushering her in with a practiced warmth until Taylor leaned into her ear and whispered, "It's Oisín."

Emmett had been expecting his call, looking forward to it, even. She excused herself from Noa, who stood dumbly until Inga—sweet Inga—swooped in to show her to her room. From the moment Oisín funded Emmett, he had always been careful to remain two steps behind her and her company objectives, maintaining a safe-enough distance that he could claim ignorance when her ideas weren't strictly aboveboard, or legal. Until the *Technologist* piece forced him to step in, Oisín's role on the board had been largely honorific. She knew he would be less than pleased that Emmett had subverted his efforts to fire one of WellPod's lead engineers by smuggling Noa into her home, and looked forward to the satisfaction his panic would bring her.

Emmett collected herself, then tapped her wrist to the Reader in the doorframe of the control room, leaving Taylor at the door as she entered. Oisín's face took up the entire wall of screens, so that every hair in his beard, every pore and micro-expression was magnified.

"Hi, Emmett," he said, his soft tone surprising her.

"It is entirely within my right to hire her," she answered, sidestepping niceties with immediate defensiveness.

"I know," he said. He held up his palms, gesturing to disarm her. They were so large in the projection that they spanned the length of Emmett's body. "That's not why I wanted to speak with you."

Emmett walked to the desk at the center of the room and leaned a palm against its surface, straightening as she heard Inga showing Noa to her room in the hallway behind her. She had expected anger, but Oisín's eyes held pity, which was so much worse. She could hardly stand it.

"Just tell me," she snapped. "What is it?"

"Something came up in Noa's check that I think you should know about."

In the days following the keynote, Emmett had asked Oisín to use his connections at Pohvee to conduct an extensive background check on all of the head engineers and product managers on the WellPod team, in exchange for her peaceful step-down from the company. Every employee went through rigorous checks before beginning at WellCorp, but what Emmett was asking for went beyond any professional protocol. She was far more interested in the personal secrets that only Pohvee's extensive database could provide. The things people did when they thought no one was watching: affairs, well-concealed addictions, family secrets, deep-seated insecurities. It was astounding to Emmett that every single person held a concealed, dark core if you dug deep enough. Unearthing them was one thing, but understanding when and how to use them could yield more power than any other business strategy. A good founder had to be tactical and subversive, unafraid to ruin someone's life if it meant progressing the company.

Emmett had only needed to know about Noa, of course, but asked about the entire team to evade any suspicions, which Oisín was careful not to raise. Emmett knew about Noa's affair with Maya from listening in on her sessions with her Emmie, but there were still entire topics Noa never spoke about, even in the privacy of her WellNest. She would speak about her father, for example, but skirted the immediate weeks following his death, when she lived with her mother in New York. In fact, she never even mentioned her mother, which was odd for anyone—but especially so for someone who had lost their other parent.

Emmett knew what it was to be left by a father too young. Like Noa's, hers had fought to stay, but instead of losing a battle to cancer, he'd lost to Emmett's mother. Her parents had been like oil and water, Emmett the improbable combination of the two. On the morning her father finally left, Emmett woke to his careful footsteps, his body too large to navigate the squeaky stairs of her grandparents' old house undetected. He stood at the threshold, and looked back as if they had planned to meet there. The rest of their house was still fast asleep. He bent down to hold Emmett's face between his rough palms.

"Promise me you will never be like her," he had said, and Emmett understood that he meant her mother. She also knew it was the last time she would ever see him. "Promise me you'll be bigger than everyone."

When Emmett's mother came downstairs an hour later, Emmett was still standing in the open door's frame. Whether her mother had been suspecting it, or simply understood the moment she saw Emmett, she knew immediately that he was gone. She took her daughter into her arms, dampening her hair with her tears.

"I'm so sorry, my little bird," she said, using the nickname bequeathed to Emmett from her days spent reading in her nest beneath her grandfather's workstation.

When the world shut down later that year, sending everyone into collective isolation from fear of viral infection, Emmett's mother was let go from her part-time job. As with her unexpected pregnancy, she took the shift in stride, embracing the opportunity to take care of her parents full-time and further immerse herself in nature, deepening her intuitive connection with the land. Each morning she returned from her walks along forest trails with leaves, flowers, feathers, bones, and stones that she would learn the names and functions of, then decorate the house's exterior with. She loved magpie feathers in particular—the blues and greens reminded her of the ocean. Neighbors began to stop and chat from six feet away, admiring her natural menagerie. As soon as it was safe to do so, her mother started to work a few hours each week for an herbalist, learning the art of creating tinctures and natural remedies. She began to supplement the traditional Slavic dishes her parents favored with hormone-supporting recipes and ingredients grounded in traditional Chinese medicine and Ayurvedic practices she learned from books.

At the same time her mother drew from thousands-year-old traditions, Emmett heeded the echoes of her father's warning. The best way to be bigger than everyone, she decided, was to beat them at their own game. In high school, she was admitted to an accelerated course for young entrepreneurs interested in science and technology. Even then, the class was still dominated by boys, and Emmett felt like she was somehow making her father proud as she learned their language and proved her belonging there.

Emmett's relationship with her mother might have fallen apart completely, if not for the ocean. Every Sunday her mother would pack them each a sandwich made with her homemade seeded bread and drive them to the coast. They would walk for hours along the shore, even in sleets of freezing rain, both drawn by its untamable power, keeping an eye out for unbroken sand dollars and sharing their disparate wisdom, but never once speaking of Emmett's father.

Oisín was the only person Emmett had ever told about seeing her father that morning, though she'd kept his words of advice to herself even as she allowed her pain to flow out in sobs after one too many beers on a rainy night that broke that summer's heat spell in San Francisco. It was the last time she would ever drink that much—she couldn't afford to lose control in that way again.

As Emmett stood listening to him now, Oisín's words began to blur together. It was worse than she could ever have imagined, but it was her own fault. She had trusted Oisín. Then Thomas. She'd thought she could trust Noa, was even willing to look past her imperfections, but of course Noa had betrayed her too. How many fucking times did she have to make the same mistake? *No one can be trusted.* It was another of her father's lessons. Oisín was still speaking when she turned to leave the room.

Emmett walked down the hallway to Noa's door. She pushed it open quietly, her entrance concealed by the sound of the shower running. She considered confronting Noa in that moment, but the sight of the book on her bed stopped her. It was a common printing, but Emmett had no doubt it was the same one she had held decades before. She picked it up, keeping her ears peeled for the sound of water turning off, and walked over to the open window, thumbing the book's pages until they caught on the familiar piece of cardstock tucked between.

A sound like a raven's four calls, slightly quicker and sharper, called her attention up to the white breast of a bird perched on the eave of the natural hillside above the window. Emmett stood there, listening to its song. When she heard the water from the shower click off, she lingered a moment longer, reluctant to turn away.

"I promise," she whispered to the bird, then left the book on the bed and slipped out before Noa could see her.

19

Noa

The fog that had ascended the hill the day before was the only thing Noa could see out the window. It obscured the ocean and the entire campus, but parts of the sun had filtered through, reflecting against droplets to lightly saturate it in hues of pink and claret. Noa searched for a sign of the incoming storm that would hit Maggie any moment, but it was impossible to see anything beyond the thick, clouded pane.

Noa rolled her sleeve up and pressed two fingers into the flesh of her inner arm as Maggie had so many years ago, like a ripe peach. The wing of the magpie bent in as if broken. Noa held her fingers there, imagining its tiny bones, thinking of the bird she'd seen Maggie grieve for and the feather tucked into the fence at the simulation of Emmett's childhood home. Emmett saying, *She really is a wild bird*. The wing recovered as soon as Noa released it, except for two red marks where her fingers had pressed.

She had woken up in a cold sweat, after a night of endless tossing and turning at the hands of a fever, dreaming, of all things, about her mother and her childhood in Brooklyn.

Noa hated the Community Center in Greenpoint the moment she'd stepped into it: the assault of primary colors on the peeling mural, a map of the world where leering animals stood on top of their countries of origin, wasn't enough to distract her from the fact that the room didn't have a window.

Her mother gave her hand a squeeze as Noa scanned the daycare for another child to share her outrage with, but they were all blissfully unaware. A toddler compulsively pressed his sticky fingers into a button that emitted a goat's bleat from a cardboard book, while children closer in age to her drew flowers and rainbows from paraffin wax with names that imitated nature: *Sunset Orange, Forest Green, Pacific Blue.*

As her mother spoke with the daycare manager, a woman Noa remembered only from her exasperated sighs of stale breath and the silver clamshell earrings that tugged down her lobes, Noa wrapped her arms around her mother's leg to bury her head into her snow-dusted jacket. The down was perfect for muffling conversations she didn't want to hear, like when her mother explained how to administer Noa's insulin or when her parents lied about the "better life" Brooklyn's gray streets offered. What part of this room was better?

They had visited Brazil that summer—the only time Noa would ever go—and from the moment they returned, Noa had been acting out. She threw her food and screamed for her grandfather, the feral cats who would come to the door and rub against her legs, the narrow streets of Olinda, the colors that burst from every building, and her grandmother's moqueca, filling the air with the scent of garlic and coriander. Her mother cried too, though only when she thought Noa wasn't watching. It made her mother's reprimands—to *stop being so dramatic*, to *get over it*—all the more confusing. Noa began to bottle her pain at home, eager to show her mother how well she could hold it, for the both of them, but she couldn't prevent it from bubbling to the surface anytime her mother dropped her off. The daycare manager called it "separation anxiety," even though Noa felt the exact opposite.

Weeks later, the manager told her mother at drop-off that Noa's cries were too disruptive to the rest of the daycare for them to admit her. She could have told her the evening before, but had waited until morning so that her mother had to scramble to find a sub, phoning around from a park bench across the street. Noa sat cross-legged on the ground beside her, smoothing the bud of a plucked, still tight spring daffodil with the pad of her thumb, sensing her mother preferred the company of her students, who never cried, but clamored for her attention.

Shaking off her thoughts, Noa cleaned up and then headed to breakfast. She had no idea what time it was. She hadn't seen Emmett since their walk, and there had been no sign of Taylor, though she hadn't looked hard. The fever must have begun the day before—she could hardly remember getting back to her room—and either she had missed the call for breakfast, or Inga had never come to summon her, not that Noa could blame her.

The professor sat in his usual chair, as if nothing had changed. Noa walked past him to the kitchen, relieved to find a full carafe of coffee on the counter. She rested the backs of her fingers against it, gauging the time of day through its temperature, and poured herself a cup, unsure if she could stomach anything else. It was lukewarm. The chair to the professor's left was the only one that offered a view of both the kitchen and the fog-enclosed window. Noa set her coffee down, then lowered herself into the seat.

"Arthur." As soon as she said it, the light returned to his eyes and he greeted her as warmly as he ever had. Noa recognized clearly now the holographic signs that had always been there. He never moved, never touched anything, and lit up only after being addressed.

She had so many questions for him but hadn't given much thought to phrasing them. She needed to ask them before Inga stepped in, in case she put an end to them. Noa had already upset her enough. She took a sip from her coffee, feeling awful.

"Do you remember telling me," she asked, "to fear the fog?"

"Oh, my dear," he said, "I didn't mean to scare you."

"Can you tell me more about the storm?" she asked, trying to keep her voice calm.

She had always known to be afraid of the ocean's powers, of its waves, but had never considered that the real power was held in the invisible banks of wind that traveled across it.

"If my calculations are correct, it should hit the western shore of Hawai'i two to three days from now, then California."

"On what date exactly?" She suspected she knew the answer, but could barely process what it meant, even as he said it.

"Oh, I suppose"—he counted the days in his head—"December twenty-fourth, Christmas Eve."

"What year?" Noa asked, steeling herself for his response.

"Twenty fifty-seven," he responded, laughing at the absurdity of the question, even as he delivered a day years in the past.

Noa thought back to her last meeting at WellCorp. The researchers there had mentioned a storm, but off the coast of Hilo, to the east. They were talking about different storms; different levels of barometric pressure and, most importantly, damages. When Noa had spoken with the professor about the hurricane on her first morning, it had been about a much larger storm. The whipping winds Noa had seen pushing the fog were coming from the east, pushing southwest. It wasn't an indication of a hurricane, but a windy California day, the Santa Anas pushing their way to sea. If a monstrous hurricane was brewing in the Pacific, which Noa was nearly positive now it was not, the storm they were experiencing along the coast had nothing to do with it.

This entire time, he had been projecting a storm that, in reality, had already taken place. She could even remember the exact one. It was the first-ever Category 5 hurricane to survive in the Pacific for three full days, long enough to reach and badly damage parts of the California coast. She and Maggie had just moved into WellHome, so they never saw the damage firsthand.

Noa stood up so quickly her vision faded—she had to reach for the back of the chair to keep herself from falling.

"It's going to be okay," the professor was saying. "We're safe here."

He couldn't possibly understand the danger she was in, that Maggie was in, even as Noa struggled to grasp it. If the storm was smaller or, she realized, even nonexistent, what possible reason could Emmett have for Maggie's descent into the Pod?

At any moment, Maggie would find the note and follow its instructions to go into the Pod's system, written with the intention of her surviving a storm that didn't even exist.

Noa sprinted through the living room toward the control room, even as her vision wavered in and out. Blurred black edges threatened to close in completely, but she didn't stop running until she reached the door, throwing it open.

Taylor was supposed to be watching Maggie, but he was missing. On the bay of screens, Maggie was awake and speaking to her Emmie, already following the carefully laid instructions Noa had written. Was it already the afternoon? *How late did I sleep?* Noa reached under her desk to release the haptic gloves from their holder, pulling them on as soon as she had strapped the infrared LEDs to her shins.

As soon as she had the headpiece on, she was in the room with Maggie, inhabiting the Emmie's perspective.

"Maggie, it's Noa," she said into the mouthpiece, but nothing came out. She was on the verge of overriding Emmie's voice controls, but hadn't fully hacked the system yet. "Maggie," she repeated, louder, more frantic. It felt like screaming in a dream—nothing she said registered from the Emmie—though she was still able to control the Emmie's movements.

"I just need a moment," Maggie was saying as she walked toward the shelf of towels that had risen from a floor tile, following the instructions Noa had left for her. Noa felt a stirring of hope from the fact that Maggie still trusted her, was doing exactly what Noa had told her to do—but now she had no idea if she'd led Maggie correctly. Without the threat of the storm, Noa didn't understand what Emmett's motivation could be to get Maggie off the Pod, to control her actions. Noa had to stop her.

Maggie swiftly curled into the tile as Noa-as-Emmie dove to catch her shoulder, forgetting she couldn't actually stop her.

From this close, Noa could see the mix of strength and determination so clearly behind Maggie's eyes. They were the last thing to disappear as Maggie vanished into the heart of the Pod.

With Maggie gone, the only sign of movement in the Pod came from the furniture shifting to prepare for bedtime. Noa remained still for the entire process, her haptic gloves and goggles tossed to the side, as the bed emerged from the floor and the tread flipped forward, replaced by a smooth white tile. The NutriStation pinged and the door opened to reveal an evening latte. She could see every detail of the room in painfully crisp detail, but Maggie was the only thing Noa no longer had access to. WellCorp kept the inner workings of the Pod so confidential that even if cameras existed there, Noa had no idea how to access them. Even Emmies were restricted so that they couldn't function below the top level of the Pod. It was the second time Noa had let Maggie slip from her grasp.

Slowly she rolled over and brought her hands under her shoulders to push herself into standing, making her way unsteadily toward the door of the control room, afraid that if she moved any faster, she'd pass out. The fog had been so disorienting that it wasn't until she finally remembered her Device in her pocket that she realized what time it was. She had thought it was morning, maybe early afternoon, but it was already close to midnight.

Outside the room, the hallway looked longer than she remembered it being. Her mouth felt dry, and the darkness that had threatened to take over her vision earlier remained, even as she stood perfectly still, urging her racing heart to slow down. She made her way toward the end, stopping at each door to rap her knuckles against it, too exhausted to shout Emmett's name. She tried a few handles, but even her own room responded with the same blinking red light until she reached the end of the hallway.

She needed an explanation, to understand what was happening to Maggie, why Emmett had created a false sense of urgency to send her down into the Pod.

Emmett had walked down this way a few times, but now that Noa was standing at the end, she couldn't see a door. The only thing in front of her was a black wall. She leaned against it to catch her breath, but where she had expected to feel a solid surface was only air. Her shoulder smashed into the ground, and when she opened her eyes it was as if they were still closed.

It was so dark she couldn't even see her own hand, or tell which way she'd fallen from. She crawled on her hands and knees until she caught sight of a glimmer of light. It wasn't until she was completely out of the black hole that she could see she was no longer in the same hallway, but at the top of a dimly lit staircase.

Noa slowly brought herself to her feet and turned back toward the darkness. When she reached her hand into it, it disappeared completely. The inky-black swallowed it whole, like it had the hallway, making her arm look like it had been amputated at the elbow.

She descended the stairs carefully, leaning against the central column for support. Every few steps, she came across a small wooden figure embedded into the wall, each more intricate than the last. Noa passed a swan with a head bowed into its feathers, a ram with dramatic curved horns, a medallion that looked like a crest, the head of a dragon.

The dim lights illuminating each object were the only lights in the stairwell, so Noa kept her eyes trained on each figure as she made her way deeper, placing her hands against the wall and the center banister for balance. She could see the bottom of the stairs when the final figure caught her eye.

Noa stopped in front of it, then reached out for it, to hold it in her hand. It was a chess piece. She picked it off the shelf to examine it more closely. It was a near replica of the one Maggie loved, which she had collected from Gamma's apartment, only in black. Maggie had mentioned once that she had left its pair there with Gamma—she always liked the idea that they each had one. *What is it doing here?* Noa turned the piece over in her hand, too distracted to notice Emmett, watching her from across the room.

20

Maggie

"Is there any way to do the same walk as yesterday?" Maggie asked Emmie.

She was sitting on the floor of the Pod, facing the ocean and rubbing her growing belly, but her mind was back at the evening of the keynote. Applications for WellPods had opened the next morning and she'd begun hers immediately, answering every question on the written portion truthfully. At "Are you pregnant or nursing?" she was surprised when her selection of "Yes" didn't immediately disqualify her, but instead revealed a dropdown of further questions, like a Russian nesting doll: "How far along are you?" "Is the father your primary partner?" *Does your primary partner know you're fucking Thomas?* The last thing she had expected was admittance to the next rounds, the physical health and psychological evaluations.

After the Pod became a mantra to her. She would tell Noa *after the Pod.* She would begin to prepare for the baby *after the Pod.* The Pod took on a mythical role in her mind of a space where she would have room to think, to breathe, to organize her thoughts. She had no doubt that she would arrive home a month and a half later with clarity, even if it meant surprising Noa with her bump. She had hoped she wouldn't be showing, but now she knew she would be—and based on her walk from the day before, she now had reason to suspect Noa could already see her.

Even this morning's gratitude journal prompt had felt weirdly familiar. *Do you have any scars you don't remember getting?* it asked, echoing a question Noa had asked during their first year of dating.

Maggie had been lying in bed, with her palm wedged between her cheek and the pillow, as Noa traced lines between the freckles on her back. As soon as she asked it, Maggie's eyes landed on a raised scar just below the base of her hand, only slightly whiter and barely decipherable from her pale skin. She remembered sitting in an online class shortly after Gamma died, pushing the sharp end of a pen cap into a soft piece of skin between an artery and bone, patiently working it back and forth until it broke skin. She didn't stop until the pain screamed up her nerve endings, blinding enough that she thought she might pass out if she pressed on. For weeks afterward, she picked at the scab until it became a scar. She had showed it to Noa and said, "I can't remember how I got this one."

Noa's fingers had paused on their interstellar journey, mapping the constellations she called "the Milky Way." Noa was the only person besides her mother ever to call the dark freckles that cascaded into a sea of lighter freckles on her forearms that exact name. She'd rolled Maggie over by her hip, pulling her in to kiss her wrist. On some level, she knew and embraced Maggie's imperfections; yet Maggie couldn't bring herself to tell Noa about the pregnancy, even after she told Thomas the night Emmett announced the Pods.

Maggie had been grateful that the auditorium was so dark, and that her seat was so close to the exit. The room hummed in anticipation of the keynote that would finally, publicly announce the project Noa had been working on all this time. It was a project so secretive, Maggie'd had to pull details, just to learn the codename for it. "Operation WP" offered little to guess from, but Noa had slipped a few days ago and said the true name, "WellPods."

The name had initially made Maggie think of a drug capsule—everyone was looking for a way to escape, one way or another, from reality. But from the little information Maggie was able to piece together from Noa's slip-ups and Thomas's vague descriptions of his interviews, she gleaned that it was a bubble; a manufactured physical retreat. The Pod gave the general public access to what most WellCorp employees and family already had. Inside, there was no methane crisis, nuclear threat, or food shortage. But for Maggie, it would also mean no longer concealing her whereabouts from Noa or trying to collect her thoughts around Thomas. It sounded to her like paradise.

When the Pod rose from the bottom of the stage, cresting like a rising sun, Maggie couldn't help but shift uncomfortably in her seat. Noa was sitting inside with her back to the audience, wearing a white uniform. Maggie felt a wave of embarrassment for her as she stood up to retrieve her dinner, then brought her plate to a small desk, miming actions as Emmett introduced the technology.

Maggie tried to see Noa the same way everyone else did, as undeniably beautiful and ethnically ambiguous, which Maggie guessed were large factors in her selection for the task. Her makeup was designed to look like she wasn't wearing any, but it sat unnaturally on her face. Maggie had never seen Noa wear mascara, and her titanium dioxide–slicked lashes made her look like a marionette. Maggie could barely look at her.

"WellPod has everything you could possibly need to flourish for weeks at a time, even years, in one of the most isolated places on earth," Emmett said. With the exception of the awkward two-minute meet-and-greet an hour before, Noa was as close as she'd ever been to Emmett, separated by glass like an animal at a zoo.

As Noa sat to eat the dinner onstage, Maggie tried to pinpoint the moment she'd started feeling so disconnected from her own fiancée. Her mind went to the evening she'd tried to show Noa her painting of Gamma, and all the subsequent nights Noa had chosen work over her. She needed time to think. Lost in thought, she spun her engagement ring around her finger.

"They are the complete escape you've always yearned for," Emmett said, just as Maggie felt a wave of nausea so strong she had to get out of her seat.

She barely made it out of the auditorium and into the lobby's bathroom before throwing up in one of the sinks, allowing the building pressure to spill out of her. She ran the water, rinsing down what she could, then washed and dried her hands.

The nausea had been the first sign she was pregnant. When it began a month earlier, it arrived in waves, and she was lucky she'd been able to conceal it from Noa so far.

In the mirror, her eyes should have looked watery and red, but reflected back to her as dry and bright. Her skin also appeared unnaturally polished. In the corner, she noticed small text:

This SmartMirror™ is running AutoBeaut™,
a correcting system to help us see the best in ourselves.

After steadying herself with a few deep breaths, Maggie exited the bathroom and saw that people were spilling out of the auditorium. Perfect timing—the keynote must have just ended. She grabbed a glass of something bubbly off a tray and stood with her back against the wall waiting for Noa, smiling at some of the faces she recognized from WellHome's social mixers. A message came in from Noa, promising she would be there soon. She hoped she was right. She needed to talk to her. They had spent so little time together lately, Maggie felt like she was going insane.

She allowed herself a small sip from the glass intended for Noa, drinking another every few minutes. When she reached the bottom, she set it down on a roaming tray and messaged Thomas to meet her. He responded within seconds.

The crowd had dispersed like a cloud around the lobby, but Maggie was relieved to see that the paths around WellCorp's campus were nearly empty. Most people selected the most direct underground route to the main building, even on nights as beautiful as this one. Out here, the path looped lazily toward the bridge and was illuminated by small lights.

Thomas arrived a few minutes later, coming from the same direction she had. She wanted nothing more than to bury her entire body in his arms. Instead, he stood next to her at the apex of the bridge, in case anyone saw them, mirroring her posture so that their forearms rested on the handrail, both their bodies angled toward the ocean. When her hip tapped his, he pressed his side into her, making her entire body feel warm.

He picked a peeling turquoise paint chip off the rail and held it between his thumb and forefinger, passing it from hand to hand. It was still barely conceivable to Maggie that this was the same bridge she had studied in photographs of Monet's oil paintings, had never thought she would have the opportunity to see in person. For a long time, neither of them said a word, but when Maggie turned to face him, he turned toward her.

"Did you give Emmett the article?" Maggie finally asked. Thomas had always played his articles close to the vest until they were published, a superstition he'd held even in college, though Maggie knew him well enough to understand that this article was not like the rest.

"Yeah," he said, lost in thought. Maggie could tell something was weighing on him. It was part of what made telling him so hard.

"I'm pregnant," she said finally, emboldened by the wine.

A wave of shock cascaded across Thomas's face, and then he was wrapping his arms around her. She loved the way her head rested perfectly under the crook of his neck. When he pulled away, Maggie could tell he was searching her face for the emotions she so carefully kept inside. His brows were furrowed, his mouth slightly open, but his eyes darted back and forth, as if reading her expression like a book. Whatever form his face took next, Maggie knew it would mirror her own. She wanted to beam at him, to allow them both the fantasy of a clean, simple break from her life. A family of their own.

At the same time, she clearly remembered standing in the exact same spot a year and a half earlier when Noa had dropped to one knee. Her face had been so full of hope, too. Maggie wondered again what had broken. She couldn't even say for certain whether she loved Thomas more than Noa, or if she had simply been seduced by his availability during Noa's long hours at work.

Instead she said, "This isn't a good thing."

"Of course. I mean," he stumbled, his face dropping, "it isn't the most ideal world to bring anybody into, but it's possible. Things are changing."

She wasn't used to seeing him ramble, unsure of the answer.

"I can't do it to Noa, I mean."

"How far along are you?"

"Two months, I think. Still early." Though they had met a handful of times since that first night, whenever his schedule allowed, Maggie knew she had gotten pregnant from that first time they'd had sex at the house.

He took her face into his hands and kissed her. His lips rested on hers for what felt like too short a time, but nothing would have felt long enough. Her head was buzzing from the wine. Neither of them noticed the person walking down the path toward the shuttle, until they felt the bridge vibrate with the approaching steps. They pulled apart quickly to let him pass.

"What are you going to do?" Thomas asked, once the stranger was out of earshot. Then, as if she didn't understand the question, "Are you keeping it?"

"I don't know yet," she admitted. "I just need time to think." *It's still early*, she thought. *There's still the chance that this entire thing goes away.*

They stood silently for another few moments, neither of them acting like themselves. She could still terminate the pregnancy. Even though it was nearly impossible to secure an abortion off campus, it was easy enough at WellCorp, especially if she did it within the first trimester. Technically, all she needed was a pill and some pain tolerance. But she wasn't sure that she wanted that, either. She had made so few choices in her life, and always assumed she would end a pregnancy if she had one, but was surprised to realize she was leaning toward keeping the baby.

"I think I'm going to apply for the Pod." The idea came to Maggie suddenly.

"No," Thomas said, surprising her, "you can't do that."

"Why not?"

"Maggie, the article I wrote—it's all about how unsafe they are. A source literally called them 'death traps.'" Just like when he would offer edits to her college papers, Maggie felt immediately repulsed by his infringement in her decision, even if he did likely have more information than she.

Before she could change her mind, Maggie kissed him and told him she had to get back, just as headlights began to approach them. She had to be alone, needed time to think clearly. The ocean felt like the only place she could do that.

When the headlights were close enough that he squinted in their brightness, he finally nodded and said, "I'll message you."

Something in his expression was different, like there was so much more he wanted to say. Maggie walked past him. Noa would be waiting for her by now—but as she approached the auditorium, it suddenly felt impossible to head inside. She continued past it, unsure of where she was headed even as each step led her toward the ocean, allowing her flats to slip off as she reached the sand. When she was close enough that the ground felt wet under her feet, she pulled her dress over her head and waded in. She stood, letting the waves pull the sand out from under her toes until she was standing in a small hole without ever moving. Finally, she took a few steps and dove, allowing the Pacific to envelop her entirely. Underwater lights illuminated the waves she created in the murky water.

It was the feeling of isolation, inches below the breaking waves, that had cemented her decision to apply for a spot on a WellPod, even after she read Thomas's article later that night. She would need more time to think, regardless of whether she decided to keep the baby or not. She still didn't know, even as she carried Thomas's child, whether he was her future, or if Noa was. If Noa understood how lonely she was, how desperately Maggie had needed her all those nights, Maggie felt hopeful she would cut back her hours, maybe even quit. Where would they even live, though, if they ever left their WellHome?

Maggie had seen from her drives with Thomas that it was possible to live outside of WellCorp, but a key to his survival was his connection to the tech companies he covered, as well as his adaptability to scarcity— something Maggie had admittedly never experienced herself—a connection that would be severed after tonight, as soon as his article went live. Sure, a baby would mean more food rations, but there was no way to guarantee that those would be sufficient. Most of the food in LA came from outside the state after water shortages finally turned the soil into a nonviable dust bowl.

Even Thomas's home, so inviting that first night, had turned out to be an unsustainable sanctuary. He was allotted three gallons of water a day and got around the dark house with a solar flashlight at night. When the country had invested in coal, instead of wind or solar power, it was based on the false assumption that it would take millennia to run out, but even electricity was rationed now as the failing government grasped for any possible solution. Thomas had to defend his house from looters and rarely left it for anything outside of work or Maggie. It wasn't the apocalypse, but it also wasn't a world Maggie wanted to raise a baby in.

If she stayed—if Noa let her stay—she would have access to pediatricians, childcare, and the essentials like food, water, and diapers. She had seen a few children on campus, walking in lines of pairs. There weren't many, maybe twenty, so their ages were always mixed. But Maggie felt a surge of joy each time she saw the three-year-olds toddling behind the eight-year-olds. The campus had existed for just long enough that some of the eight-year-olds wouldn't remember a time they'd lived anywhere else. The first time Maggie had the thought, she was horrified, but how different was it, really, from growing up in a small village? Humans used to stay in their communities their entire lives.

The message arrived from Thomas a few days later, as promised, though from someone else's Lens. In a short video recorded and sent by a stranger, he explained that he had been excommunicated from WellCorp and his Lens ID had been blocked from reaching anyone inside campus. He was safe, and on a new assignment from an anonymous tip.

The fact that Thomas was literally banned from seeing her did little to dampen the sting. Instead of doing anything he could to sneak on campus, or set up a life for them off it, he was researching another article. Maggie struggled to reconcile how real their two-month romance had felt with the fact that he had left her again. He would be back, he assured her, but that didn't change the fact that he wasn't there now. Like the mother who had raised her, like Noa, he had chosen work over her. She had never missed Gamma more in her life.

As soon as Maggie asked for the walk, Emmie nodded, though Maggie had never requested the same exercise program more than once. "I'll set that up for you."

It wasn't long before Maggie found herself standing outside the house overlooking Whites Creek in exactly the same place she had before.

This time, she walked straight toward it, past the real estate sign with its familiar message, *Lembre Se*. The sliding doors opened easily, and Maggie realized the reason she couldn't see through the glass from the outside was that the house was filled with a thick gray smoke spilling from the fireplace. It gave everything in the room a dreamlike feel, with blurred edges. Without actually having to breathe in the smoke, she was allowed to appreciate its beauty, how it coiled, then released. Being inside gave her a thrill like she was witnessing a piece of Noa's past firsthand, the home where she had spent the happiest days of her childhood, if Maggie was right. But Maggie also understood that she was supposed to be there, that Noa had placed it there for her to find.

The room was shaped like the letter *L*, with two large, mismatched reading chairs in front of the fireplace. One was covered in a soft beige fabric, frayed at the arms as if a cat had spent years stretching and extending its claws against it. Clouds of cotton burst through the forced-open seams.

The other chair had an attached footrest that was extended all the way. A splayed book rested in an upside-down V on one of the arms. She walked toward the kitchen at the back of the house. Cast-iron pots sat on the stove, and a wallpaper runner above them, blackened from years of cooking, looked like an illustrated film strip. A jockey held on to a horse frozen in various moments of a gallop.

There were two doors out of the kitchen and Maggie got lucky on her first guess, opening it to reveal two twin beds atop shag carpeting. One looked recently slept in, but a quilt neatly covered the bed closest to the room's small window. A small needlepoint pillow rested against the yellowed, coverless one behind it, with an *N* that joined two rounded loops. Maggie thought of the little girl who had slept there, exhausted from her adventures along the creek and the meadow that surrounded it.

As she got closer, she noticed crisp white corners peeking out from behind the pillow. She picked up the piece of paper, and a haptic sensation registered on her fingertips as she unfolded it to reveal a letter. Maggie read it hungrily at first, in gulps of letters, then more slowly, until she had memorized the list of instructions it contained. The signature at the bottom contained the same letters from the pillow: *Noa.*

She rested her hand against her belly, feeling her baby move, like a fluttering of bubbles breaking at the surface.

21

Noa

Noa stood at the edge of a windowless room no larger than the control room, but much darker. The only light came from an old-fashioned fringed lamp. Its dim glow illuminated a few tables and shelves crammed within the concrete walls, all covered in books.

Emmett sat straight up in a chair against the far wall at the edge of the light's reach, her eyes softly focused on Noa. Her palms rested facedown in her lap, her fingers curled around the edges of a book. She made no acknowledgment of Noa's arrival and, despite feeling so desperate to find Emmett just a few seconds earlier, Noa suddenly felt like an intruder. She stood frozen at the base of the stairs, still gripping the chess piece from the niche beside the stairs.

"Emmett," Noa ventured barely above a whisper, "what is all of this?"

The packed room was the antithesis of the minimalism that dictated the rest of the house, and several degrees cooler.

"Noa," Emmett replied, a subtle smile planted on her lips, "come in." She lifted one hand out toward Noa, then brought it to her chest, her fingers folding into her palm like a fan.

Noa stepped over a fallen pile of books that lapped at the edge of the staircase. It looked as if they had multiplied by mitosis, slowly taking over the space of their own accord. The pain from her head obscured her vision as she made her way as carefully as she could over and around the volumes until she was just a few feet from Emmett.

She hesitated, glancing around for a chair, before sinking her weight onto a makeshift seat of hardcovers. She was so tired. As Noa settled on top of it, Emmett said, "My mother would have loved this room."

"Can you just tell me what's going on?" Noa begged, her headache throbbing behind her eyes, competing with a wave of nausea for her attention.

"I got my love of books entirely from her. She never graduated from college but knew twice as much as anyone I've ever met, and she learned it all from these."

"Is Maggie safe?" Noa tried again. Maggie was inaccessible as long as she was deep in the Pod, but Noa wanted to be in the control room in case anything happened or Maggie emerged early.

"Her favorites were memoirs. I think she appreciated how much you can learn from someone else's life. The quickest way to her heart was to open up to her, to tell her your secrets." Emmett paused thoughtfully, as if considering a question Noa hadn't asked her. "I always preferred fiction. It feels more honest. You can't trust someone to tell you the truth, but authors can't help but leave their deepest emotions in novels. Their characters are always, on some level, projections of themselves."

Noa could feel the panic in her rising as she tried to connect the person sitting in front of her with the same one she had met months earlier at the keynote. It felt almost impossible to draw a single similarity between the CEO she had admired and worked for from afar with this woman, sitting in a cave of her own making surrounded by books. If she wouldn't answer her questions about Maggie, maybe Noa could start with something smaller.

"Where are all of these from?" she tried. She loosened her grip on the wooden piece, regarding the red indents its crown left in her palm. Noa could only move one space per turn, while it seemed Emmett had been gliding across the board like the queen Noa now held.

"She didn't always approve of my choice in reading. I loved Russian philosophers and speculative thinkers like Huxley and Vonnegut, but she was always less tech-inclined." Emmett paused, then addressed Noa's question: "All of these belonged to her. I had them shipped to Los Angeles when she died."

"Who?"

"I already told you. My mother. They were covered in debris when her house collapsed in the '48 earthquake, but most of her books survived. Much more durable than—"

"I thought your mother was driving through Palo Alto, on her way home from visiting you," Noa interrupted.

"No, that's what you *assumed*. She moved when I was twenty to Northern California, and lived there until her death."

For as many times as Noa had heard Emmett share her story, she had never heard this part of it before. She didn't know why it hadn't occurred to her until now, but she must have always assumed Emmett's mother had either still lived in Portland or was tucked away in a WellHome apartment.

"Do you know that no one has ever asked me that?" Emmett said, as if reading Noa's mind.

"Asked you what?"

"What happened to my mother," she said. "I learned how comfortable people—even reporters—are with accepting a small part of a story as the entire thing, as long as it has a strong lede or confirms their own worldview. But the rest of my mother's story became irrelevant as soon as mine took off. Isn't that always the case?"

Noa's mind raced to connect the dots, to uncover the significance Emmett was hinting at.

"My mother moved to Palo Alto to be closer to my daughter."

It was as if a thousand lines of code fired in Noa's mind at once. *Daughter?*

"What?" Noa could barely manage the single syllable as she studied the expressions on Emmett's face, the mannerisms and eyes that had struck her as so familiar. The room was swaying slightly now, and she had the sensation that she was sweating through her clothes but felt removed from her body.

"Oh, you're too smart to play dumb," Emmett said, then cruelly, "I know you've put the pieces together." She let out an exasperated sigh, annoyed that she had to explain.

"When I found out I was pregnant at the end of my summer internship in San Francisco, I told Oisín, but the idea of keeping the baby was never even brought up." Emmett didn't bother to enunciate the hard *e* sound, so his name came out like *Ocean*. "We were so young, and an ambitious woman choosing a surprise pregnancy over her career was as unheard of then as it is now. I couldn't let any of my investors or business partners think that I was choosing family over my business, especially as I was just starting to lay the groundwork. Even as she became the single most important thing in the world to me."

Noa could barely believe what she was hearing, even as the pieces clicked into place. She remained quiet, wishing the pounding against her temples would stop.

"I left for LA at the end of the summer to keep the pregnancy a secret, and I don't think Oisín ever once questioned that I had taken care of things. The obsession with telecommuting, email, and our Devices became the greatest gift I could have hoped for, and I was able to work freelance and communicate all day with clients and continue coding and developing WellCorp, up until the day she was born. The only person who knew my secret was my mother. She acted as my conduit with the adoption agency in Palo Alto.

"I wanted my daughter to grow up surrounded by technology. Even then, I knew it was the only hope I had of keeping in touch with her. The adoption was closed, the only stipulation being that I choose her first name."

Magpie, Noa thought. Maggie's name was the only clue her biological mother had ever given her. It had always been sacred to her. It was the reason, Maggie had told her after they began dating, that Noa's tattoo made their meeting feel destined.

"My mom moved next door to the family, to Maggie, as they called her. I didn't ask her to, and my daughter's adoptive parents never put together the connection, but it turned out to be a sort of gift. Maggie loved my mother like a grandmother, which of course she was, and I received daily reports from her, read the same books Maggie did, watched her friends' Pohvees. And I truly thought that was all I would ever need."

Emmett paused, then said, "I know you're thinking I loved her less than a real mother should. That a real mother would never abandon her daughter like that. But most mothers can only dream of the access I had to her. I could be everywhere. My mother never fully understood—she always disavowed technology, preferred to control the narrative and my access to my Magpie, but I was far more present than even her adoptive mother ever was. You said it yourself."

Noa thought of the photo Emmett had shown her. She had seen photos of Gamma, yet had missed the resemblance in the younger photo of her holding Emmett as a baby.

"I could never have known my own mother would be taken from us so soon, but I always knew she wouldn't be there for Maggie forever. I built WellNests for everyone, but added Emmie as a way to look after Maggie once my mother was gone, to communicate with Maggie as an intermediary for me. When my mother died, I was able to rush the production of a few betas, to get a WellNest into Maggie's home through her parents' connections."

Noa remembered Maggie describing her first experiences in the Nest, how it had taken time for her to trust her Emmie, then how quickly she began to take Emmie's advice on nearly everything: It had been her Emmie's suggestion that she move to LA after college. That she work at the gallery. Her Emmie had even encouraged her to go to the farmers' market the day she met Noa, to apply to be on a WellPod.

"Did you set us up?" Noa asked, even though it sounded ridiculous.

Emmett shook her head. "I wish I could take credit for that, but you were a surprise, Noa, a gift. When you came into our lives, it finally gave me a clear way to bring Maggie closer to me." Noa's own Emmie had made suggestions too: she'd brought the job listing to Noa's attention. Noa had been naïve enough to believe that, out of thousands of qualified candidates, she'd landed the position because she was the best.

"My job . . ." Noa said dumbly. Her mind felt so foggy.

"I'm not saying you didn't deserve the role, but a recommendation from the founder certainly gives one a competitive edge. When Maggie moved into WellHome, I suddenly had so much more access to her, not just when she was in a Nest. I could finally mother her."

"Why didn't you just tell her?" Noa asked.

"I always wanted to, and nearly did a thousand times, but it never felt like the right moment. We were launching WellNests, Injectibles, Lenses, the Pods, and"—she paused—"I was afraid of what would happen. I had everything to lose—not just the company, but her. It's incredible how much she takes after me. We both have that side of us, the side that would be content to swear off all technology, to go Analog—we get that from my mother. It was always my worst fear, that Maggie would go Dark."

"Out of anger toward you?"

Emmett nodded. It was strange to hear her say that word. *Analog.* It was the first thing Noa had thought of when she stepped into this room, filled with art forms from decades past. Emmett's company had been built with measures that eliminated mess, replaced books, and perfected home technology, yet here she was in a room that practically embodied the Analog movement, with its disavowal of modern technology.

"I was afraid," Emmett continued, "that if I told her the truth, it would be the last time I ever saw her, so I built a house of cards around her, to protect her and curate a happy life."

It wasn't so impossible to understand. Hadn't she done the exact same thing to Maggie? Noa had lied to her countless times for the sake of protecting her. At least, that's what she'd told herself. Emmett turned over the book she held in her lap. It was the book Noa had hidden behind her WellNest: *Song of the Lark* by Willa Cather.

"I was reading this when I was pregnant with Maggie. I learned early that she was a girl, and it helped to imagine her as a wild bird when I knew I couldn't keep her. I marked the passages that reminded me of her, then gave it to my mother as a gift along with the bracelet I had engraved with our initials."

Noa turned over the bracelet, still clasped around her wrist, that Emmett had commented on her first day at the house. Its gold plaque now faced up. She regarded the text she had confused with a word, reading it now as initials: *ENMESH.*

"Emmett Neal, Magpie Endsall . . ." Noa began slowly.

"And Sansa Hîncu, or Gamma, as Maggie knew her." *Three generations, enmeshed.* Emmett opened the book and began reading from a marked passage: ". . . *the arrow-shaped birds swam all day long . . . The only sad thing about them was their timidity; the way in which they lived their lives between the echoing cliffs and never dared to rise out*—"

"Why did you let her on the Pod?" Noa interrupted. The bracelet felt hot against her wrist, and her brain felt like she had to swim through mud to put the pieces together.

"Oh, Noa." Emmett's face was lined with false pity as she closed the book and looked up.

"You tried to stop them from going out," Noa insisted. "You knew it was unsafe."

Noa recalled the messages she had read between Emmett and Oisín on the Device. *doesn't this feel a bit fast?*, Emmett had written. Oisín was the one to ignore her caution: *It has to be now.* Except maybe not—

"That was Oisín. Everything you read was true but"—Emmett paused, as if searching for the word—"doctored. That conversation took place, but I switched our names. Oisín was the one begging me not to send the Pods out, but I always knew they were perfectly safe. I was able to convince him in the end though, or rather Arthur was, and Oisín was all too happy to have his concerns allayed. At the end of the day, his primary motivation has always been profit—that part was true." Noa thought back to the messages, how the hurried grammar and typos were so unlike the way Emmett messaged her. Emmett had everyone eating out of her hand.

"But they clearly aren't safe. And Arthur was *dead* at the time he convinced Oisín." Noa knew now that the storm wasn't real, or at least that it had been exaggerated. She almost didn't want to ask her next question, for fear of the answer. "What's inside the Pod, Emmett?"

Emmett had convinced Noa, and appropriated Maggie's trust in her, to send Maggie into the lower levels under the guise of bringing up the emergency safety equipment stowed within: a personal flotation device, shortwave radio. If she wasn't heading into the Pod for her survival, what was Emmett *so* insistent Maggie go down there for?

Emmett smirked. *Is she enjoying this?* The cruelty felt unwarranted—as if she was punishing Noa, but for what?

"I loved Oisín," Emmett began as Noa tried to remain patient, "and I really believed he loved me. When I gave him the chance to be Maggie's father, he didn't take it. But he was always a *perfect* father to his sons, the perfect husband to his wife. She made none of the sacrifices I had to, but had everything I never had. Lived on the campus I built, used the products I created."

Emmett looked perfectly calm, but something was off about her. Just below the surface.

"One thing that has never changed is people's discomfort with a single woman in power. I knew I'd have to act quickly if I ever wanted to have a real relationship with Maggie, so I pushed for the production of the Pods and increased your access to them, your understanding of how they work."

"You imprisoned her so you could have a relationship with her," Noa said, wanting to be wrong.

"Maggie was desperate for a place to go"—Emmett's tone had suddenly shifted, anger pooling into the cracks of her calm demeanor—"a moment to breathe. If you remember, Noa, she practically begged for your approval to go. I *wish* I had this opportunity when I was her age. I'm giving her—all of the Travelers—the chance I never had. A do-over, a rebirth."

"You're insane." Noa could feel her heartbeat quickening, the pounding in her head getting louder.

"Oh, *I'm* insane?" Emmett sounded more manic by the second. "*You* helped me reach her, *you* helped me gain the trust that would embolden her to see the rest of the Pod, to understand how long she can truly live there."

Noa swayed, catching herself just before falling off the books she was still perched on.

"You already know there's no storm," Emmett said, "at least nothing large enough to do any damage, but that doesn't mean there won't be more things that can hurt her."

"What are you saying?"

"The safest place for her, and my grandchild, is on the Pod."

"You never wanted to help her off. . . ."

"It's the only place she can't be hurt, that I can finally *help* her, *be* with her."

"Even without a storm, WellCorp will be bringing them home soon. The six weeks is nearly up."

"Yes, but Maggie was never on the map of Travelers. I thought you would have noticed that. When it's time to bring the Pods home, I'll be out there, with her."

"Someone will find her," Noa said. Even though the storm wasn't as large of a threat as she'd understood it to be, the Coast Guard had been alerted to ensure the Travelers' safety. Although . . . was it possible that Taylor planted the false storm warning in the meeting? Now that Noa was pulling the thread, everything was unraveling. She thought of the news clip she'd seen at Emmett's that first day, realizing it could have been fabricated too.

"The ocean is larger than you can imagine. The chances of coming across a Pod in the middle of the Pacific . . . not to mention that they're coded to escape the path of larger vessels—for safety, of course. They're slim, at best."

"You can't just keep her out there forever." This entire time, Noa had been counting down the days until Maggie's return. It was news to her that Emmett hadn't been doing the same.

"Not forever," she said. "I'll bring her back through the Pod's manual navigation system as soon as she and the baby are stable."

No. Noa could barely believe what she was hearing.

"You're planning on allowing her to give *birth* on the Pod?" Noa felt like she was shouting, but the words came out like a whimper.

"Maggie deserves to be with her true family." Emmett folded her hands in her lap, the way she had when she explained WellCorp's health initiative to Noa her first night there. Noa shifted in her seat, feeling less and less stable on the books. "She needs her mother."

"I *am* her *true* family." Noa's voice came out ice-cold. Her mind was spinning. Where did she fit into this equation?

"They say family history always repeats itself. My mother's father—my grandfather—isolated himself from the family when they immigrated to the United States. He never even spoke the same language as my mother. Though he had his reasons, my father left us as soon as he could, and Maggie never knew her father—her real father. We were all women raised by women, so I was thrilled when Maggie met you, when I saw the potential for a nuclear family entirely made of women. It felt too good to be true. You seemed to genuinely care for her. I allowed myself to imagine what life would look like, how we could all come together as a family, once Maggie got over the initial shock of meeting me . . ." She paused. "But I know now that was wishful thinking."

Emmett leaned forward, leveling her eyes with Noa's before continuing, "You hid it better than most, but you also made a lot of lazy mistakes—not that I judge you for that, affairs cloud judgment. But you called her from WellNests, met on campus where your Injectibles could track you, and you both spoke to your Emmies about each other. I saw you with her the night of the keynote. Did you know that? You held her hand while Maggie waited for you. It was almost sweet, how obsessed you became with Maya. But how could you abandon Maggie like that? She loved you. I really thought you two would make it."

She and Maya had been smart enough to meet in areas that even Well-Corp's ubiquitous cameras didn't have access to, but Noa had spoken to her Emmie about the rising tension between them, the guilt she felt about cheating on Maggie with their best friend, the inarguable connection she felt with Maya.

"You know, at one point I thought Thomas was the answer. Their connection was brief but real," Emmett was saying. "It's been that way since they were teenagers."

Maggie had met Thomas at nineteen, the same age Emmett had met Oisín. Both Emmett and Noa had been left by their fathers too young. Even in her state, Noa could see that this was more than just a mother protecting her daughter. This was a mother correcting all the mistakes she had made in her own life by manipulating her daughter's. All mothers were guilty of it, but this was another level.

"You brought him back," Noa said, piecing it together. "You brought Thomas back into Maggie's life." It had always seemed too convenient that he had appeared on campus to write about WellCorp. Where was he now? Noa knew from the news coverage after the keynote that he was last spotted in a WellCorp security vehicle, then nothing.

"I did. Until he betrayed me," Emmett said. Thomas had turned his back on Emmett when he wrote the *Technologist* piece. She continued, "What Thomas did was unforgivable, and I took care of him, hooking him with an 'anonymous tip' that I knew he wouldn't be able to resist, or prioritize Maggie for.

"You know, I'm so tired of hoping people will do the right thing." Emmett stood. She was no longer looking at Noa but gazing beyond her, transforming into the Emmett who gave keynotes and interviews. She spoke to an invisible audience as she walked back and forth, stalking her prey. "I tried. I really tried, but who is there to trust but myself? Oisín was right. The Pods offer a unique environment clear of variables, of people. I wanted to help people, but what's the point of all of this technology, all this money, this power, if I can't use it to help myself and my family?"

Noa had no idea what Emmett was talking about. *What is she going to do to me?* Noa stood up, knocking over the pile of books she'd been sitting on as she backed away. She had never seen this side of Emmett and it was beginning to scare her. Her disillusionment verged on psychosis.

"Maggie and I have both made mistakes, but we've never stopped loving each other." Noa meant to sound bold, but her words tumbled out defensively. She was begging Emmett now, but hadn't she proven she would do anything for Maggie, just as Maggie trusted Noa enough to follow her blindly into the Pod? In spite of their faults.

"Yes, you both did, which is why I considered looking past your little tryst." She turned to look at Noa, her eyes blazing. "I brought you here, didn't I? Even arranged for *her* to be the one to send you off. My plan was to build a relationship with you, have you help out with the code and feel like you contributed to saving Maggie, have us all live under one roof as a family, which I believe is worth protecting. But that was before I learned what you did, just in time, really—the day you arrived. And thank God." Emmett sat back down with the serenity of someone who knew she had the upper hand.

Noa stiffened. What did she know?

"It's big of you, Noa, to sit there and judge me for being a less-than-perfect mother. To talk about family and loyalty, when you stabbed yours in the back."

It had been over twenty years since Noa had made the worst mistake of her life—the two minutes that would change everything—but even then, the only way to trace anything back to her was the anonymous tip she had made in a moment of hormone- and grief-fueled anger. It was so blindingly shameful she could still barely stand to face what she had done. Not a day had gone by that she didn't feel terrible about it, but she had been so young and desperate.

"I can see you're surprised. Maybe you thought you could keep your secret hidden. And maybe you could have, if Pohvee had been invented even a year later. But it was there, and it captured everything."

Noa searched through the layers of pity, concern, and anger on Emmett's face as she tripped over another pile of books, her reflexes reacting too slowly to break her fall. A paperback cushioned the blow as her side hit the ground.

"I didn't—"

"No, *you* didn't have one then, but with Pohvee, well, it's easy to forget now that Oisín's first major client, before it became a social media device, was the US government. Every soldier, officer, and government employee was outfitted with that first prototype that year. The little teardrops worn at their hairlines replaced body cameras and maintained at least the illusion of accountability. Pohvees began recording and cataloging every act of violence, every trigger-happy cop, every act of corruption, every call made to emergency services that year. Including yours."

Everyone was talking about accountability back then. The entire country was coming out of two decades of being collectively gaslit by deep fakes and opinion programs parading as "news" in the lead-up to the '36 presidential election. Unalterable, live-streamed trust became a bipartisan priority, which was exactly what Pohvee delivered. Only Noa had never realized it could be used against her until Emmett hit play on the recording.

Noa's own voice, twenty-four years younger, flooded her EarDrums. "Make it stop, Emmett," she begged, but the sound of past-her only grew louder, and suddenly she was back on the fire escape of their Brooklyn apartment, speaking into her Device.

The man in their kitchen that morning, Isaac, never left after that day. Instead, he had manipulated Noa's mother for weeks with stories about the airplane hangars he worked in and his access to private jets that ran on electricity and could take her wherever she wanted to go. Noa gathered that he had once worked as ground crew at Newark Airport, unloading luggage from commercial aircraft, before the entire air travel industry collapsed in on itself from climate change, gas prices, and greed. Her mother was too strung-out on the steady stream of uppers he gave her to see through his lies.

It was easy to blame Isaac for what happened next, but the kindling had always been there waiting for a spark from the already volatile nature of their relationship. Noa made the call on the heels of her biggest fight with her mother. It had taken on the same themes of every argument they'd had since Isaac disrupted their fragile, unspoken peace: another mention of Brazil, a wounding comment, hurled words that escalated until exhaustion finally won out. But on this morning, Noa had shouted the words that would haunt her the rest of her life, "Fine, you want to go to Brazil? Let's get you back there."

In the recording, she heard herself spell her mom's name, then repeat the address of their apartment. Her parents had never legally married—the prejudice against immigrants and the bureaucratic hoops so heightened at that point, it felt pointless to even apply for citizenship. Noa's mom had flown beneath the radar for decades, but the government in office at that point had been consumed by what the media was calling "deportation fever." Noa could hear the agent in the recording thanking her. Had she been aware then what an unforgivable mistake she had made? Or did it only hit her the next week when two Homeland Security officers arrived at their door to take her mother away? She would never forget the look of betrayal on her mother's face, could never know if she really wanted to leave, or even if she had ever made it to Brazil. Noa wanted to believe she was happy, though she'd never heard from her mother again.

"Terrible, isn't it?" Emmett said as the recording clicked off.

Noa struggled to get up, but couldn't. It was as if weights had been strapped to her and were pulling her down toward the floor.

"What are you doing to me?"

"I'm surprised you didn't catch on earlier," Emmett said, almost bored. "You're in an advanced stage of hypoglycemia."

Noa let out a small sound. *My insulin.*

"It was easy, really. I changed your normal biometric parameters of insulin levels so that your patch has been feeding you a dangerous dose of insulin over the past several days." Emmett delivered the diagnosis as calmly as a disaffected doctor. "It's easily treated with glucose, but without it, you'll enter into a coma. From there, your brain will be deprived of the nutrients it needs to survive, causing irreparable damage to your cerebral cortex after about fifteen minutes. Left untreated, it's lethal."

"Wh-what?" Noa stuttered, her wooziness confirmation of Emmett's diagnosis.

"I've been altering your doses of insulin, Noa. People used to do it with insulin pumps, which isn't advisable since it's far from a perfect crime and the effects of hypoglycemia are easily diagnosed, but who would report you as missing? As far as your manager is concerned, you were fired for your little outburst. I imagine Maggie won't care that you've vanished as soon as she learns about your affair with Maya. Didn't you have some idea that something was wrong?" Emmett asked.

It was true that Noa had suspected something was off the past few days, but it was just an additional inconvenience she couldn't deal with. All of her attention had been directed toward Maggie. She had never stopped loving her, had let herself imagine a future where they forgave each other and moved on. But that hope for the future felt more distant, more impossible with every passing second.

Noa had let herself believe that she and Emmett were a team, that she had some control over the situation, even as she sat in the palm of Emmett's hand. She pushed herself onto her elbows, leaning against one of the tables until she was standing, and peeled the patch off the back of her arm. Noa moved slowly toward the door, her vision coming in and out as she braced herself against the table. She could make it, she could get to Maggie, just as long as she kept moving toward the exit.

"It's no use, Noa." Emmett's voice had shifted into something more comforting. "You're too late for whatever your plan is. Mine was put into motion before you ever had a fighting chance."

Noa fought the weight of her eyelids coming down. She just needed to rest for a moment, to gather her strength before ascending the staircase. Before telling Maggie how much she loved her. How sorry she was. How hard she had tried to save her and bring her home.

She slumped down and rested her forehead against her forearms, positioned unevenly on a stack of books, tilting her head so that she could still see Emmett, who was now stepping past Noa toward the staircase.

Her eyelids felt so heavy. She curled her knees into her chest, then let them fall to her side. Something in her hand caught her eye. A chess piece. Her head fell to the side and an empty chair came into her line of vision. She remembered the chair, but could no longer remember what she had to do.

The back of her hand lay against an open paperback. *Yours, O,* the blurred inscription read. *Yours,* the word lodged in her mind. *Yours, yours, yours.*

She was falling asleep, but had the sense she was supposed to stay awake. For what?

Yours, yours.

Noa let the heaviness seduce her into darkness, thinking again of the day she'd spent in the park with her mother. She wished so badly she could go back and sit there together until the daffodils unfurled.

Breath

22

Maggie

Zone 874, Pacific Ocean
43 Days Post-Launch

Dear Mags,

There are a lot of things you don't know and clearly a lot of things I didn't either, and the worst part is: I can't tell you everything quite yet, but right now we need to trust each other.

Maggie had stood in the re-created cabin holding the letter, not quite understanding what she was reading, even the third time through.

I need you to follow these instructions to ensure you and the baby remain safe.

"You and the baby," she'd written.

Please trust me. I love you.

The rest of the letter had included instructions to exit the simulation and head into the underbelly of the Pod as soon as possible. There were seven lower sections built into the Pod's below-water galley, but she only had to get to the fifth, which was supposed to be encouraging? Maggie had always known she lived in only about ten percent of the Pod, but had barely given any thought to the other ninety. She imagined it as an endless room of wires and servers, with food supplies and mechanisms that could make lattes, organize and deliver medicine, wash and fold laundry, and make her bed. As long as those things continued happening, she didn't need to dedicate much time to wondering how. She'd felt the pull to pack for a trip, but didn't even know the first thing she would bring—the instructions suggested she could be in there for as long as two days.

Noa had asked Maggie to trust her, as she always had. So much had changed between them, and she wasn't sure where their romantic relationship stood, but Noa's quiet confidence had been the first thing to draw Maggie to her. Trusting her, even now, felt as easy as breathing. She knew she would follow the letter's instructions.

Even as she defied her Emmie and squeezed herself into the shelf, the reality didn't hit her until, for the first time in forty-three days, Maggie didn't recognize her surroundings.

The shelf came to a stop at half the height of the room, so that it hovered in midair. Maggie unfolded herself and hopped down just as a small robotic crane, maneuvering on wheels efficiently through the tightly packed space, shoved more folded towels into the shelf she had just inhabited.

Her landing had been padded with something soft, which Maggie now realized was her bed, stored beneath the Pod's smooth floor. She scrambled aside as the crane, which included two robotic arms attached to a torso, rolled past her, reaching down to pull the edge of the duvet smooth.

The room was like an upside-down version of the one she had inhabited every single day, a holding space for the furniture she wasn't using. Her stationary bike hung suspended on a smooth white tile, poised to flip into a ready position at any moment.

She heard the familiar low hum of a tile opening directly above her. Its wide mouth gaped, allowing in light as her bed began to ascend into the Pod's main room. Everything had changed, yet the Pod was still going through the same motions.

She hopped off the bed as it rose, glancing up through the hole in the ceiling into the room that had been her entire world for weeks. Maggie would be back, but for now, there was nothing left to do but follow Noa's instructions: make her way down into the Pod, one level at a time, until she reached the Emergency Supply Hold. The fact that the Pod's engineers had made the supplies so inaccessible indicated how remote they'd considered the potential need to actually access them.

It felt unnatural to no longer be able to see the ocean, which had been her grounding point for the past month, changing colors from gray to blue to black, and moving so quickly under the Pod she probably never saw the same drop of water twice. But it had always been the same, a constant she could rely on as cells divided in her own body to create an unknown.

The crane was busying itself a few feet away, arranging and rearranging something Maggie couldn't quite see. She moved closer to the shelves, which formed a circle around the column that extended down from her room like a chimney. A soft blue light emanated from each panel of the shelves, which Maggie could see held tiny capsules and bottles, several of which were connected to IV bags that hung from the center, overlapping like scales. The crane picked up a vial, completely unaware of, or at least unconcerned by, Maggie, who was moving toward it slowly.

She touched one of the vials, etched with a barely legible name, and lifted it from the soft, refrigerated crater embedded into the shelf to get a better look; instantly the blue light that had bathed everything in the room turned red. The crane turned to face her, and she quickly set the container down, nesting it as well as she could back into place. Maggie ducked as the crane reached out a claw that resembled a human hand, but with seven fingers instead of five, and delicately nestled the vial back into its hold. The shelf turned blue again and the crane moved away unconcerned, as if Maggie had never disturbed its order.

The word on the vial was one Maggie didn't quite recognize, but sounded like a type of medicine from its suffix. She leaned in toward the shelf, close enough to see the labels without picking up another, and saw that every one of them contained a different word, connected to the thin tubes Maggie guessed were a sort of drug delivery system, attached some-how to the IV she had used ten feet above.

A few feet away from her, partially obscured by the curve of the shelves, the crane delicately picked up a vial from a row and brought it toward the NutriStation column, a narrower version of the column in the upper Pod.

With one hand, the crane pressed a button at the top of the Nutri-Station and the door opened, revealing her evening latte in her usual mug. It felt disorienting, like running into a familiar face in an entirely new context. The crane uncapped the vial and poured its contents into the steaming latte, discarding it into a trash chute beside the NutriStation. A metal rod appeared from the side of the Station's interior to stir the drink, as the door closed. In just a few seconds, it would appear from an almost identical door, a few feet above, ready for Maggie. She could envision herself in an alternate reality opening the hatch with the click of a button and receiving the drink, as she had every night in the Pod.

The crane had already moved on, busying itself with some other do-mestic duty Maggie had benefited from, but never actually seen before. She walked back to the shelf containing the medicine, from which the crane had taken the vial. The labeled vials on either side of the empty spot simply said EVENING LATTE.

She picked one up, this time unsurprised when the shelf glowed red, and turned it around. The etchings on the back were almost too small to read, but Maggie could just make out the ingredient list: doxylamine succinate, and cannabidiol. Sleep aids, Maggie assumed. There were no quantities, but Maggie knew it couldn't contain too much, since she had never felt groggy, just relaxed. She wondered how she would feel tonight, her first time without the medication in weeks. A part of her wanted to reach back into the NutriStation and retrieve the latte, let it bring her back to the warm, naïve comfort she'd found in her Pod.

She replaced the vial, which summoned the crane to come back to fix it as she made her way to where it had been standing. It was darker here—the light from the shelves was the only light in the room—but she could make out that it was some sort of washing station for laundry and dishes. A soft *ping* from the NutriStation alerted the crane, which retrieved the untouched latte.

Maggie watched as it turned the mug upside down, pouring the untouched liquid down a drain, then placed it onto a conveyer belt to be washed.

The baby kicked and Maggie made a soft "Oomph," looking down to hold her abdomen. She could hear the soft beat of a heart, just out of sync with her own, but she wasn't sure where it was coming from.

When she looked up, the crane was angled toward her, as if looking at her. Maggie backed up, the spell of curiosity broken, suddenly afraid that the machine could see her after all. In an erratic but swift motion it began to move, spinning toward her. She backed away, tripping clumsily over her own feet, throwing her arms behind her just in time to brace herself.

She heard the crash before she could see where it was coming from. Her palms plummeted through the thin, intricate shelves, passing through them as easily as paper, as the painstakingly placed vials plummeted to the ground, uncapping around her like tiny glass water balloons. The pillowed IV bags hanging from the column broke her fall. She recovered quickly, pushing herself off and away from the near-disaster she'd created. Aside from the sharp pain coming from her bruised thigh, she was unhurt—the vials and shelves were made from shatterproof plastic.

The crane was moving so quickly to fix the mess it looked like it was short-circuiting, and maybe it was. Maggie didn't have time to think. She had to get out of this strange world, to move on to the next one before it collapsed around her.

She ran past the washing station toward the orange PVC pipes she had spotted earlier, which folded back and forth into themselves to form a ladder. As soon as she touched them, a hatch below her opened. She scaled the pipes down into the blinding light below.

23

Noa

Location Unknown

[Device cannot be accessed.]

24

Maggie

Maggie squeezed her eyes shut to give her pupils a chance to contract against the bright light that filled them as she descended the ladder, away from the chaos that had ensued on the level above. This level was taller, but slightly narrower, so it took her feet longer to hit the ground. She estimated she was about thirty feet below the surface of the ocean. When she was finally able to open her eyes fully, she found herself staring straight at a vine growing out of the wall like a parasite.

She leaned in to examine it, parting the green leaves with her fingers to uncover the fruit that lay hidden beneath. Fluorescent lights lined the underside of every shelf, and she could see now that they were all stocked with food: flowering, growing fruits and vegetables, but also containers of premade smoothies and soups, canned ground meat, feta suspended in oil. Above her, the trapdoor had sealed, containing the cold air that recirculated through the room, maximizing the survival of everything but bacteria inside it.

She hugged her arms around her bare shoulders, freezing in the refrigerated room. The sound of the steady heartbeat was louder on this level, though she still couldn't identify the source of its rhythmic, dull thump. She released a hand to grip one of the leaves between her thumb and forefinger, plucking it from its stem with a gentle tug, then turned it over to expose its soft underside. She pressed the leaf between the heels of her palms, crushing the delicate trichomes against her hands, as if casting a spell to summon a memory.

"Nature's perfume," Gamma would say anytime they passed by a gardenia or rose, or while leaning over one of her garden boxes. She only grew edible plants with smells she loved so she could enjoy them three times, she'd say, admiring their beauty, their smell, and finally their taste. She'd pressed dried petals into cookies and folded roses into saffron rice. Her garden had overflowed with so many plants that Gamma spent the majority of her time outside cultivating them, then cooking and preserving them.

As a child, Maggie had asked her mother how old Gamma's garden was. They'd been eating breakfast at the kitchen counter while watching Gamma lean over a raised planter with a small trowel.

"Who, Sansa?" her mother asked. She rarely acknowledged Maggie's honorary name for Gamma. "I guess around eight years," she'd said after giving it some thought, "she moved into her house a few months after we brought you home."

The answer had surprised Maggie. Everything about Gamma's house had felt as timeless as a fairy tale, especially her garden. Maggie had expected her mother's estimation to be measured in centuries, not years. She couldn't wrap her head around the idea of Gamma living anywhere else but her home with the river-rock columns and flower beds bursting with overgrown but well-tended blooms.

She'd never once thought to ask Gamma where she came from, but after that day she asked time and time again. Each time, Gamma would offer some unsatisfactory response, though sometimes she would describe glimmers of a place not far from where they lived.

Maggie cupped her palms over her face, breathing the scent of the hydroponic tomatoes into her lungs, pushing the air down as if the more she breathed in, the closer she would be to Gamma's garden; the farther she'd be from here.

It was the first time, Maggie realized, that she had smelled a tomato vine since moving to WellHome. How could she have gone so many years without realizing the absence of such a simple pleasure? She had the sense she had been that way, sleepwalking, for many years and was just now waking up. The smell ignited a flashback of being in Gamma's garden. She must have been three, maybe four years old. In the memory, the fluttering leaves unfurled above and in front of her, and she could see a cascading cluster of small green and yellow tomatoes. A hand materialized and plucked one of the yellow tomatoes off, its stem yielding with a firm tug. A woman crouched beside Maggie, her face coming into view.

"Here, have the first tomato," the woman had said. "I'll have one too."

The woman placed one into Maggie's chubby palm as she popped another into her own mouth, smiling at the sensation of the sun-warmed fruit bursting between her teeth. Maggie was still holding hers when the woman lifted her up into her arms and began to carry her down the street. When they reached the end of the block, the woman squeezed Maggie close, then released her, leaving her alone on the corner without a word before briskly walking away. And then, as if it had never happened, she was back in Gamma's arms. The only evidence that anything had taken place was the crushed tomato in Maggie's hand, smashed into a sticky mess of seeds and goo. She remembered that she had been inconsolable, crying even after Gamma showed her all the others still on the vine.

A crane glided through the room, picking tomatoes beside Maggie and trimming basil leaves as another stood by the NutriStation's column. At first it looked like they were working in tandem, but the longer she stood watching them, the more obvious the patterns of their routine became, and a delineation of power emerged. One was clearly the assistant to the crane closest to Maggie, which was situated at a ring that protruded from the base of the NutriStation at about hip height, a prep station. It was the smallest, but also the tidiest kitchen Maggie had ever seen.

It didn't contain a single traditional appliance. Instead of hands or claws, like the crane one level above, these cranes' hands rotated through appliances. Maggie watched as the sous chef, as she dubbed it, dropped the tomatoes into a basket at the end of the primary chef's arm, followed by herbs. As soon as a bit of salt was added, the basket crushed the tomato mixture and added it to a pot that had protruded from its abdomen. It mixed the pot with a silicone spoon at the end of another arm, as the sous plucked frozen ground turkey from a shelf and placed it into a drawer that emerged from its own abdomen, then removed it, thawed, a moment later to add to the simmering tomato mixture.

Every movement was so perfectly timed, Maggie felt like she was watching a ballet. On impulse, she plucked one of the small yellow tomatoes off the vine, closing her eyes to taste it before moving on.

As she skirted the two culinary cranes, they remained too immersed in the meal preparation to notice the recipient of their efforts slipping past them, toward a thin strip of shelves that didn't contain any food.

It was hard to believe this entire production was intended for her alone, and once again she hesitated. As much as she trusted Noa, how well could she guarantee that Noa understood the situation, really? How could Maggie be sure Noa's instructions were the safest move? Noa had never even stepped onto her Pod. She felt a pang at betraying Emmie too. She'd known her for decades, nearly three times as long as she'd known Noa, and had never once contradicted her advice.

She placed her hands against the empty shelves, comforted by the fact that on either side of her was far more food than she would ever be able to eat in months, or even a year. She curled her fingers around the shelf and the floor opened below her, slowly enough that she had time to secure her feet upon the ladder's rungs. As soon as it was fully open, she began scaling down the shelves, moving swiftly down each rung into the warm air below.

For the first time since she had descended, Maggie knew where she was. She had heard Noa talk about it enough times to understand she now stood in the room that was responsible for everything—the programmed dance of the cranes cooking dinner, the refrigeration, organization, and administration of not just the food but the medicine, all of Emmie's actions. The servers were among the most sophisticated ever built. They contained everything, and communicated it all back to campus.

Though WellCorp's engineers had nicknamed it "the heart," it felt much more akin to a brain. Maggie was careful not to touch a thing as she maneuvered herself through the banks of servers, delicately stepping over the wires that connected them, consolidated in thick tubes that wound around the machines like a black snake.

As she sidestepped the banks, Maggie felt a wave of tenderness well in her. Noa had been a key part of the team that designed this, that turned numbers and symbols from code into a living, breathing system that could think and create its own novel ideas and reactions. It didn't feel so different from what she and Thomas had done, the life they'd created that was growing inside her. Noa knew about Maggie's pregnancy now—that much was clear—yet she still wanted to help her. She thought about Noa's eyes darting across her face when she had boarded the Pod on Launch Day. She thought Noa had been memorizing her, but she had been waiting for her to say something, offering Maggie the opportunity to tell her the truth, not only about Thomas but about their entire relationship. Neither was willing to admit that something wasn't working.

Maggie almost felt disappointed when she found the rungs that would take her into the next level. She wanted to stay here, safe in the warmth Noa had created, but she knew she had no choice but to continue into the next unknown, which Noa's message had made clear was the only way to save herself. And her baby.

She climbed down into the next smaller room, away from the quiet hum of the server toward the source of the heartbeat she'd been hearing.

As soon as the door opened, the noise became almost deafening, a walloping *WOOMFPH WOOMFPH* that inhabited every part of Maggie's body as she dropped down into the room. It forced its way through her ears, her pores, until it felt like her own heartbeat had submitted to its rhythm. Her entire body pulsed in time with the low mechanical beat.

The source, Maggie could see now, was two enormous metal bars that took up three-quarters of the length of the room, backpedaling like a giant's legs. Each deafening stride powered the aqua-propeller, navigating and pushing the entire Pod forward, maintaining her position amid the tens of millions of square miles of the Pacific Ocean.

Maggie only stood looking at the machine for a moment, stunned by its magnitude, before the sound became too much. This time, there was nowhere left for her to run away from her fears. She had to keep moving, into the heart of them. She continued her descent into the floor's open mouth, the legs of the machinery cresting as she moved down into the final level of her journey, following the plan Noa had laid out for her.

It surprised Maggie how quickly time lost its meaning. Smaller markers were the first to slip away. Seconds and minutes turned into hours so quickly they became irrelevant. Then another. Just yesterday, she had been so anxious to get back to Noa, to know what her reaction would be, but the note had blanketed her in a sense of calm. Noa knew she had slept with someone else, that she was pregnant, and she *still* wanted to help her.

Without sunrises and sunsets, rituals, and meals, Maggie fell into her own rhythm. With every descent, she became a little more comfortable with following the cues from her body and the Pod until they became second nature, something she hadn't needed to do since receiving her Injectible.

When she felt hunger, a clenching that came from deep in her stomach, she paused to eat in the Food Storage Room. She scooped handfuls of vineless blueberries from the hydroponic system they floated in, licked the salty cultivated vegetable cells from a bioreactor off each finger, and nursed a jar of still-warm marinara sauce the cranes had placed back on the shelf for storage. She used the waste chute when she needed it and drank water from the desalinization spigots. When she felt tired, she briefly lay on the ground between the servers, their warm air coating her like a blanket, serenaded by the heartbeat emanating from the floor.

It had been years since she'd felt the freedom of not needing to follow any schedule but her own, and she was surprised how at-ease she felt. From the first day she'd moved into the apartment at WellHome, her Emmie had begun to suggest a schedule for maximum performance. She had been told when to eat, when to shower, how often to exercise, and when to sleep. The Pod had done the same, but down to the second. Maggie's sole responsibility was to follow its choreography. Her connection to her own wants and desires had been systematically removed, without her ever noticing.

She had no idea how much time had passed—anywhere from a few hours to a day, and measured her progress by the height of her growing pile in the top level. She had been told to bring everything up from the Emergency Supply Hold, and began with the heaviest items, strapping the handles of a life raft to her back as she climbed up past the propellors, servers, and walls of food storage.

The Hold was exactly as Noa had described in her note, a trove of necessary items strapped in perfect geometry to the walls and ceiling. It could have been any organized storage unit or shed, filled with black plastic utility boxes in nearly every imaginable shape and size, carefully labeled with their contents. There were the items she expected to find with any emergency supplies, such as paddles, personal flotation devices, and signaling devices, but also everything she would need to remain on the Pod if she had to, which the first few boxes indicated she might.

On her second descent into the room, she took her time mentally cataloging the boxes she would need. She drifted around the room, admiring each box like a piece of art in a gallery, looking but not touching, until she reached a short box balancing on its narrow edge, carefully reading the white letters printed into it:

Bassinet (Ages 0 to 6 Weeks)

She tore the lid off and found a small fabric-lined basket, then did the same to the boxes on either side of it. There were reusable diapers next to a changing pad, as well as folded clothes and linens. This entire time, the Pod had been stocked with everything she would need to raise her baby, even though she planned on leaving in just a few days. It didn't matter that the letter had mentioned she should bring up every item that might be useful to her in the next few months—Maggie hadn't realized that any alternative existed where she would be raising the baby on the Pod alone, more importantly, *having* the baby on the Pod.

By her estimate, she was just shy of twenty-four weeks along. The baby wasn't due for another four months. The idea that *she*—Maggie caught herself thinking—would come while she was still in this Pod was too terrifying to mull over. Maggie wasn't sure which was more frightening to her: the idea that she would have to leave in a storm, or that she would stay.

She lost herself in the work and exertion of moving the supplies up. In the event of sinking, the necessary supplies were meant to dislodge from the Pod itself and float to the surface of the water—there was never a reason for someone to go down and get them themselves, so the work was awkward and stilted, if satisfying in the way it required her full attention. When boxes didn't fit through the holes in the ceiling, she unpacked them, tossing them to the side and carrying their contents in her arms.

On her final ascent, she carried up a light load, a few teething toys and a flashlight she'd stuffed into a water-resistant duffel she slung across her back. In the Food Storage Room, she loaded bread and cans of food into the bag until she was barely able to close it. There was no reason to believe that the automatic mechanisms that fed her would not still be working— the cranes were, after all, still cooking—but ever since that first tomato in the Culinary Chamber, Maggie had realized that she wanted to have the option to eat what she wanted when she felt like it.

The pile she had amassed reached the handlebars of the stationary bike hanging from the ceiling. The only thing left for her to do was ascend into whatever was waiting for her at the surface.

The bed was still raised, her only indication that it was evening, so she sat on the floor amid her pile, leaning against a box and tearing off a piece of bread that she dipped into a jar of olive oil–marinated eggplant to soak up the flavor from the layer of sun-dried tomatoes at the bottom. When she reached the bottom, she filled the jar with water from a spigot that ran from the freshwater hold, downing water and floating remnants of olive oil in a few gulps, then refilling it.

The only time she could remember feeling hunger or thirst like this was when she finished a hard workout, gulping down electrolyte-fortified water, but this felt different. That had been calculated; this was craved, animalistic. She watched the medical crane, which she'd named Dr. Larch in honor of one of Noa's favorite movie characters, cap and uncap vials, mixing some into larger containers then placing those back on the shelf too. Every few minutes, it checked the waste chute for soiled clothes, but of course there wouldn't be any. She would be the only person to drop clothes into the chute, but she was down here.

The sound of the tiles opening above woke her up, and she watched the bed descend back into the furniture hold. She waited for the crane to maneuver toward it, in the space she'd left for it beside her mountain of items, to determine that it didn't need to be made. Maggie thought she saw a small divot before it pulled the duvet taut, smoothing any evidence she thought she'd seen.

She didn't know what to expect when she came back to the surface. The version of Emmie she had seen just before descending had scared her. There was a look of desperation in her eyes that felt almost too human. Maggie wasn't sure if Emmie would still be there when she arrived at the surface, or how she would greet her. But she still had all day to think about it.

She worked methodically, stripping the bed down and placing the sheets in the basin of the waste chute, then flipping the curved mattress onto its side so that all that was left was the sloping frame.

The largest boxes went onto it first, followed by duffels that she squeezed into the space between, then padded with the smallest items: batteries, first aid bags, a basket of swaddles, the soft pad of a changing table. By the time she was finished, she was drenched in sweat. She drank down more water, then sat in the center of her nest, waiting to be lifted back to the surface.

25

Emmett

Emmett knelt beside Noa's body, pressing two fingers against her neck to check her pulse. Satisfied, she unfurled Noa's hands to retrieve her mother's chess piece, then checked her Device. It would be another few hours before Maggie's bed raised to the surface of the Pod. Inga and Taylor had strict instructions where Noa was concerned. Emmett messaged them to let them both know it was done and they could begin preparations as she walked up the stairs, gingerly placing the queen back onto her throne, before continuing down the hall.

The clunky haptic pieces Noa had used to access Emmie were still on the floor of the control room, but Emmett needed something more sophisticated for the next part of her plan. Emmett stepped into the glowing room where she had taken Noa on their walk two days before. The chairs had been specifically built for long-term VR experiences, something of a WellNest next generation, though she never planned to release them to the public. Aside from her brief walk with Noa, she was the only person ever to benefit from their all-encompassing illusion.

A mirror materialized from the wall and Emmett removed her clothes in front of it—the chair worked best directly against skin—leaving them on the floor for Inga to retrieve later. She looked at her naked body in its reflection. Her unfailing dedication to her workout routine had kept it from ever revealing the secret that it had carried a child, but her body was changing. Where her skin had once stretched taut across her abdomen, it sagged slightly into the thin frown of her cesarean scar, which puckered out slightly as she sat down. The chair automatically detected her body and wrapped around her, enclosing her like a second skin from the neck down and orienting her to a standing position. It was vital that the chair be outfitted with weight-bearing features to minimize muscular atrophy while she was in it. Air modules also minimized the risk of bedsores.

"Check Vitalities," she said.

In front of her appeared her ECG, EEG, temperature, oxygen levels, and even mood, detected from levels of serotonin and other neurotransmitters.

"Continue actively running Vitalities."

If anything dramatically changed, the VR would immediately stop running—the chair had fail-safes in place to stop the program.

She felt for the cannula embedded in her arm, and clicked the tube that ran from the ceiling to deliver the hydration, electrolytes, and nutrients she would need to survive. Waste disposal was built into the chair. She had designed it to be able to live in it for months, which was exactly what she planned on doing, though this was the first time she would be testing it for that long. A person could technically spend an entire lifetime in its illusion.

She had run through her plan a million times, but it was beginning to feel more and more real. Without the help of the larger Redocking ship, it would take as long as six months for the Pod to make the journey home. In the meantime, she would be in it with Maggie and the baby, getting them ready for the moment they could join their family—live together in the home Emmett had built for them. Meanwhile, Inga would manage the house as Taylor kept an eye on Oisín and the company.

"Ready," she said, as the helmet rose from the back, covering every inch of her skin in millions of LEDs.

The silence was the only thing she could hear, until it was replaced by the sounds of a crashing wave and the bed rising from the floor into the Pod, carrying her daughter.

She let her arms hang in a low V, assuming the role of Emmie for one final night before she finally revealed herself to Maggie, the moment she had been waiting nearly three decades for. Anything could still happen, but this time Maggie was fully swaddled in her nest.

26
Maggie

The first thing she saw as she crested was Emmie. A subtle but warm smile spread across the projection's face. Something about her felt different. She was almost unrecognizable from the Emmie Maggie had escaped to descend into the Pod. But it was more than that. Emmie contained none of the desperation of the previous day, or had it been days?

Maggie remained seated in the center of the bed, waiting for it to come to a full stop, protected by the fortress of items she had carefully collected from the Hold. The sky was completely dark, except for the stars piercing through the gray clouds that moved quickly as if on their way somewhere. She kept her gaze trained on the week-old moon that hung low over the horizon. Half of it was illuminated by the sun; the other half swallowed by the night sky. Emmie wasn't the only one who had changed.

Maggie felt more powerful, less afraid of Emmie, now that she knew what the rest of the Pod contained and how to listen to herself, should she need to. She had found her rhythm. If she ever felt unsafe, all she had to do was trigger the Pod into lowering her back down. The bed finally came to a stop.

"How long have I been gone?" Maggie's voice sounded strange, unpracticed.

"Just over a day. It's the evening of day forty-four of your Journey."

Maggie considered this. It had felt both longer and shorter than that. Time moved differently without any ability to track it.

She stretched her neck from side to side, letting her body wake up, keeping one eye on Emmie, who remained perfectly still. She could stand there for hours without any effort, free from the limitations and weight of a human body. Maggie moved her stiff legs out from under her, then stepped over the items and off her bedframe. She lowered the nearest box off it, onto the floor by the bed.

Her muscles were sore from the effort of the previous two days, but they felt good, capable of unloading the items.

"Were you here the entire time I was gone?"

"I was gone for a while," Emmie said, "but returned just in time to see you arrive."

"Where did you go?"

"I'm always with you," she said. It was the same answer she'd given Maggie when she was a teenager, when Maggie had asked where Emmie went when she wasn't in the WellNest with her. Maggie felt herself physically relax at the familiarity of the banter. She had been so afraid to come back up to the surface of the Pod, of seeing her, but she had known Emmie for practically her entire life. At least her entire adult life. She could trust her.

Maggie continued moving boxes, spiraling them in from the glass walls toward the center column, sacrificing floor space instead of blocking the ocean view. She worked until they were all unloaded, then pushed the mattress down into the frame. Once finished, she became aware of how dirty she felt and was suddenly desperate to take off the sports bra and leggings she had put on what felt like days before. As if anticipating this, Emmie triggered a tile with fresh clothes to rise, and Maggie pulled her bra over her head and stepped out of her leggings and underwear, not bothering to turn away from Emmie as she changed, too exhausted to shower.

"Why don't you sit down? You look tired," Emmie said once she was dressed. It struck Maggie as odd that Emmie hadn't asked about the supplies. She had assumed that Emmie would put up resistance to her tinkering with the Pod, but she didn't want to ask any questions. What good would they serve, anyway?

Maggie walked toward her desk, retrieving her box of personal items, then set it in her lap as she sat on the ground with it. She removed the lid and sprayed her mother's perfume before placing it back inside, breathing in the warm sandalwood that bloomed from her wrist, and retrieving the item she'd been looking for. She flipped her thumb across the pages of the worn copy of Mary Oliver's poetry until it fell open to the photo of her and Thomas.

She turned it over and carefully peeled back the tape to remove the photo of her and Noa, holding it in her hand as she turned to Gamma's favorite poem, resting both photos on her belly. Noa and Thomas gazed back at her as she let her eyes rest on a line from "This Morning."

Emmie moved so quietly that Maggie barely noticed when she began walking toward her. She lowered herself to the ground next to Maggie. Maggie let her eyes travel across the same page Gamma's had lingered over so many years before, feeling strangely at peace alongside Emmie when she finally let them close.

27

Noa

Location Unknown

[Device cannot be accessed.]

28

Maggie

Zone 649, Pacific Ocean
159 Days Post-Launch

Sleep came in six-minute increments, which Maggie only knew from the vivid, hallucinatory dreams it brought.

Each time she woke from another contraction, she'd press her hands, spread wide across the small of her back, down and in, to release the tension building there. As soon as the wave of pain crested, she'd sink down into another dream. The air felt thick with delirium, as if every exhale filled the Pod with the fog of not only her pain, but the intensity of every woman who had ever given birth before her.

In her dreams, women visited her. The mother who'd raised her. Noa. Emmie. Gamma. Emmett's face leaned in from the obscurity—but that wasn't a dream, was it?

Another wave crashed.

"I have to tell you something. Everything, actually," Emmett had said the morning after Maggie had emerged from the Pod's internal system.

Maggie had fallen asleep on the floor beside Emmie, but when she looked up, Emmett Neal sat in her place. Emmett, in a cashmere set, her hair pulled back, looking exactly as she had the evening of her keynote.

I have to tell you something. Everything, actually.

"Where's Emmie?" Maggie had asked, though the truth was that she already knew, at some level. It was like a thought you'd had a million times, but didn't realize having until it became conscious.

"We don't need her anymore," Emmett said as Maggie sat up to face her. "Maggie, I have always loved you, though I admit I didn't always know how to. I wanted to build a life that would protect us. Do you understand what I'm saying?"

Maggie nodded, her body responding before her mind could catch up. On a certain level, she had always known.

The adoption had been closed, but Emmett's sole requirement was that her daughter be named Magpie. She had selected the name from her own mother's favorite bird, known for its audacity and intelligence. Its black feathers over a white breast became her calling card. Emmett was photographed almost exclusively in a black blazer over a white turtleneck.

There had been other clues too, if you knew where to look: The magpie feather Emmett kept in her office that was often mentioned in features and included in photographs; the diminutive name of the Emmies that was also a combination of theirs, *Emmett* and *Maggie*; the gifts of Monet's bridge on campus in honor of Maggie's thesis and a campus built against the ocean.

"That day in Gamma's garden . . ." Maggie began to say, remembering the flashback she'd had below in the Pod.

"That was the only time I've ever held you." Emmett immediately picked up the thread. "It was so hard at the beginning. I sacrificed everything and nothing was working—I was working on other people's projects, but I couldn't get anyone to listen to my pitch, to understand my vision"—her voice clipped a hard edge—"and so I went to visit my mother, which is when I saw you. She didn't see that I was there, so when she went inside briefly, I walked straight toward where you were sitting on the soil between the planter boxes."

Maggie remembered her—a younger version of the woman sitting in front of her now—carrying her.

"I was going to take you, and nearly did until I realized what I was doing. Instead, I redoubled my efforts then to take care of you, watched you grow and later guided you through Emmie."

There had been so many parts of Maggie's life that had simply worked out in her favor—Emmett was always watching over her. Her parents had excelled at their jobs, receiving unprecedented promotions, even given their hard work. Her family had been chosen to receive a beta of the first WellNest. Noa had beaten the odds when she landed her job at WellCorp, and Thomas had found his way back into her life, even when traveling from New York to California was unheard of. Maggie wondered how many accomplishments had ever truly belonged to her. How many things Emmett had meddled with.

"You brought back Thomas—" Maggie said, at the same time she wondered, *Has a part of me always known?*

"A grant that I funded did, yes. I could see how much you were struggling. You had stopped painting."

"But I loved Noa, I was with Noa," Maggie said. And she *had* loved Noa—at one point. But over time, that love had morphed into something else. Maggie had always craved stability—someone who would never leave her as Gamma and Thomas both had—and Noa had needed someone to take care of. It was a kind of love—maybe even the most common type of romantic love—but they had performed the roles well enough to forget that it was no longer true love. When she was with Thomas, even if he didn't feel the same, always chasing after the next assignment, she didn't have to do anything. She could just be. But he had left again, enticed by a new potential byline.

"Maggie, I'm so sorry. She left WellCorp as soon as she knew you were going to be safe, that I was going to take care of you." Emmett explained that while Noa had acquiesced to coding the messages for Maggie, the pregnancy had been too much for her.

"Did she say where she was going?"

"I arranged a Courtesy Drop for her, headed south."

The tears that followed came for days.

Maggie didn't know whether to feel grateful or betrayed, but gradually both feelings were overridden by the single overwhelming emotion: Emmett was her mother. Maggie had always thought her birth mother had left her, but maybe she was the only one who never had.

Maggie's parents had never hidden her adoption from her, and had told her everything they knew about her birth parents, but that was close to nothing. Maggie had grown up wondering whose womb she had been in, imagining her in countless situations. But most of her visions had been limited to the most common; her imagination too limited to go beyond a young mother without the financial means to raise a baby. At least she'd been half right.

From the moment she hit puberty, she'd begun to imagine what it would feel like to be pregnant, and to give that child up. At every birthday, she wondered, *Could I keep a child at thirteen, at sixteen, at twenty?*

When she met Noa, she finally stopped counting. For the first time, she had hit a birthday where she could begin to imagine the possibility of raising a child: *twenty-five.* But Noa didn't want one. At thirty-eight, Noa had seen countless friends go through the challenges of raising a child and decided it wasn't for her. She didn't want to bring another person into a world that couldn't support one. And Maggie thought she loved her enough to convince herself that she didn't want one either. For a time, the clock in her mind quieted as birthdays came and went, without any acknowledgment of having a baby. Until the night she saw Thomas. It felt like the doors to every possibility swung back open the moment she saw him in the gym.

Another contraction came; they were now five minutes apart. She could hear Emmett—her mother—speaking to the AR nurse. They were both projections, and the thin line they skirted between reality and illusion only fueled the delirium. Her actual mother was thousands of miles away, wrapped in a haptic suit, but Emmett's mind was here with her. None of it was real, but what could be more real?

By the time the sun crested the horizon, Maggie's contractions were arriving in tandem with her breath, just a few seconds apart. Not enough time to dream, though reality felt hallucinatory too.

She had no memory of lowering herself from the bed onto the floor, kneeling with her face pressed into the mattress. Her knees rested in a pool of water. *Did my water break? . . . Has the ocean finally found its way into the Pod?* She pushed with every few exhales, following the waves of her contractions, resisting the same urge that carried her from one crest to the next, until she finally turned herself inside out.

Emmett told her later that she'd never heard anything so loud or guttural, but in Maggie's mind, it was perfectly silent. She caught her daughter in the cradle her hands instinctively made, pulling her to her face so she could see the blue-tinted skin and waxy vernix. As she did, the rest of the world came back into focus. The blood-filled cord tugged the placenta still inside her, as her daughter's first snotty, furious cry rang out, piercing her heart, turning her right side out.

It was the first real human sound she'd heard in months.

29

Sansa

Los Angeles, California
April 29, 2031

The baby was born small enough to need help, but not so underdeveloped that she was in serious danger of dying.

The nurse had told her in a hushed whisper that a premature birth was "normal" in "mothers like her," nodding toward her daughter. *Because of the stress*, she'd explained. It was as if the body knew to expel it, or the baby knew better than to stick around where she wasn't wanted. If only Sansa could explain to the nurse how badly the baby was wanted, that it was society's expectations that kept her daughter from raising her own child.

Sansa had spent months researching the restorative foods to cook for Emmett to aid in her recovery, but hadn't thought to research the complications of a premature birth until Emmett went into labor two months early. As she sat next to Emmett, sleeping in her hospital bed, Sansa borrowed Emmett's Device to pull up potential issues her granddaughter might encounter: *underdeveloped brain, weak immune system, difficulty latching*. Her own mother had told her once that the way a baby is born is the way that baby will live. So far, she hadn't experienced anything to disprove this: she had come out screaming, while Emmett had been patient, arriving into the world swiftly and gracefully. So then what did it say about Magpie, that she was breech and born eight weeks early in an emergency cesarean section?

At some point, Sansa excused herself from Emmett's room and took herself for a walk, which was when she saw the couple in the hallway. The man held her granddaughter, who was being kept in the hospital for observation. The mother was disheveled, with her blond hair piled into a bun, jacket pulled over jeans and a white shirt painted with a coffee stain. She had raced to get here. Their emotions hung like signs from their faces: Relief, Concern, Excitement.

"Hello." Sansa gave a warm smile as she approached. "And who's this?"

"Hi." The man smiled sheepishly, then introduced himself and dipped Magpie toward her. "And this is Maggie." He beamed, anointing her granddaughter with her new name.

The woman stared forward, not unkind but possibly annoyed that her husband had broken this private moment with their new family. It took Sansa a moment to realize that she was not ignoring her, but listening to a call coming through her EarDrums.

"Wrapping up work," the man explained, noticing. "Are you waiting for someone to—"

"Oh," Sansa said, "I just—my niece is about to have hers. She's in labor, so I took myself for a walk." She was a terrible liar, but it worked.

The wife must have been twice as old as Sansa had been when Emmett had made her a mother, which would make them similar in age, though this woman looked at least a decade younger than forty and Sansa looked a decade older from long days spent in the sun on trails and coastlines. As soon as Magpie—she would have to remember to call her Maggie now—was healthy enough, the adoption counselor would send her home with this woman, but never place her into Emmett's arms.

That had been Emmett's decision, even if Sansa would never understand it. Looking at Maggie, she couldn't imagine *not* being in her life. Emmett had kept her eyes averted as the doctor lifted her daughter out of her open wound and handed her to the nurses. Emmett was so dogged in her arrogance, convinced that she would get to know the child another way—through technology. They had always disagreed about technology, but Sansa tried not to fight with her daughter about their differing views, *especially* during pregnancy when Emmett's cortisol flowed through

Maggie's veins, but now that Sansa stood extending a finger toward her granddaughter's tiny hand, she knew: she would do anything for this child.

Sansa made polite conversation with the man, extending her time in Maggie's presence, as his wife wrapped up her meeting, then asked, "What are you reading?"

She gestured toward the book Sansa held, bewildered to see the physical version of an e-reader.

"My daughter gave it to me." Emmett had marked every passage that compared the women in the story to birds, knowing her mother would appreciate them along with the nod to her granddaughter's name. Sansa always had a pen tucked into any book she read, primed to jot down ideas. She was grateful for it when the first few lines of a poem came to her, almost out of thin air. Sansa excused herself from the new parents, retreating down the hallway, and then propped up the book at a nurses' station to jot down a few lines on its last page. She wasn't sure if it was about her own daughter or Maggie's new mother, even as she read it over.

She who is perpetually unspooling and reforming
tinsel and twine and a blue plastic thread
into a nest for her wren
has more to teach us than
any book could.

She looked up at the couple walking down the hallway, their heads bent like swans over Maggie. Her own mother had told her no one looks closely at a woman past a certain age. She'd said in Russian, *You become invisible.* Sansa hadn't imagined then that what her mother was referring to was power, the power to go unnoticed. Ever since, she had welcomed her premature wrinkles.

Sansa wasn't supposed to have their address, but a file left lazily open on the counselor's desk had exposed it to her: a beautiful modern house in Palo Alto. Still far enough north to deliver the misty weather she had loved so much in Portland, and before then, Georgia. She could live in this town, halfway between her daughter in Los Angeles and her community in Portland.

She pulled up listings, feeling a mix of fear and hope that blended into a sense that she was doing something illicit, almost how she had the day she brought home Emmett. She pushed open the door to the private room where Emmett was recovering from the operation, and felt thankful that she was still asleep. Sansa settled into the chair normally reserved for partners.

There it was: a house, not just in the neighborhood as she had hoped, but directly next door to the modern home. Her parents had left their Portland house to her a long time ago—its value would be just enough to cover this one.

She emailed the listing agent. If she couldn't be this child's grand-mother outright, she would still be in her life.

30

Noa

Brazilian Airspace
46 Days Post-Launch

"Passenger, prepare for landing."

Noa woke with a sharp gasp that flooded her system with adrenaline. Her eyes brimmed wide as her heart beat wildly, flapping against her rib cage like a trapped bird. She fumbled automatically for her Device, horrified to find that her arms were strapped to the leather seat, pinching into the gold bracelet. An IV line trailed from her arm, and she craned her neck to follow it to where it disappeared into the plush headrest behind her. Noa thought back to the basement where she had lost consciousness. Whatever was flowing from the IV into her arm now, just in time for landing, must have revived her.

It took her a moment to realize she was hyperventilating. Her Lens wasn't on—how long had it been disconnected?—and she was unaccustomed to hearing her body's cues. She took a deep breath, concentrating on the sensation of the air hitting her lungs, counting each inhale and exhale to ten, then looked around.

Above her, the domed glass that encased most self-driving cars revealed an endless swath of sky. She leaned forward, the leather squeaking slightly, to get her bearings. She had expected a horizon, but had to crane to see the ground thousands of feet below: a swath of coastline hemmed in by a belt of green sea that made her wonder if she was dreaming.

The only flight Noa had ever taken as an adult was the one to California twenty years prior. Even with the price of her ticket, she had been wedged like a sardine into the standing-only section for six uncomfortable hours. The few she had taken as a child were unremarkable, with row upon row of passengers too engrossed in their tiny rectangles of entertainment to recognize how temporary it all was; that humans were never meant to fly so close to the sun. Both bore little resemblance to the craft she sat on now.

She was, as far as she could tell, the only passenger or person on the plane, which was barely larger than a car. A matching leather seat sat empty across from her. As the plane descended, Noa felt her stomach rise up to her chest—as much from the drop as from the realization of where she was headed. She knew the coastline below. Emmett, mercifully, hadn't killed her; she had sent her home. The sight of the coast alone brought back her grandmother's thick stew and the bossa nova her mother's family put on, then drowned out with their conversation. Noa had only understood pieces, but was calmed by the chatter. It felt like the antithesis to the silence WellPark curated: an artificial world, no more real than the virtual trail Noa had coded for Maggie.

Noa arched her back, straining against the seat belt to take in the cluster of high-rises—there were so many more than she remembered from her time there as a young child—strangling the tiny, historically protected town her mother had grown up in. Noa had always assumed she would never see her mother again and, after a few feeble attempts in her early twenties to track down her information, had never tried again. As far as Noa knew, her mother had never attempted to reach out to her either, which pained her at the same time it helped clear her conscience. Maybe she was happier without Noa.

A memory came back to her, from the years they'd spent in Reno. Her mother had worked tirelessly to arrange playdates with the other little girls who attended Noa's small elementary school. Though friendly, the other moms had politely declined her mother's repeated attempts at connection until Noa was finally included in a birthday invitation for the entire class. A few minutes before they were meant to leave, Noa quietly slipped out of the sliding glass door and ran toward the birches behind their house.

She edged deeper into the forest as her mother's calls for her crested into desperation, beating aside the low thorned bushes and hanging branches on the other side of the creek.

She could still see the house in the distance behind her when she heard a loud bird call, and followed it to a clearing. A magpie lay supine on the rock, with its white chest up as another stood sentry over it, raising its beak to call loudly to others. The flock arrived silently, a few at a time, to regard the dead bird, hopping around it in what looked to Noa like reverence, before flying off. By dusk, the visitors had waned, and Noa finally began to approach the bird on its granite catafalque with the same care she had witnessed in the procession that preceded her. Just as she edged toward it, her mother grabbed her arm, violently pulling her back.

"Aí está você!" she admonished so fiercely that Noa reacted with childish petulance, shaking free to run deeper into the forest, determined for the first ten minutes to spend the night there, until she got cold and walked home to her mother's full reprimand.

Noa knew at some level that her mother was using her as a golden ticket into the insular world of book clubs and wine nights attended exclusively by the white mothers who stood in tight circles at pickup and drop-off, and she resented her for it. But she had never stopped to consider how lonely her mother must have felt in that cabin tucked in the forest, as Noa found community in the trees and the birds and her father immersed himself in his work at the university. It was impossibly sad to Noa that they had spent their short time together locked in cycles of fierce misunderstandings.

Most children had the opportunity to, at some point, meet their parents as adults, but Noa's relationships with both her father and her mother would forever be frozen in time, caught as they were when she was seventeen. Noa leaned forward to gaze out the window again at the approaching coastline. It was rare enough to see an airplane—rarer still to see a nonmilitary jet—that Noa could imagine the people below stepping out of their houses to watch her descent. Was her mother among them? Did she know Noa was coming?

Noa had no idea what her reaction would be. She had long since accepted that she would never see her mother again, which was, she realized, her greatest mistake. It entirely excused her from hoping for or imagining their reunion. She hadn't even let herself consider the most basic questions: What kind of life had her mother built in Brazil? What kind of woman had she become in her seventies? Did she resent Noa? Regret her own role in things?

The plane vibrated as its wheels lowered.

Noa would, she decided, stop at nothing to return to Maggie as soon as she found her mother. Or, at the very least, Noa refused to accept that she would never see her again. She was finally old enough to understand how many twists and turns life contained, and that "never" was an invented concept. You can't know a story's ending, or the paths it will take to get there, and assuming you can is a self-fulfilling prophecy that only limits your options.

Prepare for landing, the voice had said. How could anyone?

31

Maggie

Zone 128, Pacific Ocean
233 Days Post-Launch

The sound of birds chirping announced the sunrise, but Maggie kept her eyes closed even after she had woken up. She had removed the swaddle at some point before dawn, to change her diaper and feed her, and had never bothered to put it back on. Maggie curled in closer, encircling her limbs around her daughter's tiny, nearly naked, warm body, pressing her soft skin against her own, inhaling the buttermilk-sweet, animal scent back into her body. She opened her eyes when she felt her begin to stir, to squirm.

Her daughter's lips hung open in a perfect O that barely fluttered with each breath of filtered air she drew into her tiny lungs. Maggie watched her open one eye, then the other, then pulled her daughter into her chest. Her heart exploded as it always did when she latched onto her breast as if it was the most natural thing both of them had ever done.

She knew now that her own mother had stopped producing milk a week after Maggie was born. Her breasts became heavy with it, then crimson with mastitis, until one day her nipples stopped leaking the food intended for her daughter, as if they understood that she was hundreds of miles away. Her body adapted quickly, but her mind had never learned how to stop being a mother.

Emmett walked over to her as Maggie's latte rose from the coaster in her bedside table. Maggie sat up, cradling her baby in one arm to reach for the mug, bringing it to her lips as they both drank.

"Could I have some yogurt and berries?" Maggie asked, triggering the Pod's internal system.

The Pod had continued its routine, but Maggie had become more comfortable with requesting the things she actually wanted. It felt good to step into her hungers, after an adulthood of denying them and trusting technology's recommendations over her own.

She moved over to give Emmett some space to scoot into the bed with them.

Maggie slipped her daughter's arms into the tiny onesie, then held her up to her shoulder, gently tapping the baby's back while looking out at the ocean.

"Look," Emmett said, gesturing her head toward the horizon. Maggie's gaze followed the line she made toward a ripple of land.

Emmett had been in her haptic suit for 189 days. It was the longest she had ever stayed in an AR simulation, and soon she would have to leave. She needed to return to her body to begin preparing for Maggie and the baby's arrival. She had no way of knowing the toll the suit had taken on her human body or what the situation would be like on land. It had been months since she'd had any communication with her company.

Emmett had gone over her plan with Maggie countless times. As soon as the Pod was as close to shore as it could get, before its hull dragged in the shallows, Maggie and the baby would take the life raft to shore, where a car would meet them, then take them as far as it could get on the above-ground route to Emmett's house. From there, the walk was only a mile to her door.

They had cleared Hawai'i as Maggie's daughter turned a month old, the island appearing as little more than a raised bump on the horizon as they made their way south around it. Outside of a few smaller fishing boats off the coasts of small islands and some cargo vessels, they hadn't seen any sign of human life.

Maggie got out of bed, still cradling the baby, her eyes locked on the horizon. She had been entranced by Hawai'i, but the familiar silhouette of the Channel Islands made her feel something else entirely. Noa had never failed to point them out on clear days, and she tried to remember now if they had been visible the morning of the Launch.

Her mother walked behind her, placing a hand against her shoulder.

"It's time for me to go," Emmett said. She would leave them alone for a few days to make preparations for them. She didn't anticipate it taking longer than two days.

Maggie nodded. They'd gone over it so many times there was nothing left to say.

32

Emmett

Malibu, California
233 Days Post-Launch

"Resume form," Emmett said, and her vision gradually returned to the room in which her physical body had existed for the previous six months. As the helmet of her chair lifted, she could see the hues of the room, designed to gently welcome back its user. The chair, already oriented so she was standing, released its grip on her, and Emmett was concerned for a moment that she would collapse, but her muscles held steady—the chair had worked. The cannula that had kept her fed over the previous months released and Emmett stepped out, stiffly stretching as she crossed the room to a small window.

She couldn't see the Pod yet, but it would be in view soon. She turned around, passing the other chair, which held another figure, then through the door, locking the room behind her. She had no need for it anymore.

33

Maggie

Maggie stood with her face to the glass until the lazy ridge of the California coast crested the horizon, rising into view above the thin layer of fog that rested on top of the water. It was the strangest feeling, to know that eight months ago she had felt desperate to get away from California, to have a break. Today, she would finally return—just not to her life as she'd known it. All of her concerns felt impossibly far away the closer she got to returning, to realizing what she had lost.

Emmett's AR had dissolved as she left the Pod and returned to her own body, somewhere on the coastline Maggie stared at now. For the first time in months, she was alone. But that wasn't entirely true.

She looked down at her baby, whose gray eyes stared back up at Maggie. The only thing that meant anything to her right now was the infant gazing up at her.

The only thing that meant anything to her was her daughter, Noa.

Acknowledgments

The idea for this book arrived to me as a brief vision of a woman standing alone on a floating pod in the middle of the Pacific Ocean, and it may have ended there, if not for the support I received in the years that followed.

I am endlessly grateful to my writing group—Madeleine Englis and Alice DuBois—who read my earliest pages and encouraged subsequent chapters with thoughtful notes over many months and rounds of waffle fries at the Guest House in Los Feliz. Thank you to Jonah Ollman for believing wholeheartedly in this book and reading many early drafts. Emily Seerey, Haley Westervelt, and Drew Boulos all engaged in heated debates and contributed insights that made these characters more well-rounded. Thank you, Tikhon Markov for answering my many clarifying questions about Moldova. Any mistakes are mine. A special gratitude goes out to every friend who kept me grounded, loved, checked on, fed, and sane: Alice Ann Clark, Wendy Wilson, Caroline Bentz, Hanna Vietor, Willa Bachman, Elaine Carpenter, Mayrah Udvardi, Alexandra Lopez Zavaski, Rachel Lomax, and Betsy Schell, to name a few. I finished this book while earning my master's in counseling and my professors' and cohort's support, in challenging me to grow personally and professionally, helped me to understand Noa, Maggie, and Emmett and their mothers as complicated and real people. Thank you especially to Briana Gabel, Nicole Moussa, Skye Anfield, and Quinn Bailey. Your presence in my life has been expansive and your impact is woven into every page. Thank you for modeling true friendship to me, accepting me with all my own neuroses, and being my confidantes, cheerleaders, and readers.

This book literally never would have made it into your hands without my agent, Claire Friedman, who saw its potential from a blind email query, then guided me every step of the way. My editor and friend Taylor Rondestvedt championed its earliest drafts and always *got* it. Her sharp insights and edits made this book so much stronger. Our initial meeting, so many years ago in the dorm she shared with Sabrina Giglio, feels nothing short of kismet. Thank you to the team at Scout Press: Lucy Nalen, Bianca Ducasse, and Kelli McAdams.

Countless authors and journalists inspired this book in big and small ways. Elizabeth Kolbert's books and articles and David Wallace-Wells' research in *The Uninhabitable Earth* provided me with a jumping-off point for imagining 2060. His line, "That the sea will become a killer is a given," still haunts me. There are nods to my favorite authors all over these pages, but a few provided direct inspiration and I recommend their books to any who enjoyed mine: *The Dreamers* by Karen Thompson Walker, *A House Between Earth and the Moon* by Rebecca Scherm, *Miracle Creek* by Angie Kim, and *A Taste for Poison* by Neil Bradbury; also Mary Oliver, Elizabeth Gilbert, and Ann Lamott. Boundless gratitude goes to my friend and literary cheerleader, Thao Thai. This book was written almost entirely to Rachel Portman's soundtracks, especially "The Duchess." Rachel, I am literally your Number One Fan, a fact corroborated by Spotify every year.

There is no one I am more grateful to than my family whose love, curiosity, and creativity has been my longest and greatest source of inspiration. To my parents, Tracy Fairhurst and Norman Stephens, for instilling in me a deep love of stories and giving me every opportunity to write my own. To my brother, Josh Stephens, who has always been a role model of a friend, writer, and explorer. To my family in Los Angeles and Guatemala: Of all the families, how did I get so lucky to be born into this one? And of course, to my grandmothers, Leslie Hempstead Fairhurst and Evelyn Kent Stephens, who are no longer with us, but would get on famously with Gamma.

Thank you, finally, to my readers. I am humbled by and grateful for every single person who reads my weekly accounts of stumbling through life, over on *Morning Person* newsletter. This gorgeous community wouldn't be possible without your support, conversations, and comments. Thank you for the joy and insights you bring me every Tuesday.

I completed this book during a transitional and difficult period of my life, where I found myself in my own floating pod, so to speak. My personal challenges found their way into these pages, as some of you may have surmised. It was only by asking people for help, and being comfortable with receiving it, that I was able to find my way back to shore.

Thank you to those who guided me, near and far.

About the Author

Leslie Stephens is the creator of the popular newsletter *Morning Person*. Her work has appeared in the *Los Angeles Review of Books*, *Eater*, and other outlets including *Cupcakes & Cashmere*, where she worked as an editor. A graduate of Wellesley College, she is currently earning her master's in counseling, with specializations in addiction and ecotherapy, from Lewis & Clark College in Portland, Oregon, where she lives with her pit-mix, Toast. You can find her at LeslieStephens.com and subscribe at MorningPersonNewsletter.com.